Dodge-20

When Hindsight Becomes Foresight

Book 1

Amy Joy Hess

Dodge-20
When Hindsight Becomes Foresight Book 1
Copyright © 2024 by Amy Joy Hess
Created in the United States by Ocean to Mountain Publishing

Originally printed in January, 2020 as *2020: When Hindsight Becomes Foresight*.

Books published by Ocean to Mountain Publishing are available at special discounts for bulk purchases in the United States.

Ocean to Mountain Publishing
PO BOX 1116
Wallace, ID 83873
www.otmpub.com

This book is a work of fiction. Any references to historical events, real people, or real places are used fictitiously. Names, characters, and places are products of the author's imagination.

ISBN: 978-1-962532-05-1

To all the children,
old and young,
who long for a devoted family

Times

Table

PART I

1 I

1980

It was supposed to be 2020, and I was supposed to be an adult.

I noticed the doorknob first. You'd think the carpet would have warned me, the shag carpet under my feet instead of smooth hardwood. That should have registered something, but the pain in my bladder bothered me more than the creepy fact that my flooring had changed overnight. I had to pay attention when I reached the door, because it felt like – it *felt* like – the ancient brass knob jumped up and flung itself at my face. It stuck out all, "Hello!" right at my eye level and jolted me back against the bed.

I browsed my room in the dim morning. The ceiling pulled away from me. The walls shrunk backward, and an unfamiliar bookshelf loomed high above me like the Times Square JumboTron.

I flipped on the light and blinked at the peculiar changes to my bedroom. No shock or fear; only a mild confusion fuzzed at the edges of my brain. A teenager had silently, cleverly redecorated my room while I slept. Posters of Foreigner and AC/DC patched the walls, and another bookshelf climbed beside the window – but no books. Just a lava lamp. A gooey green lava lamp. And sports trophies and board games. A series of Star Wars action figures stood in game-on poses across the top shelf.

I gripped a wad of sweatpants in my fist; they'd grown ten sizes too big and threatened to fall off me. I'd walked up into the legs, so I dropped the wad and stepped free. A gray T-shirt hung to my knees and draped over one shoulder, leaving the other shoulder exposed to cold morning.

My bladder kept pestering, so I trudged from the room that was no longer my bedroom and down the hall into my bathroom, which was so obviously not my bathroom. Brown and gold linoleum. Yeesh. Orange Formica swamped the sink. The linen curtain that guarded my bathtub had disappeared, replaced by one of those opaque sliding glass doors. You know, the plastic and metal kind that always get stuck in the metal runner when you try to slide them? These invaders who'd remodeled my house had super tacky taste and had taken the whole 1970s retro thing way too seriously.

Giants. Giant invaders. The new toilet was so huge, I almost fell into the bowl, but at least the ultra-soft toilet paper provided comfort.

I might have fussed more, but I'd just woken up. My brain hadn't warmed to an ambient temperature. Morning dew hadn't evaporated from between my ears. I couldn't reach the knobs to wash my hands, even on my tiptoes, and that's when I decided to investigate. I climbed onto that toilet to increase my height by 18 inches, and my chest and face appeared in the mirror above the sink. I stared across the vanity at a little kid version of me, chubby cheeks and all. My bangs stuck up all cockeyed because of my cowlicks, and when I poked out my tongue, the little girl in the mirror did the same.

I laughed. I laughed out loud, and a child's laughter bounced around the bathroom. "Oh, that's fun." I leaned halfway over the sink to wash up and watched the water run. Wait. If I'd shrunk into the form of a small child, it meant I'd entered a lucid dream. And I'd peed in a dream-toilet... which meant I'd wet my bed.

I had to wake myself up.

I hopped down and headed to the living room. How? How to wake up? It didn't feel like a dream; I moved freely with no sense of pushing through water. I recognized every crisp detail of this 1970s version of my house, and the red shag carpet fibers caught between my toes. I clambered onto the couch with its green, leafy upholstery and bounced up and down. Then, I grabbed my face with all ten nails and dug the tips into my cheeks, and it smarted. My small fingernails gouged with ten pokey pricks.

I tried to levitate, to rise through the ceiling – not a problem in dreams. Nothing. No flight powers. I catapulted from the couch and crashed into the carpet on all fours. It banged my knees with startling roughness, and I sat in that fuzzy field of red shag, genuinely puzzled. Legitimate rug burns peered up from my knees. Rug burns that hurt.

A shout bounced out from behind Hudson's bedroom door, right off the living room.

"Shane! It's Saturday! Go back to bed!"

I frowned at the door. A man's voice barked at me, not the voice of my 12-year-old son. "It's Sunday," my brain said, and I wondered if that mattered.

The burns on my knees called for my attention. Slamming into the carpet had knocked off a thin layer of skin, and the high definition damp, raw marks amazed me. They cried in discomfort, and the pain of reality started to prod and shove its way into my brain. I refused to accept it, because people don't fall asleep in their beds and randomly wake up in shag-carpet-land as a little kid.

I hopped up and searched the living room that was no longer my living room, seeking out the object I knew would answer questions. A newspaper. Didn't these people own a newspaper? No. No they didn't. The fireplace sat cold and empty. No papers piled on the brick hearth, ready for kindling fires. A small TV perched on a stand across from the couches, but if I clicked its knob to a news station, the guy behind Hudson's door would yell again.

"I'm trespassing." I shook my head. "This is someone else's house."

Well, I couldn't leave, because I wore only a baggy T-shirt. I pushed aside drapes and peeked out the living room window at snow piled high on both sides of my driveway. Heat emanated from the water radiator under the window, and I briefly rested my chest and arms against its lovely warmth. We always used the wood stove downstairs, because the gas furnace stabbed us in the bank account, but Shane's dad obviously didn't care.

I stood and rotated slowly in that living room to absorb its details. Couches. Coffee table. Family photos on the walls, two parents and three boys.

"They don't own a single book."

I needed something with the date on it! A phone, a day planner. Something.

I trotted through the dining room into the kitchen, where hands on the wall clock read 6:50. No wonder Shane's dad had yelled at my failed flight efforts, the weekend morning hadn't even rubbed the sleep out of its eyes. But, good grief, this ugly version of my kitchen! What was the obsession with linoleum and avocado green? Green counters. Green curtains. Green wall paper. Gross.

I searched the walls for the item that absolutely had to be in a

1970s kitchen. There! Haha! A yellow phone had been mounted on the wall like a big banana, and next to it a wall calendar smiled down at me. The page hung open to February. February of 1980.

I shook my head, slowly slowly to myself. I had landed in 1980 as a four-year-old child. And this wasn't a dream.

2 ℥

Short

I felt no anger or horror. I didn't panic or collapse into tears. The calendar stared down at me, calm, unyielding, and I matched its lack of emotion. 1980? I hadn't done a thing to get myself shot back in time, reverse-aged.

My baby hand twisted slowly back and forth before my eyes. I turned it over and examined my palm, my soft, perfect little palm. The deep scar from my accident on Diamond Lake had disappeared. I hadn't reached age 11. I hadn't fallen through the ice and gashed open my hand, so that scar didn't exist. The nitric acid burn had vanished from my wrist. I was a chemist, and I'd dripped nitric acid above my glove line in December, but the burn mark had disappeared. The multitude of white nicks that usually populated my fingers had moved their family elsewhere, to older hands.

Was I a time thief? Had I stolen my childhood body? Were my parents going to wake up in Everett, Washington and wonder where I'd gone?

"Do I still know things?"

I expected a brain filled with Oscar the Grouch and Little Bo Peep, to have lost my decades of learning, and this was the thought that finally zapped shock through my gut. No no no! All those years of school! Scrambling around in my mind, I tried to sing the Preamble to the Constitution. "We the people in order to form a more perfect union, establish justice, insure domestic tranquility…" I knew it. Oh, thank God.

I pictured the entire world in my head with its oceans and land masses. Earth rotated in my mind and the continent of Africa spun into view. Egypt, Somalia, Ethiopia. Chad, a face with a flat hat on top, and there sat Cameroon like a deformed kangaroo.

I travelled through different subjects: the Periodic Table and the history of Rome. Phew. My body was young, but the filing cabinets in my head hadn't emptied. All those years of living, of studying. I dropped my face into my baby hands, relieved it hadn't all vanished. I was still me. In a four-year-old's body.

"I'm four-years-old!" I muttered into my palms. "How do I handle being four-years-old!" I couldn't absorb it. It didn't compute.

I pulled at my giant gray T-shirt and recognized a problem. This might be my kitchen in the future, but it wasn't my house yet, and I didn't want to be half naked when the guy in Hudson's room rolled out of bed. I gazed past the calendar through a doorway and up steep wooden stairs; the second floor required investigation. I grabbed the handrail and climbed one step, then another, because children lived in this house, and I needed those children. I knew they hadn't grown up and left home, because the man had blamed Shane when I made noise on a weekend morning.

I reached the bedroom and gently pushed the door inward. Two beds sat on opposite sides of the room under the slanted ceiling. One boy slept deeply on his stomach, his face half buried in a pillow, his arm wrapped around his head. I found another boy curled up in a bean bag chair at the end of the second bed. He raised his eyebrows at me, and I raised my eyebrows back at him.

"Are you Shane?"

He nodded, thumb deep in his mouth. He wore Scooby Doo pajamas, the polyester kind that stick to your skin.

"How old are you?"

He didn't bother to take the thumb out. "Ixth."

"Six?" I nodded hopefully at him. "You're six?"

He nodded.

The sleeping brother looked bigger than Shane. Maybe Shane had clothes he'd outgrown.

"Are there any pants I could wear? I only have this shirt."

Shane finally let his hand fall from his mouth and wriggled to stand up.

"Maybe in the closet?" I pointed at the closet door.

"Yeah. There's clothes in there. Not girl clothes, though. Only boy clothes."

"It's okay. I don't care."

I flipped on the light and waded through the garments that littered the walk-in closet floor, checking tags for sizes. Good good. Shane's mother hadn't done a thrift store run in awhile. I found a white T-shirt and a pair of size 5 jeans and a green sweater.

"Shane!" I hissed through the closet door. "Could you get me some underwear? Clean underwear!"

A minute later, I tugged on clothes and felt a lot better. The pants bagged on me a bit, but I tucked in my T-shirt, and they stayed up. I rolled up the cuffs so they hung to the top of my feet.

Shane didn't seem the least bit worried that a little girl had marched into his room at 7:00 a.m. on a February morning. He just watched me. Finally he said, "We have to stay quiet. Dad likes to sleep in."

I nodded.

"How long are you here?"

"I don't know," I shrugged.

"You want some cereal?"

Down the stairs I cautiously carried the socks and Velcro shoes Shane gave me, because we had to stay quiet. We reached the kitchen, and the wall calendar appeared again. I thought to ask a question.

"Hey Shane. What day is today?"

"Saturday."

"Not Sunday?"

Shane shook his head. "Nope. It's Saturday."

"What's the date?"

"Oh. I guess… Yesterday at school was February one, so I guess it's February two."

February 2, 1980. I'd travelled back in time 40 years. The day I left… it would have been 02/02/2020.

"So many twos."

And it was Groundhog Day. I glanced up at the ceiling. "Oh, so funny," I told God. "That's just hilarious."

How…how was I supposed to get back home? I mean, this was my house, but 40 years in the past. How could I return to my life in 2020, to my kids and my stupid cats and the chemistry lab I managed?

I worked it over in my mind. 1980. Jimmy Carter presided in the Oval Office. The Berlin Wall still stood, keeping all those unhappy people locked away in East Germany.

Earthquakes. What earthquakes loomed ahead of us? I couldn't think of any right away. The big Santa Cruz quake, the one during the World Series, when did that take place? Shoot. It was… it was my sister's 11th birthday. October 17, 1989. Nine-plus years away.

Weird. So weird.

Shane and I ate Fruit Loops in the kitchen, cross-legged on the floor with our backs to the cupboards. I crunched away on the fruity circles, astonished at the lack of nutrition in that house. The pantry offered Apple Jacks and Fruit Loops as our lone, sugary choices for breakfast cereal. In the refrigerator I'd found a half loaf of white bread, rubbery singles cheese and bologna. Sunny Delight. I mean, I liked an occasional bologna sandwich on white bread, but these people had no vegetables, no whole grains. They were determined to die young.

Shane seemed happy I was there. "Let's play Hot Wheels today. We can bring them down to the living room and set them up when Dad gets up." He got a little excited. "I can make the track reach all the way to the kitchen!"

I honestly thought that sounded fun. I liked Hot Wheels, but I needed to figure out how to get back to 2020. Maybe if I went back to sleep in my room, I'd wake up in my own bed again. Maybe my bedroom was an anomaly in the fabric of space-time.

"When does your dad wake up?"

"Like eight or something."

My bedroom an anomaly? I'd slept in that room for 18 years. Eighteen years! Not once had I been sucked through a time portal. What on earth?

Then, I had an unpleasant thought: if Shane's dad got up and saw a little girl in his house, he might send me home. I couldn't explain that we owned the same house in different decades, and I didn't want to get kicked out of the house.

"You want to play Hot Wheels, Shane?"

Shane nodded. "Yeah. It'll be fun! The cars go so sooo fast! And I have loop de loops. You'll see, it's a lot of fun."

"Okay. But, we can't make noise yet, and I'm tired. I'm gonna take a nap in your brother's room first."

Shane's eyes widened. "Oh, you can't! Todd will kill you. You can't go in his room."

I groaned. Yes, Shane. I have to go in his room.

"When does Todd get home? He doesn't have to know."

"He'll know," Shane bobbed his head up and down. "And then he'll yell at me, and Dad'll get mad."

Good grief, buddy. You're entirely too concerned about people getting mad at you.

"Fine," I said. "I gotta go to the bathroom."

I shoved my empty bowl onto the counter by the sink, and I can't tell you how ridiculous it felt to be so short I couldn't even see the sink itself. I had to stand on my toes and push the bowl with my fingertips to move it farther back on the counter. Then, I slunk to the bathroom to find scissors.

If I were going to be stuck in 1980 in boy's clothes, then I might as well have a boy's haircut. People were more inclined to protect a little girl. They might feel obliged to walk a little girl home. A little boy, though… they might simply tell me to get lost. I had to cut off all that long blonde hair, because I needed to stick around long enough to go back to sleep in Todd's bed.

I slowly, quietly slid open each drawer in the bathroom and found toothpaste and baby powder, extra toothbrushes and dental floss – the old kind of waxed dental floss, not the stuff that floats between your teeth. I found vapor rub and aspirin and extra combs and all the stuff people keep in their bathrooms. Finally, in the bottom-most drawer, I found a leather bag containing hair clippers and a variety of attachments. Woot!

I heaved the bag from its drawer and returned to the kitchen. "Shane, buddy, we're gonna buzz off my hair."

Horror widened the boy's eyes. "I cut my own hair once, and Dad got so mad!"

"Your dad's not gonna get mad, because I'm not his kid. He'll think I'm a boy. See?"

Shane shook his head warily. "I don't think you should."

I felt a twinge of guilt. Here they had Shane trained so well, and I wanted to jump-start his corruption.

I plugged the cord into an outlet near the ground and stripped down to my new underwear. I turned on the clippers and proceeded to run them above my right ear. The fine-textured hair couldn't withstand those sharp razor edges, and blonde chaff rained down on the brown linoleum floor. I had to grapple the clippers with both fists, but I ran them through my hair until row after row of locks showered down around me.

Shane stared.

"Would you help me?" I held the clippers to him. "This is hard."

He shook his head. "I don't know how."

I started to hate this family. They stocked sugar breakfast cereal and white bread, had no books in the entire house, and raised kids too scared to watch cartoons on Saturday morning. I struggled to run those heavy clippers over my head until my arms ached.

Shane watched in fascination.

"Please do the back," I begged him. No parents had risen to the morning light. They hadn't noticed the buzzing noise clear across the house. "I promise you won't get in trouble. Please get the back of my head where I can't reach."

When I woke up in my own time, would I have a bald head? I didn't think so, but whoopsie if I was wrong. That would be wild to explain at work. "So yes, I buzzed my head. I still need that report from you."

Shane's lips bundled up with anxiety, but he finally took the clippers from my hands and whispered, "Turn around."

I bent my head over so he had easy access to the area around the back of my neck, and he clumsily buzzed back and forth until the hair gave up from sheer abuse.

I reached up and felt around my head, looking for missed tufts. "There," I pulled out some stragglers "Get these."

Within five minutes, I had an easy-to-manage fuzzy bald head. I grabbed the hand towel from the stove door and brushed myself off, wishing I could take a shower. I found a broom to sweep up the light hay fluff all over the floor, but I kept giggling, because the broomstick poked into the air far above my head.

"I'm so short!" I couldn't get over it. Shane towered over me by four monstrously huge inches.

He held the dustpan for me, and we dumped my hair into the trash bin under the sink. I pulled pop cans and a mashed potatoes box out of the bag to place on top so nobody would notice the hair, then I tugged all my clothes back on, complete with socks and those cool Velcro shoes.

"Do I look like a boy now?" I asked.

Shane nodded.

"Would you even think I was a girl?"

"No. Not in a million years."

"Or at least eight years." I smiled to myself.

3 ɜ

Dodge

Half an hour later, Shane's parents walked out in bathrobes. Not remotely scary people. They didn't seem concerned that I'd appeared in their house, except the mother said, "Oh. Shane has a sweater like that."

Wait. First she asked my name, then she said the bit about the sweater. She saw me in the kitchen when she went to make coffee. "Hello there," she stood above me. "What's your name?"

My eyes blinked several times. A name. I hadn't thought about that. I needed a new name. A boy's name. I paused to drum up something amazing.

"It's okay," she said. "Don't be shy. Did you move in a few doors down? The blue house?"

I shook my head. What was a good name? Bemus. LL Cool J. Taylor. Dakota. Frankenstein. I laughed. It came out as a cute, little kid giggle.

"Does your mom know you're here?"

"Dodge. My name is Dodge."

"Oh. Like the car?"

I shook my head. "Like Dodge City. You know. Get out of Dodge?"

She smiled, but I could tell she didn't get it. She must not have loved *Gunsmoke*.

"That's a nice green sweater you're wearing today, Dodge." At least she was polite. "Shane has one that looks exactly like it. Maybe he can get his and you can be twins."

I ran into the living room. Four-year-olds can get away with anything. They don't have to make small talk.

Shane and I dragged down boxes of Hot Wheels tracks and set them up while his parents got dressed for the day. Shane's nine-year-old brother Elroy shoved the coffee table out of the way, and the boys built tracks up and down all over the living room. They ran them up the couch and down the other side, and soon cars flew off into the dining room.

They got engrossed, and I saw my opportunity to sneak away into big brother's room. I shut the door and clambered onto Todd's bed to send myself back to my own time, my own family.

As I lay there, a sadness crept over the bed with me in it. Nobody gets to fall asleep and wake up in 1980! I had a new name! Dodge. The Artful Dodger. To be absolutely dog honest, I was fascinated that 40 years had rewound overnight. I'd trotted around all morning pretending to be a preschool-aged child, but I had 44 years of information stored in my head. I knew the future! I might declare, "I, Carnac the Magnificent, in my divine and mystical wisdom, will ascertain the answers before even knowing the questions!"

I could make some money.

I snuggled beneath the covers and considered my place in history. Had *Raiders of the Lost Ark* appeared in theaters yet? Darn. I didn't know. "Hindsight's not always 20/20," I said to myself, and I laughed again. 2020.

Weariness tugged at my eyes. I'd risen early in a child's body. The pillow felt good. I snuggled into Todd's bed and flashed through the 1980s as sleep took over.

I awoke several hours later because a 13-year-old boy threw his coat on the bed. I sat up and looked around.

"Hmm. That didn't work."

At my voice. the boy jerked up his fists, startled. He barked, "What are you doing in my room!"

I wanted him to relax. "It's okay. I'm a time traveler. In the year 2020, this is my room, but today I woke up in your bed."

He didn't appreciate the gravity of this miracle at all. "Shane knows he's not supposed to be in my room. Get out of here."

"He didn't come in." I slid off the bed with a thump. "He told me not to, but I was trying to return to the future, so I went back to sleep in your bed."

"Look, I hate little kids in my room," Todd pointed toward the door. "Get out!"

I dashed away and ambled around the house. Hot Wheels tracks slashed back and forth across the living room, but the parents and younger boys had disappeared while I slept.

I stood in the kitchen, desolate. The clock on the wall said 1:10. "Wheel in the Sky" by Journey emanated from Todd's room.

I made myself a bologna sandwich on white bread and ate at the dining room table, confused. It hadn't worked. Falling asleep in Todd's bed hadn't sent me home to my own time. What was I going to do? This dining room was no longer my dining room, and I couldn't stay here. I mentally scanned the town for any friends who would have lived nearby in 1980. Not a person. Nobody. I chewed on my bologna sandwich and pondered.

"Oh!" I realized I hadn't answered one of my first questions. Had I stolen my body? Were my parents looking for me, or had I manifested as an entirely separate being? I stuffed the final crust in my mouth and dragged a chair into the kitchen to climb up to that banana-colored phone. I remembered one phone number from my childhood, one number, and I needed to call it.

My mom had moved us and changed numbers every year or so, but my forever friend Suzie had lived in the same house for 14 years when we were kids. I knew Suzie's number, no problem. I punched the numbers. "Dum dum-de-dum -7-4-1-3-6."

Suzie's parents always answered on the third ring. It was their thing. If they had to walk across the house, they answered on the third ring, and if they chewed on pizza next to the telephone, they answered on the third ring. I held that yellow phone to my ear with both of my small hands and waited for those three "brrrinngs" in my ear.

"Hello?" Judy answered. Suzie's mom.

"Hi, Mrs. Moss." I paused for several uncomfortable seconds.

"Hello," Judy said again, kindly. "Do you want to talk to Suzie?"

I didn't know exactly how to handle this, so on impulse I asked for myself. "Mrs. Moss, is Sadie Cook there?"

"Just a minute. I'll go get her."

"Okay."

I didn't *actually* want to talk to little me! I'd expected Judy to say, "No," so I could follow up with, "Oh. Do you have her number?" Then I'd call my house and talk to my mom. Of course, it made sense that the four-year-old me would be playing with Doozie Suzie on a Saturday afternoon. But I worried. If I talked to my younger self, would the universe unravel? Would time fold in on itself? Would I be blasted to pieces?

"Hang up," I told myself.

No, I needed to make sure.

A child's voice spoke into the phone. "Hello?"

The second hand ticked away on the wall clock. No implosion ripped my world apart. Space-time didn't crack open to suck me into a void.

The little voice repeated, "Hello?"

"Hi," I said cautiously. "Um. Are you Sadie Cook?"

"Uh-huh. Who is this?"

"Do you have a little sister named Kiersten?"

"Huh? No."

"Oh." Stupid me, Kiersten hadn't been born yet. "Do you have a sister named Lila?"

"Yes."

"Hey. You know dogs named Baron and Shadow?"

"Oh yeah. They live next-door."

"Okay good. Your mom is going to have babies soon. She thinks they're gonna be girls, because the doctor said they'd be girls. When she has boys instead, she won't have names for them. You should say to name them Baron and Shadow. Okay?"

"Oh! I like those dogs."

"Cool. Well, um. Goodbye."

"Okay. Bye."

I hung up. Honestly, Mom should have named the twins Baron and Shadow.

I plopped down on the chair and rested my face in my soft, soft, small hands. "This is absurd. This is crazy. This is crazy. This is crazy. This is insane." I hunched there as Journey songs poured from Todd's room down the hall.

I had gone back in time. I had gone BACK IN TIME! I sat on the chair, mentally sucking on that like a Lifesaver. I couldn't go home to my parents or even visit my grandparents. I couldn't interact with my original life at all, because I didn't want to risk messing it up. I still wanted that original me – that little girl on the phone – to grow up and meet my husband and fall in love. I wanted our kids to be born! I couldn't do anything to interrupt our lives.

What was I supposed to do?

I needed to write. I rummaged through the drawers in the kitchen until I found a spiral notepad and a pencil. I tore a sheet off the notepad and leaned on the chair under the phone to use like a desk.

"All right!" I said to myself. "What are my challenges?" I wrote the word "Challenges" at the top of the paper. Under it, I wrote:

"1. Short."

What else.

"2. No money."

What else.

"3. No identity." I had no birth certificate. No social security number. I did not exist on paper.

I don't exist.

I looked at the words I'd written, big words with nice straight lines. I drew a line down the center of the page for a second column. At the top I wrote "Assets." I realized that things in the first column had the potential to be assets, except for "No money." I couldn't see anything good about that.

If I had managed to return to 1980 with the mind of a 44-year-old, I could find ways to take advantage. That is, if I had enough *time* to take advantage, and that was the question. Would I continue from this point onward, or would I – pop – disappear from the past and reappear in the future in an hour or a day or a month? It all depended on how long I was stuck here.

What if I had to repeat the next 40 years?

That thought overwhelmed me, and I didn't want to imagine it. Had I duplicated? Was the original me still living on in the future while a second me split off into the past? I had no way to know.

"If I just live on and on, when I reach Groundhog Day in 2020, I'll have to show up here and take over my life again. I have to make sure my kids still have a mother."

Unless I returned to 4-years-old again. An eternal loop from ages 4 to 44 over and over. That seemed a bit miserable and pointless.

And that's when a realization power-punched me. Right then, right as I pictured myself looping through eternity, an outlandish idea smashed through my brain like a train engine, obliterating all other thoughts in its way.

I stood up. "I can go anywhere."

I had complete freedom! I had no house. No car payment. No bills! I had no parents looking for me or a job to go to. I absolutely had no responsibilities in the entire world. I couldn't go home to my childhood home in Everett, but I also didn't have to live in the frozen mountains of the north.

Jeopardy! I could head to Los Angeles and make my way onto Jeopardy! If I were stuck back in time in a small body, I might as well use my brains and win Kids' Week on a game show. I could make a ton of money and stick it in the bank so that it would be waiting for me if I suddenly popped back to the future again.

Los Angeles. Los Angeles in 1980 looked a world different than it did in 2020. Far more smog. Far fewer homeless people. A smidgen of sanity. Visions of ocean and palm trees - a wonderful shortage of snow - washed through my mind. I needed to catch a ride to southern California.

The clock had ticked to 2:00. It would be getting dark in a couple of hours.

I rummaged through the hall closet and found a small coat that fit me. There was a nylon bag on the closet floor, and I grabbed that too. In it, I stuffed a Nutty Buddy and a can of sardines from the pantry. I pulled a fuzzy hat and mismatched mittens from a box by the door. Finally, I grabbed a new toothbrush from the drawer in the bathroom.

I tugged on my stolen hat and mittens, slung my stolen bag with my stolen food and toothbrush over my shoulder, and headed out the door and down the icy steps. One day those steps would belong to me. One far far away day.

4 ᚦ

Oldsmobile

No great concrete freeway marred Wallace, Idaho in 1980. The snowy hills rose into the blue sky clear and white, unblocked by the overpass that 12 years would bring. Trucks rumbled through town all day and night, and the brick buildings of the mining town were locked back in time, as though the 1950s had refused to let go. Or the 1850s: working girls still populated the town's brothels.

It took me 30 minutes to walk the half mile from my house to the center of town, and I recognized familiar buildings. Fat snowflakes drifted into wide alleys. It was like I'd entered a giant copy of the Wallace I knew, a painting of monstrous old cars and towering old buildings come to life.

A 1970s truck splashed by me, so huge, so tall.

"I'm short," I told the sidewalk. "I'm little and weak. I can't walk fast, but my size can be useful." It meant I could hide in small places. I could sneak into a car or truck and nobody would notice me. Maybe I'd slip into the cab of a semi truck? No, that was ridiculous. I couldn't reach the door of a monster like that.

I hid behind the gas station dumpster and looked for something very specific: a small car with California plates that drove in when the place was empty. That was my brilliant plan, and I figured it would work because there were no credit card readers on the gas pumps back then. The numbers rolled mechanically, and folks flipped a lever to get the gas going. I assumed every single driver would have to pop inside to pay for their gas.

I hadn't realized something, though. An important something. The town of Wallace still had full-service gas stations in 1980. From behind the dumpster, I watched in deep disappointment as one driver after another sat in their cars while the station attendant walked out to serve them. I couldn't go sneaking into anybody's car as the attendant pumped their gas!

I grieved over this development when a train blared on its way through town right behind me. A train!

No. Such a bad idea. First, I'd freeze to death. I imagined my tiny body climbing the icy metal of a train ladder and falling right under the car where the great wheels sliced me in half. They'd find me in two frozen lumps like a Tootsie Roll bitten in half. And I didn't want to go to Chicago or something. I wanted to land somewhere warm, where I could sleep in playground equipment at night.

I leaned against the metal of the dumpster. Pillowy cold flakes landed on my neck, and I appreciated the real danger of my situation. Serious danger. The sun glowed beyond the snow clouds on the west side of town, but night's darkness would soon dominate Groundhog Day in North Idaho. I had no friends to hunt down. I didn't want to hide in somebody's house or camp out in the library, because that only delayed the problem. I needed to jump into a car on its way west, and there wasn't a better time than now.

I pictured all the shops along Bank Street, walking mentally past them to the end of town. And that's when sunshine glowed on my sad little form by the dumpster. The end of town. The grocery store. That was my ticket out.

Thirty minutes later, I hid behind a giant Buick and surveyed the store. Ten cars dotted the parking lot in two rows facing the front doors. Plenty of folks had stopped to shop for dinner, and I hid and watched them enter and exit. I hoped they wouldn't notice me while focused on their lists of milk and lettuce and burger.

Slop slop slop, I dashed through the half-frozen slush, hopping from car to car and checking plates. Idaho. Idaho. Montana. Idaho. Wisconsin.

"Wisconsin? What the heck?"

I had reached the end of the row.

Groan.

I didn't want to try the next row, the one closer to the front door. I hated the idea of all that exposure as people pushed carts through the swinging doors. I ran back the way I'd come, peeking between rows at those other cars.

I growled, "This is the worst! The snow!" Dirty slush half-coated the license plates and blocked my view. I fell back behind the lamp post and hid there in the dusky evening shadows, watching as cars left and others pulled in. When each drove past, I eyed their plates in the dimming light.

My slush-drenched feet had long passed the numbness stage when a Washington plate finally passed me. Washington! That might get me to Spokane or Seattle, which were both warmer than Wallace. I'd mostly seen Idaho plates and didn't dare hold out for California at this point. I scurried to get into position behind my target and watched a lone man climb out. He slumped through the snow and entered through the store's automatic doors. They weren't sliding glass doors like in my time. There were two doors, and they opened inward and outward. He disappeared inside, and I cautiously dashed to his driver's side door, praying he hadn't locked it.

All my plans had failed. California plates? No! Small car? Not a bit. "It's like my father's Oldsmobile." A big, huge, metal Olds.

I used both thumbs to press in the fat button on the handle, and magically, wonderfully, the mechanism clicked inside. I pulled on the handle with both hands, leaning away from that huge metal door with all my 35 pounds of weight, and it eased open just enough for me to wriggle inside. I climbed onto the blue vinyl bench seat and heaved the door shut.

"Clunch."

"Thank you, Jesus," I said wholeheartedly. "Thank you."

I jumped over the bench into the back and dropped to the floor. The fuzzy carpet on the driveline hump made a little bit of a pillow while I waited.

Hopefully this guy headed west. Hopefully he hadn't taken off from Spokane on his way to Bismarck or Fargo. My grandmother had grown up in North Dakota, and we were durable Scandinavian folks, but I didn't care. The North Dakota wind and I made bitter, hateful enemies.

I rested on the floor a solid 10 minutes. The longer I lay there, the worse I feared discovery. If he bought a lot of groceries, the guy might open a back door to shove bags in and see a little kid piled in a heap on his floor. The warm car air and my body both cooled as the minutes ticked by, and I noticed the wet of my clothing, my socks and shoes and mittens. I longed for the guy to return, to start the car and warm me up. But, I also feared he'd spy me. Grab me and drag me out. Hold me up and ask, "What are you doing in my car?"

"Please don't let him see me," I begged, hardly noticing the old vinyl smell in my face. "Please. Pleeeease." Tears blubbed up and over the lip of my eyes. Salty warm drops mixed with melted snow that burned my cheeks.

A crunching sounded outside the car, and anxiety tightened every one of my small muscles. There were no squeaky wheels of a cart, just the slushy stomp of footsteps, and I listened to his movements. Shuffling. The passenger door creaked open and cold snow blew in. Icy fresh air mixed with the vinyl odor. Two paper bags scraped across the front passenger seat. The heavy door slammed shut. Slomp slomp slomp, he walked around the front of the car. The driver's door creaked open. Keys jingled. A heavy woven seat belt whizzed out, and the buckle clicketty clunk, snapped into place. The keys jingled again, and rum rumm... that beautiful engine growled to a happy rumbling life.

In a moment, the radio turned my dark vinyl cave into a bubble of merriment. The Beach Boys sang that we'd have fun fun fun now that Daddy took the T-Bird away. Potholes and mush under the tires bounced and vibrated up into my face, and I stuffed a damp arm up under my head.

Right or left? East or West?

Left. West. Thank you.

I rested in relief. Go west, young man!

5

Trialogue

That big boat of an Oldsmobile drove through the evening. We pulled onto the freeway, and I took my opportunity to ease onto the back seat. I slid across the smooth surface, first body, then legs, then shoes. Ahhh, that felt better. Small or not, I'd gotten cramped curled up on the floor. The car warmed, and I almost got snuggly.

The guy occasionally reached around in his paper bags. A potato chips package rustled, and he crunched and crunched. A root beer can popped open, and the sweet aroma wafted over me.

We passed the glow of Coeur d'Alene and Spokane, zoom zooming beyond the city lights until dark night swamped that Oldsmobile. Vibration from the engine and warmth from the heater and sounds of oldies soothed me as the miles passed. I soon fell into a damp, warm sleep.

Bright gas station lights flashed into my face hours later. My driver filled his car and continued into the dark night. Eventually, he turned his dial through the entire array of stations and only an occasional crackle or faint words behind white noise greeted us. He finally gave up and started singing.

My chauffeur's songs were…hilarious. His voice wasn't good, but it wasn't bad either, and he sang songs I knew. Then, he changed them up with his own lyrics, sometimes rhyming and sometimes not. I'm certain he'd never have crooned freely if he knew he had an audience in the back.

I decided I liked him. I liked Olds Driver.

"I had a girl, and her name was Sal, and she left me colder than the Erie Canal. She's a mule and she's a sow, and she left me colder than the Erie Canal. I hate her face more than a boil. I gots an Olds that burns up oil. Oh, Sal's a drag and she's the worst, and I hope her next car's a big black hearse!"

He chuckled to himself. I stuffed my face into an elbow crook and breathed in and out, in and out, until the urge to laugh faded.

"Oh Sally, Sally what went wrong, oh so wrong!" He started again at full volume. "We went together for so long! Oh yes we did. I never thought a guy could die, until you made with Fred the Pie… face. Oh Sally, you went and left me alone. Hurts so bad! Sally, Sally left me alone. I hope you fly to Bermuda and have a fiery crash in the ocean."

Wow. He wasn't bitter at all.

He sang a few more songs then tried the radio again. I hadn't seen a single light for an hour and expected we'd hit the mountains soon. Had we crossed the Columbia River while I slept?

As my driver sang, I scooted to the window behind his head and peeked outside. I'd forgotten how difficult it was to look out windows as a little kid, because you're too small. I could see upward better than outward, and I gazed at the dim stars above us. I thought we were driving west toward Seattle, and that meant my window faced south. I expected to see Orion, all huge and bright in the southern sky, but no Orion appeared out my window. Which meant … which meant we weren't driving west.

Where was Olds Driver going? I felt momentary concern that we headed north, toward Omak, toward Canada. I eased onto my knees to look out the back window. A full moon washed out most of the twinkles, but the Big Dipper smiled faintly at me. I followed its pointer stars to Polaris.

Okay, then we drove due south. Well, that was fine. South was good.

I settled onto my back with my hands under my head while my driver again twisted his radio dial through the stations. He finally gave up and drove for a long time in silence. He reached into his bag and unwrapped something that filled the car with a spicy, meaty aroma. Pepperoni? No, pastrami. And pickles. My stomach grumbled at me, and I thought of the stolen Nutty Buddy in my bag. I hoped we'd stop soon. I had to use the bathroom.

I'd almost fallen back to sleep when my driver started talking to himself. Muttering at first. Then outright talking. He did both parts of a long conversation with himself. Sometimes three parts.

"Nah, I dint say that."

"Oh yes you did."

"No I dint. You always gots to put words in my mouth."

"Don't say 'gots.' You cain't talk right."

"Hesh yo mouth. You smell like kumquats."

"Don't you say that about her! She's a lady!"

"She's not a lady! She's a toad that smells like kumquats."

"Kumquats. What the world's a kumquat? You make no sense."

"That's cuz I ain't got no cents. I spent 'em all on kumquats."

"Don't say 'ain't.' You cain't talk right."

"Hesh yo mouth. Jo mama's got jowls that would make a saddle-bag proud."

"You leave my mama out of this."

"Oh no. Jo mama ain't gots a chance when I'm around."

"Seymour, you be nice."

"Now now now… I'm not nice. Don't you go tryin to change me."

"You cain't change!"

"Nope, I cain't! I done spent all my change on kumquats."

And that's when I giggled.

It was like the time back when I was five. I talked and talked and wouldn't shut up, so my Uncle George said, "Hey Sadie, I'll bet you five dollars you can't stop talking for an hour."

I said, "Okay! It's a bet!" Then, I retired to the rec room upstairs, where it was easy to keep quiet while watching Bugs Bunny.

In the middle of my second show, Uncle George called up the stairs, "Hey Sadie!"

"What!" I answered.

"Haha! You lose!"

Oh! That rat tricked me! He waited until I'd forgotten that I was supposed to keep quiet, then he called out to me.

Seymour made that last crack about kumquats, and I laughed. I had forgotten! For one single moment I forgot I had to keep quiet and let a laugh fall out.

And his foot lifted off the gas.

I froze, my eyes wide in the back seat. I could hear him stretch, listening. I could hear him wondering if he'd simply imagined a child's giggle behind him. I knew he concentrated on his rearview mirror, but all he saw behind him was darkness. Blackness.

Olds Driver pressed the gas and drove onward, but he no longer entertained us with his spastic trialogue. I lay absolutely still, taking slow breaths to avoid suffocation.

I started to relax. Maybe he'd shrugged it off.

Then, without warning, the car slammed over to the side of the road, and I slid involuntarily to the floor with a thump. We skidded to a stop in the gravel, and "clunk," the gear lever moved to Park. His door slung open and the dome light came on, shining like a veritable sun through my dark vinyl bubble.

I hunched into a ball on the floor, tucked into the smallest space possible, trying to look like a lump of rags. It didn't work. The door opened behind me, and a hand grabbed me by the back of my stolen coat and plopped me onto the back seat.

A variety of unmentionables burst from the man's mouth.

"What's wrong with you!" He spun and stomped around outside his car on a snow-crusted, lonely road, cursing at the moonlit sky. In a moment, his face appeared again in the doorway. He looked about 30, both young and grown up at the same time. He hadn't shaved, and his five-o-clock shadow had darkened into something like a two-day-o-clock shadow. His dark hair stuck up all messy.

"Where do you live? I can't take you home! I do not have the gas money or - or - or the *time* to drive you home! You stupid little kid! Where do you live?"

He did not strangle me, and relief spread through my chest. I needed him to get on a page with me as quickly as possible.

"What's your name?" I asked. "Is your name Seymour?" He had used that name in his trialogue.

"No!" He shook his head. "No, that's... that's just one of my - I - I just have made-up names for - That's not important. What's your name?"

"My name is Dodge."

"Dodge, I need to know where to put you." He got angry again. "Why did you do that! Why did you climb into my car! Do you realize how far we've driven? Wait a minute. Did you get in at Kennewick ... or Wallace... or Missoula? How long have you been stowed back there?"

"It's okay, Seymour," I said. "You don't need to take me backward. I don't want to go back."

"Mike! I'm Mike. Don't be stupid. You can't run away. You have to go home."

"That's the thing," I tried to explain. "I don't have a home. I don't have parents. Nobody is looking for me. I'm going to California."

"What do you mean you don't have parents! Of course you have parents."

"Not anymore, I don't. And I'm a genius, with ridiculous, super genius powers. And I don't want the CIA to get ahold of me and stick me in a little room and do electroshock on me to control me. I really don't want that to happen. Please calm down and just keep going to wherever you were going, and we can talk while you drive."

I'm sure that whole spiel sounded other-worldly spilling from the mouth of a tiny kid. I should have been crying and snotting on myself like a respectable child, but I met Mike's stare and waited for him to make a decision. I knew he wasn't going to leave me alongside the road, and that was the only thing I couldn't handle at the moment. He'd have to keep driving with me somewhere. Somewhere that wasn't the middle of nowhere.

He glared at me. "You're a super genius, huh? And you don't want the CIA to get you?" He sounded less than convinced.

I nodded. "But, I have to poop. Can we go somewhere sanitary so I can do that?"

Mike gave up. He sort of wilted, like he had no energy to fight about it.

"Okay, listen up. You're going to sit in the front seat and answer every question I ask. And you're not going to be a little jerk about it, okay?"

I nodded.

He grabbed his two bags of groceries from across the front seat and stuffed them past me into the back seat. Then he slid me out by my coat, physically picked me up and slung me over his shoulder around the front of the car to the passenger door. His flannel jacket bounced against my face fuzzily as he walked. I couldn't see anything until he had uprighted me, and the dashboard came into focus as he dropped me into my new seat.

"Where are we?"

"No. I ask the questions." Mike slid the broad seat belt across me to click it into place. The shoulder strap hit me in the face, so he tucked it behind me and tugged on the lap belt until it snugged against my middle. Then, he slammed the door.

Half a minute later, the Oldsmobile rumbled back down the road.

"I'm ticked off at you," he informed me. "I don't care if you're a super genius or an alien or a secret government weapon, I am so sooo angry you sneaked into my car."

I didn't say anything. To be honest, I felt victorious. We'd driven too far for him to turn around, and I no longer had to hide in the back. I didn't have to curl up on the floor, breathing exhaust.

"What did you say your name was? Dodge?"

I nodded.

"Dodge?"

He couldn't see me in the dark car. I had to answer.

"Yes."

"Dodge what?"

"Dodge Journey." It was the first thing that bounced through my head, and I laughed. I'd just given myself a car name after all.

"What's funny?" Mike asked. "That's not funny. Nothing about this is funny."

"I'm sorry, Mike. I really am. I know you're upset I got in your car, but I think you're fantastic. I'm glad I stowed away with you and not some psycho. I like you a lot."

I sensed the scowl on his face as he focused out the windshield at the road. It's hard to return "You're fantastic," with "You're a little twit," but he managed it.

"Well. You're a little twit," Mike growled.

"Probably. Still, you saved my life. I was going to freeze to death in the slush, and getting into your car saved me. So! Ask me questions."

He drove in silence for a few moments. "Okay. Where are you from? Do your parents beat you up? Is that why you ran away?"

"No. I don't have parents."

"Are they going to report you missing? Am I'm gonna get charged with kidnapping?"

"I. Don't. Have. Parents."

"Are you a science experiment?"

I hadn't thought about that. "You know…Maybe I am."

"You don't know?"

"No. I don't. But I'm a real human being. I'm not a robot or an android or anything."

"How old are you?"

"Forty-four."

"I told you not to be a jerk,"

I sighed. This whole thing was going to be difficult. I hated lying, but the truth didn't sound believable. People weren't going to believe the truth. I'd have to give them amended truths and sound relatively reasonable - offer stories that made sense to them. I didn't want to tell Mike I'd fallen asleep the night before in 2020 or that I had 40 years of memories not accounted for by my small body.

"I was born in July of 1975," I said honestly.

"Okay. And where are you from?"

"I was born in Saugus, California. But I've moved about 25 times since then." That was true. My four-year-old self had only moved two times, but the full me had jumped all over the country before settling back home in Wallace.

"Like where?" He sounded doubtful.

I took a deep breath. "Washington, Idaho, Texas, Colorado. But I woke up this morning in somebody else's house where I didn't want to be. So, I figured I'd head to Los Angeles. At least, south where it's warm. Maybe Santa Monica. Doesn't Santa Monica sound nice?"

Mike squinted at the snow dusted road. "What do you mean. You woke up in somebody else's house?"

"Exactly that. I woke up in some other kid's bed, and I have no clue how I got there. It wasn't my bed, and it wasn't my house. But, I have no parents or guardians, so nobody is missing me. It's not like I'm a lost child. I'm telling you, not a soul on this planet is looking for me."

"That doesn't make any sense. What happened to your parents? Like... they're both dead?"

"Whether they're alive or dead really doesn't matter. I don't have them."

"Did somebody kidnap you? Who has been raising you?"

I scratched my nose. "That's a good question. Mike, I really have to go to the bathroom. Is there a town nearby at all? Can you tell my pelvic muscles how long they have to hold on?"

Mike snorted. I think he tried to stifle a laugh, and it came out wrong. "You're a pain, you know that, right?"

"Yes, sir. I'm certain of it."

"Okay. We're about ten miles north of Grass Valley, Oregon."

The dark world passed by outside with only the occasional light in the distance.

"Oregon? You have Washington plates."

"Until a little while ago, I lived in Washington."

"Like... a month ago?"

"I don't know. Two years? I'll get them changed one of these days." Then he snapped, "And no questions about me! I'm interrogating you! I think you're a big fat liar. But, if you're a super genius, I want to know how much you actually know."

I sat silent when he said that. I realized that I could spit out all kinds of impressive things, but I suddenly felt shame in it; I was a humbug, the Wizard of Oz, pretending to be something I wasn't.

"Can you do algebra?"

"Yep."

"No you can't."

"Yeah, I can," I said dispassionately. "And I can do geometry, but I mean… I think any four-year-old should be able to do geometry. It's long division that's a pain in the neck."

Mike chuckled. "Tell me about it." He thought for a moment. "Can you read?"

"Sure."

"Spell something for me, then."

"Okay."

He sucked on his lower lip. "Spell cow."

"C-O-W."

"Spell Frankenstein."

I laughed. Frankenstein. "Okay. F-R-A-N-K-E-N-S-T-E-I-N."

I could tell that impressed him. "Not bad. Spell chrysanthemum."

"Whatever. I bet *you* don't know how to spell chrysanthemum. Even if I spelled it right, you wouldn't know."

"I do, as a matter of fact."

"Okay, fine then." I tried to think of Anne of Green Gables from the show. Gilbert Blythe had spelled it wrong, and Anne got it right. "Okay. C-H-R-Y-S…A-N-T-H…E…M-U-M." That E in the middle was important.

Mike started laughing for real. "That's pretty awesome. What's 18 times 6?"

"Ow. Um. That's 60 plus 48. So. 108."

"What's the square root of 121?"

"Eleven."

"What's 20 cubed?"

"So, 400 times 20 is … 8000."

"What's the capital of Minnesota?"

"Minneapolis. No, wait! St. Paul."

"Who is buried in Grant's tomb?"

Really? "I never understood why people ask that," I said. "Isn't it Grant? Like. It's a question to stump stupid people?"

"Yes. Who was the 40th president?"

"Ronald Reagan."

"Ahah, you got me," Mike said. "That's a good guess, though."

That's right! Ronald Reagan hadn't been elected yet! I was tempted to tell Mike I knew Ronald Reagan would be the 40th president. I wanted to tell him what would happen in the future.

"You don't think he can beat Carter?" I asked.

"I mean, sure. I think a dancing duck could beat Carter."

Mike no longer grimaced at his windshield, and that cheered me. Maybe it wasn't so bad to be a humbug.

"You want to know what's really weird, Mike?"

"What?"

"You were probably born in 1950."

"1949."

He was the same age as my mom. He was this young guy, and in 2020, Mike would be 70-years-old, maybe already 71. In my world, he was legitimately an older fellow, and here I was driving in a 1960s Oldsmobile with him as a 30-year-old young man. It felt so strange, I wanted to cry.

"Why's that weird?"

I shook my head. "I just feel older than somebody who was born in 1975."

I could sense him nod in the seat next to me. "Yeah. I can see that."

A few minutes later, we drove into a little town. The few lights glowed dimly, and I doubted that any gas stations stayed open that late. It had to be nearing midnight.

"I really have to go. Are there any places open?"

"No," Mike said. "But I have an aunt here. We'll sneak into her place and you can use her bathroom."

6 ∂

Aunt Mindy

I realized that age had changed me, had softened me. I'd come to appreciate how few things were worth fussing about. When I was 12, sneaking into a stranger's house in the middle of the night, potentially waking her up, that would have mortified me. Now? Now, I'd gotten exceptionally practical, and I was perfectly happy if I didn't have to do my business in a field. I didn't care if Mike's aunt yelled at us for waking her up. I didn't care if she chased us out with a shotgun - as long as I could use her bathroom first.

Or, maybe I felt that way because I'd returned to early childhood and had no sense of propriety.

Mike turned down one road and then another before he pulled in front of a small house with a separate garage. The moon shone bright in the northeast, almost a full round circle, but an electric candle still glowed in the darkness of the big window out front.

"Come on," Mike hissed. "Let's make this quick."

He pulled me up concrete steps and through an unlocked front door, and I welcomed the warmth inside the house. Mike led me through the living room, then used his whole arm to point to the left, down a hallway where a cheery night light lit the bathroom.

"Go. And try to be quiet."

I gently shut the door and handled things. So relieved. I felt like Mike had saved my life again. I owed him the world. I owed him a million dollars. One day, I would bless his grandchildren.

Of course, Auntie heard us, because old women are like owls and cats. Old men sleep through atomic bomb testing, but old women wake when the dog shifts its weight on the couch. I emerged from the bathroom to find Mike in the kitchen past the living room, chatting with a middle-aged woman. She sat in a white terry cloth bathrobe, her short brown hair in the process of going silver. She'd flicked on the lights and put a kettle on the stove. It hissed as it heated.

She asked, "You mean, this little child?"

Mike nodded.

"I'm Dodge." I reached out my hand to shake hers.

"My! He's just a tiny thing! And he's soaking wet, Mike! Here, baby. You take those things off."

Oh, I liked this aunt! My clothes weren't soaking, but they were damp enough. She started pulling off my excess cover: my mismatched mittens and hat, my jacket and sweater and pants and socks. When she'd peeled me down to my T-shirt and underwear, she stopped. That's where the wet seemed to end.

"I don't have dry clothes."

"Don't worry about that," she said. "We'll throw these in the dryer and get them nice and warm. Mikey, hon, why don't you both sleep here tonight? I can wash his things and dry them, and you can have breakfast and drive the rest of the way in the morning."

Mike protested. "It's only two more hours."

"It's past midnight! And this little one needs dry clothes. Don't you, Dodge?"

"Yes ma'am." I smiled, because I knew I looked adorable, standing there, acting super polite in a T-shirt and baggy underwear.

"Are you hungry, Dodge?"

"Yes, ma'am."

She grinned, tickled. "Well, baby. I'll make you up a grilled cheese sandwich, okay? And you don't have to call me 'ma'am,' Dodge. You just call me 'Aunt Mindy.'"

A hot sandwich sounded awesome. The last thing I'd eaten was that bologna thing hours earlier, and my poor tummy cried in its emptiness. As soon as she said, "grilled cheese," I felt I'd die before she'd finished making it.

"Do you want to take a bath, Dodge? You can get nice and warmed up, and I'll wash your underclothes too."

My discomfort showed. Aunt Mindy read my face and assumed I was shy, not guessing I wanted to hide the deeper realities of my identity.

"Don't worry," she said. "I have jammies for my grandson here. You can take those into the bathroom with you, and you can have all the privacy you need. I'll run a bath for you, okay?"

"I can take a shower. I can do it."

In a few minutes, I hugged a pair of footie pajamas with the feet cut out AND a set of Captain America Underoos. I cannot tell you the excitement those Underoos gave me. When Aunt Mindy placed the briefs and undershirt in my hands, I gaped with my mouth half open. "These are amazing," I breathed. "I love them."

Aunt Mindy grinned, pleased at my delight. "You go ahead and keep them, baby. My little Charlie's outgrown them."

I carried my garments into the bathroom and took a hot shower that chased away every last shiver I had. After I toweled off, I borrowed the hair dryer from under the sink and dried out my ears and enjoyed the wonderful warm air. With every bit of dampness gone, I girded my loins and chest with the noble Captain America and climbed onto the counter to study myself in the mirror.

Haha! That was so fun. I looked like a little boy with a fuzzy head. I made muscles and laughed at myself. Then I hopped down, pulled on my pjs, and trotted into the living room.

Aunt Mindy grabbed me and swooped me into a seat at the table in front of a large grilled cheese sandwich on whole wheat bread. Mike sat opposite me, pulling apart his own grilled cheese and stuffing it into his mouth. He still looked disgusted, as though I'd gotten him into this. I had forced him to visit his sweet aunt and eat a hot, gooey sandwich and sleep instead of driving through the night.

Aunt Mindy had used cheddar, and I enjoyed every creamy bite. I paused between mouthfuls. "May I have some water? I'm awfully thirsty."

She set a glass of water before me and returned to the counter to make our cocoa.

"Aren't you tired?" I asked. "I'm sorry we woke you up. I just had to go to the bathroom."

"Listen, I'm glad you had to go to the bathroom, baby. Mikey hardly ever stops by, and I love to see him. I don't mind that you had to drag him here in the middle of the night."

I smiled at that wonderful lady, then set down my sandwich to gulp water. So so thirsty. It soothed my mouth and throat, cool and delicious, and my tiny tummy swelled.

Aunt Mindy settled down beside me with her own cup. She poured milk into it from a quart container. "Would you like some milk to cool your cocoa?"

I nodded. She had only filled my mug halfway, wise woman.

I wiped my mouth with the back of my hand. "What did Mike tell you about me?"

Mike focused on his food and didn't even look up.

She poured in a bit of milk that swirled and lightened the brown in my cup. "Oh," she finally answered. "He told me that he was friends with your dad. That you had a little trip to visit your grandparents, and he's taking you home. And, he tells me that you're very smart."

I tried to thank Mike with my eyes. I didn't want Aunt Mindy to know about my homeless status. I didn't want the cops to appear at Aunt Mindy's door in the morning and cart me away with my cool new Captain America underwear. I wanted to thank Aunt Mindy for being such an honest, open person who willingly believed her fibbing nephew.

"He says your dad is an engineer at his company. He thinks you might be an engineer one day like your dad."

I shook my head. "I'm going to be a chemist."

"Really?" Aunt Mindy raised her eyebrows. "What does a chemist do?"

"Well. The kind of chemist I'm going to be is the kind that can tell what's in rocks." I didn't want to sound too smart to Aunt Mindy. I might talk quantum physics with Mike, but Aunt Mindy needed to see me as a child who liked shiny things. "Miners are looking for gold and silver, and they need to know if they have them in their rocks. So, that's what I wanna do."

Mike slowly shook his head. He recognized I was pretending to be an almost-normal little kid. Smart, but normal. Well, he was the one who had outright lied! We were a pair, both of us telling stories to his precious Aunt Mindy. Except that I did want to be a geochemist. Or rather, I'd been a geochemist in a future life.

"Mike, are you an engineer too? Like my dad?"

Mike took a bite of his sandwich and chewed for awhile. "No." He swallowed his food and drank down his cocoa. "I'm in sales. I sell the machines your dad designs."

"Oh. That's right."

"That's right. Aunt Mindy, my dear. I love you, but I'm heading to your spare room. Feel free to talk to Dodge, but don't tell him my secrets. He's a sneaky little guy. He'll be figuring out how to empty my bank account if you're not careful." Mike reached over and gave his aunt a kiss, then he disappeared into another room.

"I like Mike," I said when he'd gone. "He's funny."

Aunt Mindy's face warmed into a big smile. "Yes, he is."

"Thank you for drying my clothes. I was running around in the snow before I got in Mike's car. It wasn't Mike's fault, it was mine."

"Well, that's what little boys do. But, don't feel too bad if you need to throw a snowball at Mike." She leaned forward and whispered, "I think you should. Tomorrow, you throw snow at him for me, would you?"

I snickered. "Okay."

"Okay," she smiled.

At that very moment, a feeling of longing swept over me so strong and sweet that tears blubbed up in my eyes. I thought of my own three children, separated from me by decades. I thought of all the people I had lost in one strange day. I tried to hide my face in my sleeve, but that lovely woman saw my emotion before I managed to cover it.

"My goodness! What's wrong, Dodge?"

"Nothing." I took a long draw from the cooled cocoa and wiped my eyes. That cured me a little. "I just..." I wanted her to know part of the truth. "I just think you're so kind and nice. I wish I had met you before today."

"Aww, Dodge. Well! Maybe you can come back and visit me. Make my nephew come and see me."

That didn't sound too bad. "Hey!" I thought of something. "I have an idea. What's your address? I'll write you a letter!"

"That's a wonderful idea! I would love to get a letter from you."

Without thinking, I reached for my cell phone, but only patted the sides of my footless pajamas. That's right, no cell phones. Aunt Mindy had a viable alternative for keeping her address handy, though. She disappeared into another room and returned with a miniature red notepad, just my size.

"I'm going to give this to you, Dodge. It's your address book, and every time you meet a friend that you want to write letters to, you just put their address in here. Okay?"

"Okay." No cell phones. No Internet.

She wrote her name and address and phone number on the first page, and her information filled the little paper.

"Will the sheets fall out easily?" I didn't want to lose Aunt Mindy's address.

She tugged on several of the pages. "They seem pretty well glued in there. Just don't get it wet. Don't go dropping it in the snow."

I turned the tough pages; the book contained 25 small square sheets in total. I had an address book! What a splendid thing. Much better than writing on a single sheet that would get dropped or run through the laundry.

"Thank you, Aunt Mindy." I took the cup of cocoa and drank it down deeply. Then, I wiped my mouth on my sleeve.

Geez. I really was a child again.

7

Bradbury

I awoke from a shove and Mike's smooth face over me.

"C'mon, get up."

I sat up in the couch cushions, still in Aunt Mindy's living room, still in 1980.

Mike had shaved and combed his hair and dressed in a button-up shirt. The flannel hobo had transformed into a respectable adult.

"Hey, you look sharp!"

"Put your clothes on. We need to get going."

My clothes lay folded in a neat pile on the coffee table, and I quickly shed the pjs and pulled jeans over my beloved Underoos. I tucked in my T-shirt to keep my pants from falling down and folded the sleeves of my green sweater up one roll.

Aunt Mindy had produced orange slices and scrambled eggs, and I stuffed my face at her table while Mike drank coffee and munched a piece of toast. She and I chatted and laughed until Mike stood and said we had to leave. Aunt Mindy gave me a warm hug and kissed my cheek before I climbed back into Mike's car.

In the light of day, full of food and dry, I felt pretty darn good. Mike headed south, and I didn't have to walk those long miles that his blue Olds ate up at 55 miles-per-hour. As we drove through the Oregon countryside, still white with snow, Mike looked over at me and shook his head.

"Your legs hardly stick past the edge of the seat. Did you tell Aunt Mindy you could do trigonometry and calculus and stuff?"

"I never told you that I could do trig and calculus and stuff."

"Yeah, but you just called it 'trig.' You didn't tell her you knew the nuclear strike codes either, but you probably do."

"I might."

"That's what I thought," he nodded. "Listen. The biggest question is this: what am I going to do with you?"

I shrugged. He'd helped me plenty already, and I was happy. "Look, I appreciate the ride, and you don't have to do anything with me. When we get to wherever you're going, I'll be very naughty and run off. I'll disappear, and you won't have to bother your head about me."

"'Bother my head?' Who *are* you? No, young stowaway. That right there is a terrible idea. You might be a genius with your finger on the nuclear button, but don't run off. We'll figure something out. Do you have any relatives in Santa Monica where you intend to land?"

My mom's family all lived north of L.A. I had aunts and uncles down there, but I couldn't go see any of them. I sighed, overwhelmed again by loneliness. I'd been cut off from everybody I'd ever known.

"My situation is abnormal, Mike. When I said I lost my parents, I was telling you the truth. I don't mind going into foster care, but I need to live somewhere down near Hollywood."

"Near Hollywood? Why?"

"Or Burbank, or wherever it is they film Jeopardy. They have Kids' Week on Jeopardy, don't they?"

Mike gave me a half smile. "Sorry to break it to you, kiddo, but Jeopardy was cancelled."

"What! No Jeopardy?" I couldn't believe it! I realized I didn't know the exact dates for things. I imagined Alex Trebek out there right that minute, walking door-to-door to beg for a job. "Mike, listen. Jeopardy will resurrect like the phoenix, and I want to get on it. No matter what, I don't want to be stuck in the icy north."

Mike frowned. "How were you planning to go to Hollywood, anyway? Were you gonna stow away in random cars until you finally got there?"

"Well. Gandalf owes me a favor. I could hit him up for a ride on his eagles."

Mike only grimaced above me.

It was a joke, Mike. Laugh. "Fine. Yes. I figured I'd sneak into a car with California plates next. With or without Gandalf, I was pretty much winging it."

Haha. Winging it. Hahaha.

Mike shook his head. "That was bad."

I couldn't help giggle. "What are you talking about? That's funny!"

"So bad." Mike kept shaking his head.

We must have drifted toward the shoulder, because he abruptly straightened the car. He did smile then, embarrassed. "It's really weird. You're this little bitty kid, but then you talk, and I feel like we should be sitting somewhere having a beer. And it doesn't do any good to watch the road and not look at you, because you have this baby bear voice, this tiny Chip and Dale chipmunk voice, and I can't get over it."

I could see his point.

We drove for two more hours, and Mike answered some of my questions. He lived in Bend, Oregon. No, he wasn't married. Yes, Sally had dumped him.

"Nooo," he groaned. "You heard me singing, didn't you?"

"I loved it. It's when I decided I liked you. 'Sally. Sally what went wrong, oh so wrong...'"

"I can't believe you heard that."

"What was her problem anyway?"

"I was gone all the time for work, and she wanted me home. Her family is in Camas, Washington, and she begged me to take a job at the paper factory there - they're trying to modernize. But Dodge, have you ever been to Camas?"

I had, actually. "Camas is pretty. It's nice and green there."

"Yes, but it's a paper factory town, and paper mills plain stink. The stench covers the whole area, and I didn't want my kids to grow up having the Papermakers as their school mascot. So, I told Sally I wanted to try something else, and she decided to try *someone* else."

"That's cheeseball. You should be glad she moved on. If she didn't love you enough to wait a minute for you, you shouldn't spend the rest of your life with her." That was a fact.

"Oh, I know." He curled his lip in more of a pout than a snarl. "I know. But, Fred! He's got the personality of a ski jump. It's totally insulting that she dumped me for Fred. He's probably already chained up there in Camas, happy with a life of shoveling paper pulp."

Mike's lips popped the p's in "paper pulp" so that they sounded even pulpier.

I tried to soothe him. "There are nice girls out there. Shoot, I'd tell you to marry my mom. But, of course, you can't. And now I'm sad."

"Thanks, twerp. I appreciate that."

I stared at my smooth, tender hands again. At that moment, at that very moment, my mother's stomach swelled like the Goodyear

Blimp, 32 weeks pregnant with my twin brothers. In three years, she'd leave my dad and stumble through a series of lousy relationships and never ever happily marry. I doubted Mike wanted to wait three years to take on a woman with five small children.

"Mike, I know I can't stay with you. I have other things I need to do, and you didn't ask me to climb into your car."

He stared straight ahead, his smooth chin slowly bobbing up and down. "These things are correct."

"But." I thought about it. "I don't intend to lose you forever. One day you might get a note from me, maybe 20 years from now, and it would be fun to have that beer with you."

Mike smiled, and a wry wrinkle tugged at the corners of his eyes. "Okay kid. Sure thing."

We reached Bend about mid-morning, and Mike pulled into an apartment complex and parked his car. He grabbed his bag of leftover groceries and a suitcase from the trunk then directed me to follow him up the exterior stairs.

"Here's the deal, Dodge." He set down his suitcase to unlock the door. "I need to go into work, and you need to stay here. Normally I wouldn't leave a little boy alone by himself, but you're not normal, right? You are not, under any circumstances, to leave this apartment. Do not run off. Understand?"

"Yes. I got it. Do you have any books?"

"I have books. Look. I have books, see?" He led me into a living room that included shelves filled with histories and mysteries! The place boasted a kitchenette and a round table, a bedroom and small bath, and that was it. Just a one-bedroom cubby hole.

"Wait. Why are you going to work on Sunday?"

"I just need to check on something." Mike placed the bag of food on the table, tossed the suitcase onto his bed, and shut the door to his bedroom. He glanced around and felt his pockets for important things. Wallet? Yes. Keys? Yes.

I saw Mike's shoebox of a television and thought of the flat-screens of the future. We didn't have hoverboards or flying cars in 2020. We didn't have regularly chartered flights to the moon. We had to grow our apples on trees the old-fashioned way. But! We had monstrous, vast televisions and a world of movies on demand. We had smart phones that could give us videos on polar bears or cheese making or DNA transcription whenever we asked. Or cats. So many cat videos.

I wanted to tell Mike. I wanted to tell him about flat-screen TVs and the Internet and smart phones. But I didn't.

"All right." He opened the front door again. "Stay out of trouble. If you're hungry, eat something, but clean up after yourself. If you so much as open the front door, I will kick your rear end, got it?"

I crossed my heart. "I got it."

"Hope to die, stick a needle in your eye?"

I grinned. "Yes."

"And stay out of my bedroom!" The key clicked in the lock.

I turned around and around in the entryway. Where was Mike's Atari? Where was his Rubik's Cube? See? That was my problem. I didn't know when things became popular. Maybe the Rubik's Cube hadn't multiplied across the country yet. Maybe it hadn't descended on the masses, a cruel Hungarian device of torture meant to brutalize the West.

I looked through Mike's groceries: the rest of the root beer and chips, some oranges and pretzels. Not a single kumquat.

I skimmed his bookshelf next. *The Rise and Fall of the Third Reich* jumped up all bold. Hmmm. He had a set of Dickens. Books on selling things. Books on home repair and wood working. U.S. Civil War history. So much Civil War history. The man must be a Civil War fiend. No westerns, although he did have a Time-Life collection on *The Old West*. No philosophy. No Voltaire. No Stephen King or Michael Crichton or Sue Grafton. No biographies. He did have *The Complete Sherlock Holmes*. And George Orwell's *1984*. Ha.

When did Tom Clancy start publishing? I'd read *The Hunt For Red October* my freshman year of high school in 1989. Had he written anything before that?

I browsed the titles on the bookshelf and none of them interested me, not even the phenomenal Ray Bradbury. *Something Wicked This Way Comes* stared at me, and I plain didn't feel it. The bottom shelf held vinyl records, though. Records! I spent a bit of time fiddling with Mike's turntable and stereo. Then, I walked my fingers through that record collection, and Marty Robbins' *Gunfighter Ballads* soon mellowed the air. I lay on the couch and stared at the ceiling. Those familiar old ballads made me think of my dad.

I wondered what secret developments Mike had going on. Were the cops about to show up? If I'd found a genius child in my car, I'd have called the police to check if he were missing, no matter what he said. I'd have expected a genius child to deceive with more skill than a normal rotten kid. I honestly kept waiting for the cops to arrive.

When Mike finally returned two hours later, he found me resting on the carpet under the crooning of Three Dog Night, hunting for pictures in the sprayed popcorn on his ceiling.

"Hi Mike." I waved lazily from the floor as he returned the record player needle to its cradle.

"Okay kiddo. To business. Come sit up here real quick."

I rolled over. "Did you tell the police on me?" I climbed onto the couch beside him. "Are they going to come take me away?"

Mike shook his head. "No kidding, I want to know where you belong. Somebody somewhere has got to be looking for you."

"Nobody is looking for me."

He rolled his eyes. "But, I also considered a certain possibility. I realized that if somebody *is* looking for you, they might not be the good guys."

"Nobody is looking-"

"Shhh." Mike took hold of both my hands, and his serious blue eyes looked me in the face. He appeared so respectable with his jaw shaved smooth and his dark waves combed back like Superman. I'd pulled off Shane's green sweater, and I sat there in a white T-shirt and jeans. Mike lifted my arms up and down and checked my ears. He had me open my mouth to say, "Ahhhh." He took his index finger and pressed it slowly into my left cheek, as though testing to see if I were real. He worked his fingers over my neck and fuzzy skull. Then he gently squeezed down my arms like he was giving me a massage, first my left arm and then my right.

"What are you doing?"

"You seem okay." He frowned, monumentally puzzled.

I smiled. "I'm not injured."

"No, I don't think you are," he murmured.

"I'm not a robot either."

Mike sat up. "Okay. Here's the deal. In two days, I have to drive down to San Francisco. You can stay here two days and drive down with me. You want to land in Los Angeles. Right? We'll get on a plane, and I'll deposit you in Los Angeles, but I can't stay. I'll have to turn around and go back to San Francisco."

"Really? Thanks. That's... that's amazing."

"But, here's the catch. At the other end, child protection people will pick you up and find a home for you."

I slumped. I didn't like it, but it made more sense than dropping me off on the streets. "Thanks. That works."

"Unless there's a relative I could send you to."

I thought of Uncle George in Saugus and Aunt Shelly in Palmdale, but I shook my head. "Honestly, there's nobody I can go to. I mean, I would go see my grandparents if I could. But, I can't."

"Why not?" Mike asked more gently than before. "Why can't you go home? What trouble are you in?"

I shook my head, miserable. "I'm not in trouble. I'm not. I just plain don't have a home."

I looked up at him, and he looked back at me. And that was that.

8 8

Redwoods

The next day, Mike and I made chicken and dumplings together. He wouldn't trust me to cut up carrots and celery, but in the end we both enjoyed a feast. Mike photographed me standing on a chair next to the pot of chicken soup.

"Do you want to prove me to your friends?"

He shook his head. "Nope. I want to prove you to me. Once you're gone, I won't believe you ever existed."

He even got out an ancient Super 8 camera and filmed while I read *Oliver Twist*. "Now read about Hitler." He handed me his giant book about the Third Reich. He filmed while I penciled out fractions and decimals. I didn't offer to do any trigonometry or derivatives, because that seemed obnoxious.

On Monday, we visited a thrift store and Mike bought me a pair of jeans and a hooded sweatshirt, three shirts and a pack of socks. I found an L.A. Dodgers backpack and jumped up and down I was so excited to buy it.

Tuesday morning, we packed up and drove to California, but Mike did not take the most direct route to San Francisco. I knew we chugged about 100 miles out of the way, because I had charge of the map book. Mike directed us through the northwest corner of the state, and we ate our lunch under the redwoods. How great was that? A fellow explorer agreed to take our photo under those magnificent trees, and Mike swooped me onto his shoulders. We grinned at the camera - two ants at the base of a vast wood tower - and we didn't say, "Hi there, Mr. Tourist. We met four days ago."

On and on we drove until we reached the hotel about 10 p.m. I awoke briefly when Mike carried me up and tucked me into bed.

San Francisco sunlight shone across my covers the next morning. This was the day. Mike drove us out to the airport and led me through ticketing and security. He firmly held my hand while we walked along.

"Wow," I said without thinking. "You don't have to take off your shoes."

"Why would they make you do that?"

"Because of shoe bombers..."

"Shoe bombers?" He laughed at me. "Seriously?"

As we trekked through the plane to our seats, guilt wriggled its whiny little head through my thoughts. Mike had spent a large sum of money to make sure I reached Los Angeles safely, and he didn't have to do it. He could have taken me to social services back in Oregon.

"Mike." I buckled myself in beside the window. "Mike, do you have a sheet of paper? There's something I want to write out for you. I want to tell you something."

"Yeah? I bet you have a lot of things to tell me."

"I'm not saying where I came from," I warned him. "But, I do want to write things down. Only, don't read them until after I leave."

Mike reached into his briefcase and pulled out a legal pad. He tore off a sheet of lined yellow paper, folded it in half, and placed it on the small tray in front of me. Next, he handed me a pencil.

"Thanks, Mike." I hoped my eyes expressed how deeply I meant it.

"You're welcome, twerp."

"No, really. You saved my life. You really did."

"I know. Go ahead and write your deep, dark secrets."

I turned my back on him and hid the paper with my body. I'd been thinking about what to tell him, what details to give. When did Steve Jobs' brilliance materialize as Apple computers? Microsoft. When did Microsoft go public? My hindsight was not 20/20.

I did remember certain dates. Just a couple. November 22nd stuck out bold in my mind because of the Kennedy assassination. On that same date in 1963, C.S. Lewis died and my grandmother turned 40. On November 22nd in 1986, my dad and I watched Mike Tyson knock out Trevor Berbick to become the heavyweight champion of the world. Dad said Tyson also won exactly one year earlier in 1985. I remembered significant events that took place on November 22nd.

What else? What else! I could say, "Hey Mike! Invest in Bitcoin!" I didn't want to make him wait 30 years, though. What important 1980s events could be valuable to him?

I finally wrote a simple note:

Dear Mike,

I can't tell you everything right now, but I want to give you treasures. The first things in the list are to let you know the others are real. Pay attention and you might hit gold.

-January, 1981, Iran hostages freed.
-Rubik's Cube, ALF, Fraggle Rock.
-IBM, Apple, Microsoft, WalMart, Amazon. Buy, don't sell.
-Mike Tyson, November 22, 1985 and 1986, 2nd round.
-October 17, 1989, Giants vs A's. Don't watch from Candlestick Park! Watch from Grass Valley!

Give Aunt Mindy a big hug for me.
D.J.

I studied my print, big and blocky, like somebody who needed more practice. My brain knew things my little hands did not. Dear small hands. I smiled at them, all cute and chubby. With my cute, small, chubby hands, I folded the paper and handed it to Mike. He tucked the yellow rectangle straight into his left breast pocket.

"All right. Now, look out your window."

I did. I looked out my window - and fell asleep.

Of course, Mike hadn't *promised* not to read his yellow prophecy-present. I awoke an hour later when he shook my shoulder, because airlines still fed people in the 1980s.

"C'mon Dodge. Here's your lunch."

I gazed around, bleary. The clouds made a white blanket beneath us. Mike had already cut up my plate of Salisbury steak and added butter to my mashed potatoes and soft wheat roll. He placed the tray in front of me and watched me eat.

"So!" Mike confessed. "I read it."

I shook my head, horrified, mouth full of soft steak. I tried to protest through the food. "I said no!"

"I didn't agree. Besides. You might get sucked into a whirlwind next week. I want a couple of answers. What, do you bend spacetime with your powerful mind? Is that what you do? You pull the future toward you and look at it and say, 'Yeah. That's it! That's when the earthquake happens.'"

I stuffed the steak into my cheek, amazed at his insight. "How did you know it was an earthquake?"

Mike's whole head flicked in response, and I realized I'd slipped up. He didn't know anything, he'd just tossed out an imaginary idea.

I muttered, "I mean. I didn't say anything about an earthquake."

He frowned on the yellow paper. "There's an earthquake in here?"

"Stop. Forget it. I'm not explaining the clues on your treasure hunt. I'm not cheating."

Mike gave me an amused sideways glance. "Okay. But, one day, I'm going to find out what you are, Dodge Journey. I'll figure it out."

"You do that." I bit into my roll and took a few chews. "Just don't forget about me."

He laughed, an honest cheerful laugh. "If only I could. All right. Don't talk with your mouth full."

The plane dipped down through the clouds, and a rising ache grew in my heart. I didn't want to leave Mike. Sitting beside him, walking hand-in-hand with him, his presence had grown so comfortable, so normal. I plain liked my new friend; we'd become real buddies in those five short days.

Now, Mike led me through an airport to meet the woman sent to register me in the system of orphans and abandoned children. He waited with me until she arrived, and we sat in silence. We'd agreed that he'd hand me over to her, that he'd leave and return to San Francisco, that I'd stay here in Los Angeles. We had agreed, so that's what happened. We found the woman, and she and Mike spoke for a few minutes.

Then, Mike did something he hadn't done before. Not really. He picked me up and kissed my forehead and pulled me into his cotton shirt in a tight hug. His heart thudded away in that warm chest of his, and I absorbed the comfort of those precious seconds.

"Go save the world, kiddo," he whispered in my ear.

He squeezed me one last time before setting me down. Then, he picked up my backpack from the concourse floor, handed it to me, and thanked the woman. With a final wave, Mike walked away.

I watched him go and held my Dodgers backpack close. "I have your Aunt Mindy's address," I whispered to him. "I'll see you again one day."

And I started to cry.

9

Ashlynn

If I'd truly had prophetic powers, if I'd really had the ability to bend spacetime and pull the future toward myself, I might have run after Mike and begged him to keep me. I could have traveled across the country with him while he sold office machines and we'd have had a blast. If I'd seen the future, I'd have raced away from that social worker, grabbed Mike's hand and convinced him to keep me.

I didn't even try. I *let* him let me go. He left me behind, and I let him walk away. Neither of us understood. We had taken for granted the kindness of strangers to children.

Welfare workers spent the next few days deciding what to do with me. I had no records. I had no parents. I realized too late I was a perfect snuff film candidate, but this team clearly wanted to do right by their orphans. They talked about finding my birth certificate and social security number. They talked about school.

I told them my real birthday, because there's something personal about a birthday, but I had little else true to tell them. I decided I needed a third name, though. A last name. Nothing against Chrysler, but "Dodge Journey" might eventually get awkward, so I chose a final name to cap it off, a surname on my Grandmother's side that went back to the Revolutionary War. "Spicer." A solid, zesty name.

"What's your name?"

"Dodge Journey Spicer." I liked it.

They asked me plenty of questions, but I had few answers. I told them my mother's name was Madeleine and I was born at home in a little house in Saugus, California, and that was it. They let me get away with coloring at a table. They must have worked it out, because

I was assigned to a family in the suburbs: Ted and Ashlynn Cresson.

Ted and Ashlynn. Ted and Ashlynn Cresson.

Even now, I'll cover my face with my hands when I think about them. I've had to tell this story over and over, and I hate it. I didn't know completely disturbed people slipped through the foster care screening process.

If you want to skip the next five chapters, that's okay with me. I'm serious. I wouldn't want to read them.

Ted and Ashlynn amazed me with their acting skills. They could pretend to be whatever people wanted them to be. They lived in a pleasant bungalow on a grassy, tree-lined street in Pasadena, and both earned good incomes. Ted worked as the accountant for a large law firm, and Ashlynn sold makeup to rich socialites. They smiled at the right times. They said the right things.

I stared at them during that first meeting, when Cheryl my case worker brought me into the Cresson home. I studied them, focused on his face, then her face, and puzzled over what was wrong about them. Ashlynn's auburn hair bounced with natural curls, and Ted dressed like he'd come in from the racquetball court. They were young and respectable, but there was something odd, some quiver of discomfort. I sensed it without knowing how to label it. It was like holding onto someone's wrist and feeling no pulse. I kept pressing the fingers of my emotional intelligence here and there, and I couldn't find a heartbeat.

Ashlynn bothered me the most with her plastic face. As Cheryl spoke in the living room, I waited for her to notice, to recognize that Ashlynn's smiles hung empty between her cheeks. It was like Ashlynn understood, "This is the time to do that upward bend thing with my mouth." No joy warmed those glossy lips, and it amazed me that Cheryl didn't cringe at Ashlynn's mannequin coldness.

Ted seemed better, a normal businessman. I felt safe taking his hand as he showed me to my room, a perfectly excellent boy's room. Blue stripes ran down the cotton comforter, and a fuzzy brown bear greeted me from the pillow. A box of blocks had been tucked under the bed, and kids' books filled the bookshelf by the door. Rock on.

As soon as Cheryl left, though, the walls seemed to close in, like I'd been left in a cave with tigers. It wasn't the house itself. This home had wide open, brightly lit rooms, modern for 1980. Tiled floors, white area rugs and cream sofas. No shag carpet. No floral print couches or green counters. A light lemon scent lingered in the air, fresh and clean. Still, a danger lurked there, as though the tigers weren't hungry yet.

I thought maybe demons possessed the house, or aliens had slurped clean the bodies of the original Ted and Ashlynn and donned their forms like Halloween costumes. I sensed that I had to be aware, to be on guard. That was it. I had to be on my guard.

Later, I wondered if my reluctance to talk had earned me that spot with Ted and Ashlynn. Maybe the Cressons had requested a quiet child. I'd felt free to jabber on and on with Mike, but Ashlynn and Ted sucked all the chatter right out of me. I took in information but didn't share in return. That seemed the wisest approach.

Cheryl brought me to the house mid-afternoon on Friday, the 8th of February, and Ted returned to racquetball or whatever he did after Cheryl left. Ashlynn led me from the stylish living room into the kitchen, where she had me sit at a small glass table and wait while she cut up food. Afternoon sunlight flooded through open shades and shone cheerfully on clean, white-tiled counters. Ashlynn set a plate of carrots and apple slices in front of me, and I thanked her before crunching quietly. Otherwise, Ashlynn didn't talk to me. She didn't seem interested in me at all.

A knock came at the front door as I chewed away, and Ashlynn unlocked it for a little girl with long, blonde, curling hair. The pale, pretty child saw me at the table eating carrots and apples and happily sat across from me. I thought she might be six or seven - a little older than I was. I said, "Hi," and the girl smiled at me.

She looked up at Ashlynn again, and we both waited for Ashlynn to give her a snack too. When it became clear that Ashlynn wasn't making the little girl her own plate, I offered her mine, and the child picked up a piece of apple.

That's when Ashlynn did a bizarre thing. She snapped, "No! No, Donnielle, you don't get any. Take your jacket and go to your room!"

Donnielle's eyes rimmed red, but she obediently slid off her seat with her windbreaker. She slunk down the hall while I smoothly slipped two carrot sticks and two apple slices into my hoodie sleeve with one hand. I crunched calmly on my last chunk of apple.

When I swallowed, I asked, "May I go?" Ashlynn nodded, so I strolled through the living room and down the hall, past my door and into the open door of Donnielle's room.

"Shhhh," I put my forefinger to my mouth and carefully closed the door. I pulled carrots and apples out of my sleeve, and the girl's eyes brightened. I waited while she ate my small food offering, pleased at her enjoyment. She opened her mouth and showed me her food all chewed up, and I mimed for her to eat with her mouth closed.

"I'm Dodge," I pointed at myself. "What's your name?"

Donnielle dropped her chin, her big brown eyes hidden by blonde hair. She didn't answer me. I wondered if she knew how to talk.

"Is it Donnielle?"

She smiled shyly at the yellow rug that covered the hardwood floor.

"That's a pretty name. Can I call you Donny for short?"

She nodded, her smile bigger.

I reached out my hand to shake hers, and she looked confused. I tried to take her hand, but she pulled away.

"It's okay. It's okay, Donny. You don't have to shake my hand. You're my friend anyway. We're friends."

Panic splashed Donny's face, and she slid silently beyond the foot of her bed, against the back wall. I blamed myself until I heard the footsteps down the hall. They passed Donny's door and turned into the last bedroom, the master bedroom.

"Should I go away?" I whispered.

Donny nodded frantically.

I scooted to her door and listened for noises. All was silent, so I eased out. Just as I placed my hand on my own doorknob, Ashlynn stepped back through her door and saw me.

"What are you doing out of your room! You're not permitted to run around the house!" She shouted this. She shouted. Much louder than necessary.

I nodded. "Bathroom."

That wasn't good enough for Ashlynn. "No. No no. You should have gone after snack time. You'll just have to wait until Ted gets home. I can't have children out loose like ferrets."

Wide-eyed, I closed the door to my room and leaned on my bed. Wow. Good thing I didn't really have to use the bathroom. Between my stepping across the hall and using the commode like a civilized person or wetting my pants, Ashlynn would have chosen wet pants?

At least I had my blocks. I heaved on the wide wooden box, and it slowly rolled out from under my bed. I admired the multitude in that box and knelt to separate their sizes and shapes into quantities. They were old and oak and had the rich brown tone of wood that had spent hours and hours in the hands of small children. Happy hands. Hands full of creative inspiration that rubbed oils into the surfaces of those big, durable blocks, blocks just right for building a castle.

I kicked my small blue rug to the side and set base blocks on the hardwood floor. I stacked happily and considered the possibility that I'd misunderstood myself. Yes, I had the memories of an adult, but there was far more *child* in me than I'd realized. I didn't simply have a child's body. I had a child's tastes. I even had a child's reactions to things. I'd felt genuine excitement when Aunt Mindy produced those Captain America underclothes and wanted to wear them as much as possible. I delighted in the oak blocks from the box beneath my bed. I *remembered* that I had been an adult, and I remembered that fool's gold is pyrite and that pyrite is an iron sulfide. I could reason like an adult, but there was a great deal of me that felt four-years-old. I felt four and old at the same time.

I missed Mike, but it hadn't entered my mind to say, "What a handsome, sexy man." That hadn't occurred to me, not at all. What had I thought? "I like Mike. I wish he'd marry my mom."

How many times had I been stripped to my underwear? And it didn't matter at all - no smidge of embarrassment. I liked it when Mike carried me on his shoulders and slung me upside down and plopped me into the front seat of his car. That felt like a natural thing. I loved that last hug he gave me, but I loved it as a little child, and I grieved when he left as though I'd lost a dad.

I'd wanted to listen to music rather than read Ray Bradbury. I'd listened to music and looked for Yogi Bear in the popcorn ceiling.

As I stacked my blocks, I decided I wasn't exactly a normal child, but I wasn't an adult either. I'd converted into a strange mixture, a baby with a big brain. A little kid with memories of the future.

I contemplated these things while I constructed my castle, solidly placing each block until I had a structure large enough to crawl into. My base had two rows of blocks, but the building slimmed as it grew taller, topped with pillars and wooden triangle flags. I laid out long flat boards along the tops of the walls as ramparts and added small blocks with spaces for my archers to shoot through the cracks. There were no toy soldiers to use as archers, so I had to imagine them.

I set up triangle blocks as the invading army. "Pew pew pew!" I shot down my enemy invaders.

My castle had no roof, though. The long, slender boards didn't stretch far enough. I'd made the castle too large, and no one block reached across the gap at the top. I stood back and frowned. Hmm. I'd start over again.

Time for real fun. "Oh no! The oliphaunts are coming!" I took a karate stance and kicked the castle right in the middle. CRASH, the blocks tumbled and bounced over my hardwood floor. Boom! Haha!

"Bring in the bulldozers!" I shoved the blocks away with my arms to make room. This time, I'd keep the castle small so I could build a proper roof. I'd add a full courtyard and build a wall. From there I could set up the enemy armies all around and plan my defenses. Gosh, what I wouldn't do for some Lego men. Lego guys would fit up on the ramparts and stand as guards, ready with their crossbows to shoot invaders.

Fwwwack! I had just finished bulldozing when my door crashed open. I knelt on the floor when a wind fluffed over my head. The door banged against my bookshelf, and Ashlynn burst into my room like a cannon explosion.

Her behavior didn't fit the scene at all. I knelt there with a block in my hand and tried to make sense of the sudden invasion. Armies of wooden triangles still lined the floor, and she kicked through them so that one breezed my ear and clapped the wall behind me. She moved faster than my emotions could keep up! Before I'd finished turning to see where the block had gone, she pounced and dug angry fingers into my ribs, and a moment later I bounced across the bed and into the wall. Was she joking? No. No, this wasn't a joke. I spun myself around, hardly noticing the jarring smart on the ridge beneath my eye.

Something had enraged Ashlynn, and I puzzled as fast as I could to work out what it was. The blocks. Something about the blocks. I'd infuriated her with the blocks. I mentally scrambled to figure it out as she reached down and grabbed one of the boards I'd planned to use as my castle roof. It wasn't quite four inches wide and it wasn't quite a foot long, but it rose like a sword in her hand.

Fear finally caught up. Alarmed, I shoved away, but Ashlynn grabbed my leg and dragged me across the comforter. My sweatshirt rolled up under my stomach, and blue striped cotton smothered my face. A hand pressed hot on my head. Hot. Hard, hot fingers. I kicked and kicked again, but the hand didn't yield. It held me, forced the soft comforter against my cheek I couldn't roll over or get her hand to loosen. Crack! The oak board called out about two seconds before the pain hit my brain.

"You!" Whack.

"Will!" Whack.

"Not!" Whack.

"Make!" Whack.

"Loud!" Whack.

"Noises!" Whack.

"In!" Whack.

"This!" Whack.

"House!" Whack. Whack. Whack.

She flung the board back against the other blocks with a clatter. "Put these back before Ted gets home, and I don't want to hear any of it!" She swept out of the room and slammed my innocent door again.

Joan Crawford and *Mommy Dearest* flickered through my head. I always hated that movie. Ashlynn had thrown all her strength into those blows, and they weren't funny. I wriggled in misery, trying to rub the hurt out of my back end before crawling up to my pillow and climbing under it. Humiliation mixed with my physical suffering. All she'd had to do was ask, she didn't have to wail on me like a dusty rug. Good thing she didn't carry bags of concrete for a living, or she might have broken me in half and crumbled me into pieces.

The combination of injustice and injury overwhelmed me, and I curled under my pillow and sobbed. Softly. Because I believed that if I cried loudly, Ashlynn would have returned to beat me all over again.

I rested for about 30 minutes before I felt able to tackle the blocks. Quietly, gently, still sore, I stacked all those wooden squares back into the box. I organized them by size and type. Large rectangles, large squares, large triangles, small triangles. long rectangles, half circles, cylinder pillars, little half squares, and arches. I organized them in the box, then shoved with all my strength to roll it back under the bed. My feet slipped somewhat on the smooth floor. That done, I climbed back onto the comforter and curled up to go to sleep.

I woke an hour later when Ted's keys jingled, and the front door swooshed open. Voices rumbled in the living room, and after a bit Ted's head poked into my room. "Can I come in, Dodge?"

I nodded and rolled up onto my knees.

"I heard you got into trouble today. Did you?"

Ted stood over me, all frowny in his racquetball outfit. I wanted to plead my case. I wanted to describe the unfairness of the whole thing, but something in Ted's face said he plain didn't care. His visit to my room meant Ashlynn had complained about me, and my comfort didn't matter to him. I saw it in his eyes before he spoke a word: this was a moment of, "Don't you dare upset Ashlynn again in the future. Do you understand?"

"What did you do?" It was a demand.

"I made noise knocking down my blocks."

"Yes, that's what Ashlynn said. She was not happy with you about that. Will you ever do it again?"

"No," I whispered.

"Okay. That's good. Because if Ashlynn tells me you've upset her again by making noise, I'll punish you when I get home. Do you have a handle on that?"

I nodded. I had an excellent handle on that.

I gazed through my wall and imagined the child in the next room over. No wonder poor Donny never talked. She'd forgotten how to do it.

10 OI

Train Book

My days at preschool started Monday, and I rejoiced to escape that awful house for the land of crayons and graham crackers. I hoped I could find a sympathetic teacher who'd let me snuggle in the corner and read C.S. Lewis; a sudden urge for *The Lion, the Witch, and the Wardrobe* overwhelmed me. I felt a kinship with Lucy, who had grown to adulthood in another world only to tumble through the wardrobe as a child again. That was me. I'd become the ward of a real live witch, and a cruel wizard stood at her back to zap me with his powers, to paralyze and hold me down while she tortured me.

I refused to speak to Ted and Ashlynn all day Sunday, and they seemed content with that. I figured their bliss would be complete if I went completely mute like Donny. I sat in the back of the car as we drove to school on Monday and pondered over what had possessed these two people to seek out foster children. Did the state pay that well? Ashlynn clearly didn't like children, yet she and Ted had collected a second one.

How bizarre. How bizarre.

The school tucked me into Mrs. Borglum's room, and she seemed as jovial and plump as a sugar plum fairy. A nice, happy lady. Not overtly crazy like Ashlynn, not at all. I spent the morning doing as she said, and it was all pleasant. I heard stories and crayoned pictures and sipped apple juice, but my heart hurt me under it all. I had planned to wait some days before exposing my brains, but I couldn't bear it. The longing to read about Narnia overwhelmed me until I almost started crying again. I finally drew away by myself and picked at the carpet.

Mrs. Borglum eased over and stood beside me. "Hello Dodge. Are you having fun your first day here? Are you making friends?"

I gazed mournfully at Mrs. Borglum. "Mrs. B., I need your help."

I hadn't spoken a word all morning, and the head of my plump teacher perked up. "You do talk! I wondered." She smiled.

I smiled back. "But, I have a secret. Can I trust you?"

"Well, of course you can trust me."

"Will you promise not to tell anybody unless I say okay?"

"Yes." She clearly didn't know what she was getting into.

"Okay," I said. "Promise that you won't send me to another class."

"Well, of course, Dodge. Is that your secret? That you don't want to be sent away?"

"No, Mrs. B. My secret is bigger than that."

"Okay." She nodded, curious.

I took a deep breath and leaned up into her ear. I whispered, "I … can… already… read."

I sat back and watched her eyebrows pop up. "You can? That's wonderful. Let's get a book, and you can show me."

She led me to the storybook corner and asked me to pick out a book. I found a collection of *Aesop's Fables* and read "The Lion and The Mouse." I didn't stumble or guess at words, and Mrs. Borglum laughed, such an easy laugh, just as easy as butterflies flitting through the air.

"Now, you promised," I said. "You promised you wouldn't send me away. You promised not to tell anybody. Nobody."

"Dodge, this is a good thing to tell people. You might get to go into the first grade. Wouldn't that be fun?"

"More fun than preschool?" I grimaced. "I'm too jumpy for first grade. And you promised."

I didn't let her renege on our deal. I made it clear that all I wanted was a set of *The Chronicles of Narnia* to read during my free time each day. While the other children stood at easels and painted trucks with fat brushes, I sought the freedom to read to myself. Mrs. B. obliged me, and I curled up in the pillow corner and soothed my heart with talking animals and Aslan.

I liked preschool. I liked finger-painting and bouncing balls in the gym. I enjoyed resting in the pillow corner with my books, and I adored my freedom from Ashlynn for four hours a day.

Did I tell Mrs. B. about my home life? No. I did consider tattling on Ashlynn right then, but I saw that going poorly for me. Ashlynn would lie convincingly. I did have light bruising from her board, but if the authorities believed her story over mine, it would end up much worse for me.

It took me a bit to figure out Ted and Ashlynn. They confused me utterly, which compounded my suffering. I wanted to understand the monster I faced every day. What turned the crank on its cage and let it loose? I wanted to know how to shut the door and keep that thing safely behind its bars.

Ashlynn obviously had an anger problem, but she'd ebb and flow like the tide. One day she'd act almost normal, cleaning or baking cookies, letting me play in the back yard before Donny got home. By the fourth or fifth day, a sort of destructive tension had built until she had to damage somebody, and I made a convenient victim. She'd erupt and attack me, then she'd be fine for another few days. Geyser. She was like a geyser. Ashlynn Old Faithful.

Nothing I did changed this cycle. I always obeyed her, swiftly and silently, and I think that frustrated her. She *needed* an excuse to flip out on me. The second time she hit me, she had me sit in the kitchen to eat saltines smeared with peanut butter. I swear she lost her temper because I didn't chew fast enough. She started barking, "Hurry up! Why are you taking so long?" Ridiculousness. I needed to chew the crackers completely or I'd choke. I had a small mouth and a small throat, and she didn't have the decency to give me milk to wash it all down. She wanted me to eat faster, and I couldn't, so she finally stomped across the kitchen and slapped me. Bam! Right across the face with the full force of her body. The shock jolted through my head, through my cheek and nose, an orange-red explosion that knocked me off my chair. I scrambled up and ran to my room to hide until Donny got home.

Blood dripped down my lip. She'd knocked a nosebleed right out of me. As soon as I heard Ashlynn's bedroom door close, I slipped out of my room and sneaked back a minute later with pillow of soft paper wadded against my nostrils. I had spun out half a roll of Charmin and gathered it up as a bit of passive aggressive generosity to myself.

Ashlynn's craziness had one benefit. She hated noise, hated it, and that produced a genuinely excellent condition in the house: none of the doors squeaked. Ted must have sprayed WD-40 on every hinge until they opened on owl wings. I could push my door open, slip across the hall, steal a world of toilet paper from the bathroom and sneak back into my room without a sound.

Of course, when Ashlynn discovered a few drops of blood on my blue rug some days later, she grabbed a yardstick and wailed on me again. It was like that. I could expect to get punished for something once or twice a week, and she didn't have a single, favorite weapon; she'd hit me with whatever lay nearby. She even threw a cookbook at me once.

Her fourth beating wasn't too bad. She threw her energy into it, but it didn't do much damage. She'd emptied a plastic two liter of RC Cola, and she hammered on my shoulders and head with that fat bottle. The blows hurt if she caught me with the hard end of it, but they mostly made a lot of hollow bopping noises.

I felt deeply for dear Donny. So silent and scared all the time. I wondered how long she'd served as Ashlynn's venting dummy before Ted decided to protect the little girl. He didn't *stop* Ashlynn. "Hey. We're here to help children." No. He hired me for the time-honored position of whipping boy, like in a medieval castle. The golden-haired princess could not be battered, so the whipping boy took her place. When Ashlynn felt an urge to pound on somebody, she now had me to knock around.

But see, it took time for me to grasp all that.

Ashlynn didn't slap me flat across the face a second time, because bruises in the pinkish purplish shape of fingers appeared after she knocked me off the kitchen chair. Ted walked in the door that night and saw those fiery welts across my cheek, and he strode past me into the kitchen to speak quietly to Ashlynn. I stood still, terrified that he'd work me over for whatever offense I'd given his wife.

He did nothing. Ted simply returned and crouched down to my level. "You made Ashlynn mad again today, didn't you?"

Fear welled up wet in my eyes. It wasn't right.

Ted shook his head back and forth. "Okay. Your punishment is that you're grounded. You can't go to preschool. You don't get to go on walks. You're grounded to your room."

He strode out, and I thought, "You loser! You know how she is, and you don't care! You know I did nothing wrong; but you don't want the world to learn your wife's a monster."

I stayed home the next week. "Grounded." It turned out fine for me, because Ashlynn was irrational and left me alone all morning. She left a four-year-old child alone. All morning. She always booked her appointments before noon, and during my week home she still went off to remake the faces of uber rich ladies. I was abandoned with orders to stay in my room.

I should have pulled flour out of the cupboard and flung it around the kitchen or painted the fridge with jars of nail polish. If Ashlynn had left a normal child alone all day, she'd have returned home to vast destruction. Every room in shambles. Scissor holes stabbed in the couch or the walls or the child. That's right. A child dead from scissor holes. Or a choking obstruction. Or poison.

I decided to spare us all the natural consequences of Ashlynn's foolishnes and behaved myself, except that I explored every cranny of the house. I clambered onto Ashlynn and Ted's huge bed and watched their TV with their remote control. Daytime programming nearly bored me to death, but they did have HBO. I hunted through the *TV Guide* and watched *Saturday Night Fever* with John Travolta and a documentary on the 1950s. I explored the parental bathroom and discovered that Ashlynn possessed all the moisturizers and beauty creams developed since the Persian Empire. Jars and tubes and bottles littered the large vanity counter and filled her drawers, along with baskets of eyeshadows and blushes and cover-up and lipsticks and powders.

Ashlynn loved jewelry: necklaces and earrings and bangles. Her ring collection bothered me the most. All those rings. She always wore four or six different rings on her fingers, which had cracked my nose when she slapped me. I didn't touch the jewelry, worried I might turn into a gremlin - as though evil itself sprung out and danced from her gaudy trinkets.

During my investigations through their room, I discovered that Ted liked porn. An envelope under the mattress held a collection of photographs - not magazine pages - and a short flip flip flip through the images revealed some weird garbage. I absolutely didn't want any of it in my brain, so I stuffed the envelope back and searched for something on television to bleach my eyeballs.

I recognized Ashlynn's pattern of violence by the incident with the empty cola bottle, and I understood Ted had no interest in saving me from his wife. That's when I started to keep a record. I hunted through the books on my bookshelf and found an innocuous, dull book about trains, something published in 1955. I picked it because it attracted no attention – the least interesting book on the shelf. Nobody would miss an ancient yellow book with pictures all in black and grays. I opened to the back page, the empty page at the back of the book, and I began my record.

Dodge Journey Spicer of Pasadena, D.O.B. 7/15/1975. This is a record of all the times Ashlynn Cresson hit me.

2/08 – A 1x4 board – 11x.
2/13 – One face slap. It left finger-shaped bruises
   so I was kept home from preschool.
2/17 – A yardstick – 8x.
2/22– An RC Cola bottle - I lost count.

I explored Ted's desk one day, which is how I learned we lived in Pasadena. His mail held no psychiatric bills, no evidence they'd sought therapy. What was wrong with those two! Were they hiding from their obvious demons, as though everything was okay, pretending that they could handle their significant personal corruption alone? I longed to expose them, to crack apart the happy facade and let sunshine explode into their dark, decrepit world.

I did glean another useful bit of information from Ted's desk: my case worker's phone number. I copied it down and stuck it in the back of my train book along with Ashlynn's attacks.

Ashlynn's morning absences gave me something greater than the freedom to trespass into my foster parents' private domains; those mornings provided me with peace. I felt free for about three hours, free to wander and snack, free to watch TV, free to peek into baskets and boxes. As 11:00 passed, the anxiety settled in. I carefully picked every crumb off the counters, tugged on bedding to make it smooth, walked the place over to make sure I hadn't missed anything, then hid snugly in my room. By the time Ashlynn's keys jingled in the door, my emotional rubber band had stretched nice and taut, and I spent the rest of the afternoon in hyper vigilance, waiting for her to flip out over something meaningless.

11 II

Donny

I returned to preschool on February 25th after an alleged bad case of the flu. The purple marks on my face had faded to yellowish splotches, and those disappeared under clever dabs from Ashlynn's makeup brush. That was her skill set, after all.

When I walked into the classroom, Mrs. B. handed me my big pink and red construction paper valentines holder, and I realized I'd missed our Valentine's Day party! I held that big heart full of notes and tears dripped down my cheeks. I couldn't help it. I thought to myself, "This is silly. Why am I so upset?" It didn't matter, because I bawled anyway. Mrs. B. got a tissue and blew my nose. She sat down with me and helped open my cards, but I knew I'd missed the pink Valentine's Day cookies with sprinkles, and that broke my heart. After that, my face looked all splotchy from crying.

Mrs. B. helped me gather up my pile of Batman and Strawberry Shortcake love letters, and her kindness and true concern touched me. I felt that warmth keenly after two weeks of straight Ashlynn.

Ashlynn. I'd been thinking about how to escape her.

"Mrs. Borglum? Do you know if the kindergarten is full-day?" I considered the possibility that if I avoided alone time with Ashlynn, I could escape her eruptions as well.

"Yes!" Mrs. B. seemed pleased. "Yes, kindergarten can be full-day. Do you want to go into kindergarten?"

I shook my head. "I don't know. I have to ask."

Things usually improved after Donny stepped through the door every day. When my face wasn't obviously bruised, Ashlynn took us on walks through the neighborhood under the rows of leafy trees. She pasted on her fairy-tale smile and laughed with the neighbors while Donny and I stood on both sides of her, dutifully and silently holding her hands. It wasn't great, but it was better than sitting in the house with her, waiting for her to go banshee on me.

I waited several days before I dared mention the idea of moving to kindergarten. The RC Cola bottle had failed to satisfy Ashlynn; her shrieks echoed across the house minutes after I walked through the door that afternoon. She wanted my valentines off the table. Why did I put them on the table? Did I have to make a blankety blank mess wherever I went? Wooden back scratcher: pow pow pow pow pow pow pow pow pow.

Look, I knew perfectly well foster parents weren't allowed to hit children. After finding Cheryl's number, I picked up the phone to call my case worker and file a complaint, but again I stopped. I was still four-years-old, and nobody listened to children. The Cressons had big voices, and Cheryl had believed them enough to give them two children! More importantly, I worried about Donny. Even if Cheryl decided to move me, she might leave Donny behind, and I couldn't risk that.

It wasn't just Ashlynn's awful temper. Ted had his secrets too, and I carefully watched his attentions toward Donny, his special interest in the child princess with her golden curls. He brushed her hair at night and tucked her into bed and told her bedtime stories, and that was good and all. It was the way he looked at her that concerned me. I never saw those two adults hugging or kissing each other, and when I found Ted's porn pictures under the mattress, I worried that pictures of Donny would appear. Mortified, I stuffed the pictures back, but they increased my ugliest fears about him.

An idea slowly wriggled into my head: Ashlynn hated Donny, but Ted wouldn't let her hurt Donny anymore. Ted wanted Donny, and Ashlynn knew it. She couldn't hurt Ted, and he wouldn't let her hurt Donny, but Ashlynn had to be pacified and so she focused her anger on me before they came home.

"These people are sick," I told my train book, and the train book agreed.

At night, I gazed into the darkness of my room and tried to decide what to do. I couldn't call the authorities with accusations and no proof. Even if they believed me, they might require Ashlynn to take parenting classes, then turn around and place other children with her and Ted, and I couldn't risk that either. We were trapped, Donny and I. I had to put up with Ashlynn's abuse until I could figure out how to keep the Cressons from taking children into their home again. Ever.

I did grow weary of my role as family piñata, so I finally suggested the move from preschool to kindergarten.

Leap Day evening, I caught Ted's eye across the table. Softly, I said, "Mr. Cresson, my teacher wants me to go into kindergarten." I'd waited all those weeks to talk at dinner, so this large number of words surprised both adults.

Ted raised his eyebrows. "Why is that, Dodge?"

"She thinks I'm smart."

Ted nodded, interested in the idea. "Well, that sounds fine."

Instantly, Ashlynn's face twisted, and a rage flushed up tense through her body. "What are you talking about, Ted! He can't go to school full-time yet, he's just a little kid."

Ted frowned at her. "What? If they want to put him-"

"Kindergarten is full-day, Ted!"

"Oh! Yeah, Dodge. You can't go to kindergarten. You're too little to go more than half-time."

Holy smokes, Ted knew. I'd suspected Ashlynn needed me around, but that's when I realized Ted knew she needed me there. I served as a ready victim constantly available to her, and in a warped sense that made me a fix, a security blanket, always within her arm's reach. And that satisfied Ted.

I was safe on the days she felt calm, but I couldn't hide myself well enough on Ashlynn's stressed days. As February rolled over into March, her fury days tumbled at me more and more frequently, and that increased fretfulness obviously ramped up to something awful.

On March 3, Ashlynn clocked me in the arm with that cookbook, and I realized something was up. If Ashlynn's central source of angst had everything to do with Ted and Donny, that meant Donny was in trouble. Which is why I decided to start sleeping with my gentle foster sister.

That next week ranked among the worst in my life. Ashlynn prowled on the edge of a mental breakdown, and I don't want to talk about it. I watched her fall apart during the day, but I slid out of bed every night and tiptoed down the hall to Donny's room and climbed into bed with her. My foster sister surprised me by throwing her arm over me. Our cheeks snugged up together, cozy and happy, and we both slept through the night, big sister and little brother cozy bear.

Every night and every night, I slipped into Donny's room.

The sixth night, a harsh jerk on my back awoke me. I swiftly came to consciousness levitating in the dark. Ted had caught me up by the back of my pajamas, and he hauled me down to my own room while I dangled like a kitten. He dropped me on my bed and grabbed my shoulders.

Light from the hall washed the left side of his face in gray and shadowed his right side in semi-darkness. Veins pumped up around Ted's eyes, furious eyes, wide and wild, like a man awake from dreams that gave him no rest. Like a man unable to sleep because of terrible ideas that slashed around in his head. Maybe he had been fighting himself. Maybe he'd been fighting for years, and he hated the things he longed to do. But he'd also allowed that enemy to set up residence in his head, and he'd carefully hid and fed it.

"She's not yours." It was a feral sound from his throat. "Stay out of her room, Dodge. I mean it, stay *out*." With that, he shoved me against my pillow and left.

In and out I breathed. In and out. I lay flat on my bed and stared into nothing as my mind replayed Ted's intense face above me. I saw the bulging of his eyes in the gray light and the desperation of his words.

Wait. Wait! Oh no. I had to stop him!

I slid out of bed and toed open my door. I needed a golf club. If he went back into Donny's room, I'd have to fight him. No, I didn't have the strength! I'd have to call 911. I listened in my doorway, my chest heaving. Donny's door remained ajar.

Ashlynn had awakened. Her voice murmured, high-pitched and irritated. Ted's voice rumbled back. Okay good. He'd returned to his own room.

Ted's smothered rage terrified me. Tension shook through my body, and all I wanted was to hide in my own bed and stay safe. But I couldn't make decisions based on fear. I'd remained in the Cresson house to protect Donny, so that's what I had to do. I had to protect her.

Ignoring every rigid muscle in my body, every screaming warning in my head, I slipped out of bed the next night and climbed under covers with the little mute girl. Donny wrapped her arms around me, but I lay awake, hyper-aware, listening to her deep breathing as the hours drifted by. My heart pounded in my ears until I finally dozed off, only to be jolted again sometime after midnight.

This time Ted carried me to my room upside down by one leg. When we got there, he flicked on the light and dangled me in the air for a good ten seconds so his form swayed in front of me. His wrong-side-up boxers filled my view, and I wondered what thoughts ground through his mind. Finally, Ted caught hold of my other foot and swung me through the air. I expected to connect with the wall, but Ted body-slammed me into the bed instead. This time, he grabbed my shoulders and forced me into the mattress. He leaned over me so that gravity pulled at the skin on his face - his dark, enraged face.

"Do you want me really angry at you, Dodge?"

I shook my head.

"Don't you go into Donnielle's room at night. Ever. If I catch you in there again, I'm going to hurt you."

He spoke the word "hurt" meaningfully, and the heat from his face warmed my cheeks. I peered into his dark eyes and knew he hadn't slept again. A million red spiderwebs laced through the whites of his eyeballs, and I felt the frustration that pulsed blood through his heavy skin. I believed him. I believed he'd hurt me.

In that moment as he leaned over me, his restrained fury no longer scared me. A collage of bruises already decorated my body, because of his wife, because of what she did, and a rage crept up in me to match his. If he felt frustrated, I felt the desperation of my small size and helplessness. His job was to look after us, to care for us, to love us, and what did he do? This. He threatened me to keep me away so he could have unhampered access to a little girl who couldn't talk.

I met his hostile eyes with my own, and I said the worst thing I knew how to say to him.

"Do you have a small dick, Ted?"

He jolted. He hadn't expected those words from my young mouth.

"It must be small if you want to have sex with a seven-year-old."

That did it. The red almost blistered his face. I expected him to choke me to death right then, but instead he took several deep breaths in and out, in and out, just as I'd done in my fear the night before. He swallowed, sniffed and swallowed again, my arms still gripped in his fists. I cringed, wound up, waited for destruction. But Ted made a decision in that moment and let me go.

"I swear, Dodge." He stood straight and swallowed once more. "If I catch you in there with her, you won't be going to school for a long long time. I'll have to tell them you moved."

12

Ted

Don't you know, things calmed down after that? They really did. Ashlynn relaxed and seemed almost happy. The list in my train book grew slower.

I didn't give up. I still slept in Donny's room every night, and every morning I awoke early and slipped into my own bed. Nobody yanked me out of sleep in the middle of the night. My bruises almost healed. Well. I mean, Ashlynn was still Ashlynn. She still had crazy fits, but her rain of fury eased into a sprinkle.

Then, one Friday evening Ted suggested we go to the movies and watch *Coal Miner's Daughter* with Sissy Spacek and Tommy Lee Jones. Ashlynn seemed to spark with real enthusiasm, and Donny and I perked up, excited to see a show.

"Will you be good, Donnielle?" Ted asked. "Will you sit still and watch the whole movie?"

Donny nodded happily.

"Dodge?"

"I'll be good."

Ted acted so pleasant, so friendly that night, I almost thought he'd turned into a human. Maybe he'd had a heart change. Maybe he'd finally sought out counseling and wanted to make us a family.

He bought a huge popcorn for Donny and me to share, along with Red Vines and Milk Duds and cups of Coke. Donny and I ate our popcorn and candy and guzzled our soda pop. I have no idea what happened in *Coal Miner's Daughter*, though. Loretta Lynn became a big star, I guess, and Sissy Spacek won an Oscar, but I have no idea what happened, because I zonked right out.

Hours later, I awoke in my own bed with the horrible impression I'd been tricked. I listened to the house and heard no sounds but the clock ticking in the living room. I lay still, irritated that my teeth felt fuzzy and unbrushed after all that sugar.

Through the wall, Donny gave a muffled whimper, and her springs squeaked a little. Silent Donny. I'd snuggled with her every night for weeks, her teddy bear, and Ted had tricked me into falling asleep at the movies and had put me into my own bed.

My stomach hurt, hot and tight. I dropped lightly onto my rug and crept out the door and down the hall. We had no locks on our doors, so I turned the knob on Donny's room and pushed the door inward without a sound.

I felt it as soon as the door opened. Something about the room had changed; there was more presence, more warmth. I'd expected the worst, but my brain still refused to recognize it. My eyes dilated to allow in light, and as they focused, I finally saw him there on the bed with Donny. With Donny.

A second of shock passed, two seconds, and then every ounce of fury and indignation available seethed up inside me. I wanted to pound on him with a baseball bat and break all the bones in his arms and legs and back. I wanted to kick him into a ditch and smother him, remove him from the world. I stood in the doorway, appalled, aware I had absolutely no physical power to stop him. So I used the best and only weapon available to me. I screamed. I screamed with all the wrath that can erupt from the heart of a four-year-old child.

Ted stumbled out of the bed and tripped and fell on the floor.

"You disgusting low life! What's wrong with you? You pedophile loser!" I bellowed a string of insults as he scrambled to his feet and tugged up his boxers. My voice echoed around that room, even as his hands wrapped around my arms, lifted me into the air and shook me.

"Shut up!" Ted roared into my face. "Shut up!!"

I kept screaming. I wouldn't stop – couldn't stop.

"That's it!" He caught me under his arm, muffling my curses with the skin of his ribs. In a moment he launched through my bedroom doorway, and my head smacked the doorframe before he tossed me on the bed. Dizzy, forehead singing, I watched Ted tower between me and the ceiling light.

Donny. Was she okay? I wanted to run back down the hall to her.

"I told you, Dodge!" Ted's face twisted with the intensity of his frustration, of waiting and waiting, always tripping on this little kid in his way. "I told you! What did I say would happen if you upset Ashlynn by being loud? What did I say! What did I say about staying out of Donnielle's room! What did I say!!"

Ted kept spinning in place, looking, hunting around and around the room. He grabbed my reading lamp in the crook of his elbow and ripped the cord right out. It was an old lamp with a thin but heavy cord, and he snapped it free with one jerk and endzone slammed the ceramic base into the wall. Bash! Drywall buckled, and the lamp crunched against the floor.

I backed to the corner between the headboard and wall and searched for an escape route. Ted was preparing to kill me. He had that cord and he was going to strangle me and string up my body as a warning to other defiant toddlers.

"You want to go into Donnielle's room?" He grabbed me by the shoulder, and I punched and kicked, fighting for my life to break free. "You want to ignore me and disobey me! Is that what you want to do?"

Ted tossed me onto my stomach and yanked the back of my shirt up over my face, muffling me in cotton cloth. I wriggled, but I was blind and my arms couldn't move freely.

"You want to make noise? You want to scream and wake up the neighbors!" He held my neck through the fabric, and the terror of exposure prickled hairs across my back.

I heard the first crack, but it took time for my brain to process. My nervous system jolted, spurted, couldn't rightly relay the points of contact. When the signal did hit my brain, the scalding shock radiated out to my fingertips. I'd never whimpered when Ashlynn attacked me, but I shrieked then - into the muffled cotton of my shirt.

In *David Copperfield*, David's stepfather caned him half to death in an upstairs room of the house. David flashed into my mind in that moment, and I wondered about Dickens and how much of his own suffering he'd written into his books. I thought of Tommy Traddles, crying and drawing skeletons all the time, or Roald Dahl's years in the brutal British school system, long before he wrote *Charlie and the Chocolate Factory*. I watched the world pass by, back through time, past the Spanish Inquisition, on to the Apostle Paul and Jesus Christ Himself. I had to. I had to focus outside of me, because Ted Cresson had made me the whipping boy of his family, and he meant it.

13

Locks

I honestly don't know how many times Ted whacked me with that cord. The blows blended together in a searing symphony. My body offered Ted a small piece of real estate, and it didn't take long for him to plow across most of it, snapping certain spots over and over. When he finally left me alone, I had no energy to move, no energy to sob. I lay there in the dark, arms tangled in cloth above my head as tears leaked into my shirt prison. My back burned and burned, raw and tender and damaged. I rested, lying still until the torn sensation dulled to steady throbs. Bub bub bub bub, my heart beat in every wound.

Voices rumbled in the other room, first loud, then low-grade. People wandered through the kitchen, and the odors of fried eggs and toast filtered into my room. After a time, Ted opened my door and placed his face near mine - I think he wanted to check on whether I'd stopped breathing. I let him hear me. I let him hear long, even breaths, then he disappeared and closed my door. The house grew quiet.

Resting gave me time to think about Ted's crimes. I worked it over in my mind and realized an important truth: he'd made a mistake. A critical one. My back thudded, but flames of victory joined together in my chest, and they helped me ignore the all-over hurt. Ted had lost, and Donnielle and I had won. The only thing I had to do was slide off that bed.

Slowly, slowly, I worked my shirt the rest of the way over my head and freed my arms from the sleeves. I didn't want anything to touch my skin, and the night offered soothing cold air. That cord had caught the whole of my body from my shoulders to the backs of my legs, but

Ted had focused on the middle of my back. Painfully, carefully, I eased off the bed, pulled my train book from its hiding place, and tucked it under my left arm. He had lashed the ribs on my right side, but the left side had hidden safely from the storm.

Out in the hall, only the living room clock ticked. I crept lightly to the door of Ted and Ashlynn's bedroom and waited a long minute. Silence answered my careful question.

Donny's door opened easily, but I had a sense this would change. Ted planned to buy new doorknobs for our doors - knobs with locking mechanisms. Maybe that had been one of the rumbles from the kitchen. It meant I had to get Donny out of the house. I had to get her out now. Right now.

I moved up to her face and whispered. "Are you okay?" I felt the wetness on her pillow, on her cheeks, in her hair.

She grabbed my hand and squeezed it.

"It's okay. We have to leave. Will you leave with me?"

She hesitated, always so afraid. So afraid, poor girl.

"I'm going now," I breathed near her ear. "Come with me."

She held my hand as I led her off the bed. I didn't dare bend over, so I briefly knelt, back straight, to grab her shoes. Donny followed me into the hallway, and we padded out to the front door in our sock feet.

I couldn't reach the deadbolt or even stretch to try. I pointed, and Donny cautiously reached up and turned it slowly, slowly. And then the doorknob. I eased the door open a crack, then another centimeter, and then another. Dread almost deafened me. The blood pounded in my ears and pumped through my back with such tremendous thuds, I worried I wouldn't have heard Ted if he stomped over the couch like an elephant. Donny glanced backwards every three seconds while I focused on easing that door open.

Stiff. My skin felt so stiff.

The door had half opened when I heard a murmur in the room down the hall. Outside air wafted into the entryway, the air of liberty. We stood silent, though, because somebody had stepped out of bed.

"Go," I breathed to Donny. "Go."

I grasped the book under my left arm and clung to Donny's shoes with the fingers of my other hand. Near panic, I urged her down the steps, across the grassy front yard, onto the pavement. We needed to get off the street and out of sight. Donny followed me into the grass of the Simmons' yard across the street, where we dropped into the shadows between an oak tree and a hedge. It hurt to hold Donny's shoes while I ran, and I knelt in the dirt to offer them to her. It hurt to move, period. Stiff soreness had replaced the searing sensation that had first tormented me, but every step jarred my injuries.

Donny and I peeked through the hedges back across the street at the prison we'd escaped. It appeared so calm, a bungalow like a thousand others. I watched the house as Donny pulled on her shoes, and a yellow light glowed through the window of Donny's bedroom. Moments later, my bedroom light popped on.

"C'mon!" We hopped up and ran. I had no clue about the time. I didn't know where we could find refuge in the dark morning, but we couldn't stay put. The front door slammed behind us, and I knew Ted had emerged to bloodhound us down.

I led Donny through yards across the fronts of houses. We had taken walks all over this neighborhood with Ashlynn. We knew it. We knew the people here, because she had stopped to fake-talk with them over and over again. I visualized the blocks around us and focused in on each home at a time, on each group of people. People with little kids. Who had children? More importantly, who had dogs? Who had dogs that would bark when we trespassed through their territory, dogs who could alert Ted to our location?

A rock bounced down the street and skittered to the curb. I pulled Donny beside the hydrangea bushes under the Taylors' living room window, and we huddled there in the shadows. Ted approached at a light jog, and we ducked our heads down. Ted might see us if a little light caught our golden hair, but we didn't move. We waited as the enemy's tennis shoes dap dap dapped past us. Guttural sounds choked from his mouth, and I thought, "What a stupid man. He should be listening. He can't listen if he's cursing at us."

Donny and I huddled like rocks in the shadows. Could we sit there all night? No, we had to move soon. I could hope that Ted ran on and on all night, but it was likely he'd double-back and explore each yard carefully, one set of bushes at a time.

I shuddered, shirtless in the crisp night air. The temperatures had pushed into the 70s during the day, but the nights remained chilly.

I dashed around the neighborhood in my mind, trying to decide where we should go. We had to have a plan, a specific destination! The Rogers, were they in town? The Winstons... no... What about that house with the swings in the back? They had children there. The kids at that house had been splashing in puddles on the weekends, two little girls and a boy about my age. They lived a few houses farther down.

I grabbed Donny's hand and pulled her into the Taylor's side yard to huddle and listen. A privacy fence guarded the back yard, so we couldn't just zip behind houses. I tried to draw in sounds from the neighborhood, straining to hear Ted's shoes on the pavement. I had horrible visions of racing to somebody's door and banging, shouting, only to have Ted arrive a few moments later. He'd punch me and knock me out, then carry us over his shoulders back to our personal penitentiary.

I didn't know the time - no cell phone or watch - but we waited in that side yard awhile. I didn't know whether Ted lingered out there in the street. I couldn't hear him anywhere. We only needed to travel three houses farther down the road.

Donny bowed her head, and I wondered if she was praying.

I shivered and thought hard. I knew Ted wouldn't stop walking, walking and hunting all night, and the approaching dawn already warmed the gray sky in the east. That's when we heard a dog barking. Two dogs now. Where? The next block over. Yes! The dogs could tattle on Ted just as easily as they could tattle on us!

Those faithful pets gave me the courage I needed to make a final dash. I led Donny along the edge of the house and peeked out into the empty street. We took the chance and ran swiftly around a front porch and across a driveway. We slipped from bushes to tree trunks and finally made a run for it, bolting the last fifty feet to the house I'd had in my mind.

A short gate guarded the front yard. My hands shook, but I flipped the latch and opened it for Donny, and we skirted around the house to the back door.

I had no fears about getting caught by the house owners. I didn't worry they'd call the cops, because I needed them to call the cops. No matter how they reacted to our invasion, none of it mattered as long as Ted didn't reach us first. I trotted up the steps and tried that back door. Magically, it opened.

14 ℲI

Bill

The door creaked as I pushed, but I didn't care. I pulled Donny in after me and gently closed and locked the door behind us.

We stood in a sort of coat closet entryway. Donny didn't want to move, but I tugged her hand and led her around the corner into the kitchen itself. A dog growled then, a deep rumble in its chest. In the light from the stove hood I spied a yellow Labrador in a doggy bed just past the fridge.

"Hi there," I put out a hand. "We're your friends."

Being short had its advantages. The shaggy dog eased up and clicked across the kitchen to sniff at us. I could tell she took care of children. That's what she did. That was her purpose. I sat with her and rubbed her ears and hugged her. That hugging stretched the skin on my back, and I gasped in pain when I did it, but a massive relief breathed life into my heart. Donny finally relaxed and petted the dog too, and that plain made everything better. The adults of the house could help us when they woke up in the morning. I didn't think they'd call Ashlynn and send us back. They couldn't. I wouldn't let them.

Weariness weighed on my eyebrows, and I rubbed my arms, chilled after spending too much time outside. I led Donny through the kitchen into a front room with couches. She climbed up onto the biggest soft sofa, and I joined her. I pulled a fuzzy afghan off the back of the couch to drape over us and cautiously snuggled up.

I had hardly dozed when a cat stepped on my head, but it didn't matter. Coffee brewed in the kitchen, and the aroma brushed comfort across my face. I removed Donny's soft arm from my neck and rolled onto the carpet. Easing to the doorway, I peeked around the corner on the lord of the home. A man stood at the stove in sweatpants, his back all hairy. He'd buzzed away the hair on his head, unable to hide the fact that hardly any grew on top anymore. Eggs sizzled as he cracked them into a cast iron pan. Aside from those light sounds, the house sat silent.

What if this guy acted like Ted? Normal outside but brutal inside, willing for adults to batter children? My back hurt all over, a bruised, stiff throbbing. I halted in the doorway. Tears bubbled over and gushed down my cheeks, but I had to try.

"Hello?" I whispered tearfully. "Good morning?"

The man didn't spin around. He kept frying his food.

"Good morning, bud. You're up awful early. Jump up to the table and I'll give you some scrambled eggs."

"No. I mean." I tried to speak up, tried to make my voice heard. "I mean, I live down the road. I need you to call the police for me."

The man turned and frowned down. From the front, I looked like a normal little boy in pajama bottoms. The two of us made a pair of shirtless, balding guys. Except that my hair had grown and poofed a bit.

"Well now. Where'd you come from?"

"I need you to call the police." I started bawling for real. I couldn't hold it back. All the stress and pain and fear rose up and spilled out of me, and I had no more ability to be strong. "Call the police. We need the police to come!"

Do you know what he did? That dear man stepped over and got down on his knees and gently brushed the tears from my eyes with his thumbs. Concerned, he said, "It's okay, buddy. It's okay. It's okay. What's the matter? You sure have a big egg on your forehead. You must have whacked your head pretty hard."

I couldn't breathe. I pressed my hands against his hairy chest and rested my head and sobbed big shuddering sobs.

He placed a large, warm hand on my fluffy hair. Then, he went to wrap an arm around me to give me a hug, but the insta-agony jolted me.

"Don't. Ow! Don't!"

And that's when he saw my back. I didn't know what it looked like, but I imagined the alarm that zapped through him. The man took me by the top of the head and turned me around. Curses breathed out of him, and I don't think he even heard himself.

"Who did this to you? What happened?"

"He was hurting Donny." I had to keep my explanation PG. Short. Childlike. "He was in bed with her, and I screamed at him. Please call the police. Please."

Confusion washed over the man's face, but he nodded and grabbed his phone off the wall to punch the buttons.

"Hello. It's 608 North Michigan Avenue. Yeah, a beat up little boy is in my house. Bruising all over him. What? He just showed up in my kitchen. Huh. Someone did a real number on him. Yeah, that would be great, and an officer to take a statement. No, no he's conscious and breathing. He can walk. Thanks. Another child might be injured too, so -" He paused for a few moments, listening. "Okay. Okay. Thanks."

He answered a few more questions and hung up.

"They're gonna be here in a few minutes, buddy." He got down on my level again, anger in his face.

"You're not mad we came in your house, are you? He was trying to find us, so I thought we could hide here."

"Oh no." The man shook his head. "No no no, I'm not mad at you! Not a little bit. Come sit up here and have some eggs. Are you hungry? Do you want a warm cloth for your back?"

I shook my head. I didn't want anything to touch my back, and I had no desire to eat. "I'm so thirsty. Can I have some water?"

"Sure. Sure, you can have water." He quickly filled a plastic cup at the tap. Then, he picked me up and set me at the table and handed me the cup. My butt hurt. Everything hurt, but I could sit.

"Is the other child still back at your house? Where's your brother?"

"My brother?"

"Who did you say? Uh...Donny?"

"Oh, no. She's my foster sister. She's in the other room on your couch."

That surprised him. He looked into the living room where little Donny slumbered in her nightgown.

"Foster sister," he nodded. "Was it your foster father who did it?" He pulled up a chair and settled at the table beside me.

The cup blocked my mouth, and I kept gulping and gulping. I tried to nod.

"Who? What's his name?"

I pulled the cup away and breathed out. "Ted Cresson." I took

83

another breath and returned to my water.

The man's anger rushed up again, and I understood that he knew Ted. He knew him. He shoved his chair back, and I saw the violence in his movements.

"Don't!" I choked on the water, and a painful coughing fit shook me. "No." I tried to breathe and drew my air slowly. "The police will take care of it."

The man glared in the direction of Ted's house, but he pulled the chair under him and settled back into it.

I finished coughing. "The police will take care of it." I wiped my eyes. "He tried to do bad things to Donny. They'll get him."

"The police will get him," the man repeated. That seemed to calm him down.

"They will. I'll tell them everything. I'll tell them he was hurting Donny, and that's why he whipped me."

"Ohhh, I see. He was hurting her, and you wanted to stop him." The man looked at me in a new way. "What's your name?"

I set my cup down. "Dodge." I reached out my hand.

"Bill." Bill grabbed my small hand in his huge, rough hand, and we shook.

I wiped the tears off my cheeks, then I placed my hands on the table and rested my face on them. I had no more energy.

Bill kept shaking his head, staring at my back. "I should kill him."

"It's bad, I know." I didn't move. "Am I bleeding? Is there blood?"

"Some. Honey, what did he use?" Bill studied my wounds, clearly puzzled. "What did he hit you with?"

"He tore the cord off the lamp. He threw my lamp against the wall, and I thought he was going to strangle me to death."

Bill closed his eyes and shook his head. "Yeah. Yeah, that's what it looks like. A blasted cord. Geeeez."

He got up and disappeared into the other room. He returned with a Polaroid camera. "I'm going to take some pictures, okay?"

He took snapshots of my back and had me drop my pants enough to get my backside. He got shots from the side to show my ribs.

I studied the photographs as they slowly brightened in the kitchen light, and I couldn't understand what I saw at first. I expected stripes, but the full force of the blows had concentrated at the rounded end of Ted's doubled-up cord; it had created a cascade of swollen, darkening violet marks, some split open and blood-crusted, each shaped like the top half of a paper clip - like long fish scales. Most would heal as the weeks passed, but the worst ones never disappeared altogether. Ted had given me a series of permanent scars across the right side of my back that honestly looked like repeating stamps of the Nike swoosh.

The police arrived. They didn't use sirens, but we heard them pull up outside.

I sat up in earnest. "Bill, listen. The police need to have Donny tested right away. At the hospital. Because Ted tried to ... to do bad things to her in bed. He made her cry."

I figured I'd entered Ted and Ashlynn's home at a key moment in Ted's relationship with Donny. Donny always feared Ashlynn, but she seemed perfectly calm around Ted. The little orphan girl needed somebody to love her, and she'd enjoyed a father's attention as Ted doted on her. I'd watched Ted fight with himself. He'd tried to satisfy himself with brushing Donny's hair or holding her on his lap, but rather than calming his desires, they only stirred him up.

Ted should have sent us back and kept a fat barrier between himself and little girls. He should have sought help, gotten his monster out in the light, anything to ensure he didn't hurt that child. Instead, he danced at the edge of the sarlacc pit with Donny. His self-control had broken down. He'd slid slowly slowly into the pit with her, into the toothed mouth of the beast, and he'd punished me for standing in his way.

I hoped I'd broken into her room and interrupted Ted in time. I hoped Donny had been crying from fear more than anything else. She didn't run or move like she was injured, and that encouraged me.

Bill said, "Okay, okay. I'll let them know."

"Because I don't know what he did to her."

Again, Bill held back his rage. "We'll tell them. We'll tell them to take very good care of your sister."

The law men knocked at the door, and Bill led them into the living room. I woke Donny, and she perched in her blue nightgown on the couch while I tried to smooth her messy hair.

"The police are our friends, Donny. They're here to help us." I held her hand and patted it. Then I warned the law men, "Donny can't talk. Please don't scare her."

Donny hid her face in my neck most of the time. She didn't even sign to communicate, so I explained things the best I could.

"Ashlynn is bad too. Ted wouldn't let her beat up Donny. So, she beat me instead. Oh! I have a book! I wrote it all down!"

I set my train book on the coffee table and opened it to the last page. Embarrassment heated my cheeks. I didn't want Bill to see my list, all those things Ashlynn had done to me, so I ducked my head and handed the book over to the police.

Bill's wife walked in about then, surprised to find officers in her living room. After Bill pulled her into the kitchen to explain, she kindly offered to let me and Donny take baths, but the cops wanted the hospital staff to examine us first.

When the officers were ready to leave, Bill sat down next to me. "Dodge, you want me to ride to the hospital with you?" It was an honest, decent offer, but Bill had his own life, his own family. He'd done everything I'd asked him to - and more. He'd given me water and taken pictures and expressed fury at Ted for me.

I started to say, "No." I started to, but then I pictured the hospital without him. As soon as I imagined being alone, fear pulsed up again. What if Ted and Ashlynn appeared and convinced the police to give us back? What if the people didn't listen to me?

I said, "Okay. You'll keep us safe." And that got the first smile from Bill I'd seen all morning.

Paramedics helped Donny and me into the back of an ambulance waiting outside. Bill pulled on a shirt, and nobody stopped him as he climbed in after us. He handed me a light jacket and guarded us the rest of the morning.

Bill left my life after that, but I made sure to write him. And I sent his family a card every Christmas.

15   ٢١

Court

They cleaned and patched me up at the hospital, but then I had to deal with legal matters. The police questioned me. The welfare people questioned me. They asked the same things 20 different ways, and I gave them the same story every time.

My train book really caused some noise. I'd forgotten that four-year-olds don't write; they draw pictures. Even worse, I'd spelled it all correctly. I should have thrown in some phonetic spellings, because little kids don't write "slapped." They write "slaped" or "slpd." I wrote much better than any small child should write.

I had to prove I wrote that list, to show them I could do it. They dictated to me, and I wrote out what they said. "The quick brown fox jumps over the lazy dog." I printed with large, unskilled letters, but I spelled the words right.

I wrote, "Once upon a midnight dreary, while I pondered, weak and weary, over many a quaint and curious volume of forgotten lore." That astonished them. They called me a "child prodigy" with far more excitement than I liked.

They asked, "How did you know to keep a record? Who told you to do that - to write everything down?"

I shrugged. "Police television shows."

I tried to... not *dumb* myself down so much as *tone* it down. I had to be careful with my vocabulary. One adult after another stared when I explained myself, and I didn't like them paying close attention to me. Whether or not it was rational, I worried I'd get kidnapped and sold to the CIA. I couldn't decide which fears were reasonable and which were silly.

The officials took pictures of what Ted had done to me, but I pointed out my other bruises too. I explained that Ashlynn's attacks were all about her anger over Ted's thing for Donny and were never meant to correct me as a parent.

"She hit me because she was mad. She didn't care if she hurt me. She *wanted* to hurt somebody - that's why she got me in the first place. Because she couldn't hit Donny, and she couldn't hit Ted, so she hit me."

They asked me to describe specific incidents.

I tried to explain. "If I did nothing wrong, she made things up. That last time, I asked to get down to go pee, and she said, 'No. You're not excused.' Then she made me sit and sit and sit at the table until I wet my pants. I held it and held it, and it hurt to hold it. I begged her to let me go. Then I wet my pants, because that's what she wanted. It gave her an excuse. See? See these bruises?"

Ashlynn's attacks were always humiliations. She had humiliated and degraded me for nearly six weeks. But only six weeks. What if I'd been a normal kid and Donny and I had *stayed* there, stuck? I couldn't fathom the lifelong damage to both of us.

The thing that bothered me most was I didn't have answers about Donny. I didn't know if the hospital found evidence of Ted's dalliance with her, and nobody would tell me the results. My biggest source of comfort was something the prosecuting attorney's assistant said to me. She said, "It's good that you want to tell your story, Dodge. Your testimony is very very important. What you tell the jury might be the most important thing to send Ted to jail."

That gave me several hopes. If the hospital hadn't found solid physical evidence that Ted molested Donny, that was good news. I wanted her as innocent and unharmed as possible. Donny couldn't talk! I had to testify on her behalf, to stand in for her.

A doctor at the hospital could have blown my cover, by the way. He checked me over and asked questions, but he didn't correct the "male" listed on my paperwork. He noted that I had no evidence of sexual abuse and signed off on it.

Cheryl rescued my things from Ted and Ashlynn's house. I dressed myself in boy's clothes, complete with my favorite Captain America underwear, and went on with life.

I attended hearings over those next months, and Ashlynn's final punishment upset me so much. A judge gave her six months jail time, all suspended. He assigned her community service, that's it. Tell you what, that enraged me. I thought back to all those awful days trapped with her, back to Ashlynn's fury face and the slaps and kicks and boards and sticks. Battering me wasn't worth quiet time in a cell?

Still, I knew she'd never get another foster child. The news had trashed Ashlynn's name, and I suspected she'd had to leave Pasadena. Maybe that was enough.

Meanwhile, they took Donny away somewhere and didn't let me see her. When I asked about her, they assured me she was receiving good care. "You don't understand!" I insisted. "She needs me! At least let me tell her goodbye!" It didn't seem to matter to them.

The court scheduled Ted's trial for May. I hoped I'd see Donny there, but they kept me in a little room so the other witnesses didn't influence my testimony.

When my turn came to testify, they led me across the courtroom to the stand. I hunted over faces in the seats as I walked to the front. No Donny. I stepped up behind a wooden barrier to the left of the judge, and the prosecuting attorney stood behind his table. Because I was so young, he had to demonstrate my competence as a witness.

"Dodge," the attorney asked me. "Do you promise to tell the truth here today?"

"Yes, I do."

The members of the jury watched me with interest. I was so small!

"Good good. Could you tell me what truth is?"

I squinted, "What is truth?" Did he really ask me that?

The attorney nodded, "Yes, young man. What is truth?"

I stifled a smile. That was the philosophical question of the ages, wasn't it? I behaved myself and answered seriously. "The truth is something that really happened. A lie is something that people make up."

"Good." He pulled out a card and showed it to the room. "If I said this card had an orange circle on it, would that be the truth?"

"No, sir."

"Why?"

"Because it's a picture of a blue square."

"Right. And if I said this is a picture of a blue square, would that be the truth?"

"Yes, sir."

"So, you know the difference between the truth and a lie, don't you? Have you ever told a lie?"

I nodded. "Oh...Yes."

Above me, the judge raised his eyebrows. I guessed he didn't often hear kids admit to lying.

"When did you tell a lie?"

"One time I cut my own hair and blamed it on a kid at school."

People in the courtroom chuckled.

I recalled that hair-cutting incident clearly, even though it wouldn't take place for another two or three years. Deep breath. Remembering my own future still gave me shots of anxiety.

The prosecutor asked, "Why did you lie about it?"

"I didn't want to get in trouble. But, then my mom said she'd talk to my teacher, and that was gonna end in a huge mess. So I just 'fessed up and told her I did it."

Titters rustled across the courtroom again.

"Is there ever a time when you *should* lie?"

I thought about the folks who'd bravely hid Jews from the Nazis. I thought about my walking around, pretending to be a little boy. But I gave the simple answer. "It gets you into more and more trouble. My mom used to say, 'What a tangled web we weave when first we practice to deceive.'"

The prosecutor laughed spontaneously at that. "My mom used to say the same thing."

"So did mine," the judge murmured.

"Do you promise to tell the truth, Dodge?"

"Yes, sir."

That ended the truth-lie portion of my testimony.

Under the prosecutor's guidance, I told them my story as plainly as I could. I explained the entire series of events that led to the horrific night Donny and I escaped. And I felt good about it. I could sense the anger, the outrage in the room. I heard whispers in the audience.

Of course, Ted's shameless defense attorney cross-examined me. He didn't *act* mean. He spoke gently and patiently, but he asked the worst things and used my intelligence against me. Really. He had to be an evil man to do what he did.

The attorney smoothed his sharp gray suit jacket. "It's clear you're a remarkably smart fellow, Dodge." He folded an arm and brushed a thumb over his lips, as though pondering deep ponders. "Before you came in, psychologist Dr. Behrmann testified that you have an IQ of 180. That's astounding. I've never been in the same room as somebody with an IQ of 180." The lawyer dropped his arms and pointed at a legal pad on the table. "In fact, he stated it was 'at least' that high and that you were actually 'off the charts.'"

I didn't respond. I stared at my foe's dark mustache and wished he'd shave it. Ted's lawyer wasn't my friend. He'd arrived to defend my enemy, the abuser of small children, and that meant I couldn't trust his warm words. He wasn't trying to prove I was incompetent or forgetful. He didn't want to convince the jury that I didn't know right from wrong. He was taking steps to highlight my intelligence. Why?

"Do you remember the reading tests the doctor gave you?"

"Yes."

"You read Edgar Allen Poe out loud and answered questions. How old are you again?"

"Almost five."

"Edgar Allen Poe. That's impressive. According to his results, you read at the same level as the average 10th grade student."

I smiled to myself. Frankly, an IQ of 180 at my age meant I had the mental age of a nine-year-old. I hoped the average 10th grader was better off than that.

Here's the thing about Dr. Behrmann: he saw through me. He saw that I'd offer wrong answers when I knew the right ones. He gave me all kinds of tests. Pattern tests. Memory tests. Vocabulary. Math. Puzzles. I suspected Edgar Allen Poe was *not* a normal part of his IQ testing repertoire, that he'd pulled out "The Raven" only because he was curious. When I purposely flubbed on words, he asked me, "Dodge, why are you pretending you're not as smart as you are? What are you afraid of?"

The evil lawyer brought my mind back to the courtroom.

"Do you remember 'The Raven,' Dodge? The poem you read?"

"Yes."

"What did you think of it?"

I blinked. It was too late to claim I was anything like a normal child, so I decided to go along with it. What had I thought about Poe's poem back in high school?

"It frustrated me."

"Why? Why does Poe frustrate you?"

"So. In the poem, the guy keeps asking the raven questions, and the raven always says, 'Never more.' When I first read it, I thought, 'He knows the raven is going to say, "Never more." Why doesn't he ask questions that would give him *hope* when the raven says, "Never more?"' I mean, he could have asked, 'Will Lenore and I be miserable? Will we be poor or sick?' Then, it would have been good when the raven said, 'Never more.' He set himself up for disappointment."

The crowd murmured, and I wondered if I'd made a mistake. I'd impressed and amused them, and the general anger I'd successfully built seemed to dissipate.

"That's very good, Dodge. You really thought that through, didn't you?"

I looked out across the audience and over to the jury. Maybe it was okay to let them laugh a little. I didn't know.

"You think things through, don't you?"

I agreed carefully. "I do."

"Your brain is more like the brain of a teenager than a preschooler. That's pretty amazing. Did you know that's amazing?"

"Sure," I shrugged. "I believe you."

The audience chuckled again.

"Do you think you're as smart as an adult?"

"What?"

"Do you think that you're as smart as Ted, for instance?"

Darn. I didn't want to lie, even to play the game.

He repeated, "Do you think you're as smart as Ted?"

I took a deep breath. "I could be."

"Do you think you're smarter than Ted?"

I shook my head. "Not necessarily."

People laughed right out loud at that, and I scowled. How could they allow themselves to think any of this was funny?

The attorney paused. "Is that why you disobeyed Ted?"

He didn't sound unkind when he asked it. He asked like he'd been puzzled and wanted to know, and I wasn't sure how to respond, so I sat and stared at him.

"I don't understand your question."

"Did you think you were being a smart boy by disobeying Ted?"

"Not even a little bit." I didn't think I was a boy at all.

"Not even a little?"

"Wise. I was being *wise* by disobeying Ted."

"It's obvious you're intelligent, Dodge. You're a very aware young man. You were healthy when the state became your guardian, so you must have been doing well on your own in the big world. Were you used to making decisions? Doing whatever you chose to do?"

"Mostly."

"Did that change when you moved into Ted and Ashlynn's home?"

"Yes."

"Was that frustrating?"

"Yes."

"For instance, when Ted took you to Eaton Canyon Park, did you run off to explore?"

This again! He'd mentioned it when we met before the trial. Ted had taken us to a neighborhood park one Saturday, and I'd rolled down a grassy hill over and over, trying to get Donny to join me.

"You ran off and climbed a hill at Eaton Canyon Park?"

It was more of a knoll than a hill, but okay.

"Did you fall down the hill?"

"I mean, I rolled down it."

"Did you scrape yourself?"

"I scraped my knee."

"Did you scrape your back?"

"No."

He spoke confidingly. "You tumbled down a great big hill, and you didn't scrape your back even a little? You lied to your mother about your hair, Dodge. Are you lying about this?"

Was he supposed to ask me questions like that? I looked over at the prosecutor. Shouldn't he be objecting to some of this stuff?

As Ted's lawyer asked about the park, it occurred to me that we were talking about two different places. I thought Eaton Canyon Park was the little park near our house. He kept talking like the hill was enormous and rocky, and that confused me. Ted must have told the lawyer I'd climbed up the side of a ravine, that I'd tumbled down the hill, banging and scratching myself.

I hadn't banged down any hillside!

The lawyer didn't care. He didn't care about the truth, because he only wanted to splash doubt on my story. That was his whole purpose, and he did a good job of it. He provided an explanation that sounded reasonable, and I'd foolishly agreed we'd gone to Eaton Canyon Park when I didn't know the actual name of the park. I'd screwed up!

I studied the jury and wondered. They had to be smarter than that. Then, I thought of Ashlynn's trial, and insecurity overwhelmed me. I could *not* let Ted get community service over this!

"Ted told you not to climb that hill, but you did anyway."

"No, sir. He didn't."

"We're getting into a tricky area now Dodge. You had a bad habit of disobeying Ted, didn't you?"

"It... it wasn't a bad habit."

"You disobeyed Ted when he told you to sleep in your own bed?"

"I did. I disobeyed him about where I slept, but I-"

"Be truthful about this, Dodge," he interrupted me gently. "You said earlier that Ted told you not to sleep with Donnielle, but you did anyway." The lawyer raised his eyebrows at me.

"*Yes,* but it was-"

"You love Donnielle, don't you?"

"Yes."

"Is that why you slept in there with her?"

I glared at him.

"She's a pretty girl, isn't she?"

I felt the heat rise into my ears. "She's beautiful."

"And you enjoyed snuggling with her every night?"

I lost it when he said that. I popped up and barked, "I object! Your honor, I object!" The prosecutor looked like he'd just woken up. Why wasn't he doing his job!

"Don't worry, Dodge," the judge dismissed my concern. "Answer his questions."

"Isn't he leading the witness, though?"

"He's allowed to during cross-examination."

The defense lawyer's eyes narrowed at me. He was good at this, and he maintained a voice of calm reason.

"I understand this upsets you, Dodge. These aren't good memories for you, are they?"

I glared. "Of course not."

"Is it too difficult for you to continue? Do you want to get down now?"

"No, I'm fine." I hated this guy.

My neck and ears warmed around my face. The other questions hadn't affected me like this. The lawyer could exaggerate my falling down some hillside, and it only irritated me. When he tried to use Donny against me, a dizzy tunnel vision clouded in and fuzzed the edges of my eyes.

The attorney had more presence than I did. His voice reached the back of the room, while I was stuck half-hidden behind that wooden barrier. I didn't have the verbal bulk to wrestle past the defensive line he was building. I couldn't force my voice over his.

"You know, it's okay Dodge. You love Donnielle, and you wanted to snuggle up in there with her. We all understand that. Did it upset you when Ted told you to stay in your own bed?"

"I had to sleep in there *specifically* because Ted didn't want me to."

"What was that?"

"I had to sleep in there because Ted didn't want me to. Because-"

"Because you didn't like him telling you what to do? You wanted to sleep there, and it made you angry that he told you to stay out of Donnielle's room?"

The prosecutor finally spoke up on my behalf. Finally! "Objection, your honor. Compound question. Counsel is not allowing the witness to answer."

"Sustained. Counsel, please ask one question at a time."

"Were you frustrated and angry with Ted?"

I had to calm down. I couldn't belt out, "Of course!" Being rude wasn't going to help my case. Take a breath. Answer the questions. Honestly.

"Yes."

"He treated you like you were just a regular little boy. He tried to tell you what to do. He wouldn't let you sleep with Donnielle. Did you want to get back at him?"

"No, I did not."

"Are you sure? Even after you felt humiliated?"

"Yes, I'm sure."

"Everybody understands, Dodge," the lawyer said gently. "You are a very bright boy. Nobody wants to be treated like a little kid when he has the mind of an adult. No more questions, your honor."

I wasn't relieved when the evil lawyer settled into his seat. I studied the jury. Had they bought any of that garbage?

Before someone had a chance to dismiss me, I spoke up. "Your honor, do you have any questions for me?" I begged him with my eyes to fix this thing. He had to fix it.

The judge lightly shook his head, and I thought he was going to make me step down. "I do want to know something, Dodge."

I nodded.

"Tell me again, why *did* you keep going into Donnielle's room?"

I flicked a look at Ted, the young, handsome accountant in his navy blue suit and tie. My eyes had avoided him all this time, but I finally dared a glance. He sat at his table, so respectable, so calm. Not a brute who abused little children. Maybe they'd believe I made it up after all.

I pictured the defense attorney's final summation in my head. He hadn't made it yet, but I saw it. He'd tell them, "Don't be tricked by his sweet face. Dodge was angry, jealous of the attention Ted paid

Donnielle, because Dodge wanted her attention. When he tumbled down the hillside and banged himself up, he determined to get back at Ted. He sneaked out to the neighbors and phoned the police so that he could blame Ted for bruises he had given himself. Dodge might be small, but he's a genius - a genius with a child's fickle emotions."

Maybe someone on the jury would ingest the poison and fight for Ted. Someone who assumed all children lied. Someone with no sense. The frustration of being blocked in overwhelmed me.

"Your honor, is it okay if I stand up?"

"In your seat?"

"Yes, sir. Please."

"Okay, but be careful."

I stood, and it made such a difference. I stood bigger, more visible. So grateful. Grateful for the judge's question. Grateful for the new height. "I went in to protect her, not to snuggle." I pointed over at Ted's lawyer. "That guy said weird things. I don't even *like* girls."

The audience chuckled again, and I wanted to laugh too.

No no no. I needed their anger!

"I was scared for Donny, for Donnielle, because something was wrong with Ted. He always woke me up in Donny's room after midnight. Your honor, why did Ted keep going into Donny's room so late at night?"

"Good question," the judge nodded.

I nodded with him. "He didn't say, 'Now Dodge. You need to sleep in your own bed,' all reasonable like a normal adult. He grabbed me by my shoulders, so angry his face was red. He said, 'She's not yours!'"

"And you kept sleeping in her room after that?"

"Yes, sir, but not because I wanted to. It scared me to go to her room every night. I'd lay awake listening, listening for so long…"

The judge studied me for a few moments. "That was brave of you."

And that's when emotion came to my rescue. I covered my face and struggled to breathe. The adult part of me felt grateful for the tears and their effect on the audience, but the child part of me just remembered the heaviness of all that fear and stress night after night. So much fear. So much stress. I recognized it more now that it was over. I wiped my face with my sleeve and kept going.

"The one night I *didn't* sleep in her room, I woke up and realized Ted had tricked me." I wiped my face again and tried hard to keep my voice calm. "So, I ran into her room, and he was in the bed with her."

Most of my lash marks had healed by that point, but the worst ones remained, five purple-red swooping scars on the right side of my back, blending together. My tender, young skin had captured that night forever like a photograph, a still-shot of cruelty. I didn't want those people to depend on little square pictures. Ted's behavior was personal, and I had to make it personal to them.

My new foster mother had dressed me in a blue button-up shirt with a collar. Standing in the chair, I turned and pulled that dress shirt up and exposed my back to the whole court.

Using all the air from my diaphragm, I projected so the whole court could hear. "These scars aren't from rocks or branches. See how the marks are swoops? The same shape over and over?"

Those angry marks told the truth, and I waited several seconds before tugging down my shirt and facing the jury again. Even the evil lawyer cringed in his seat.

"Those scars are from a lamp cord. That's what Ted did. Ted did that to me, because I found him in bed with a 7-year-old girl!"

"Okay son," the judge said. "Okay. It's okay. You go ahead and sit back down."

I obeyed him, still upset. "Your honor, please. Please. Donny can't talk! She can't tell you herself!"

"Okay okay," the judge shushed me with his hand.

"They need to put her with people who will be nice to her!"

"Dodge. Dodge, it's all right. I'll take care of it."

In the end, the jury found Ted guilty of five out of six charges. That excellent judge made Ted serve real jail time, and he ordered social services to let me visit Donny.

When it was all over, the judge said one last thing to me:

"Dodge, when you grow up, I hope you go into public service."

July 17, 1980

Dear Mike,

I'm sorry it took so long to write. Please tell Aunt Mindy I love my Captain America underwear.

I'm a super hero! Dun! Dun! I put bad guys in jail. I save little girls!

My foster parents are good and I like them a lot.

I turned 5 on July 15th. You know what you could get me? One of those Simon Says games.

Tell Aunt Mindy I miss her And tell her you're the best sort of guy. You're a guy who buys little kids Simon Says games for their 5th birthdays. ☺

Love,
Dodge Journey Spicer

Dodge

PART II

Idea

After Ted and Ashlynn, the child welfare folks moved me into the home of John and Shirley Chester, and they were good people. The Chesters had one other foster child and two biological children, and I enjoyed my cheerfully normal time with them.

I stayed with John and Shirley during the whole trial process, glad to live in a home with pleasant people, a real mom and dad. We had a party for my fifth birthday with balloons and games and neighbor children. It was a peaceful, healing time.

Something bothered me, though, and it took me time to work it out. I finally realized that I didn't want the happy home.

Wait. That's not exactly what I mean.

I enjoyed the Chester family, and I especially liked not getting beat up all the time. However, I knew other Ted and Ashlynn-types existed out there, and some little kid was getting tortured while I slept safely in my bed every night. As awful as it had been, I was glad that I'd been the one stuck with the Cresson monsters. I had a bit more presence of mind, more wherewithal to fight off tigers than a normal child with no sense of the world. When I imagined another four-year-old stuck in the Cresson house, nausea raised acid in my throat. I had to protect them. I had to look out for other kids in the system.

I called my case worker Cheryl a few days after my birthday and asked to meet with her. It took her a week, but she finally showed up.

"I need you to move me," I said when she sat across the table.

That didn't make her happy. "Why? What's the problem?"

"Nothing. Nothing is wrong. Shirley and John are super, and I love them."

"And that's a problem?" She frowned at me.

"Cheryl, listen to me. Listen. There are a whole bunch of kids out there who need a safe, happy home – like the one I have with John and Shirley. I have a different idea for me. I want you to make me a foster home spy."

Cheryl obviously did not track with me.

I explained. "See, you screen foster parents, but you don't know which ones just *look* good on the surface. Some houses are pretty on the outside but torment for the kids living there. But, I could tell you! You place me in a home, and I'll stay there for awhile and scope it out. I'll tell you if the parents are good parents, and I'll tell you if they're not treating the kids right. I can be the quality control for the Los Angeles foster care system."

My idea did not thrill Cheryl. "I'm not going to play with your life like that, Dodge."

I tried to behave like a normal child around most people. A scared, confused look always wrinkled their faces if I slipped up and started adulting, so I'd catch myself and say, "Normal kids don't say that, do they? They say I'm a prodigy. Is that what prodigies say?" That offered people an explanation for me, and they relaxed. They assumed a child genius could do amazing, impossible things and accepted that I wasn't an alien or artificial intelligence. Cheryl had gotten used to me, which gave me freedom to speak my mind to her.

"Cheryl! You already play with the lives of children in the system. Every single one. So, let me make these places safer and better for the kids who live there."

She insisted, "I can't do that! Besides, we have a lot of kids to place and not enough homes as it is."

"You can do it. I'll be a temporary. I'd be there a few days or weeks, that's all."

"You're a child, Dodge. I know you forget that, but you are. You need a stable home and a stable family. That's what's good for you."

I'd made up my mind and wasn't going to give. "I'm stable inside my head. Send me to a counselor if you want."

Cheryl frowned.

"Pleeeeeeease?" I begged. "I want to do it! Please, let's try it."

Eventually Cheryl gave in. I think she figured I'd switch homes once or twice and give up. I hugged John and Shirley goodbye and wrote down their address in Aunt Mindy's little notebook. Then, Cheryl moved me in with the Faulkners.

17 ᛁ

Trevor

I liked Jeff and Laurie Faulkner just fine. They didn't swing me up and give me big hugs, but they weren't mean. They provided me with shelter and food, a bed to sleep in, toys to play with, and books to read. Their house lacked something, though… the warm, homey quality that I expected in a family. At first, I thought the Faulkners were politely giving me my space, but they just didn't seem to get that little kids required one-on-one time. I needed people to pay attention to me, but I spent all day in my room or out in the back yard, until the lack of human interaction bordered on legitimate neglect.

I considered reporting this to Cheryl, but I figured the Faulkners weren't bad people. They meant well.

They had a teenage son named Trevor, and I liked Trevor a lot. He built Legos with me at the table some afternoons and played music in the mornings on his stereo. We rocked out to Supertramp and Pat Benatar and had a legitimately good time. Still, summer blazed in full force, and most days he drove off with his teenage friends. Laurie worked from home, but she needed her space during the day, and I spent a lot of time alone.

Which is how I came to nearly get Trevor killed. My first house as a spy ended up as Operation Destroy Trevor's Life. It was mostly Trevor's fault, and it was mostly my fault, but it was also mostly Jeff's fault.

Jeff watched baseball in the evenings, so I climbed onto the fat fluffy couch and sat next to him. Trevor wore his hair parted in the middle and feathered back, but Jeff cut his dark hair short in a quiet rebellion against fashion trends. No mustache or beard either.

"Who is playing?" I engaged Jeff. Jeff the trimmed and shaved.

He looked down, surprised to see me there. "Shhh. Just watch."

I had to act like a normal child if I were going to churn up the depths of Jeff's personality, and normal kids don't sit quietly and watch.

The pitcher walked onto the mound and threw the ball back and forth to the catcher as part of his warm-up. "C'mon. Tell me who is playing. What does that guy do?" I pointed to the catcher. "What does that guy do?" I pointed to the pitcher.

"You need to go to your room if you're gonna talk," Jeff said.

I got it. Jeff didn't want to deal with children. I slid off the couch and scooted into the other room to wait. When the commercials came on, I ran back in.

"Please tell me who is playing, Jeff." I leaned my elbows into the corduroy couch cushion beside him. "Please."

"Look, Dodge. I want to watch baseball in peace."

"But it's a commercial!" I stood on my short little legs, and he towered over me on the couch.

Jeff winced as though I didn't get it. "This is my quiet time, Dodge. I had a long day at work, and I want to be left alone."

I didn't let it go; he could spend a couple of moments with me. "You're supposed to be my foster father. Isn't that what fathers do? They teach their kids about baseball."

He stared at me. "You're not my son. Laurie was the one who wanted to do this whole foster home thing. Go bother her."

"Yeah?"

"Yeah." He raised his eyes wide at me, took a sip of his beer, and returned to the television.

I wanted to watch baseball with him! "Well, then you can go soak your head, Jeff!"

He turned back to me, disbelief on his face. "What? You go soak *your* head."

And that made me laugh. I laughed and walked away.

Laurie turned out better than Jeff and showed honest interest in me. I watched her make dinner in the afternoons, and we talked as she diced up onions or potatoes or breaded chicken. She grew warmer every day, telling me stories and laughing at my jokes. I didn't want to spoil her too much with my skills, but I buttered bread or tore up lettuce for salads. Mostly, I kept her company and talked to her. The more time we spent together, the more she relaxed. I think she simply hadn't known what to do with a new human in her house.

"Have you had a lot of foster kids?" I asked one day.

"Nope, you're the first."

"That's what I thought. Well. I like your food. I think it's yummy. But your next foster kid might be a picky little guy, so don't force food into his mouth if he won't eat."

"What! Dodge? What a horrible thing to say. I wouldn't do that!"

I believed her. "But, you might want to!"

"No," she said firmly.

"Then what would you do?" I scowled at my half-eaten turkey sandwich and scrunched up my face. "Ew. I don't like that." I looked up at her. "Okay. How would you handle that?"

Laurie just laughed. "You're so funny!"

I grinned because she was laughing, but I wanted to be serious. "Laurie! One day, you might have a little boy who is picky because he only ate macaroni and cheese every day of his life. He's never even seen a turkey sandwich. Or a cucumber. What do you do?"

Laurie squinted at me. "Where do you come up with these things?"

"Yuck!" I made faces at the turkey. "I want potato chips!"

"You're such a goofball! I'd tell him he needed to try a little of it."

"Okay. Just don't be mean to him."

"Dodge! I promise I won't be mean. I can give him some potato chips, you know. Or make him macaroni and cheese."

"He needs fruits and vegetables."

"I'll make it fun," Laurie tried to reassure me. "I'll reward him if he eats a bit of everything."

"That's a good idea. It's just...the thing is...sometimes kids get messed up. We need to feel safe, even if you have to make sure we try new food. And we need hugs."

She thought about that. "I know, sweetie."

"Yes. But you were afraid of me when I first came here. Because I'm a strange kid. Don't be afraid of me. Think of me like I'm *really* your kid. Like... I got lost in the woods for years, and you just found me again."

She rolled her blue eyes a little. "I got it."

I felt all kinds of hope for Laurie, with her naturally curly hair and naturally kind heart, but Jeff kept blowing me off, and it bugged me. It bugged me! I crawled up on the couch beside him every evening and watched sports with him, and he ignored me. If I kept quiet, he didn't seem to care what I did.

One day the Angels played the Mariners, and I shouted, "My

team! They're gonna destroy the Angels."

Jeff actually responded to me. "Are you kidding? The Mariners? They'll lose by 10 runs. You watch."

"Yeah. Probably. The Mariners aren't very good. And anytime they draft awesome players, the Yankees steal them away. But, we used to go buy cheap seats at the Seattle Kingdome, and it was fun."

Jeff sipped his beer. "I thought you didn't know anything about baseball."

"I wanted you to talk to me."

Jeff didn't respond. He watched the television and acted like I did not exist on his planet.

I tried again. "Can I like the Dodgers? They're in the National League, right? So, they won't be playing your precious Angels."

Jeff stared straight ahead. "You know what, Dodge? Sometimes you're almost cool. And then, nope, you're a brat."

"Pay attention to me! I promise I'll be cool!"

"Shhh. The game is starting."

"Hey. Would you play catch with me sometime?"

Jeff groaned. "Dodge."

I groaned back. "Fine. Do you have a ball so I can play by myself?"

"Go ask Laurie. Or Trevor. He might still have one."

I'd spent a lonely week there. I'd read through all of Jeff's Louis L'Amour westerns and resorted to issues of *Sports Illustrated*. Gahhh, I was bored!

Trevor was out, so I dug through the bottom of his closet. He had hockey stuff, which I hadn't expected in Los Angeles. I found a ball glove four sizes too big for me and no ball. Next, I dove into Trevor's drawers, and there I found a Hershey's tin box under his shirts.

I settled onto Trevor's carpet and popped open his tin. I didn't plan to harm or take anything. I just wanted to know what he'd hidden in a tin in his shirt drawer.

On top, I found several Thurman Munson baseball cards from the early 1970s, each protected in durable little plastic sleeves.

"Thurman Munson. Never heard of him."

Underneath, I found a couple of Morgan silver dollars and other old coins, like buffalo nickels and Mercury dimes. There were bone-colored dice, lead toy soldiers, a few weird token things, and four balls of white powder tied up in sandwich bags.

I took one of the small white balls and studied it. The first thing I thought - and I know this is silly - was that Trevor had a sweet tooth and kept portion-sized amounts of powdered sugar in his room. There was a heaping tablespoon of white powder in each of the bags, more than 10 grams. Closer to 15 grams. I'd been a chemist. I knew grams.

I held up a bag, and it glowed in the orange sunset light from the window. Were they part of a recipe, an unused Christmas gift? A very small gift? I tried to remember where I'd seen little packages like this before.

Oh. Ohhh. I couldn't believe it! No, not Trevor!

I tugged open one small baggie, and a sharp acetone aroma puffed into my face. Acetone, you know, the simplest ketone, the stuff in nail polish remover. The smooth powder shone pearly in the light, and when I pushed my finger into it, it felt oily. I'd never held real cocaine, and these details surprised me.

What was Trevor doing with some 60 grams of cocaine? Two ounces...one-eighth of a pound. Was that a lot? That seemed like a lot to me.

I tied the baggie back up and stuck all four balls into the pockets of my shorts. Trevor was still out with his friends, but he had to be home by 10:00 on weekdays. I replaced the lid on the tin and tucked it back into his shirt drawer, then I ran to my bedroom and hopped up on my bed to think.

And I fell asleep. Because I was a little kid.

In the morning, I got up and watched cartoons on television, and it wasn't until I heard the fridge open that I remembered the round balls in my pockets. I trotted into the kitchen and watched as Trevor lumbered from the fridge in his red Superman pajama bottoms. He set a carton of milk on the bar next to a box of Cheerios and slumped down to eat.

This kitchen was a three-sided square. The fridge and stove lined one wall, and the sink and dishwasher sat on the second side, under the window. A wide bar made the final side, separating the kitchen proper from the dining area with the table. Trevor sat at the bar and munched on his cereal while his shaggy hair hung into his face.

"You want some Cheerios, Dodge?" He glanced at me from under his mop.

I grabbed a bar stool and dragged it around to the counter by the sink. I climbed up and sat on the counter, right next to the garbage disposal.

"Be careful up there." Trevor raised heavy eyebrows. "Don't fall."

"Trevor. I like you."

"Well, thanks." He offered me a sleepy smile across the room.

"But, I need to know something."

"Hmm?" He stuffed a spoonful in his mouth and crunched.

"What are you doing with these?"

I held up all four white balls of cocaine. And I held them higher, because Trevor chewed on without looking. As soon as he did focus on me, he jumped and instantly suffered an explosion of coughing.

"Don't move." I leaned over the sink and turned on the water.

Trevor started around the bar, coughing deep chest coughs.

"Don't move!" I shouted.

Trevor kept coming, waving his arms and coughing.

In a panic, I flipped on the garbage disposal, and he magically stopped in the middle of the kitchen floor. His eyes remained fixed on me, wide with horror. He coughed a few more times and wiped his mouth.

"Dodge, don't!" He took a few deep breaths. "Don't. Don't do that."

"What are you doing with these?" I could hardly hear myself over the sound of the garbage disposal.

"Give those to me, Dodge. Please."

I put my hand out "halt" at him, then slowly reached over to flip off the noise. "Don't come closer, Trevor, or these are gone." The water - shhhhh - rushed into the sink.

"That's $6000 there, Dodge. It's a lot of money. Just... just give those to me."

"I know what they are, Trevor. What are you doing with them?"

"Quiii-et!" He dashed his eyes over his shoulder . "Give those to me. I need them."

"Why?" I demanded.

"I gotta sell them. I need a car."

"You're a drug dealer? Getting other kids hooked on drugs?"

"Would you keep it down! One time. One time, that's it! There's a big party tomorrow, and I'm selling to a bunch of rich kids."

"Whatever! Where did you get them?"

Trevor took a step, and I flipped the garbage disposal switch.

He stopped, hands up, every muscle tense.

I watched him as I reached back and turned off the noise again.

"Please Dodge. Please give those to me."

"How did you buy them?"

"Please, please hand those over before Mom comes in."

He was only 16-years-old, and this thing wasn't going to stop. There was no such thing as "one time."

I took a deep breath. Then, I dropped the baggies into the garbage disposal and flipped that switch.

The shriek from Trevor's mouth almost knocked me into the sink. He stood in the middle of the kitchen, mouth gaping, hazel eyes wide and filled with panic. Then, he ran to the sink and vomited into it. It was mostly Cheerios, and the water was still running, but I turned my face away. He leaned over the sink for long seconds as the water ran down the drain.

"I'm dead! I'm dead. I'm dead." He repeated the phrase over and over again. He scooped water into his mouth and spit it out. "I'm so dead. They're gonna kill me. I'm dead!"

I reached over the sink and turned off the water. "It's two ounces, you dolt. Not ten kilos. You're not dead."

"I am!" He turned on me, his eyes wild. Then he grabbed my arms and hauled me down the hall to his room. He closed the door behind us and walked around and around in a circle. Around and around. Finally, he dropped onto his bed and covered his face with his hands.

"Dodge. I know you think drugs are bad. I know. I know. But, I owe men money, men who are gonna hurt me if I don't give them $6000! And I don't have $6000, you psycho."

Oh. Ohhh. He was selling for somebody else. They weren't his.

"You work for drug thugs? You're in with drug dealers? Then, you have to turn them in! Call the police." I suddenly felt like I was in an *Afterschool Special*. Do the right thing, teenage boy.

Trevor looked at me like I'd squished caterpillars on his birthday cake. Trevor with his mop of hair. "Are you out of your mind!"

"It's your only chance. If they get busted, they can't come looking for you." Maybe not an *Afterschool Special*. Maybe *Magnum P.I.*

"No no no," he shook his head. "You don't get it, dude. You don't know what you're talking about. I have to come up with $6000 by Sunday. Two days, Dodge!" Trevor walked around in circles, fingers clutching his hair, cursing quietly to himself.

I'd known people destroyed by drugs during my life, but I'd never dealt with dealers. That wasn't my world Still, it seemed simple.

"Trevor, if they get arrested, they can't come after you."

"Noooooo!" He dropped his face into his hands again. "You don't understand. These are my friends, and loyalty is important with these dudes. You don't call the cops! You don't snitch on your friends. I'm not a rat, Dodge! And they're not bad." He shook his head at me. "They got families. They're just trying to make a living."

I squinted. "You're an idiot."

Trevor moaned loudly through his hands. "You want to know who gave me that coke? Mark Roper's uncle Paco. He's got connections with some Mexico cartel, and those dudes are crazy! They chop off people's arms and legs and heads!"

Send them right to jail. Skip all the scenes where Trevor gets tied up in a basement. Sell drugs to teenagers? Right to jail. Right away.

"Use a payphone." I forced myself to be serious. "Be anonymous. If you don't, I'm telling everybody. Your parents. Cops. Everybody!"

Trevor gaped at me in dismay for a good ten seconds. Finally, he clenched his fingers like claws in front of him. "You do that, and I'll tear you into little pieces. I'll tear you up and flush your pieces down the toilet!"

No, he wouldn't. "Trevor, you have to turn them in. I won't let you be a bad guy! You're supposed to be a good guy!"

And that's when Trevor slumped in the middle of the room. "I'm not a bad guy. I'm not, Dodge. I know it looks like that, but... there are really bad guys out there. I'm not the bad guy."

"Where does Uncle Paco get it? The stuff you sell?"

"I don't know."

"You do know! Nobody just gives a teenager two ounces of coke. You've been doing this for awhile. You know!"

Across the house, the front door opened, and we both tuned our ears in the direction of the living room.

"Trevor!" Laurie called. "Help me with groceries!"

I know it's messed up, but at least I wasn't bored anymore.

Sarlacc

Trevor and I sat at the counter and ate omelets his mother made, but I can't imagine Trevor tasted the food any more than I did. As I chewed, he surprised me by asking his mom to take me for a drive.

"Dodge is stuck here all the time. Can I borrow the car? I'll take him to the movies so you can get work done."

Laurie brightened. "Oh, that's a great idea! See if you can find something rated G for him."

Trevor and I left his neighborhood in Laurie's white VW Rabbit and drove through West Torrance and past West High School.

"Where are we going?"

Trevor didn't answer me. "I still can't believe you did that." He sounded miserable.

When I was originally five-years-old, 16-year-olds seemed so huge, so grown up to me. Trevor felt big and strong to me now, but I could see him for what he was: a scared teenager. I'd garbage disposaled that cocaine, but I didn't want anything bad for him. I didn't want him beaten to pieces. Maybe he wasn't selling heroin or meth, but I'd seen the destructive power of cocaine firsthand, and I hated the stuff.

I tried to explain it to Trevor. "Once upon a time, I knew a kid who got caught stealing at the corner store. He was nine-years-old, but the owners called the cops to teach him a lesson. When police talked to him, they learned he had sisters at home who hadn't eaten in two days. Two days. They weren't even poor. Their mom was high on coke and didn't buy food, so he stole to feed his little sisters."

Trevor frowned through the windshield. "You're too little to think about things like that."

"Once upon a time," I continued, "I knew this other kid whose dad overdosed in the living room. Jessica Holmes. She ran into her house after school and found her dad dead." I didn't tell Trevor I'd been with her that day, that I was still haunted by the look on her face when she saw him on the couch. I could tell he was dead, with his eyes half open in his gray face. His chin rested on his chest; he hadn't even slumped over. Spoons and lighters and baggies lay on the table, but it didn't seem real to me. It was like I'd entered a room in a wax museum where they'd posed a life-sized replica of Jessica's dad. The thing that tormented me was the awful look on Jessica's face. Ever since that day, I'd associated cocaine with the crushed, utterly defeated expression in Jessica Holmes' eyes when she saw her dead father.

Trevor didn't respond. He drove and drove, so I shut up.

We entered Redondo Beach and cruised down a main road that ran parallel to the ocean. Trevor rested his hand flat on the dash and pointed with his forefinger. "See that seafood place there on the left? That's where their shipments come in from San Diego."

I climbed onto my knees to look out his window.

"Do you know if there's anything at the restaurant right now? Is another shipment coming in soon?"

Trevor sighed. "I don't know. I don't know, okay? This was your idea, dweeb. I'm just an errand boy. I'm nobody."

"But you've been an errand boy for awhile."

"They trust me! Mark's like my brother!"

We drove right on past the restaurant, past other businesses, and I peeked between the buildings to the left, trying to catch a view of the vast, open ocean. I knew the water had to be there somewhere, and I hunted for the tell-tale masts of sailboats. The ocean always made things better.

"Hey, Trevor. How about we go to the beach? I can swim."

We slowed to a stop at a red light, and Trevor rubbed his face with both hands. "Look. You totally ruined my day, dude. I was gonna meet Mark and some girls this afternoon, but you ruined everything, because now I gotta deal with all this mess and I can't even look Mark in the face or he'll know something's up."

Puffs of ocean air breezed through the open windows of Laurie's Rabbit. The high sun still baked us in that cramped little car, and I imagined long stretches of sand and cool splashing waves, boom, just to the west of us! Trevor had lived near the beach his whole life; he didn't appreciate the treasure in his backyard.

We did not veer toward the ocean. Instead, Trevor turned right to take us eastward.

I groaned. "Where are we going?"

"I told Mom I was taking you to the movies. You wanna see Cheech and Chong?" That was his lame effort at a joke.

"You're a jerk. Let's stop and call the cops before we do anything."

"You know you're crazy, right?"

Then Trevor sat upright, as though a single thought jolted him to life. "You know what I should do?"

"Take me to the beach?"

"No! No, I should take you to Paco's house, tell him about what you did, and sell you to him. That will fix it. He can get his money from you, and I'll be okay."

I stared at him. "Cheech and Chong aren't at Paco's." It was my lame effort at a joke, and Trevor ignored me.

"Yeah! People want to buy kids, and you're healthy. Somebody would pay a lot of money for a crazy smart blond boy."

He couldn't be serious.

"I'll tell Mom you ran off. She'll be worried for awhile, but it's not like you're her real kid."

I didn't panic yet. He was just desperate. "Trevor, that won't work like you think. You'll get caught."

That's when Trevor got vicious. "You owe me, Dodge! You owe me thousands of dollars!"

That morning he'd asked if I wanted Cheerios. He'd told me to be careful so I wouldn't fall off the counter and hurt myself, and now he was contemplating selling me? *Selling* me.

"What happens if you trade me to Uncle Paco for your life? Where will I go?"

Trevor shrugged. "They'll sell you to someone who can't have kids and wants a family. It would be better for you anyway. You wouldn't have to be a foster kid anymore."

"Is that what Paco told you?"

Trevor only wanted to buy a car. He didn't recognize the pit of filth and depravity he'd walked up to. He didn't smell the stench of death. Ted was different. Ted knew he danced on the edge of a sarlacc pit, but Trevor didn't get it. The multi-toothed beast waited either way, waited to eat him up - and me along with him - and Trevor tripped along so naive, so foolish.

Billie Eilish popped into my head just then. She sang, "I'm the bad guy" all sarcastic, talking tough, but not the bad guy at all. She pulled the Invisalign from her teenage mouth and jumped around in her yellow hoodie. That was Trevor. He was playing bad guy games, but he wasn't a bad guy.

Not yet. Not yet!

"Trevor." I forced the truth on him. "Trevor, listen. People might buy babies, but nobody wants to buy a five-year-old to start a family. That's not real. They'll sell me to pedophiles."

Disgust spread over Trevor's face. "Dude." He shook his head.

"And it won't be just one pedophile. I'll be sold day after day. Like a prostitute."

"No. That's nuts. You're too little. And you're a boy."

"Has Paco sold other kids?"

"They're getting families!" Trevor shouted. "Because it's expensive to adopt!"

I shook my head.

Trevor couldn't take it. He jerked Laurie's car to the curb in front of some house and shook his head over and over. His brain refused to process and accept this idea. His eyes narrowed at me in disbelief. "How could you know that? You're a little kid. You can't know about that stuff."

I knew about cocaine. I knew about sex trafficking. I didn't talk like a kindergartner. "You have no idea where I came from, Trevor."

We sat in silence for several minutes. Trevor glared at his steering wheel for so so long. Finally, he took a breath and pulled onto the road, and I wondered what he'd decided. Had I witnessed a significant moment in Trevor's life? Was this the day he abandoned all that was good and decent?

I let Trevor drive in silence, but I expected to meet Uncle Paco that day. The palm trees passed above me as I daydreamed through several unrealistic escape plots until Trevor turned into the parking lot of a doughnut shop.

"Get out."

He didn't lead me inside. I followed him around the side of the building, right up to a pay phone. Trevor picked up the receiver and grimaced at me.

"Do I call 911?"

A phone book hung from a metal cord at my eye level. I grabbed it and held it up at him.

"Find the DEA. Maybe Paco pays off local cops."

"What?"

"Call the Drug Enforcement Administration. Look it up."

Trevor thumbed through the phone book blue pages. He kept looking up and around, outright paranoid. Meanwhile, I leaned against the store's concrete wall in relief.

"You know this is useless." Trevor pouted as he ran his finger down a page. "There is so much cocaine in this city right now. Everybody loves it. Even if they stop Paco, tons of other guys are doing the exact same thing."

With a finger on a line in the phone book, Trevor punched five numbers. Then, he cursed and hung up. Clunk. His unused quarter chinkled into the holder, and he fished it out. I nearly protested, but he thumbed the quarter back into the payphone. Chink. This time, he punched four buttons before he cursed and (clunk, chinkle) pulled out his quarter. Wow, he was scared.

Trevor plunked his quarter one last time and muttered numbers as he slowly, purposefully pushed each button. His hand shook, but he held the receiver to his ear and waited.

Poor dude. When he finally got an agent on the line, his voice quavered and he dumped information in rapid, choppy sentences, a disorganized mess of words. The agent told him to calm down and asked him for specifics. Trevor didn't name Mark, but he gave up a bunch of other people. He told the agent Paco's habits, his partners. Their locations and time schedules.

"Tell them about the child trafficking," I hissed.

Trevor waved his hand at me to shut up, but at the end he blurted, "And Roberto Romero buys and sells children."

Trevor slammed the phone back onto the receiver and leaned his hands against the phone booth, like he needed its help to stand up. His morning omelet remained safely inside him, but it took a minute for him to breathe his heart back into his body before he dragged me to the car.

Trevor's hands still visibly shook as he started the engine. "I gotta get out of here."

So, we went to the movies. You know what Trevor picked out for me? Nothing G-rated. We watched good old *Airplane!*, where Lloyd Bridges famously says, "Looks like I picked the wrong week to quit sniffing glue."

That night after dinner, Jeff watched his ballgame on the couch. He ignored me, and it bothered me even more than usual. I wanted to bellow, "You don't pay attention to anything! You don't know that your son has been selling drugs! You don't know he's worried they'll kill him! All you care about is your stupid alone time!" I couldn't say those things, so I compressed my frustrations into one insult.

"Geez Jeff, you're a loser."

Jeff did *not* ignore me for once. He jumped up and followed me toward my bedroom.

"Hey. This is my house. It is not okay for you to call me a 'loser' in my own house."

I didn't want to shine any light on Trevor, but I was furious, so I returned to my original irritation. "It's a good thing what Laurie did. She took in a foster child, and that's a good thing. You need to be part of it."

"I don't want to be part of it!" Jeff shouted into the air and walked away.

I marched into my room and slammed the door, and it didn't even slam loudly. Gahhh!

Trevor spent the next two days in tense misery. I told him, "If Mark comes over, you have to act normal!" I could tell Trevor wasn't good at poker face. Not at all.

"He's expecting the money today. Today, dude. The coke was for a party last night, and I need to pay Paco. If the cops don't do something now, I'm dead. Thank you so much."

"Haven't you saved money for your car? You could give them your car money."

"Shut up!" That's all Trevor said about that.

In the end, Trevor faked the stomach flu like a boss. When Mark called, Laurie told him Trevor was sick. Trevor got on the phone in his bedroom, and his dying-of-dysentery voice convinced even me.

"Dude, I've been puking my guts out." He confessed that he hadn't sold the cocaine for the party. "I couldn't move, dude. I thought I was gonna die. Tell Paco it's no problem, though. It's fly. I got other sales lined up. Nahhh dude. I got like three other buyers waiting."

Liar liar pants on fire.

At least he was stuck at home "dying," so we could finally have fun together. Ha I wish! I tried to get him to play board games or listen to music, but he spent all day looking at maps and planning his escape. "There's all that space in Montana." He chewed on his lip.

"If you like brutal winters."

"I'll chop wood."

"You've never chopped wood in your life."

"Shut up, Dodge. Get out of my room."

Jeff and Laurie and Trevor all ate at the dinner table, and I ate with them, but they didn't talk much. Their family dynamic seemed so cold, so boring. Maybe if his parents weren't dull as mud, Trevor wouldn't have gone tripping along the edge of the sarlacc pit for a little excitement.

No. I brushed that thought away as soon as it entered my head. It didn't matter if Jeff was boring, Trevor knew better. Stupid stupid Trevor. Still, maybe I was trying to make rocks bleed with Jeff. He had no interest in being a dad to Trevor, let alone me. I'd either destroyed Trevor's life or set him free, and I had nothing more to offer him. I finally called Cheryl and asked her to move me, and she said to give her a few days.

I announced it at dinner the next night. "Thank you for a safe place to live. Cheryl says I'm leaving sometime soon."

They all looked up in surprise, but Trevor's shock included a hint of betrayal. His hazel eyes demanded an explanation. I'd gotten him into a mess, and now I planned to take off and abandon him? It touched me that he cared.

"Cheryl called?" Laurie asked.

"I talked to her on the phone. I told her you were nice to me, Laurie. I think you're cool. And Trevor, thanks for when you played games with me."

Jeff felt the jab. "But, I'm not cool."

I shook my head. "You never smacked me, not even when I told you to soak your head. And you're patient."

"Dodge told you to soak your head, Dad?" Trevor smiled for the first time in days. He shook his head at me, "You sure are gutsy, dude."

Jeff chewed on his pot roast, not impressed. "I'm patient. But?"

Irritation spurted up and splashed out of me. "You could be a great dad! You could be! And you could rescue kids who really need to be rescued, and you don't want to do it. You know what? That makes you a twit!"

Jeff pointed at me and turned to Laurie. "Why did you want to do this? How was this a good idea?"

That wounded Laurie, who held up her hands in self-defense. "We are helping children! It's important, Jeff! And besides, Dodge is great with me. He's a big help, and he's a nice kid."

I agreed. "I *am* great with her, Jeff. I do the dishes and sweep the floor for her. You never do that. I talk to her. Do you ever talk to her?"

Jeff straightened in his chair, amazed at my accusations.

I didn't stop. "You never spend time with Trevor! You never hang out with him! He needs a car, and you should fix up an old Charger with him. Your wife is super pretty and cool, and you don't appreciate her at all. Maybe when I'm grown up, I'll steal her from you and take her to Fiji! How would you like that!"

Jeff shoved his chair back. Woah, I didn't think he had it in him! He grabbed me up under my armpits and carried me to my room. "There," he deposited me on the carpet. "No dinner for you. You stay here until you learn manners."

And he closed the door on me.

Angry adult barking erupted. Their quiet dinner had developed into a nice, loud fight, and it was all my fault, and I listened through the door in satisfaction.

The next night, Jeff ordered me to keep quiet at dinner. "Or you're going to your room again."

I ate my food in silence. And the next night too. It felt so hopeless. Jeff wouldn't hurt the children who came through his house, so maybe it was good enough that Laurie could love them. I still climbed onto the couch and watched sports with Jeff every night, but I didn't harass him. I just watched, and he softened a little toward me.

Friday the phone rang, and Laurie called out to Trevor, "It's your friend Mark!"

He picked up the phone in his room, and I thought Trevor might really puke his guts out. I knew he expected death threats, but the color gently flushed into his cheeks while he listened.

Trevor muttered into the phone, "Dude. Dude, what if they come here? What do I do with the stuff you gave me? I was sick all week. What if they knock down my door?" Trevor listened a few moments, then he started cussing into the phone, legitimately upset. "They've probably been watching us for months! Months, Mark! No dude. You're like my brother dude, but I ... I can't leave the house. They're gonna be watching all of us dude! If they drag me in, I'm not saying a thing! Dude. Not a thing. Of course not! You're my best friend! Yeah, and that's what I'll tell them."

Trevor hung up the phone, and I readied for him to strangle me. Instead, he howled into the air. Then he grabbed me and shook me out in front of him.

"Ahhhhh Hahaha!" Trevor laughed in my face before he set me on his bed. "Oh man! They flew down! Redondo Beach's finest totally busted the restaurant and invaded the houses of everybody. Paco had two bricks in his living room, sitting right out in the open! But I was smart! I was smart because I didn't name the little guys, Paco's boys like me. But Mark said to flush those two ounces I had, which is awesome."

Get wrecked, Paco!

"And Mark called to warn me, so they don't think it's me. But, he's scared. Maybe he'll get away from that stuff too."

"Maybe." I breathed in relief. I hadn't wanted Trevor battered and broken as an example to the other errand boys. "Do you really think they were watching them for months?"

"Maybe they were. But, they didn't arrest Mark."

"Still. You should stay away from him. You might give away something, and he'll figure you out, and they'll have you killed as a snitch."

Trevor shoved me off the bed. "Shut up! For real!"

Hopefully that was over. Maybe Trevor would grow up and be okay. Or, maybe not. I couldn't force him to make good choices.

The phone rang at dinner that evening. Laurie settled down and said, "That was Cheryl. They want to come get you on Sunday, Dodge."

"He's leaving? Thank God."

Laurie protested, "Jeff!"

"It's okay, Laurie," I said. "Jeff works hard all day, and he wants to watch television in peace. He's not mean. He just wants to rest."

"Why is that so hard?" Jeff looked around at everybody.

I slumped in my chair. "Jeff, I'm sorry I called you a 'loser.' I know you're a decent guy."

"Thank you."

As I snuggled into my pillow that night, I tried to think of what I could do. I wanted Jeff to understand that he mattered, that I breathed and bled just like he did, that he needed to view children as more than a pain in his eardrums. I wanted him to realize his life could have an impact, that he could be a real hero. The kids who came after me would need a lot of one-on-one care. I didn't knock over lamps and pour bleach on the sofa or vomit in the hallway in the middle of the night. I wasn't born addicted to drugs. I didn't bite or scream or break windows to hear the sound of shattering glass. If Jeff didn't care about those kids, the Faulkners wouldn't last long as foster parents.

Maybe foster siblings would be good for Trevor. He needed exercise for that protective nature inside him. It was malnourished and weak, but I saw it there. I contemplated over Trevor's heart and wondered about Jeff. I suspected Jeff had a protective nature in there somewhere too, and I wished I could wake it up. Wake up, Jeff. Wake up.

My last night at the Faulkner home, I complained of a tummy ache and excused myself from dinner early. Instead of going to my room, I slipped into the living room and climbed up onto the couch. Air conditioning dulled the L.A. summer heat to "warm" instead of "baking hot," and I was grateful for the not-sticky corduroy cushions.

During those three-plus weeks, I'd never undressed in front of the Faulkners. I'd planned to hide my ugly purple scars from everybody forever, but I peeled my T-shirt over my head and curled up smack in Jeff's spot while he ate his dinner. I tucked the shirt under my face like a pillow and tried to go to sleep.

I breathed slowly, deeply, when Trevor walked in. He stood behind me a moment, then turned around and left. I heard him talking in the kitchen but couldn't hear what he said.

Jeff entered a few minutes later, and I felt his presence more than I heard him. He didn't move me or turn on the television. He stood above me for a solid four or five minutes, not speaking, and I almost rolled over to see if he'd left. Five minutes seemed like eternity as I lay still, breathing evenly, waiting. Finally, my foster father tucked his hands under me and lifted me to his chest. He carried me into my room and pulled back my blankets. Cool sheets met me, and covers draped me gently. The door closed.

I expected to hear noises in the living room, but Jeff didn't turn on the TV. The house remained silent.

I didn't know where Jeff went. No voices pushed through the walls, and I guessed he'd left the house altogether. I lay awake for an hour, wondering where Cheryl would take me and what kind of strange people I'd meet. The Faulkners were boring, but they were good people. Who would I face next?

Around my normal bedtime, Jeff surprised me by cracking the door and entering. Then, he did something I didn't expect at all; he knelt beside my bed and put his hand on my head. My hair had grown long enough to require a haircut, and Jeff gently ran his fingers through my locks, firm and warm over my head.

"I'm sorry," he said simply. I sensed that he wanted to say more, but he didn't. He just took a breath and rested his hand on my head.

I rolled over and looked up at him. The light from the hall shone into my room and dimly lit his concerned face. I felt bad.

"Jeff?" I winced at him. "Jeff, is it okay if you give me a hug?"

"Sure. I'll give you a hug, Dodge." He took me by shoulders and pulled me into himself, and he held me for a long time. I wrapped my little arms around him and hugged him back, and it felt good. It felt so good.

"I want you to know, I'm going to do better from now on. I'll try. I'll try to be a dad to them."

"And Trevor. Trevor needs you too."

"I know. I remember."

I wasn't sure exactly what he meant, but I snuggled into him while he rubbed my back.

"I knew it, Jeff," I mumbled. "I knew you were one of the good guys."

19 19

Hopping

I hopped through foster homes for the next 30 months. In some I stayed a few days and others eight weeks. Over those years, I visited 52 foster homes throughout Los Angeles County. I could have written a television show about all those houses. Every few weeks I stepped into a new adventure. Did I live in a sitcom? A mystery? A Stephen King thriller? Each place offered a new answer to that question.

On December 11, 1980, Tom Selleck appeared on *Magnum P.I.* for the first time. Oh, my heart, I adored that man! Maybe my new life really did mirror Thomas Magnum. Good guys, bad guys, tragedy, fun, jokes, fist fights. All of it.

I didn't dare tell people I knew the future. I feared somebody would try to squeeze horse race results from me, which wouldn't work. I knew bits and pieces, this and that, but I didn't know race results. Or who won the Super Bowl or World Cup or even the World Series. They all swam together, blurs through the years. So, I protected myself and kept those foster homes ignorant to my superpowers. I could be safe as a child prodigy; I wouldn't be safe as a prodigy who knew the future.

By the way, I want to make an important point. World, listen. Please listen. Don't be quick to envy the smart kid. First, when the adults called me a "genius," other kids wanted to shove me around. Next, people are insane and expect perfection from a brilliant child, as though geniuses can magically read minds and never misunderstand intentions or rules. I knocked over my water glass more than once. I forgot people's names. I misplaced things. I lost count of the times adults scolded me when they would have laughed over any other child. I didn't usually yell at adults like I'd yelled at Jeff; I kept my mouth shut, but some parents worried I'd get *attitude* and criticized and nit-picked me in a misguided effort to keep me humble. It wasn't fair to expect perfection from me.

I told Cheryl, "*Please* stop telling them I'm a genius! I'm serious! Please!"

Besides, if I were spying on people, I needed to look like a normal boy. Sometimes I let folks know I had brains in my head, but I didn't want Cheryl to take that choice away from me.

I also hated hated *hay-ted* when adults told other children, "Why can't you be more like Dodge?" Those were the worst words ever, and I learned to nip that foolishness in its ugly infancy. After they pulled that line, I refused to listen. I refused to do what I was told. I left toys everywhere. Take that, dumb adults who compared children and made me the common enemy.

And yes, while I had brains packed with information, I struggled to control the herds of killer bunnies that trampled my soul. Wild emotions bounded all around my heart, sometimes joyful, sometimes vicious, full of passion and fury. I hadn't built up years of walls, and no callouses protected my heart. Frustration, anger, delight, gratitude, horror rushed up fresh and strong with no ceiling to hold them back. I bawled over cookies with sprinkles, for crying out loud. Insults that I'd have laughed off as an adult infuriated me as a child, and throwing tantrums came easy.

It wasn't just emotional sensitivities. Physical senses had also heightened in my backward trip through time. I heard whispers down the hall with keen clarity. I hadn't realized I needed glasses in 2020, but details suddenly appeared clear and unmuffled around me in 1980. I read road signs halfway down the block. So fantastic! Smells and tastes weren't so fantastic. Pungent aromas wafted into my face, and I could no longer ignore bad cooking; offensive flavors burned on my taste buds with vomit-inducing potency.

I scorched myself on a toaster one morning and held the injured finger on an ice cube to ease the pain. It kept on and on and on, an unrelenting wailing in my finger. I thought back to the agony of my last night with Ted and wondered how I'd survived it. My tender skin! Young, thin, tender skin.

Oh! And I had to learn to do everything again! I had to learn to whistle, to blow gum and tie my shoes. Ride a bike or skateboard. Use a yo-yo. I mentally knew *how* to do these things, but I had zero muscle memory. None. I can't express the frustration of going to snap my fingers and - nothing - no noise. So many anticlimactic moments.

Anyway. I had all kinds of homes, all kinds of adventures among those 52 families.

Hollywood people, though. Good Lord. I don't know what about Hollywood drew in all the derelicts. I had more trouble in the houses of people in the movie business than anywhere else.

Three houses after the Faulkners, I moved in with a producer for some TV show, and I liked her just fine. But her friends! I could not trust a single one of her friends. And the more attention they showed me, the weirder I felt.

"Hey there. Come here for a minute," one guy beckoned me into the living room. Bobby. His name was Bobby.

I scowled at Bobby and remained solidly in the kitchen doorway.

"Go on, Dodge," my foster mother said. "Don't be rude."

Unhappy, I sludged across the floor.

Bobby smiled too big. "Hi Dodge. Well, look at you!"

I hadn't liked Bobby from the moment he poked his handsome blond head into the house.

"You're a good looking kid, Dodge." He reached out to hold my face with one hand, and I jerked back. "Oh hoh, don't be afraid, little guy. It's cool. You just have a solid face. We should take pictures of you and get you an agent." He turned to my foster mother. "Hey Kate, have you tried to get him an agent? Look at him, he's beautiful, man."

"I'm not beautiful. I don't want an agent."

"I mean, you're handsome. You have gorgeous skin and nice eyes. I mean, really great eyes."

Kate ignored her friend's oozing over a child. "You want a drink, Bobby?"

"You still have that Beefeater gin you had on the 4th?"

"Oh sure, bottles of it."

"Then get me a Tom Collins, would you?"

Kate stepped out, and Bobby returned his attention to me. "You look strong, Dodge. You're a strong kid, huh?"

I didn't even look at him. Four of Andy Warhol's Marilyn Monroe faces smiled from a print on the wall above the sofa. In three of the pictures she had blue eye makeup, and in the fourth she was paler with red eye makeup.

"You are strong. I can tell. Pull off your shirt for a moment. I want to see your muscles."

"No." I tried to leave, but he caught my arm and led me around back in front of him.

"C'mon buddy." Bobby grasped my hands in his cold fingers and wouldn't let go. He laughed and held up my arm to expose my bicep. "I want to see you make some muscles. There's auditions right now for kids. They're making that orphan stage show into a movie. They need kids to be orphans."

"Orphans?" What was he talking about. "You mean like *Annie*?"

"That's it! They're casting kids for *Annie*."

"Yeah. Girls. Who can dance and sing."

"Boys too."

"Let go of me."

He repeated himself. "We'll take pictures of you, get you some headshots and see about getting you an agent."

I stretched my neck around and watched for Kate to return with Bobby's drink.

"I'm trying to help you, Dodge. You could be in movies. Wouldn't you like to star in a big movie and make a lot of money? You could go to Disneyland. Buy any toys you wanted."

That did pluck a string for me. If I were going to bet on Mike Tyson one day, I needed to start making cash. I could act. Honestly, I could be a great child actor.

No. No. I changed my mind. The risks outweighed every possible benefit. Especially with this guy involved.

I leaned up close to Bobby's smooth face, close enough to breathe in his cologne and chest hair. "Listen, you creep. Button your shirt. You can't take my picture. I don't want to be an orphan. Get away from me."

Kate returned, and Bobby released my arm, but he insisted on talking to me every time he stopped by. If his car pulled up, I ran down the hall and hid behind a set of golf clubs in the closet until he left. Kate yelled at me for hiding and making them hunt for me.

"Bobby's a weirdo," I told my foster mother. "You should never leave kids alone with him."

It wasn't just Bobby. Another of Kate's friends kept inviting me to spend the night at his house. He pressured me join him at parties or go hot tubbing, and I had to insist I didn't want any of it. Kate never touched me, but her friends! Good grief, what was wrong with people?

"That's just how people act here," Kate said when I complained. "They like their parties and beautiful people. You should take it as a compliment."

No. I didn't need compliments.

When she picked me up, I told Cheryl, "You cannot place any more children there. I can't tell you how serious I am. Kate is okay, but she's got a bunch of child molesters in and out of her house, and she seems totally blind to it. Or! Or she doesn't care!"

My warnings frustrated Cheryl; she needed more people to foster, and she didn't honestly *want* me knocking any off her list.

I told her. "Look! It's not my fault! Your whole goal it to protect children, but if you put them in dangerous houses where they're gonna get hurt, that defeats the whole purpose. You might as well let them live on the streets."

Cheryl agreed to warn Kate about her responsibility to protect kids from creepy crawlies. "You realize we're struggling to get enough homes, right?" Cheryl frowned at me.

I understood. "Wouldn't it be nice if parents took care of their own children?"

"Yes," Cheryl grunted. "Yes it would be. And it would be nice if you smiled once in awhile. I should hand you over to the Addam's Family."

Wherever I lived, I kept the same morning ritual. I lay with my eyes closed and listened to the sounds of the house before I started my day. There was always the chance I'd wake up in my old bed, that I'd find myself magically back in 2020. Day after day, that hope died as I opened my eyes in some strange bed, some strange house, desperately far from home. Months passed, and the pain of losing my real family wore my soul raw, until a scab developed around my tender, passion-filled heart. I wanted no emotional connections. I had a family 30-odd years in the future, and I wasn't ready to replace them.

The daily heartache mutated into a rage deep inside me, like a coal fire under the ground. I wasn't angry at anybody in particular. Not at the people who took me into their homes. Not at God for getting me into this. It kindled away regardless, a steady fury, and the role of angry foster child naturally grew on me as the months passed away into years.

I did have adventures, though, and adventures distracted me from my existential crisis.

In late October, two homes after Hollywood Kate, Cheryl handed me over to a tall, gray-eyed, gray-haired farmer named Leland whose grown daughter Shannon looked after his ancient mother. That old woman was straight up crazy. And crazy... proved interesting.

Poor, dear Shannon. Exhausted, laboring, worn-out Shannon. My first day there, Leland led me into the farmhouse living room where this old lady with wild hair sat on the couch yelling into the television remote.

"I want to talk to Hazel!"

Hazel wasn't answering through the remote control.

Shannon met us in the kitchen doorway, her dress torn and streaked with white goo. The creamy, herby aroma told me that ranch dressing had made the nice sash across her blue cotton house dress - a regular dairy princess.

"Daddy, she threw dressing at me!" Tears reddened Shannon's pretty eyes. She wasn't young anymore, maybe 40, but Grandma had obliterated that woman's confidence.

"I was making supper, and she called me a harlot and screamed for me to get out of the house. Then! Then, she launched the whole bowl across the kitchen at me."

"Hazel!" Grandma bawled into the remote control. "Hazel, get this hussy out of my house! She's trying to poison me!"

Leland swiped a forefinger through the slop on his daughter's shoulder. He tasted it and nodded. "Mmm. It's good."

"Dad!" Shannon covered her face and slumped onto a piano bench just outside the kitchen door. Leland calmly lowered himself onto the bench beside her and pulled off his boots. She shook silently, and he patted her back.

"I haven't slept in two days, Dad. Two days." Shannon sat up straight. "Supper's in the oven, I'm taking a bath and going to bed."

Leland and I watched Shannon leave her piano bench and trudge up the farmhouse stairs while his mother hollered into the TV remote across the room. Leland turned to me. "It's been getting worse. Would you do something for me?"

"Me?"

"Yes, you. I need to see what's left for making food. Would you please sit with Grandma and let me know if she goes anywhere?"

I shrugged. "Okay."

"Okay." He gave me a serious nod. "I'm warning you, though, she's sneaky."

Leland disappeared into the farmhouse kitchen, and I surveyed the room. This was one of those big, respectable farmhouses, with high ceilings and oak floors and paintings of mountains on the walls. I settled onto a red sofa that matched the one where Grandma perched in her raggedy yellow nightgown. As soon as I sat down, she shoved the remote to her chest, as though she didn't want Hazel to hear.

"And you, young man. Why aren't you in school? Were you out picking blackberries?"

That startled me. "Blackberries?"

"Don't play dumb! You skipped school again!"

"School is out for the day. It's after 3:00."

"Oh." That made sense to her. "Did you fail your math test again?"

She was crazy. I needed to humor this crazy lady.

"No, ma'am. I did well in math. I got an A."

She didn't believe me. "Don't you lie to me," she brandished the remote control. "Don't you lie. You haven't earned an A on a test in your life."

"No. No I did!" I defended myself. "I know my multiplication tables."

She weighed that, but she didn't fully believe me yet. "Then let's see it. Let's see your exam."

I didn't have a test to show her. "I left it at school. I left it in my desk. I'll bring it home tomorrow."

Her eyes narrowed. "We'll see about that!" She pulled the remote to her mouth. "Melanie. Melanie, would you give me Zetty. Stella Zetty in Palmdale. I have a little boy here lying about his schoolwork."

Wow. She'd hung up on Hazel without even saying goodbye.

I had to prove myself quickly. "Seven times three is 21! Seven times four is 28. See? I know them."

Grandma squinted at me in suspicion. "Never mind Melanie." She slowly lowered her phone remote and demanded, "What's 12 times nine?"

"It's 108." Wow, that was a mean one.

Her eyes agreed, still distrustful. I didn't know how to handle it if Grandma had forgotten her times tables.

Leland stood in the doorway, watching. I met his eyes with a "How am I doing?" look. He gave me a nod and went back into the kitchen.

Because of Grandma, I spent two months at Leland's house. Or rather, I stayed because I felt sorry for Shannon. And besides, it was a pretty place out there in the country, surrounded by alfalfa fields and lined with oak trees. I enjoyed my fall break at the farmhouse. All I had to do was follow Grandma around and talk her out of doing inconvenient things.

Nobody said the word "dementia," but Grandma had it. Her brain didn't shut off like a normal person's, and she'd walk around for two days straight and never take a nap. She constantly stole things, and I had to follow and spy out her hiding places. The TV remote. Keys. Wallets. Poor Shannon foolishly left a library book on the table, and we hunted all through Grandma's rooms for that book. And it was big! It wasn't a pair of glasses that could fit into a vase or behind a doll on the shelf. Shannon couldn't find it anywhere, and she ended up having to pay the library to replace that book. Thieving thieving Grandma.

I'd always thought dementia meant memory loss, that it was sad because mothers didn't remember their children anymore. Patients might tell stories about when they were 25, but they didn't recognize their grown sons. That sort of thing. I had no clue, no clue how wild it could get.

Leland saw that I had skills.

"I need you to stay up all night tonight, Dodge," he said one day. "You can sleep during the day, but Shannon hasn't been getting any rest. I don't care what else you do, but you need to watch Grandma. If she gets out of bed and runs off, I need you to wake me up. Can you do that?"

"Yes, sir. I can do that."

"Thank you." I saw real gratitude in his gray eyes.

"Grandma!" I followed her into the yard one night. "Grandma! What are you doing outside?"

The old farmhouse had a wraparound porch, and she knelt on the ground beside the porch with a screwdriver, digging in the dirt. Plastic tulips lay next to her. I remembered them from the table on the landing.

"Grandma, are you planting flowers?"

"What does it look like I'm doing? And why do you keep calling me 'Grandma?'"

"Do you want me to help you?"

"You should be helping your father with hoeing. Why aren't you hoeing?"

"He's gone to bed. When you're done planting flowers, do you want to go to bed?"

"Bed!" She sat in the dirt and pointed the screwdriver at me. "He's off with that Eliza woman, isn't he?"

"No Mother." *That* was the title she wanted. For now. I'd learned to be flexible with her daily whims regarding my identity. "He just went to bed. It's late. See how dark it is? See the moon out?"

She grimaced at me like I was silly. "This flower bed is terrible. All these weeds." The ground gaped at us dry and empty.

"Do you want me to help you weed the garden, Mother?"

She laughed. It was the first time I'd heard that unpleasant woman laugh, and it still sounded harsh.

"I already told you, you can't go camping with that Spalding boy. You're not going to sweeten me up."

She planted the plastic tulips, and they flopped there in the dirt beside the deck, a pitiful little clump. She gave me their vase and told me to collect water for them, so I ran to the pump by the tractor shed. I planned to return the tulips to the table on the landing, but she didn't even wait for the water. When I got back, she had disappeared. I ran up the porch steps into the house to find her banging pots in the kitchen. She sat on the kitchen floor in her dirt-smeared nightgown and pulled pots out of a lower cupboard.

"Can I help you, Mother?" That got the best response. If I tried to stop her from doing anything, she got angry and threatened me and sometimes screamed, so I'd learned to offer my help.

"These pots don't belong here. We have to put these away."

"I'll get a box."

I emptied an orange box in the pantry and brought it back to her. By that time, the cookware had been pulled onto the floor, and Grandma toted two small pots and a frying pan into the living room.

"Mother! Here's a box. Let's put them in the box."

She agreed to that, and we carried the pots outside and past the hay barn into the big wood burner in the machine shed. It took two trips, but we moved all the pots and pans. That's when I suggested we change our clothes. "We've been working. Let's get cleaned up and put on our pajamas."

She let me help her find a new nightgown and changed herself in her bathroom, out of my sight. When she came out, I said, "Please lie down, Mother. Tell me a story."

"Oh, you're too old for bedtime stories." She did climb into her bed then, but she looked me up and down. "You're filthy. Go take a bath."

"It's late."

"Don't you argue, go take a bath!"

I had to leave, but I peeked into her room from the hall. She seemed content to lie flat in her bed. Maybe she'd go to sleep.

I dared run down to collect the pots and pans from the shed. In five trips I stuck them all back in the lower cupboard, still smudged with ash from the wood burner. Next, I dashed out and rescued those plastic tulips. The whole fix-up took me about ten minutes, but when I ran lightly up the stairs to Grandma's room, she'd vanished again.

Alarmed, I looked in her closet and bathroom. I dropped to the ground and checked under her bed and behind her curtains. (I had to be thorough. Seriously.) No Grandma.

I listened; a cat mewed downstairs, and that was it. Back outside, I dashed around the entire farmhouse and then to the hay barn. The moon rose just over the trees and shone across the grounds. Past the barns, the alfalfa in the fields waved all silvery in the midnight breeze. Where had she gone?

Across the yard, the tractor sputtered to life. Oh no! I raced in my bare feet across the powdery dirt to the tractor shed, where Grandma crunched on gears. Not a good time to humor her, I jumped onto the tractor.

"Daddy said we can't do this today!" Moonlight shone in on the wooden planks of the shed wall, enough for me to see. I reached down and snagged the key from the ignition.

"How dare you, you hussy!" Grandma shoved me hard.

I grabbed at air and the tractor flew up away from me. Poof! I landed flat on my back on the dirt floor. It didn't hurt, but dust flew up around me.

"Get out of here! Get out of here, you're trespassing!"

I stared up at her. This was new.

"Get off my property before I call the sheriff!"

"It's okay, Mother." I scrambled up and stuffed the key into my pocket.

"I'm not your mother! I don't know you, some little girl dressed in boy clothes. Go home."

Oh wow. That sent a stab of adrenaline through me.

"Where are your parents, letting you bother people in the middle of the night? I told you to go home! I'm calling Herman right now!"

I changed tactics. "Mrs. Norman, Leland sent me out to get you. He wants you to go inside."

"What?"

"Leland says it's time for everybody to go to bed."

She heard that. "Well my lands. It's bedtime. I shouldn't be using a tractor now. It's late."

"Yes, it is."

"Okay. Good night then. You can go home now."

After the tractor incident, Grandma slept all day and all night. She'd finally worn herself out, but not for long. She was back at it two days later, stealing things and demanding I do my homework. They honestly needed to hire full time care for Grandma, and that's what I finally told Leland.

"She started up the tractor," I warned him. "What if she really hurts herself? What if she hurts me?"

He nodded. He'd been struggling in himself about what to do.

"Maybe you can pay a local woman to come stay the night? This... this isn't a job for a kid."

Leland nodded again. "I know. I know it." Then he smiled. "You did good, Dodge. Thanks."

It had been a rare evening that December 11th when Magnum P.I. first showed himself to the world. Grandma wanted to knit slippers, and she stuck to it for three whole hours, so Shannon and I sat down and admired our handsome Tom Selleck as a private investigator.

Before I left, I enjoyed a pleasant Christmas with them. Shannon bought me a Dodgers hoodie and Leland gave me a pocketknife. After the New Year, Cheryl came and got me.

It was time to go, but I treasured those months with Leland and Shannon and crazy Grandma.

20

Hungry

It became clear that the child who could read Edgar Allen Poe was overqualified for kindergarten. I went to school for a month, long enough to get the chicken pox, until I finally said, "Cheryl, this is stupid. Let me get my GED! I don't see the point in registering in one school after another every three weeks. I don't need to go to school!"

I took my high school equivalency test just before I lived with Hollywood Kate. My converted score gave me a 3.85 GPA, which was perfectly good enough. I thought about child doctor Doogie Howser and realized that I might be able to attend college in a few years. Not yet, though. I had spy business right now.

I still needed a place to go each day, so every set of parents had to work that out. The first week of January, right after I left Leland and Shannon, Cheryl stuck me with some ancient lady in San Marino. I don't even remember her name. She lived in a nice house, but it smelled stale, like week-old boiled oatmeal, all crunchy and dried out. Stale. The bigger deal was that she hardly fed us. The two other kids ate school breakfast and lunch. Me? That old lady dropped me off at the library every day without even an apple, and at night she only fed us ramen or mashed potatoes. She didn't want to feed us! The other kids grumbled from hunger, but I began to panic in real desperation.

I sneaked into the kitchen one night to pilfer food but only found flour and rice in the cupboard. Seriously, I stole a pound bag of rice and sucked on dry grains at the library.

The second day, I couldn't focus in my anxiety for food, so I slunk up and down the rows of library bookshelves. When a young man sat at a table, I sidled up beside him.

"Hello." I didn't even try to look cheerful.

He frowned at me, startled to see a child at his elbow.

"Can I earn a quarter from you?" I asked.

"You should go find your mom."

I trudged away. Young men were no good.

I had more hope when an older man wandered in. I followed him through rows of tall shelves and watched as he perused titles.

"Are you looking for a certain author?" I finally asked him. "Or are you studying a certain subject?"

His thick eyebrows furrowed down at me. "A certain subject. What about you?"

"A certain author. But then I got hungry for a hot dog. Is there anything I could do for you to earn a quarter? I figure if I can make fifty cents, I can buy a hot dog."

He chuckled and dug into his pocket. "Hold out your hand." Two quarters dropped into my palm. "Go buy a hot dog."

I grinned. "Thank you."

I quietly slipped out the door and around the neighborhood in search of a convenience store. Nope. Nothing. School buildings and palm trees. In disappointment, I returned to the library and pulled out my half bag of rice from behind thick books on China. Let me tell you, dry rice is miserable. My mouth grew raw from sucking on it.

The next day, I earned myself another 75 cents and trotted down the block to the grade school. When the kids ran out for recess, I dashed around and played tag with them. As they trotted back in, I washed with the crowd straight into a classroom, then slipped out the far door before the chaos calmed.

A quick walk down a breezy hall brought me to the bathrooms, where I hid until lines of children streamed from their classrooms two hours later. I casually tagged onto the tail end of a class line down to the lunchroom. The cashier accepted my $1.00, handed me back two dimes, and I filled my tray. When I sat down, two children at my table asked questions, but I couldn't answer with my mouth full of hamburger casserole. The others poked suspiciously at the meat and contented themselves with eating canned peaches and bread. Without shame, I asked for leftovers, and several trays passed in front of me before the students crowded out for lunch recess. Two stray milks got stuffed into my hoodie pocket, and I rushed out with the others, tummy crammed full. I hid in the jungle gym until every teacher and child disappeared before returning to the neighborhood library.

By the time I left that old lady's house, I felt so sorry, so sorry, for little children starving in Ethiopia.

After that, I determined to keep some sort of money on me at all times. The parents at my next house were nice, so I dared earn a $5 bill on the Iran hostage situation. It was January of 1981, and Reagan was going to be inaugurated January 20th. I told the foster father, "I'll bet you five bucks all those hostages in Iran get freed as soon as Reagan becomes president."

He said, "You don't have five bucks."

"If I'm wrong, I'll wash the floors in both bathrooms. But! If they get freed before he's president one week, then you owe me a fiver."

He laughed at me and said, "Okay. You're on."

The hostages were freed shortly after the inauguration - within minutes - so I pocketed five dollars. But, I didn't dare get too serious as Carnac the Magnificent with my divine and mystical powers.

Quoting movies didn't cause me any trouble because nobody knew what I meant, but I had to watch out when crooning pop songs. I liked to sing Journey's "Don't Stop Believing" when I did jigsaw puzzles. I didn't think much of it; it was just my jigsaw puzzle song.

"…Just a city boy, born and raised in south Detroit. He took the midnight train going anywhere…"

On June 3rd, 1981, during my foster sister's birthday party, my jigsaw puzzle song came on the radio for the first time. I sang along as I ate my cake, contentedly enjoying the music. I glanced around the table and saw the scrunched eyes and wrinkled foreheads of my foster family. Every single face gaped at me.

"It's a good song," I said.

"The radio guy said it's a new release today," my foster brother said. "Why have you been singing it all week?"

My fork stopped halfway to my mouth. "You've never heard it?"

"Yeah! From you!"

I didn't know what to say. "We used to play it in my living room?"

This convinced the family that I'd *lived* with one of the Journey band members, which pumped instant jealousy into the hearts of my foster siblings. They asked all kinds of questions about the house, and I had to invent an entire Journey-band-member world for them. Lies, all lies! I decided to be more careful with my song singing after that.

Most of the houses I visited were okay. Some parents did great, but others... neglect was my most common problem. People had this crazy, paint-munching idea that they could make money by taking in foster kids and then ignore the real-life humans who entered their homes. They wanted parakeets kept in cages. Or fish. Fish in tanks. Just throw crumbs at us once a day.

Ashlynn had physically abused me, but I could have died because of neglect. Died. Dead. Eesh.

I spent hours stuck in bedrooms with other kids. A few times parents gave us an Atari to play on, and we got to practice Pac-Man or Frogger. If the other children were small like me, we played make believe or wrestled or read stories. I taught a bunch of little kids to read, and I felt good about that.

If there were bigger kids, I led them in pushups and crunches. Stretches. "Flexibility is strength." Work our limber muscles. "If we get flexible, we can be ninjas!" Children all over the bedroom falling down, bending their knees as they touched their toes, tumbling into each other, fighting and yelling.

I wanted to get good at handstands. Practice those things. Hands down and kick our legs into the air – thump thump thump de dump – pairs of feet against the wall. Back down. Legs in the air, tha-dump against the wall.

"Hey!" A voice barked from the other room. "Stop banging!"

Tha-dump. Quieter. Don't touch the wall. Legs in the air three, four seconds. Down again. Legs back in the air, THUMP.

"KIDS! Stop banging the WALL!"

In late June, an especially loud bump brought the household adult to my door. He was a young guy, maybe 25. Skinny and shirtless. No tattoos, but his stomach bore a long horizontal scar, probably from an appendix removal. Peach fuzz on his face. I don't remember his name. He opened our bedroom door, and four children went silent. Without a word, he grabbed me up over his shoulder and walked me through the house to the back door. He set me down outside, and ziiiiishhh, the glass door slid shut. Swoosh swoosh, brown curtains swept in front of my face and rippled to a stop.

I turned and surveyed the dismal back yard. That patch of ground had retired as hard, pale dirt. Dirt. Not soil! Solid, concrete-like dirt adulterated only by the scattered carcasses of courageous once-weeds. Heat baked up from the hard pack. I didn't even have a soccer ball to kick around this barren patch of desert, and the glare boiled into my brain. Thirty seconds later, I stepped on a goathead and leaned against the block wall to pull the spiky seedpod from my bare feet.

My head already ached. No shade as the sun cooked down on my skull, not even a deck to scooch under. Could I climb out and escape? Cinder blocks had been stacked plumb and smooth around the whole yard. I picked my way around to where the blocks met the house, but I couldn't jump high enough to grab the top of the wall and toe up the corner.

The latch loomed high above me. The gate's metal frame barely cleared the ground; I couldn't squeeze under.

A merciless sun cooked my shoulders, pale and unprotected. It wouldn't take long to roast blisters all over my baby skin. I needed back inside!

I ran to the glass door and pounded on it. "Let me in! Let me in! I won't bang on the wall anymore!"

The glass door swooshed open. "You better shut up!" Whatsisface presented an alarming rage face, no humor, eyebrows ganging down toward his nose.

The door slid shut again.

I was going to die. I'd die in the hot sun like a neighbor's pit bull I'd once known. He'd chewed through his water pool and all the water drained out. They found him cooked to death on his chain. That's what would happen to me. My core temperature would rise and rise until I baked dry.

I already felt the thirst, the desire for water pulling at me. I hadn't had a drink for hours, and my body suddenly panicked and cried for liquid. Dust in my mouth. My dehydrated lips would crack, and I'd collapse. Whatsisface would find me with ants working holes through the desiccated skin on my ribs.

I banged the door again, slammed my fist on the cool glass. I had to have water! He couldn't abandon me without water! The door slid open again and cool air gushed into my face. He roared down, "I swear to God, Dodge! If you don't shut up, I'm gonna kill you."

The door swept shut again and the baking heat from the ground instantly overwhelmed me.

"Unalive," I corrected him. There were no social media, no word rules to get him sent to Facebook jail. It was my inside joke with me.

The situation wasn't a joke, though. He'd dropped me into an oven prison, and I scanned the yard and the yellow stucco of the house in hopelessness. It was over.

A spigot appeared then, out of the house, just three feet from the door. Had it been there all along? It was old and coated with dust, sprayed the same pale yellow as the house. I grabbed the hot metal and turned it clockwise. It took all my five-year-old strength, but I got that spigot handle to turn a little. And then a little more. The metal petals hurt my hands, but a dribble of water spattered onto the pale dirt, and then a trickle, and then a legitimate and proper stream.

I dropped to the ground under that flow of lukewarm delight and let it pour over my head and down the bare skin of my back. I gulped the water until I choked and coughed a fit, then recovered and gulped more. I lay on my back in the growing puddle; water sloshed up against my neck and onto my ears. I splashed my arms up and down, splush splush, a water-dust angel. Glorious water.

Mud. I needed mud to protect my skin from the burning sun. I scraped my fingers across wet dust, but the hardpack soaked up water about as well as peanut shells. I picked my way around the pokey backyard. Ooh, a chunk of concrete! I snatched up the angular hunk and carved and carved at the ground while water gushed down my back and into my shorts. Once I'd removed the upper crust, the underlying dust scraped up more easily, and I dug until the concrete chunk chafed the skin on my palms.

That mud saved me. I slopped handfuls on my shoulders and chest, my legs and arms. I streaked it across my face and piled it on the back my neck. I spent a good thirty minutes digging under the flow, occasionally packing on more cool mud before I turned off the water and lounged in my puddle. So much better.

"You can't find me, Predator. Your heat seeking powers won't sense through my insulating camouflage."

I lay back and closed my eyes under the smoldering yellow sky.

I awoke later. An hour? Three hours? The sun had dropped behind the neighbor's palm trees. Hard mud caked across my chest and arms. It weighed on my face and hair. I rocked back and forth and rolled out of the shallow trough, then laughed at my heavy, cracking armor.

"I'm the Thing!" I shouted at the red sky. "Look at me!"

Loose mud pattered away from my body. "Rawrrr!" I grabbed an imaginary car and flung it across the yard. In my mind, it smashed through the block wall like the Kool-Aid man.

Zzzzzsh, the glass door slid open and Whatsisface stared at me for a few beats, as though he didn't understand what I'd done. Then, the rageface returned, and harsh words blasted me. A lot of them. "You are not coming in here like that! You can stay outside all night for all I care, you idiot!"

The door banged shut so hard it bounced back. When it slid shut again, the lock thunked into place.

I was an idiot? Me? He'd left me outside all day to die.

I twisted on the water and once again sat under its loving stream. This time I took a shower. I washed the mud out of my hair and rinsed the layers off my arms and neck and legs and chest. I rubbed water over my face until the rough earth disappeared and only my smooth skin remained. I turned off the water and banged on the door as the evening heat evaporated away my dampness. Whatsisface didn't return. I banged on the glass, but he hid away inside.

My stomach wailed at me. The day had been hot, but the night might freeze my shirtless, shoeless body. I walked around in circles then banged on the door, over and over again. Nothing. No response. That was it. I had to get somebody to pay attention to me.

"AHHHHH!" I cried out. "Don't make me stay out all night! I'm hungry! You didn't even feed me!" I howled on and on and on. Was he wearing headphones? Had the other children gone to bed?

About fifteen minutes into my shriek-fest, the cops arrived. They didn't use sirens, but I heard a single "Whoop!" out front. My throat had gone sore, but I put extra effort into my vocal grief until I heard a voice at the gate.

"Hey! Come here!"

The latch popped up, and a hefty woman officer stood in the gateway. Shudders shook my chest. I'd worked myself up, and snot filled my sinuses. My eyes burned with swelling, and I sobbed, "I... I... don't ... want... to ... sleep ...outside."

The officer beckoned with one hand. "Come on. You're not going to sleep outside."

She picked me up into her meaty arms, dirt-stained damp shorts and all, and carried me around to the front of the house, where an even fatter officer talked to Whatsisface.

"He was muddy," my stupid foster father said. "I didn't want him inside while he was muddy."

"You locked me outside all day! All day!" I took more shuddering breaths.

The young man dismissed me. "It wasn't all day."

"You didn't give me any water! I would have died!"

"You had the water hose. You were fine!"

Not a hose, loser. No hose.

The lady officer set me down. "All right. All right all right. Look. You can't leave your kid in the back yard in the sun. You can't do that."

"It's evening. It's not that bad outside."

"The neighbor said you stuck him outside hours ago. Use your head, it's too hot."

The other officer spoke up. "Take him inside and feed him. Give him a bath, put him to bed."

I couldn't believe them. That was it? They were going to abandon me?

"He hates me!" I told the lady officer. I wanted her to hear me, to believe me. "He hates me. Please don't leave me with him."

She set me on the front step. "Listen, kiddo. You have to stay here, okay? Eat your dinner and take a bath and go to bed."

"What if he beats me up and locks me in a closet?"

"He won't do that. Just be a good boy. Okay?" She turned to Whatsisface. "You remember what it's like to be a little guy? Think about that. And don't leave him screaming outside anymore."

They left me. They got into their car and drove away, and I had to walk with Whatsisface back into the house. He didn't hit me, but he acted like I was a cockroach.

The aroma of grease and onions lingered in the air. "You fed the other kids? You had hamburgers?"

"The others were good. They didn't scream and get the cops called."

He slapped together a peanut butter sandwich and tossed it on the table. It wasn't peanut butter and jelly or even peanut butter and butter. Just peanut butter. Sticky peanut butter between two slices of white bread.

"Can I have some milk?"

A cup of milk clunked in front of me, and a dollop splashed out onto the table.

"Thank you."

But yeah. Neglect. I hated it.

21

Family

When I left Whatsisface, Cheryl picked me up, irritated like usual. "Look, it's going to take me time to find you a new placement. I have this guy who says he'll keep you for two days."

I thought back to Trevor, and suspicion sneaked through my chest. "You're not selling me, are you?"

Cheryl rolled her eyes. "I haven't sold you yet, have I?"

"If you *are* selling me, can you at least feed me first? I haven't eaten anything but peanut butter sandwiches all week."

We reached the social services office, and Cheryl made me sit in a little waiting area while I continued to starve. I flipped through a magazine, unable to think past the angry groaning from my gut. My whole body wanted food. All my cells bawled for nourishment, and I slumped in my seat, weak from another bout of malnutrition. How did anyone survive for years like that? Maybe they didn't move. Maybe hungry gnomes in the jungle conserved their energy by hiding in the shade of lilac bushes. They sat, silent, unmoving, blocked from the view of jaguars by enormous flowers that sheltered them like floral wall tents.

I wandered over to Cheryl's desk.

"Please, I'm starving."

"He said he'll be here at 1:00."

Cheryl sorted through papers, clearly grouchy. She would have to educate Whatsisface on practical childcare or knock him off the list altogether, and Cheryl hated firing foster parents.

The clock struck one. The mouse ran down. Hickory dickory dock. No guy appeared. Two days? Only two days? Did this guy want to impress some girl? Had he lied to his parents about having a child, and now they were visiting from Missouri? Two days. It made more sense some sicko wanted to rent a kid. Cheryl had always played me straight, but maybe she needed a trip to Aruba. Maybe temptation had worn her down. He might feed me, though, and then I'd have the strength to run away.

I opened a *Highlights* magazine and tried to focus while I waited. I'd found seven differences between two pictures when a voice spoke above me. "I hear you want lunch."

I knew that voice. Superman? In a sparkling split second, a reel of faces flashed through my mind. Christopher Reeves? No. My Uncle George? I looked up, and it took me three full seconds to understand who he was.

"Mike!"

I spontaneously flung my arms around his middle, and my own emotion surprised me. All the hurt and loss and anger and frustration of the past 16 months exploded through my chest at once. I buried my face in his stomach and held on.

Mike laughed a tender laugh. "Dodge. Dodge, hey guy. Hey. Hey." He picked me up, and I wrapped my arms around him and shoved my face into his warm neck.

"Dodge, it's okay. Shh shh shh. It's okay."

I couldn't say anything. I didn't realize how much I'd missed him, how much I'd shut myself off from everybody. He cracked the shell around my heart, and pain splashed out. Mike stood there a calm, quiet minute and let me hug him without letting go. When I finally relaxed, he held me out and looked me up and down.

"So. You want pizza?"

We enjoyed two amazing days, and I stared at him the whole time. He'd retired the heavy blue Oldsmobile and drove a sporty two-door Toyota Celica, all zoom zoom. We drove around L.A. together, and I tried to absorb him, to take in his face, his blue eyes, his dark hair, his five o'clock shadow. I wanted to melt him forever into my brain, the plaid of his short-sleeved button up, the gold chain around his neck like some 70s goofball. I didn't want to miss a minute of him.

"You... wanna go to Magic Mountain?"

Of course I did.

At first I didn't share anything. I didn't even want to talk, not at first. But, his presence widened the crack in my shell and soon my adventures came gushing out like water through a dusty spigot.

"There was this one lady who didn't believe in silverware. She was scared we'd stab holes in her table, so we only ate food we could eat with our hands."

"Like burritos?"

"Asian foods. Egg rolls and pot stickers and Indian curry dishes that I guess you're supposed to eat with your fingers. She made these open-faced Danish sandwiches that usually involved salmon, which I liked more than the other kids."

Mike and I spent an hour riding Magic Mountain's older steel roller coaster, away from the newest attractions. The lines were shorter for that up and down roller coaster, and we only had eight-minute waits to catch another ride. I was inches shy of the minimum height, but that particular operator didn't even measure me.

For lunch, we sat on a bench and took fat bites of sausage dogs. Filling my face with juicy food. I loved it.

"So, give me a good memory. Something you loved."

I chewed hard and thought about it until I swallowed and wiped my mouth on my arm. "I had this one foster dad, an astronomer at UCLA. He took me down to Palomar and let me gaze out at space through this huge research telescope. That was pretty cool. I had a lot of fun with him."

Puzzlement wrinkled Mike's forehead. "That sounds perfect for you. Why didn't you stay there?"

"Oh." He didn't know. "No. I ... I don't stay anywhere. I go into houses and do research. I decide whether they're good or bad for kids and then I move on to the next one. I'm the quality control of the Los Angeles foster care system."

"Quality control?"

"Yeah. The astronomer took on three kids after I left, brothers and a sister. They'd have gotten separated if he didn't take them all. Cheryl gave me a letter from one of them last week, and they're happy."

Mike frowned. "You mean, you don't get to have a home?"

Resentment spurted out of me. "I don't want a home!"

I hadn't recognized how deep it went until Mike asked that simple question, but the wound was like termites tunneling down down and shoving out their dirt, packing and packing until there was no more room.

He gazed at me, studying me.

"I lost my whole family. I lost everybody, Mike, and I don't want - I don't want the hassle."

Mike's eyebrows raised in his Superman face. "You don't want the hassle of a home? A forever home?"

I glared at him.

"You mean you don't want to lose another family."

I kept glaring.

He reached out and brushed some crumbs off my chest. Gentle. Much more gentle than that long ago night I'd climbed into his car. "What happened to your family, Dodge?"

I watched my dirty tennis shoes dangle over the concrete below our bench. "They weren't murdered in front of me or anything." They weren't even dead.

He guessed, "Car accident? Fire?"

I shook my head. I was getting them back again one day, and that was all I cared about. "I don't want anybody else."

I hadn't left behind a lousy marriage. I didn't owe $50,000 to gangsters or the IRS, and I hadn't developed some incurable disease. Leaving the future didn't save me from anything. I'd spent years and years working to build a life with a husband I loved. We'd started with nothing, with *nothing*, and we'd built something good, and I got flung back in time without him? That wasn't fair. It wasn't bloody fair at all!

My chest heaved with heavy breaths, and I couldn't explain any of it to Mike.

He stuffed the rest of his dog into his mouth and chewed. He sucked on his pop and asked, "What about your mom, though? Is that what your mom would want? For you to be homeless for the rest of your life?"

My lip stuck out on its own. Despite one year and four months of callouses to guard it, Mike stuck a stirring stick into the softness of my inner heart, raging termite nest and all.

"She'd want you to have a family to love you, wouldn't she?"

I wanted to stop him. Stop it, Mike. I'd finally gotten over the habit of reaching over to an empty spot in the bed every morning.

"I'm not ready."

I said it solidly, with no room for more debate, and he let it go. Mike stood and smoothed down his shirt. "All right then. You ever had a funnel cake?"

That was something I could smile about. "Can we? Can we get funnel cake?"

We spent two precious days together. Mike and I. Me and Mike. He bought me new tennis shoes, because the seams were splitting in my dirty white ones. Of course, he had to leave me again, but this time didn't seem so permanent. I thought of him every morning when I tied my new shoes, and this time I had hope he'd show up again one day. He'd cracked my shell, and it didn't close up right away.

It's an interesting coincidence that my next placement was a 65-year-old music composer named Dr. Wilkins. Dr. Wilkins lived in a pleasant apartment near the Burbank Studios. He wore shirts with collars and respectable vests. A trim beard garnished his face. Books and stringed instruments filled the shelves in his living room, and a white baby grand piano and cello took up most of the room to the left of his door. Dr. Wilkins fit in the category of true genius; not a fraud like me. He'd graduated from Juilliard, and when he sat down, his hands moved over the piano keys with ease and freedom, like they had their own minds, their own lives to live.

After lunch our first day together, he said, "Kick off your shoes and get comfortable. Go ahead and relax while I finish a bit of work. Do you want to draw? What do you like to do?"

I perused his collection of leatherback books. "Can I read one?"

He smiled. "Only if you like Shakespeare. Don't worry, we can go out and buy some early readers for you."

I shook my head. "These are so beautiful."

"I agree. Thank you. But listen, they're not for flattening flowers or dead moths."

He said it so funny, so warmly, I laughed out loud. Here was a good natured, brilliant man. Maybe it was safe to let him see my brains.

"I'll be careful, I promise. Last week I started *Much Ado About Nothing* at a library and didn't get to finish."

He squinted at me, a puzzled frowny face.

"How old are you, Dodge?"

"I turn six in two weeks."

"And you like Shakespearean comedies?"

"I really do. I mean, sometimes. Sometimes my brain gets tired."

He shrugged. "Okay. Whatever you want. As long as you don't mind me plunking over here at the piano."

That's all he said. No big deal at all. So, I snuggled up in an over-stuffed chair with his expensive book and relaxed while he created music. The most comfortable thing in the world.

Maybe it was because Mike had visited and got me feeling again, but Dr. Wilkins magically pierced my defenses. He wiggled past my scabbed-over heart and got through to my soul.

The next day, he gave me a piano lesson with a rare and gifted wisdom. I'd labored over the piano in my previous life as a weekly exercise in torture, but Dr. Wilkins made each moment like a game. I had no muscle memory, but I already understood sheet music, and he delighted in how quickly I picked up his lessons with my small fingers.

"I'm going to write you up some Scott Joplin." He did! He created an easy version of "The Entertainer" for me to practice, and after a few weeks I felt amazing and skilled playing it.

We walked around his neighborhood in the mornings. He told jokes and I told jokes, and we both laughed. He had no car, but we took a bus to the park, and he urged me to practice my handstands and climb trees. In the afternoons, he returned to his work at the piano, and I returned to his bookshelf.

"Dodge," Dr. Wilkins murmured one day. "Maybe you should try *As You Like it.*"

I scanned the titles. "I've never heard of it. Is it funny?"

"Oh, it's certainly entertaining. And you'll recognize the story, my dear child, even if you don't know the title. Are you familiar with the phrase, 'All the world's a stage, and all the men and women merely players?' It comes from that play."

"What's the play about?"

"It's about a young lady who passes herself off as a boy."

I turned to him at his piano and watched his face, unwilling to respond. I didn't know how serious he was. He gazed back calmly.

I found the book and pulled it down. "Well, that's a funny plot."

"Dodge." Dr. Wilkins had a little chuckle in his voice.

I climbed onto my favorite overstuffed chair. "Yes, sir?"

"How many people have you really fooled?"

I smiled despite myself. After all those months back in time, Dr. Wilkins was the first person to say something - besides Leland's crazy mother. Even Mike believed I was a boy.

"Everybody. I've fooled everybody. Please don't tell on me."

"I won't. But *everybody* must not be paying a smidge of attention to you. There is nothing masculine about you, dear young lady. You are strong and smart and brave, certainly. But you'll grow up to be a strong, smart, brave woman, and the world needs you just like that!"

I adored Dr. Wilkins. We'd found bosom buddies in each other, like daisies in a world of sod clumps, and he stayed in my heart. I knew Mike was right. I'd been in danger of hardening down, layer after layer until I'd solidified into a jawbreaker straight through to my center. So, I let Doc in, and that connection saved my heart. His friendship kept warmth and tenderness and love alive in me, and I've always regarded him as a gift of mercy.

"I can't stay," I warned the good composer a week later. "But I'll come visit you when I can." I'd found him; I wasn't about to lose him.

"I'm holding you to that, my dear. Keep the sheet music. I'll give you something else to play when next we meet."

When next we meet.

I wrote certain foster parents now and then, but I *called* Dr. Wilkins. Every week or so I called him. Any time I landed in a home remotely close to Doc's apartment out by Burbank, I'd sneak off and take a bus to visit him. I had a job to do, but he gave me an anchor point, a grounding, a place of stability in my disjointed world.

He did bug me about my spy cover on occasion. "Why are you pretending to be a boy?" he demanded during one of my visits. "You're so much better at being a girl. Just. Just confess and be a girl."

I wore a fat lip from a fist fight, and Doc frowned while he handed me a glass of lemonade.

"I'll be a woman for the rest of my life," I explained. "I'm not trying to be political or anything. It's just that...right now I feel safer looking like a boy, so I'm playing this game. Please don't tell on me."

He grimaced and pointed at a bruise on my cheek. "I think you'd be safer looking like a girl, my dear. Please please keep yourself out of trouble."

Dr. Wilkins offered an island of safety for my wounded, calloused heart. One man. One person with whom I could drop all my facades and just be me.

22

Chemistry

I spent my sixth birthday with Dr. Wilkins, but then I had to move on. And (sigh) the next lady locked me in my room and left the house. This had happened before, but she didn't even give me access to a toilet, and I realized I had to escape before my bladder filled. It took a bit of climbing, but I opened the window and scooched out enough to hang and drop to the gravel. I walked along the street until I found other young friends and played all day. So much better than being locked in a room.

I returned home around 3:00 p.m. - before the foster mother got back from work - and realized I'd made a mistake. I had no way to climb back into my bedroom. The eight feet of flat wall to the window loomed high above me, so I circled the house and hunted for a way in. Locked front door. Locked back door. Unmovable garage door. I found no lawn chairs, no conveniently placed ladders. I finally settled on the front steps and awaited my foster mother's return.

I hated that feeling, the growing anxiety of anticipation, expecting some scary lady to arrive home and flip out on me. Would this woman be like Ashlynn? She'd locked me in my room and left for the day! Who knew what she'd do if she found me outside the house.

A realization struck me. Good grief! I didn't have to stay there! With a new sense of liberty, I started walking, and I walked the next four hours until I reached Dr. Wilkins' apartment.

"Dodge!" The old musician frowned when he met me at the door. "It's 8:00 at night!"

"Yes, sir, it sure is."

"Won't somebody be missing you?"

"I don't care. I'm not going back there."

Dr. Wilkins let me in and fed me dinner and heard my little story. He made sure I brushed my teeth and tucked me into my old bed in his spare room. My legs ached from walking, but that didn't stop me from zonking right out. I knew Doc would be perfectly responsible and call the authorities and sort things out, so I let him.

Thank God for Dr. Wilkins, my dear composer friend.

But see! That's why I had to home jump. Some other kid would have messed his pants locked in a room all day. That's exactly why I'd gone undercover in the first place, to protect children from people with poor judgment.

Bad houses were easy. I could generally tell when something wasn't right within the first few days. It was easy to see if the kids were dirty or hungry or nervous. It was easy to get the truth out of them. It was easy to see that the parents got drunk every other night, or that the dogs pooped inside and nobody cleaned it up. I only stayed a few days in really bad houses.

It was the sorta-kinda houses that bothered me the most, the houses that weren't bad, but weren't good either. As much as I could, I tried to give the parents pointers, to help them out.

Two months with Leland and Shannon had given me a chance to see who they really were, but I couldn't spend two months every place. Early in my home-hopping, I realized that I had to find out how folks would react to a little rottenness. Even hideous people can be decent sometimes, and I needed a way to yank the ribbon off each house and look straight into the box. Doctors make folks run on treadmills to stress-test their hearts. I wanted to stress-test homes.

It started when one sister drew all over the cupboards and walls with permanent marker. All over. Black scribbles. So awful and ugly. My sweet foster mother wept in misery as she scrubbed stubborn marks that refused to come off. Hand sanitizer is pretty good for black marker, but I never saw one bottle of Purell in 1981. That was okay, because I knew how to find the best agent of all: methanol. Methanol wipes away permanent marker like magic!

I told the poor lady, "Don't worry, Mom. Don't worry! Wait here!"

I dashed to the garage for a bottle of gas tank additive, the kind that gets water out of the lines? That stuff is mostly methanol. I didn't find any in our garage, so I ran my short legs to the neighbor, and ten minutes later I raced home with a yellow bottle.

The young mother watched in wonder as I rubbed her cupboard doors and fridge clean. I hoped she'd stop crying, but instead she grabbed me in a hug and wept even more.

The neighbor didn't want the open fuel additive back, and I walked along with a bottle of methanol in my hands. That's when a wicked cool idea sparkled into my head, an idea for impressing other kids and freaking out the parents.

Alcohol burns. Methanol is the simplest alcohol, and I could make it burn any color I wanted by adding stuff to it. The chemist in me grew excited about demonstrating chemical properties! I hoped I wouldn't create a generation of pyromaniacs, but I almost didn't care.

To be honest, I'd gotten bitter at the boredom of my life. It wasn't good parenting to leave me in my room so much! It wasn't right! I knew I shouldn't teach kids to play with fire, but I didn't care anymore in my excitement over possible chemistry fun.

First, I got an empty tuna can and poured a little methanol into it and lit it with a match. It glowed blue in the dark garage - eerie in a pleasing way. But the tuna can was too big; the methanol spread out, and I needed tall flames. I rummaged around the house and found tea candles. Tea lights! I removed the candle from one of the small metal cups and poured methanol into it. A lovely blue flame burned in the cup. Haha! Now, I needed stuff to add to the methanol.

Strontium burns a bright red, but I wasn't going to find any in the garage, and I couldn't go on Amazon and order strontium chloride online. Lithium also burns a bright red, but I couldn't find lithium batteries anywhere (and opening batteries scared me anyway). I did find a road flare. I shaved some flakes into the methanol and lit it up. The red glowed nice and bright!

Next, I needed the color orange. Calcium. A teaspoon of garden lime went into a second little tin of methanol, and it burned orange. Sodium for yellow? Dissolved table salt.

Borax from the laundry room gave me light green. I got super stoked when I found some roach killer that was almost pure boric acid and offered gorgeous envy green. Methanol itself burned blue, but it really wasn't super visible until I turned off the lights. I found garden sulfur in the same garage as the lime. Sulfur is yellow, but it burns blue. Lime raises soil pH and sulfur lowers it, and they both gave me super pretty colors!

Purple cost me money. For purple I bought a potassium chloride salt substitute, and it worked okay, but it had other ingredients that yellowed out my violet flames. I happy danced when I found stump killer made of potassium nitrate. Yes, purple!!

Throughout 1981, I collected baggies of chemicals to go with the methanol. They were packed away in my Dodgers backpack until I had the power to make a rainbow of fire anywhere I went.

A whole show soon developed. I glued my tea light tins to the inside of a Frisbee and measured chemicals into the tins. Just before dusk, I dragged kids to sit in the driveway, because concrete driveways don't catch fire. I wore a cape lined with maroon felt and collected a shiny quarter from each kid. The presentation had more gravitas when it required payment.

In grand magician style, I swept my cape in the creeping darkness. "Behold! Prepare to be amazed! This is very dangerous and do not try this at home or you'll set your house on fire!!" (That was my effort at responsibility.) "When I pour my magical special water into these simple tins, something extraordinary will happen! In a moment, you will see the great powers in my fingertips!"

It was ridiculous, but the kids liked it. I kept the methanol in a baby bottle and squeezed the clear liquid into each tin of materials. I stirred them and with sober grandeur used a barbecue lighter to fire up the pools of methanol. As far as the kids could tell, I was setting fire to water. Real magic. Red! Bright orange! Yellow orange! Green! Blue! Purple! I spun the Frisbee (gently, lovingly), and flames blended in a rainbow swirl of light.

I cooed "Oooohh," and all the kids of 1981 joined me. Nobody asked for their quarters back.

The first time I did it, I made a huge mistake; I left the baby bottle beside me. There wasn't much methanol left, but as the fires died, some foolish kid grabbed the bottle and squirted more "magic water" on the tins.

BWOOSH! The bottle exploded out the nipple and flung fiery methanol everywhere. Splashes burned spots up the foolish kid's pants and shoes, and I tackled him to knock off the flames. The other kids pounced on me and slapped the singes in my hair. Drops had melted through my cape.

Those kids learned a lesson: never ever ever add liquid gas to an existing fire. I learned a lesson: hide the baby bottle in my cloak.

My rainbow fire show didn't work well as a stress-test, though. First, most parents didn't find out. When they did walk up on my magic trick with the colors all twirling, they were kind of impressed. I got a few lectures about playing with fire, but no real trouble. And I made $26 between the 12 houses where I performed it.

Oh wait. Hahaha... I forgot about Janie. In the fall of 1981, neighbor Janie walked up the driveway as I lit the red and orange tea tins. She'd arrived to collect her boys for dinner and nearly popped when she saw the long lighter in my hand.

"No no no!" She stomped on my Frisbee to put out the two flames. Of course, she splashed all kinds of chemical-rich methanol on her legs and skirt, and the fire leaped and turned her into a rainbow bell of flame.

I yelped, "No no no!"

Yellow, green, and purple flames swooshed in circles as Janie spun and danced. The kids all shouted over Janie's caterwauling, "Stop, drop and roll! Stop, drop, and roll!" Two older boys and I smacked at her flames until we put out her dancing fire of colors.

I *was* grounded that time. My chemicals were confiscated, and I had to go on another treasure hunt to collect them all again. Dumb Janie.

I liked my colored fire show, but it was the "swimming pool plot" that became my favorite jolt to the serenity of a foster home.

Simple stuff. I'd convince foster brothers or sisters or neighbor kids to sneak out with me in the middle of the night and go for a swim. If the family had a pool, we used their own pool. If they didn't, we found the nearest neighbor's pool. I had to have other kids involved, because kids are loud. Even if they think they're being quiet, they're loud.

I taught so many children to sneak out at night! But I mean, the whole point was to get caught, so I didn't feel too much guilt.

I thoroughly enjoyed those pool invasions. I'd back float in the smooth warmth, my face and chest exposed to the midnight sky as I gazed at lonely Venus or Jupiter in the pale light. I missed my Idaho sky filled with stars and delighted in the dim twinkles that forced their way through the Los Angeles light pollution. Hi Arcturus! Castor and Pollux, you bright twins, you.

Sometimes we got caught the first night. Sometimes it took two or four nights before the inevitable discovery. An adult would appear and shout at us. They'd lecture while we climbed out of the pool. Irate homeowners called the police two different times! So exciting! We were all super young, so the cops sat us down to explain the dangers of swimming alone. They said it wrong to use other people's pools without asking, then they marched us home.

We had a scary incident at the nicest pool I ever invaded. We'd walked four blocks, slipped over a rock wall and squeezed through an iron fence to get to it, but it was worth it. Rock work and palm trees surrounded this mock tropical wonder, and a small waterfall splashed down the rocks at the far end. A water slide had been constructed among the rocks, and over and over we slid off it and splashed into the water. We'd discovered a hidden paradise.

The cursing threats of an old man interrupted our delight. He stood at the edge of the pool, a pointy shovel raised above the dim pool lights as though he planned to decapitate every last one of us and bury us in the back yard. We never moved so fast! Three children scrambled out of the water and through the fence before that old man could snatch us. We raced home and giggled uncontrollably in relief.

I generally got caught first. I made sure to recruit older kids who knew how to swim well, which made me the youngest in the group and easy to grab. Over and over my foster folks opened the door to an angry neighbor and one or two or three dripping kids on the front steps. They apologized profusely and ordered us inside. The door closed, and yelling commenced until we were sent to bed. I heard, "What were you thinking!" so many times, I eventually brainstormed on T-shirt designs to wear for the occasion:

A picture of a stick man thinking, like a Rodin statue.

A picture of a puppy/doughnut/chocolate. "All I ever think about."

A picture of an empty box. "What's inside my head."

A smiling stick figure swimming in a pool inside the outline of a huge brain labeled "My Brain."

Some parents begged us not to do that again. One mother – I felt terrible – sobbed because her three-year-old had drowned in a pool. I hugged that dear woman and cried with her and apologized over and over.

A few dads pulled out weapons to punish us, but the moms mostly stepped in and calmed them down. Out of all the homes, the worst response was a mother who plain lost it. She shrieked and slapped us around the living room like a lunatic. I didn't stay long in that house.

The unexpected response, the one that made me laugh, were the four different foster parents that said, "You shouldn't have done that, but let me tell you about the crazy stuff I pulled when I was a kid!" We laughed and laughed late into the night as each parent entertained us with stories from his or her own wicked youth.

I'd left behind my rainy green mountains of North Idaho. Those nights of illegal swimming were a good stress test for homes, and they offered me hours of real fun.

My crazy situation wasn't all bad. I hadn't travelled into a strange world when I time jumped. It was a familiar world, one I understood, one I knew how to navigate. It was my childhood all over again, but with a bigger grasp of the world and my place in it.

As time passed, I reluctantly recognized all kinds of good things. First, I took better care of my teeth than I did my first time around. I flossed, even my baby teeth. I'd learned the hard way that cavities are forever - so many thousands of dollars on crowns and root canals, and here I'd been offered a dental do-over? That was fantastic! And, like I said, I could see and smell and taste better. I sat on a bench one memorable day and chowed down a bowl of strawberries, relishing each explosion of flavor.

I also had fun acting like a boy. I need to make this thing clear; I was perfectly content *being* a girl, but I'd always preferred baseball and soccer with the boys at recess. Most girls liked Barbies and playing dress up, but I'd never cared for all that. If I'd played with the skinny dolls at all, I'd pulled off their heads and stripped them to see what they looked like naked. I didn't collect stickers or plan out tea parties; I'd chosen football over playing dress-up every time. My mother had given me that freedom, but I no longer lived with my mother. I liked pretending to be a boy because nobody bought me dolls or tried to stick me in a dress. Without explanations or disputes, I got to play with the boys, which is what I liked best.

In the late spring of 1982, Cheryl placed me with the Jaegers in Malibu, and I didn't want to leave. We drove to the ocean pretty much every day, and I learned to surf on baby waves. I'm the whitest thing since Wonder Bread, but we smathered me up with sunscreen until I developed a real tan. My scars had faded to whitish pink by that time, and when people asked about them, I said I'd fought with barnacles. I'd claw out my fingers and roar like a dinosaur, because barnacles are so scary after all.

Look at me, I'm a surfing six-year-old! Rock n roll, baby.

I lingered at the Jaegers for six weeks, because I plain loved it there. I felt selfish the whole time, but I had more fun than I'd ever had in my life! When I finally made myself leave them, I told Cheryl,

"Place siblings with them. They want to take siblings." Boys and girls, enjoy your forever home in the Jaegers' happy land of luxury.

During those three years, I lived in a vast variety of houses. I lived with hippies and nerds, with alcoholics and addicts and artists and architects and aerospace engineers. I slept in dens and spidery garages and above restaurants. I accepted a new adventure every week or so. Sometimes they were lovely adventures, and sometimes they looked more like *Indiana Jones and the Temple of Doom*. Which hadn't come out yet.

Throughout my 52 homes, I faced all kinds of parents, but I got good at reading them. I could usually follow their thinking. Other foster children proved the most critical threats to my safety. Seriously. Children don't enter the system because their lives are Cheerios and Sugar Pops, and I had to deal with some messed up kids. Messed up kids don't reason like adults.

Most of the children I saw needed security and love more than anything. They had a range of messy medical and emotional struggles, but at the bottom of it they needed somebody to love them. A few kids, though...concerned me a lot. I had the comfort of knowing I could escape the nightmarish places, but I still faced real danger when I walked through the front door.

Jeremy

I bear three sets of scars from my years in the foster system. It seemed that any time I left an especially lovely place, I always entered a nightmare. If I'd remained at the Jaegers in Malibu like a sensible person, I'd only have the marks Ted gave me. I therefore bore some fault for the second and third sets. Immediately after the Jaegers, I moved to the Robertson home in Van Nuys, and in Van Nuys, I met Jeremy, and sweet Jeremy gave me my second installment of scars, ones I couldn't hide under a T-shirt.

The Robertsons had taken in five foster children, and I made number six. They lived in a three-bedroom apartment and packed all six of us into two rooms. As far as I understood the rules, parents weren't supposed to keep more than two unrelated children per bedroom, but I found a variety of things had slipped through the cracks in the L.A. welfare system.

The Robertson parents never harmed me. Not directly. In fact, they offered little supervision at all. I saw Mr. Robertson only once, and Mrs. Robertson left for work before we woke up. We kids ran around the streets of Van Nuys and kicked balls on the dry grounds at a sort of park off Lennox Avenue and did pretty much whatever we wanted. If we reached the park early enough, we could shoot baskets before the big kids in the neighborhood showed up and chased us away. I had a lot of freedom at the Robertsons, and we kids got along. All was fine except for Jeremy.

Jeremy fit into the special folder of genuinely disturbed children. At 9-years-old, he liked to stab pencils through dolls' tender parts. He terrorized the other kids, even 12-year-old Benny, and I mean it when I use the term "terrorized." Before I arrived, Jeremy had been tying up the three youngest kids regularly. He threatened to cut off their fingers, or he heated a butter knife on the stove burner and held it near their faces. My first night, I found fresh burns on the children's legs and learned Jeremy had done it. The boy sadist cornered me and warned that if I ever told on him, he'd stab out my eyes in my sleep. I believed him.

My fourth day in Van Nuys, I walked into the living room and found Jeremy on top of six-year-old Tim, rubbing dog poop in his hair.

"Eat it." Jeremy forced feces into the child's face. "Come on, open up!"

Jeremy heard my footsteps. He turned and saw me, but he didn't look embarrassed or ashamed. He showed no fear that I'd caught him. He glanced back at me with green, hard eyes, and he smirked.

So, I tackled him. A two-year size difference separated us, but I had enough momentum to knock him off Tim and roll him over onto his back. Before Jeremy recovered, I sat on his chest and punched him flat in the nose until blood smeared. I didn't have a lot of strength, but I threw my body into it like Ralph Macchio in *Karate Kid II*. Jeremy ripped out one arm to grab at me, but he couldn't see through the explosion of tears.

I'd learned two things by that point in my travels. First, end the fight fast. Don't threaten, just end it. Second, punching bullies in the nose makes their eyes water and blinds them. A boy who shoved dog poop in another's face had psycho-emotional problems, and I needed to get Tim out of there.

I weighed maybe 50 pounds. Jeremy could knock me over in a moment and pin me down, so I had to make a quick escape. As soon as I'd pounded on his nose, I hopped off his chest, dragged Tim into the bathroom and locked the door. I helped Tim soap up his hair and face really well, washing him clean. Then we waited for a good half hour, listening at the door. I finally shouted for the other kids to tell me where Jeremy had gone. They couldn't see him anywhere, so we crept to Tim's room.

We obviously had to take care of our Jeremy problem. I left the kids playing on the floor and hunted around for the bully himself, but Big Benny shrugged when I asked where Jeremy had gone. I plopped on my back on the bedroom carpet while Benny told me the horrible things Jeremy had been doing.

"We're gonna get rid of him," I promised Benny.

"Sounds good to me."

I was certain Jeremy had his own past of darkness and trauma, and I could sympathize. Regardless, he had to be stopped. He towered over me by at least five inches, and I considered sleeping in the locked bathroom that night.

I called Cheryl and described Jeremy's behavior.

"He's torturing these children. He is torturing them! What were you thinking putting him in a home with young kids!"

"He's been through so many homes-" Cheryl started to explain, and I didn't want to hear it.

"I knew it! He's a psychopath, but you still placed him with three little children!"

She tried to reassure me, but I insisted, "You have to move him as soon as possible, Cheryl. He needs help, and you have to get him out *yesterday*. Also, talk to these parents about supervising us. They leave us alone all the time."

I clunked the phone back onto the receiver. "C'mon, guys," I turned to the little kids. "Let's go to the park."

We kicked our soccer ball all over the dusty lot down the road and enjoyed ourselves. Smog hung over the city like a dense cloud of cigarette smoke, and I wished we had real grass to lie down in. The weather danced in the 70s and 80s, not too hot, but we hadn't had one day of rain that June. Our world had dried out, and the city didn't care to use water to keep the grass green.

"What should we do, Benny?" We kicked rocks on our way back home. "Jeremy already threatened to stab out my eyes."

"You should definitely sleep with the little kids. And block the door so he can't get in."

We never saw Mr. Robertson that night. I finally realized that he travelled for work, so he didn't appear for days at a time. His wife did walk up the stairs about 6:00 to make dinner.

"Where's Jeremy?" Mrs. Robertson asked after a bit. I realized from the way she looked around the table, she didn't recognize that Jeremy created toxic waste in her house. Benny had warned me that violent Jeremy said "please" and "thank you" and acted nice and healthy around adults. He could play the good boy role, no problem.

Before we answered her, Jeremy himself climbed the stairs, the bridge of his nose puffed up red, nice purple bruises under his eyes. Wow, maybe I was stronger than I thought.

"Jeremy!" Mrs. Robertson stood right up. "What happened!"

I expected him to rat me out, but he just shrugged. "I got into a fight. It's no big deal."

"You've got blood all over your shirt, Jeremy. Look, go change and get a bag of frozen peas from the freezer to put on your nose."

"I'm all right." He walked past us into the kitchen, poured himself a glass of water and guzzled it. He'd disappeared for most of the day and had to be dehydrated. He grabbed himself two burritos from the stove, sat at the table and chomped them down, then retreated to our room. He didn't look at any of us the whole time, and I wondered what gears whirled in his troubled mind.

"Change your shirt, Jeremy!" Mrs. Robertson called after him.

"I will."

After Jeremy left, something about his appearance bothered me. What was wrong? I puzzled about it over my own burrito until Benny said, "Wasn't Jeremy wearing a red shirt this morning?"

That was it. Yep. Jeremy had already changed shirts, and the new yellow shirt was covered with blood like Mrs. Robertson said. It made me wonder whose blood it was.

While Mrs. Robertson stood in the kitchen, I felt safe enough to approach my colorful foster brother; I didn't think he'd shank me right then, not with an adult in the next room. As soon as I washed my plate, I walked into our bedroom and casually confronted him.

"Where'd you go today?" I asked it simply, like a normal brother.

He lay on the bottom bunk with his hands behind his head. "I dunno. I went places."

"Whose blood is that on your shirt?"

"I dunno."

Several scratches raked his right forearm. New, red, flaming scratches.

"Was it a cat?" Not a wild animal, like a rat or a squirrel. But, a neighborhood kitty cat? Those come right up to you.

Jeremy finally nodded.

"Oh."

Revulsion twisted in my stomach, and I tried not to think about it. He'd murdered somebody's pet.

Jeremy rolled onto his side and stared at me, the empty stare of somebody who needed sleep. He muttered slowly, "I was practicing on the cats. I got pretty good at it too, and maybe tomorrow or maybe the next day... I'm not sure. It depends on what's going on. But, I think I can do it good enough to kill you."

I wish I could have recorded him as he said it. His face expressed no anger. He looked - he *looked* - like a boy who needed to take a bath and go to bed. He said it with a matter-of-fact calmness, as though using cats to practice murdering humans made logical sense, and he'd worked hard all day to get it right. His eyes drooped in exhaustion.

"How many cats did you use for practice?"

He yawned. "I don't know. I didn't count."

"Oh. Well, good night."

"G'night."

I turned to leave, but first I suggested, "You really should take off that bloody shirt before you fall asleep."

Sick to my soul, I decided that Benny should sleep in the room with me and the little kids. I couldn't predict what Jeremy would do, and I didn't want him to practice on Benny in the middle of the night.

Our foster mother had retired to her bedroom, so I knocked on her door. "It's Dodge. Can I come in?"

"Sure."

I entered and closed the door behind me. Mrs. Robertson had changed into her nightgown and sat in bed with a crossword puzzle.

"We have a problem." I got right into it. "Jeremy is a dangerous person. That blood on his shirt? He spent all day killing cats."

She didn't believe me. "What?"

"Hold on, be right back." I ran to the little kids' room and grabbed the six-year-old and brought him back with me.

"Show her, Tim," I told the younger boy. "Show her the burns on your legs."

Tim shook his head. Jeremy had threatened him with gouged eyes too.

"It's okay. I won't let Jeremy hurt you. Show Mom the burns on your legs."

It took some coaxing, but I finally got Tim to pull up his shorts and expose three ugly burns on his thigh. The scabs had torn off and raw, weepy wounds glared at us. We needed to bandage him better.

"Tell her what happened, Tim."

Tim didn't want to, so I asked him questions.

"Did Jeremy do that to you?"

Tim stared at the carpet. After a moment he gave a small nod.

"Did he burn you with a butter knife he'd heated on the stove?"

Tim nodded again.

Does Jeremy do bad things all the time?

Tim gave his third affirmation.

I turned to the woman on the bed. "Mrs. Robertson, I already called my case worker and told her that Jeremy needs to go to a special home. He needs one-on-one care. He's scary and dangerous, and he told me himself that he spent the day killing cats. Do you know why?"

Mrs. Robertson sat dazed. She didn't process this information quickly. "I … I can't believe he would do something like that," she murmured. "That's not like him."

"That's not like him? What? Because he *looks* like a nice boy? Ted Bundy looked like a nice person too. Until he bludgeoned women to death."

Confusion froze on Mrs. Robertson's face.

I took a deep breath. I didn't want to freak her out, but I needed her to be the adult.

"Look. Jeremy told me he killed cats all day because he planned to kill me, and he wanted practice. Please *do* something. Don't leave tomorrow and abandon us. Because if you come home and find me stabbed to death, that's going to be your fault, and they'll charge you with criminal negligence."

She started crying then. Mrs. Robertson started crying. Tears dripped out her eyes and down her face, and a sob heaved from her chest. "I told Rick it wasn't good for him to be gone all the time. I can't do this alone!" She covered her face and shook there on the bed.

I watched in disbelief. She hardly spent time with us. She left us alone all day and made dinner at night, and she hadn't even made sure Jeremy changed his shirt! Benny did more to take care of the kids than she did, and she felt sorry for herself? She wasn't crying because there was a murderer in her house, or because I faced real danger of death by knifing, or because Tim wore torture burns on his legs. She cried because she was forced to handle it.

I gave up. "C'mon Tim. Let's go to sleep." He stood next to me, almost my height. Only about six months separated us, but he was a little kid, and I was his protector. I grabbed his hand to leave, but I warned our foster mother, "You should put something in front of your door tonight, to block it in case Jeremy tries to come in here. Maybe he wants to kill you too."

I had the little ones brush their teeth and go to the bathroom and get a drink of water before hiding in their room. Benny and I pushed their bunk bed against the door, and all five of us slept in there.

In my original childhood, I'd played soccer and baseball and climbed trees. If I skinned my knees, I hopped up and kept going. But I'd never had a fist fight. The girls I knew never tackled other kids and punched them in the face. During my second childhood, I walked around looking like a boy - and quickly learned boys were different. Some boys wanted to assert dominance, and some boys wanted to find somebody they could hit, which forced the other boys to deal with them. Jeremy wanted to kill somebody. He'd been practicing.

We survived until morning, but Mrs. Robertson left to work like usual! I called the child welfare office again and waited and waited for somebody to show up for Jeremy. But they didn't.

That's when I had the idea to offer Jeremy a distraction. I searched through the Sunday newspaper until I found show times for new movies. What movies were coming out? I needed one I recognized, a movie I *knew*. I planned to talk to Jeremy that night, to reason with him and try to be his friend.

Benny and I walked the little kids to the park that afternoon, and we all ran around in the sun, getting red-faced. I jogged down to the pop machine to buy a few cans of 7-Up for us to share, but the others had disappeared when I got back. I searched the main road, hoping to spy the others, awkwardly cradling cold cans in my arms.

"I told them I was going for pop." Why had they left? I enjoyed the pleasant cool against my chest, but those three cans were heavy. I figured the others had headed home, so I started north.

Lennox Avenue was a quiet street lined by small trees in front of two-story apartment buildings. I strolled down the sidewalk with no reason to worry about Jeremy. My eyes hunted for the little kids while cold cans chilled my chest, and I plain did not hear three pairs of sneakers run up behind until they were on top of me. A sudden shove knocked the pop out of my arms so that the three cans bounced and rolled against the concrete. Thin, foamy spray shot out the side of one 7-Up can, and somebody kicked me onto my hands and knees.

I ignored the raw scrapes from the pavement and snatched up a can to launch. It clocked one of Jeremy's ratty little friends right above the eye, and the kid fell on his butt. I quickly hucked a second can, but it missed Jeremy altogether and bounced and rolled out onto the main road. At that point, I scrambled up and ran, ran super speed down the narrow driveway toward a cinder block wall in the back. That enclosed area roared "danger" at me, and I planned to race around the building and out the other side, but my legs chewed up the yards slower than the bigger kids behind me. They caught me within about six seconds.

I wrenched and kicked in a panic. I knew Jeremy didn't want to tie me to a telephone pole and slap my stomach with grass stalks. He didn't want to give me a wedgie or stick my head in a toilet or take my lunch money. That's not what Jeremy wanted.

The three boys wrestled me along and shoved me into a cave-like doorway in the back of the apartment building. They blocked me in, and Jeremy and Rat-Boy shoved me back when I tried to break free. The biggest boy dragged an old wood and metal chair to the doorway and forced me into it, and Jeremy pulled strips of cloth out of his pocket and handed them to the others. I didn't plan to go all gentle into that good night, so I kicked somebody in the knee and elbowed somebody's stomach and jumped up to bust Jeremy's nose again, but he punched me in the chest with his palms and knocked me back into the chair. He stuck his knee into my crotch and caught my arms as I swung at him.

"Tie him. Tie him, guys." They wrapped strips around the metal frame of the chair and around my wrists to anchor them down at my sides. I kicked the big kid in the mouth as he stooped to tie up my right leg, but I had no real chance. One almost-seven-year-old against three bigger, stronger boys? It wasn't sporting at all.

"They'll put you in jail forever, you know that, right?" I glared into Jeremy's puffy eyes. "They'll know it was you."

"Mmm." Jeremy stood back and checked my bonds. Then he leaned back and smashed my nose. Bam! And he punched me again. It was all explosions of orange and crunching pain and instant tears. I'd already lost one upper tooth, and the final punch knocked out the other one. That's what I got for being almost-seven.

Those cloth chains held my wrists, and I couldn't stop the blood from my nose and mouth. It dripped and drained over my lips and off my chin and down the back of my throat from my sinuses. Saltwater rolled down my face as Jeremy stood - so calm, so sickeningly calm - in a blurry form above me.

"I'll see you guys back at our spot," Jeremy told his two friends. "Give me a minute."

Rat-Boy's mouth dropped open in dismay. "I wanna watch! You said I could watch!"

Good grief. The psychopaths abounded.

My whole face cried at me, heavy and clogged. I told Rat-Boy, "He can't kill me." I leaned at my shoulder to wipe the blood off my mouth, but I couldn't reach with my hands tied at my sides. I had to lick my lips and spit at the ground. "He can't chop me open, because Mrs. Robertson and Benny will know. He'll go to jail forever."

I lisped a lot in those few words without my top teeth. I won't write out the "th" sounds, but it's hard to sound tough without front teeth.

The rat asked, "Can I punch him? You said I could punch him."

Jeremy pulled out his knife and shoved it in the other kids' faces. "Get out of here!" He chased them, and the two boys ran off.

Soon enough, Jeremy marched back, and I started talking before he even reached me. I wanted to get out what I had to say before he started belting me again.

I blurted, "Jeremy. Jeremy, wait. I have a superpower!"

"Shut up," he kicked me in the shin. Hard. Then, he kicked me in the other shin for good measure. I couldn't reach over to rub out the pain, but at least he evened it all out. My OCD appreciated it.

"Owww... no I do!" I groaned, "I can tell the future."

That's when Jeremy picked up his kitchen knife - an old, dark steel paring knife. He held it up so I could see it, hard humor in his face. "It's sharp," he informed me. "I sharpened it good."

Don't think panic didn't dizzy my brain and give me tunnel vision, because it did. I couldn't breathe well, and his knife blurred before me.

"Jeremy, I can tell the future," I tried again in desperation.

"That's impossible."

"I can. It's my secret, the thing I don't want anybody to know. And now you know."

He could have done anything to me while I sat tied to that chair, dripping blood onto my shirt. Dear God, I did not want to wear an eye patch for the rest of my life. I needed my depth perception!

"Jeremy, I swear, if you gouge out my eye, I'll scream and scream and the adults will come and catch you." I tried hard to keep my voice from pitching upward, but it sounded squeakier than I liked. I couldn't stop the lisping at all. "If you wait, I'll tell you something nobody else knows. I know who will be the next president. And the president after that. I know when the *Batman* movie comes out and when terrorists blow up buildings."

I wondered if Jeremy didn't suffer from boredom. I wondered if this whole torture bit interested him, and that's why he did it. He stared in fascination at the blood that dripped off my chin. He scraped the tip of his knife across my upper lip and studied the smear of blood.

"Did you ever notice how red blood is? It's so red."

I still couldn't reach my shoulder to wipe the wet away.

I stopped to spit again. "There's a movie, Jeremy. A movie comes out tomorrow. It's the first of July, right? *The Secret of NIMH* comes out in theaters. It's a cartoon." I tried to say the S's through my back teeth, and it came out, "The Shecret of NIMH."

Jeremy didn't care, still focused on his knife. He wiped it on his pants and held it up again. Warm, gritty fingers grasped my chin. The blade pressed against my right cheek, harder and harder until it broke the skin. I forced myself to hold still, because I didn't want him to slip and stab my eye. I ignored my terror and the slicing pain, fighting the urge to pull away. More tears gushed as Jeremy drew the knife slowly across my cheek bone. My arms shook. I grabbed the wooden seat of the chair with both hands and forced myself solid and still as he split my skin cells in a slow trail. He pulled the blade off the end of my face, and it occurred to me he'd used his left hand.

"The cats had hair in the way. Your face is smooth. It's easier."

As soon as he released my chin, I tried again, my eyes squished shut. "Put the knife down, Jeremy, and I'll tell you what happens in that movie. I can give you quotes. You can tell people that *you* know the future." I opened and closed my eyes to press out the water. "If you tell the future, they'll think you're so great."

Jeremy still didn't believe me. "Tell me what I'm going to do to you next. Tell me that."

I imagined an array of horrors in a flashing montage. "No, because that's your choice. You can choose what to do. But, the movie – they already made it. It is what it is."

Jeremy grasped the hair on the back of my head for a better hold. "I dreamed all last night about cutting you up." Again, he held the knife against my right cheek, and blurry knuckles gripped its handle. The warmth from his skin conflicted with the cool sharp of the blade. I stiffened every muscle, clenched my eyes and waited for the fiery slicing to end as he drew the blade through my skin again. Two stripes.

Jeremy puzzled me. He didn't seem moved by anger or hate. He was motivated by, I tried to decipher it, a hunger maybe? I knew he had watched my skin split and my blood bead up and run down my face. I felt the obsession ooze from him like the blood oozed from me. I wanted to offer him something else to hunger for, something else to fascinate him.

The whole right side of my face flamed. The bridge of my nose and cheeks pulsed. I blinked while Jeremy rubbed his arm across his mouth.

I spit again - badly, a bloody spray. "You want to cut me up more than you want to know the future? At least listen."

Jeremy considered that.

"Cut me again, I won't tell you a thing!"

Cautious belief narrowed his eyes. I didn't bawl and beg like a normal kid. "Okay. Tell me."

"You might not remember everything. Let me write it down."

He poked out his lower lip, insulted. "Yes I will. I'll remember."

"There's too much. I have to say lots of things."

Jeremy walked off without explanation. He just walked away, so I tugged at the cloths around my wrists to pull my hands free. Most kids can't tie good knots, and if I could just get one loose…

No good. My captor returned and produced a used envelope and broken pencil stub.

"Okay, stupid. Tell me. Then I'll let you go."

"Could you plug my nose? The blood makes it hard to talk."

Jeremy surprised me. He cut two squares off the end of my cloth bonds, rolled them, and stuffed them one at a time into my nostrils. He even used the front of my shirt to wipe off my lips and chin. It hurt a lot because he was rough, but I was grateful to have my lips clear.

Jeremy got ready. He sat down cross-legged on the pavement and set the envelope on his leg. "Okay. Talk."

I'd probably watched *The Secret of NIMH* 48 times growing up. I knew every voice lilt in every scene, but I made a show for Jeremy. I closed my eyes to concentrate, flicking them rapidly back and forth under their lids. Accessing my superpower. "Okay. Write small so you can get it all." Eyes still closed in prophetic concentration. Nose stuffed. Teeth missing.

"Go already!"

"I am. It starts with an ancient old rat saying, 'Jonathan Brisby was killed today…while helping with the plan.'" I dictated the words slowly, carefully. I couldn't have spoken fast anyway. "'It is four years since our departure from NIMH, and our world is changing.' You spell it 'N-I-M-H,'" I clarified. "National Institute of Mental Health."

"…NIMH, and our world is changing." Jeremy wrote each word with surprising diligence.

I provided a sentence at a time, and Jeremy scribbled down the words. "'Jonathan, wherever you are, your thoughts must comfort her tonight. She'll be waiting, and you will not return.'"

"And you will not return," Jeremy finished up.

I repeated the entire monologue so that Jeremy could make sure he'd gotten all of it.

(And the whole time I was thinking, "My cortisol levels have got to be so high right now. My adrenal glands are rock stars." Then I thought, "That's so ridiculous, thinking about cortisol.")

"Okay," he said. "Something else."

I quoted the heck out of the movie for Jeremy, painfully, slowly, and he filled the front and back of the envelope, tore it open, then wrote on the inside.

"When I close my eyes, I see the movie scenes. So, can you untie me?" Hope. I had hope for about two seconds.

Jeremy laughed. "Yeah. You can stay here until after I go see the movie."

Thumping in my cheek. "It doesn't open until tomorrow night!"

Jeremy didn't answer. He bent over and tugged my knots tight, then he pulled out additional cloth strips and bound my hands more thoroughly. Finally, he stuffed a dirty gob of cloth in my mouth and wrapped strips around my head to hold the gag in place.

"Don't worry, I'll be back." He patted my head unnecessarily hard and walked away.

Cloth wads blocked both my nose and mouth. Jeremy left me like that, all primed for suffocation. Violent, foolish boy.

I had no intention of dying in that doorway. I leaned my chair backward until my head rested on the door behind me and rubbed my head up and down until the binding around my mouth dropped onto my neck. Aching for oxygen, I chewed and wet the gag until I could spit it out. I listened while sucking air. Then, I awkwardly rock-walked that chair out of the doorway cave.

No humans anywhere. I listened for Jeremy but suspected he'd gone off to find his friends. I rock-walked a few more feet. Nobody.

As I rocked onward, I sang the theme song from *The Secret of NIMH*, which Jeremy would have found mushy. I liked the song, so I sang it to myself. I didn't sing loudly; it put pressure on my face, and my nose was stuffed anyway, but I murmured out the words and did my heart some good.

I wish someone had been filming me, lyrics lisping from my mouth, tied to a chair, spattered in blood, rocking my way to freedom to save my life. The song and the scene did not mesh.

Rock. Rock. "'Love it seems made flying dreams so hearts could soar. Heaven-sent, these wings were meant to prove once more that love is the key. Love is the key.'"

Rock. Rock. Rock. I had to stop and cough up the blood that drained into my throat. I couldn't stand and walk with my feet tied to the chair legs, but I dug my toes into the pavement to keep balanced, keenly aware that if I tipped forward, I'd break my face. It took a lot of energy, and I stopped to rest several times during those next 10 minutes, but I'm sure the cortisol helped.

I finally reached Lennox Avenue and scanned the street for help. Plenty of parked cars jammed up next to the sidewalk, but no people appeared in the middle of that hot, dry day. It didn't matter if drug dealers or pimps walked up, I felt certain that any Tyrone or Charlie on the street would cut me free if he saw me tied to a chair. That's all I needed. Just one person.

I wobbled out and rested for a minute. Trickles of blood itched as they dried on my jaw. "Bueller?" I muttered. "Anyone? Anyone?" I searched up and down the road for one stranger. Up and down, up and down. Of course, the first people I did see turned out to be the very three I didn't want.

Jack

My enemies spotted me out there in the open, out of my den, and my heart sagged. I liked my face whole! Desperate, I wobble-walked into the middle of the avenue where heat billowed at me from the sun-baked pavement. The boys bolted my way, and I watched helplessly as they grew larger. It was no good.

Then a car skidded to a stop beside me. Shiny bumper a foot from my arm. Thank God. Thank God a car almost hit me. A toweringly tall guy emerged from the driver's side, and I thought, "Haha! Get wrecked, Jeremy!" The boys stopped as relief drained the last of my energy.

Most of the truly important moments in our lives fly by us, and it's not until years later we can look back and think, "Wow. That was pivotal." We can't see our future; we have little capacity to recognize when a happenstance meeting or simple event will completely redirect our trajectory. That July 1st in 1982 was different for me, because the next thing that happened I knew, I *knew*, was significant. As soon as that driver got out of his car.

A giant man blocked the yellow sky, and his nose stuck out like a great hooked beak above me. I stared up at him, that distinctive, tall, balding fellow with his prominent honker, and I squinted.

"Wait. I know you."

His eyebrows furrowed down. Was he angry at me? No. Upset. Concerned like a decent human being. I made a strange sight, a child covered in blood, tied to a chair in the middle of the street, but I didn't worry about that. I focused on his face, trying to remember his name.

"Jack?"

I was born in L.A. County, and around 1976 my mom had been sitting in dead stopped traffic on the freeway on a boiling day, and she said to herself, "I am not raising children here."

My parents relocated to Washington where the rain fell constantly, and Mom loved it. She eventually moved us to North Idaho where her child support lasted longer, and I learned to resent the tedious cold of forever winters. I didn't mind hot summers, but Mom hated them. She relaxed happily as the weather grew cold and nasty every fall.

Mom had lived in Van Nuys before she'd married my dad, just a few blocks away from where I sat tied to that metal chair. I didn't know that. However, I *did* know Mom had attended a little church on Sherman Way, and the fellow who stood above me with his healthy nose served as pastor of that church. The church exploded into a huge congregation known across the country, but Mom knew Pastor Jack as a young pastor, back when the assembly remained small and personal, and Mom and Dad had asked him to dedicate me as a baby.

Basically, the guy who picked me up, chair and all, and placed me on the sidewalk happened to be my first family pastor, and when I saw him, it felt like the hand of God had settled him right there on that road to rescue me. Jeremy and his friends evaporated into the dusty afternoon, and we didn't see them again.

"Pastor Jack, you amazing, beautiful man!" Wow, he looked young! When had I seen him last? April, 1999. At the Pontiac Silverdome in Michigan at a conference when I was a youth leader. I'd found him and given him a hug - two decades from now.

He leaned over me in alarm. "You're bleeding all over the place." I saw the anger, the distress in his face. He kept looking me up and down, but I wanted him to rejoice with me. I was safe!

"Do you have a pocketknife or anything?"

He felt his pockets then yelped, "Wait!" He returned to his car and pulled a leather satchel of tools from the trunk. "Hold on. Hold on. There's something in here I bet." He found a box cutter, and that lanky man knelt on the ground and sawed through my cloth bonds. It didn't take him long, and I stood up, woozy, my heart still beating in my face. I helped him gather all the strips off the ground, and he left my chair on the sidewalk.

He handed one cloth wad back to me, "Here, young man. Press this against your cheek. There you go. Those cuts might need stitches."

"I'll butterfly bandage them." I loved butterfly bandages.

He shook his head. "This is just sick. Who would do something like this? Can I give you a ride? Is your mom home?"

I started toward his car, words tumbling. "Mom's not here. I'm so glad you are, though. I haven't seen you in so long!"

I climbed into his car, glad for the air conditioning, glad for the refuge. Pastor Jack slid into the driver's seat and paused to study me again, shaking his head. "Was it other boys? Other boys did this?"

I wasn't upset at all, and I could tell my excitement confused him. "Pastor Jack, listen. I'm not a boy, I'm a girl. I'm Sadie Cook. My mom is Madeleine Cook." I gently pulled the wads out of my nose and wrapped them in the cloth Jack had given me.

He squinted for a moment. "Oh wow!" He stared at me while the car idled. "I'm sorry, I thought... Wow. You're little Sadie?" His eyes widened at me. "Your mom is going to pitch a fit when she sees what those kids did to you!"

I chewed crusted blood off my upper lip. "Look, um. I want to talk to you about something super important. Do you have a few minutes? Can we go someplace and talk?"

"Let's take you home. We need to get you cleaned up."

"Okay, but then can we go talk?"

He thought about it. "I need to call the police and report this. I was heading back into my office for a little bit. Where is your mom?"

I thought of Benny and the kids. "Mom is in Washington State. I'm staying up the road."

I directed him to our apartment and briefly described my Jeremy problem on the way. I asked if we could get the little ones, because I didn't want to leave them alone with Jeremy still prowling around.

Twenty minutes later, I left Benny with the others coloring in a classroom at Jack's church. I'd cleaned and taped my face and changed my shirt and half-filled a sock with ice. Jack led me into his office, and I sat on the padded edge of one of his large, comfortable chairs. My toes just reached the ground.

"You want some water?" The pastor handed me a cup from his water cooler.

I gratefully took the paper cup and drank heavily. The ice-sock cooled and soothed my nose, and the throbbing calmed.

Jack dragged my chair - with me in it - over to his desk. Then, he sat behind it and picked up the phone.

"Don't call the police yet," I begged. "Please wait."

He frowned down at me. "I need to call them."

"Okay, but wait a minute. I need to talk to you about something really important."

He sighed. "I need to call your mom at least. How's she doing these days? It's been years."

I set my cup on his desk and put the ice-sock on it. "Right now? She has five little kids and Dad is trying to find a better job. Sorry. Sorry. That's not what I want to talk about. I've been carrying a huge secret, and you're the only person I can tell. My mom doesn't know. Dad doesn't know. Nobody *nobody* knows this."

I know he saw a scruffy, taped-up child in his chair, and I slumped in my seat. The past 29 months were impossible! It didn't sound real! But, I also couldn't think of anybody I felt safer telling. If anybody would believe me, Jack would.

Concern wrinkled in the corners of his eyes. "What don't they know, Sadie?"

I hesitated. It sounded so crazy.

He suggested, "Whatever is going on with Jeremy?"

I shook my head and heaved out a deep breath. "No. Jeremy is small potatoes. Here's the thing," I tried to confess. "I... I..."

It didn't sound real!

"It's okay. Go ahead." Jack waited for me to finish.

"Pastor Jack. Here's the thing. I... I know what happens in the world for the next 38 years."

That wasn't what Jack expected, but he didn't give me the basic adult, "C'mon" look. His eyebrows wrinkled, puzzled. That was it. "You know what happens in the world? What?"

"In the future. I remember the future... like it's history..."

I felt more confident with Jack than I would most people, because he believed in things like prophecy. He believed God still performed miracles through regular, everyday people. Of course, that didn't mean I was telling the truth. I expected doubt. But, I had been keeping my secret for so long!

"You remember the future? You mean, you see the future?"

"No, it's worse than that. Much worse." I winced. "I've already *lived* through the future. All the way up to the year 2020."

"Lived through...?"

"I already grew up once. I got married in 2002, and I have three kids. I lived into the future to age 44."

Jack didn't know how to take that. He chuckled at me. "Sadie, honey. Those kids punched you in the head a lot, and you're hot. Drink more water."

"Jack, please listen. Please. I have to tell somebody! It's killing me having nobody to tell. I've already lived my life once, all the way to the year 2020. This is my second time through 1982, and I know that President Reagan will be reelected in 1984, George H.W. Bush will be elected in 1988, then Arkansas Governor Bill Clinton becomes president. The Berlin Wall is going to fall in 1989, and the USSR will collapse. I'm not inventing these things. I remember them."

Jack sat there, silent, his eyebrows all wrinkled up.

I needed to hammer my point with ideas that would never come from the mouth of an almost-seven-year-old.

"In 2003, the Human Genome Project will finish mapping out all the base pairs in the human genome. They'll be able to use DNA to detect genetic diseases. You know, like Huntington's."

Jack listened to this flood of words and stared at me the way all adults stared at me, but his face relaxed and I saw a spark of interest. I had intrigued him.

"Well, you're bright anyway. You say the Soviet Union collapses? Is the Cold War over, or do we destroy them with nukes?"

"Nope. Not one nuclear weapon is sent to blow up one city. But there's the Chernobyl thing. Has the Chernobyl meltdown happened yet?" I squinted at him. "The Chernobyl nuclear disaster? Did that happen yet?"

I saw in his face he had no clue what I was talking about.

"It's a Soviet nuclear power plant accident. It has a meltdown."

Jack shook his head. "Wait. So, you say you lived until 2020. You lived it in your mind?"

I shook my head back. "No, I lived it in real life. I was expecting to wake up on Super Bowl Sunday in 2020, but I'd travelled backward in time and turned into a child. I woke up in 1980 as a four-year-old all over again."

"They still have the Super Bowl in 2020?

I nodded with energy. "Yep. We wear jeans and T-shirts and Chuck Taylor sneakers. We eat hot dogs and pizza."

Jack stared at me for a full 20 seconds without saying a word. He was processing, trying to work out what I'd just told him.

"That's nuts. Give me a moment, Sadie. I can't quite wrap my mind around that." He was not accepting the truth quickly. "Are there time machines in 2020?"

"No. I don't know how it happened. I checked if the original Sadie Cook is at my home, living with my mom and dad, and she is! The original me is home in 1982! I'm perfectly safe and going into the second grade this fall. If you called Mom and said that you had me in your office, she'd say, 'That's impossible. Sadie's right here with me.'"

I wanted to gush and gush. I had stifled myself for so long, and it felt good to erupt the truth all over another person.

Jack didn't accuse me of lying. He squeezed his eyes shut and got up to grab himself another cup of water. He poured the water from his cooler and took a few big gulps.

"You're saying that you grew up, then woke up one day as a child again." He repeated these basic facts, because they were new and strange to him. He wanted to get it all straight.

"Yeah! Here I am! People think I'm a genius, but I'm a big fat fake, because I really had to go through all those years of schooling once upon a time. I have a master's in geochemistry. And I read up on DNA and genetics for fun."

"All right," Jack said. "All right all right all right. I'm sorry, honey, but I… can't… I can't… this sounds like something out of a movie. You definitely talk like an adult. I hear it."

"Even with my lisp?" I joked.

He smiled. "And you're clearly *educated*. Most adults don't read up on DNA for fun. Right? But there's a disconnect between what you're saying and anything like normal reality. Can you give me a minute?"

"Sure. Get some coffee."

He didn't go for coffee. He walked back and forth a few times, then sat down and leaned forward on his elbows, still tall and lanky even when sitting. "Can you prove any of it?"

I thought about it. "Well. I can talk about analytical chemistry for an hour. Or. You could call my mom. I'm there with her – the original me is there. Ask her questions and hear her answers. It's a good test."

I gazed mournfully at the pastor as he sat above me, thinking.

"I just wanted somebody I could tell!" I burst out. "I need another person to know the truth!"

"You haven't talked to your mom about all of this?"

I'd never even considered this simple idea. "Absolutely not. I can't disrupt the original me in my original life. I want to meet my husband and have my kids, and I don't want to do anything to mess it up, so I've stayed far away from little Sadie Cook and my whole family."

Jack reached up with both hands and laced his fingers atop his balding head. "You say you just woke up one day, back in time, forty years younger? Do you think God sent you back on purpose?"

That had crossed my mind. "I've thought about it. I'm able to do things a normal child couldn't do. And I'm able to do things a normal adult couldn't do. It's a unique situation."

"All right. Okay. So, you know all about the original Sadie, who has no clue that she's got a beat-up doppelganger running around?"

I grinned. "I know about the original Sadie, and we don't want her to know she has a beat-up doppelganger."

"Where do your parents live right now?"

"Everett, Washington."

"And what's the area code there?"

"Right now it's 206."

He asked me questions about my brothers and sisters, our house and neighborhood there in Everett. About my father's lousy job and whether I had a bicycle. He asked about notable events my mom would know about. I told him everything I could think of.

"Okay." Jack picked up the receiver from the cradle of his desk phone and called directory assistance for my parents' number, then he called my house.

When Mom answered, I heard her voice through the phone for the first time in years, and it gave me a warm wave of real comfort, like a soft sweater on my face. Like she'd been brought back from the dead. I couldn't talk to her, but at least she lived out there in the world.

Mom and Jack had a good conversation, and I felt his gladness in catching up with her. I returned the ice sock to my face and rested while Jack cleverly dug into my old life. By the end of 15 minutes, I think she'd satisfied him. Which was good, because a toddler started crying, and Mom had to hang up.

I wished I could have spoken to her.

"I always thought your mother had a great sense of humor," Jack chuckled as he returned the phone to its cradle.

I agreed.

"Okay, young lady." He shrugged. "You check out as far as I can tell. You have the freckles. You have the cleft chin. You have three or four cowlicks on your hairline, which she says makes it impossible to give you a good haircut. Can I see your left hand?"

I shook my head. "There's no discoloration in my hand." I knew what he was looking for. "A few months ago in Everett, I flipped off my bike and broke my hand, but a few months ago in Los Angeles, I *didn't*. I remember losing control and flying over the handlebars and how my hand swelled up so huge, so fat, I thought it would pop. I remember how it hurt and hurt, and the doctor couldn't cast it right away because of the swelling. I remember all of it. But, I remember it from 40 years ago, not from this spring."

Jack hunched over his desk and shook his head. "That's so strange. I've never heard of anything like this before. It's a peculiar thing!"

I nodded.

He pointed at the top of his desk. "Teach me some chemistry."

I grinned. I had to ask for a pencil and paper, and I wrote out a few chemical formulas and did simple reactions and conversions for him. I described the work we did at my chemistry lab. He took notes the whole time, and I helped by spelling out certain words for him.

"A-Q-U-A R-E-G-I-A. Aqua regia digestion. We add 0.2 grams of sample to a mixture of hydrochloric acid and nitric acid and cook it for 15 minutes. Then we bulk it to 200 milliliters with deionized water. Metals like silver or lead will go into solution, and we can run that solution through instruments for analysis."

"What's deionized water?"

"It's 'empty' water. Water that has had all the ions removed from it, so they don't interfere with the analysis."

I definitely did not sound like a seven-year-old. I imagined what I looked like to him, a cut and bruised little kid with short hair and scraped knees. I know it felt crazy to hear words like "deionized" and "solution" dropping from my mouth, let alone "aqua regia digestion."

Jack shook his head slowly back and forth. "There's got to be a reason for it. There's a reason you were sent back in time!"

I nodded. "Well, I've been doing my little part to improve the lives of children in the L.A. foster system."

"That's noble. I just wonder what else God has for you. I don't think He sent you here to get battered by the Jeremys of the world."

I frowned at him. I hadn't even thought about it. "He sent Jesus to get battered, and He's way more important than I am."

Jack cringed, and I wondered what the cringe was for. With one hand, he beckoned me over to him. He took my chin in his warm hand and peered at my damaged cheek. "Have you even seen yourself in the mirror?"

I nodded. I looked swollen and bruised, sliced and taped. The ice had soothed the throbbing, but my face still hurt.

"Thank you, kind Jack. But listen, I could have played things safe, and I didn't. I could have stayed with my second foster family, and I'd have a nice, happy life with good people. I chose this instead, with all its increased risks. But even though I got popped in the nose today and my face got cut up, you showed up. I didn't get stuck in some closet to be stabbed to death."

His lips tightened together in the long face before me. Jack didn't look convinced.

I kept going. "That's your job, to help save people's lives. I figure my purpose is to save lives too, and that's what I'm doing. And that means I get into dangerous situations."

"Okay okay!" He pushed himself back. "I give. Is there anything I can do to help you?"

"Yeah. Don't tell anybody about me. Not a person, except your wife. She's okay, but nobody else."

He agreed.

"You promise?"

"I promise."

"And call in a complaint to social services about Jeremy. I'm not my case worker's top priority."

"Sure. I can do that. And I *am* going to file a police report."

"Fine. But one more thing. Please let us all stay at your house until they come and take Jeremy away."

"All of you?" That request startled Jack. "Those other kids too?"

I made large nods. "Please. Please call Anna and warn her. There's five of us. By the way, you two live long lives."

"What?"

"You and Anna. You both live into your 80s."

"Really? Are...are you supposed to tell me that?"

"I don't know. Nobody gave me a rule book."

Like a brick, Jack called his wife and told her we were having an old-fashioned sleepover. He could have pawned us off on some church members, but he didn't. I called Mrs. Robertson at work and told her we were all staying at a friend's because we were afraid of Jeremy.

That night, Jack's dear wife Anna fed us and read to us and tucked us into various spare beds and couches. As we went to sleep, Jack prayed for us, which was the best. I knew that God parted the waters and calmed the storms when Jack prayed. And the next day, Cheryl picked up Jeremy.

I never talked to Jeremy after I gave him all those quotes for *The Secret of NIMH*. I wondered if he got to see the movie at a theater. I wondered how many people thought he knew the future.

PART III

25

Home

Something changed inside me that summer night, the night that Pastor Jack rescued us all from Jeremy. I lay awake in the darkness, listening to Benny's steady breathing on the other couch, and I had a new thought, one I hadn't had during the previous 29 months.

"Could I bond with Benny? A real bond?" I'd purposely kept house-hopping, but I knew Mike had a point. Eventually I needed a real home. What if Benny and the little ones were my permanent brothers? What if I tried to have a family again?

I recognized the frustrated loneliness of my life. My heart still hurt far more, far worse than the wounds on my face. As I lay on Jack's couch, the deep resentment oozed away inside me, and a sadness replaced it. I had waited and waited to bounce back to the future, to wake up one morning in my adult body. It took all that time to accept the cruelty of reality; I'd been forced into this new life permanently.

I replayed Jack's conversation with my mom. A tough heart was no good. I'd become a serial killer myself if I spent the next 37 years alone, walling myself off, moving from people to people all the time. I needed to open myself to another family, a long-lasting family. I should try to bond again.

Not the Robertsons. I liked Benny, but he didn't need me, he just needed Jeremy gone. Not Dr. Wilkins either, even though I loved him. I needed a home with kids, and Doc was best one-on-one.

"Lord," I prayed for the first time in a long time. "Can I have a real family again, one for this new life?"

These little kids with Benny - they needed somebody to love them. I'd met a bunch of other children who needed dependable, solid brothers and sisters, and I kept leaving them. My home hopping had benefits, but maybe there were kids out there who needed me to stay. Who needed me to stick with them and be with them forever.

It didn't happen overnight. The softening of my heart took a few more months. Slowly, slowly, the longing for a home grew, and after 51 placements, I'd finally had enough. On the third anniversary of the day Mike dropped me off in L.A., in February of 1983, I decided it was time to stop. I could not possibly vet all the foster homes in L.A. County, and I'd given Cheryl a taste of the problems to look for. It was time for something different.

I thought of my own mom raising children as a single mother. Single moms needed help, and if I couldn't be there for her, I'd be there for another woman in her honor.

I made the call.

"Cheryl, I'm tired. I'm not going to home hop anymore. Can you find me a family in North Hollywood? A place I can stay long term? A place where there's a single woman with a lot of kids?"

For a few moments, I heard nothing through the phone. Then, Cheryl said, "You're serious? The jumping bean wants stability?"

I'd planned what to say. "I want to go to school. If you help me apply to Los Angeles Valley College, I can start attending classes next fall. I'll find grants or scholarships and take a few credits at a time."

During my years at local libraries, I'd studied whatever interested me. I'd read all the *Little House on the Prairie* books and I'd pushed through a whole set of Jane Austen. For two weeks I had poured over everything I could find on solar power, and another week I learned to fold origami. I focused on genetics and quantum physics or crayoned on pictures of ponies and birds. All along, I'd expected to pursue a degree at some point. I could have my PhD by age 16.

"Dr. Dodge Spicer." That rocked.

I wanted to attend USC, the University of Southern California, but it cost a bazillion dollars. On the other hand, Los Angeles Valley College offered an exceptionally inexpensive, low-key means to earn college credits. It sat in a convenient location between Pastor Jack and Dr. Wilkins, the two men in my life who came closest to knowing my deepest secrets. If I lived in North Hollywood, I could easily take the bus to either one of them.

Cheryl did it. She hooked me up, and that's how I managed to get locked into a foster family a few blocks south of Burbank Ave, a short bike ride to LAVC.

"Here's the thing," Cheryl called me back later. "I found you a mother in that area. She's already fostering four children. George is almost eight. Shamisha and Tamika are five-year-old twins, and Jason is two. Mia says she's already maxed out for her space, but she needs help, and I've already bent so many rules for you, why should today be different?"

"Yep," I said.

"She's in North Hollywood like you asked. I had to push hard to get Mia to take you, though, so you'd better be good. You hear me?"

"I'll be good, Cheryl."

"No swimming pools?"

"I'll be good."

"I explained that you'd be a big help to her, and you will be, right?"

"Cheryl, I promise. She'll be glad I'm there."

"Okay. But you should also know that she's black and the kids are all black and Latino. Are you okay with that?"

"Of course."

Cheryl seemed weirdly uncomfortable. I wondered if her department tried to place white kids with white parents and black kids with black parents. That probably made sense, but it didn't matter to me. In fact, I felt an unexpected excitement about this move. I was about to walk into my home. My home. I'd have a long-term mom and long-term brothers and sisters. I needed to peel that scab off my heart and open up to somebody, or I might as well go turn myself into the CIA and start my training as an assassin right now. Love people or become a Terminator. I didn't see a happy medium.

"When do I meet them?"

"I'll take you over there Friday."

The next day, I boarded a city bus to visit my Dr. Wilkins. I always expected the bus drivers to say, "Where do you think you're going, little boy?" But they never did. I climbed up the steps and boldly told the driver the stop I needed. I plugged in my coins, and the old black man just pointed at the seat nearest him and said, "Sit up by me." As long as I knew where I was going, those bus drivers took me there. Mind you, I didn't tell them how many times I wanted to change buses, I merely told them my next stop and sat near the front of the bus until we got there.

When I knocked on his door, Dr. Wilkins grinned big and wiped his mouth to brush crumbs off his trimmed gray beard. "Dodge! You've practically abandoned me the past two months! I thought you'd been hit by a truck."

I hugged his stomach and dropped into my favorite overstuffed chair between his piano and packed bookshelves. I liked Dr. Wilkins' cozy apartment with its maple floors and tall shelves and plenty of lamps lighting the big chair where I plopped every time I visited.

I plopped there now. "I've got good news! From now on, I'm living in North Hollywood, so I can get here easily. And I'm not gonna leave. I plan to stay there forever, so what do you think about that!"

Dr. Wilkins didn't answer me; he'd disappeared into the kitchen.

"Doctor!" I shouted.

He shouted back, "Just a moment! Tea! You need hot tea, dear girl."

He returned a minute later with a tray and mugs of deliciousness. Doc always added plenty of milk and sugar to mine. The rain gushed down outside, and the 50-degree weather had chilled me. I sipped on my hot tea and breathed in deeply; I'd finally lost my northerner's cold tolerance.

"Did you hear me? I'll be living something like four miles from you. I have a permanent home, so I can see you all the time."

"You must like your new family, then." Disappointment tinned his voice. I knew the good doctor wished I'd made my permanent home with *him*. He'd wanted me, and he'd rarely taken another foster child since I'd left.

"I haven't actually met them yet. I don't know." I said honestly, "They might be a disaster."

Dr. Wilkins' eyes narrowed with worry behind his round glasses. "I know you're joking, Dodge, but they really might be a disaster. You haven't met them, but you've decided you'll stay there forever?"

I shrugged. "It's a single mother with kids. It means a lot of work for me, that's all."

"Well, that's different. That sounds like Christmas morning." Doc settled into his own leathery recliner and frowned at me over his tea.

"I asked for it. That's what I wanted. I wanted a family I could love on. A family that needs me."

He shook his head. "I don't understand you, young lady. You could live here in your own cozy room, and we'd have great larks all the time. You'll be an esteemed concert pianist in no time, and we should go on the road and make millions of dollars."

I laughed.

"But no," he kept going. "You abandon me to go off to odious places where they carve holes in your face."

I started to protest, but he waved me away with his hand. "I know I know I know. I know all about it. You've already told me."

I jumped up and gave his old cheek a kiss. He pretended to push me away, as though affection was too sloppy for a respectable gentleman like him.

"You're the reason I've been able to bear all of it, dear doctor. I'd have descended into a pit of despair if it weren't for you. But, I'm excited!" I flopped back into my chair. "I plan to make them my real mom, my real little brothers and sisters. I mean, if she turns out to be a monster, I guess I'll tell Cheryl, and she'll have to move all of us, but I don't think it will be like that. I'm honestly excited, like Christmas morning really is coming."

Dr. Wilkins shook his head again. "Okay. I'll give my blessing, but only under certain conditions. First, you tell me the truth. No matter what. You won't pretend everything is glorious if it's not."

I sucked down my lovely, just-sweet-enough tea and wiped the back of my hand across my lips. "I can't fib to you anyway. You see through everything, right through my guts to my backbone."

Doc laughed out loud at that. "Okay, and the second condition is that you come see me every week. I'll buy your monthly bus pass. You promise you'll come?"

"Bus pass? You don't have to do that."

"I'm not leaving you an excuse! You'll say to yourself, 'Oh, I have a dollar, and I could spend it on bus fare, or I could spend it on crayons for the children. I must buy crayons.' Yes! Yes, that's what you'd do! While I sit here all lonely, bored out of my mind, starved for charming conversation."

I nodded from behind the rim of my mug. I didn't tell him my bus fare had dropped to 20 cents, because he was right anyway. I filled my mouth and throat, and the comforting liquid warmed my eardrums from within. I did love him. I needed him too.

The old composer and I enjoyed our time together. We joked and laughed and talked about books and news for a solid hour before I had to stoop and pull on my shoes.

"I'd better go. I'm living practically out in Thousand Oaks until Friday, and people will worry if I'm not home by five. They think I'm at the library."

"Thousand Oaks? You took the bus all the way here?"

"Well. Canoga Park."

"Child, you're going to kill me. You shouldn't be riding the bus all over the valley by yourself. It's not safe. Those scars on your face." He grimaced. "I can't believe you let some barbarian do that to you. Next time, you throat punch him. Do you hear me? Throat punch him under my orders."

"I'm not keen on getting hurt any more than you're keen on my getting hurt. I'll be okay."

He frowned. "Call me when you get home tonight, please? And call me on Friday when you get settled in. You worry me."

Friday morning, February 11th, Cheryl drove me across town. We rumbled past apartments and single-family homes to the front of a squat house with tan stucco siding. A few shreds of grass wearied up at me from the patch of dirt in front of the house, and weeds poked out from the cracks in the walkway. I glanced with longing at the green, tidy yard of the neighbor next door, where a mature tree hung heavy with ripe oranges. In my new yard, toy cars and a dented Tonka truck made their grave in a dried-up muddy patch near the front steps.

Cheryl led me up the walkway, and two small brown faces peered at us out the window. One of the little girls had a runny nose, and she rubbed her arm across her face. I didn't want Cheryl see me cringe, but I did, because the mucous of earlier arm wipes had smeared and dried on her cheeks. Somebody needed to wash that child's face.

Cheryl knocked, and a plump black woman threw open the door, her bosoms bursting from a red floral blouse. As soon as words left her mouth, I knew this woman had been raised in a Hispanic home. Puerto Rico? Cuba? Venezuela? I studied her, with her big Afro hair and blue eye shadow and pink lipstick, and I tried to pin her origin on the world map in my head.

"Come. Come inside," she urged us, the Spanish accent thick on her bright lips. "Come in. Jorge, baby you get Cheryl some a*gua, pronto.*"

A Hispanic boy about my age trotted to the fridge and pulled out a chilled jug of water. He poured two glasses and placed them on the oval kitchen table before the two ladies.

Mia pronounced the boy's name, "Hor-hay." I learned that Jorge liked being called "George," but Mia used the Spanish pronunciation.

Jorge had big brown eyes and a dark birthmark on his right cheek. Skinny kid, but cute. I smiled at him and waved. He didn't smile, but he lifted one hand in greeting.

Cheryl stood beside the table and ignored the water Jorge had brought. "Mia, this is Dodge. Dodge, meet Mia."

"Oh, he can't call me 'Mia!'" Mia declared. "Everybody calls me 'Mama.' You call me 'Mama,' Dodge."

I am not joking. Mama Mia.

I giggled, and Jorge's thin eyebrows frowned. I quickly converted my amusement into a nod. "Okay, Mama."

The two little black girls crept from the living room window and peeked shyly into the kitchen. I wanted to pour warm water on a washcloth and clean their crusty faces. The black hair of one girl had been plaited into two braids in the back, and the other wore braided pigtails high on her head, both tied up by those elastic bands with the big pink balls at the ends.

"Those devils are Shamisha and Tamika. They're not this quiet ever. You just watch! They'll turn into spinning gyros in a minute. Light will flash out their eyes and we'll display them at Carnival." Mama placed her hands on her hips and laughed at herself. Then she turned and barked, "Hor-hay! Take Dodge and show him the house."

Dishes piled in the sink under the dusty kitchen window. Black drops spattered the tan tiled floors into the living room and down the hall toward the bedrooms, as though various cups of Kool-Aid had splashed across the room, were badly wiped up, and leftover drops had collected little dust coats. A layer of grime dulled every room. Grimy fingerprints on the once-white walls. Grime on the windows. Even the couch's floral upholstery looked sticky. I wanted Mary Poppins to appear and wiggle her nose.

"Here's our room." A set of bunk beds dominated the wall just inside the door, and the carpet hid under clothes and toys and a pile of other nonsense. I peeked around the corner into the girls' room. It was the same thing, but they had two separate beds on opposite sides: pink framed children's beds, the kind with vinyl-covered mattresses. The whole room smelled of urine, and whatever belongings those girls owned were piled and scattered over the middle of the carpet.

Yep, this was home.

Jorge grabbed my arm and hauled me back into my new bedroom. "I sleep on the top bunk. You sleep with Jason on the bottom bunk."

I pulled back a gritty comforter and found a small boy underneath in just his cloth diapers. His little Afro poofed out all fuzzy over his head and his chest rose and fell slowly in sleep. Kissable baby cheeks.

"Jorge!" Mama called from the other room. "Get the girls ready for school! The bus comes in 10 minutes, and I can't be late for work."

"Bianca's not here yet!" Jorge called back. "Call her!"

"Find the girls clean shirts!" Mama called.

"They don't have any! Bianca needs to do laundry!"

I wandered back to the kitchen.

"Our laundry machine has been broken," Mama sighed to Cheryl. "I've called the landlord to get it fixed, but I hear nothing from him. We have to go to the laundromat tonight."

Cheryl raised her eyebrows at me. I smiled and shrugged back.

"Jorge!" Mama shouted again. "Find something these girls can wear to school! Hurry!" She marched over and grabbed the little girl with the ponytails and tucked her up under one arm. "Tamika baby, we're going to wash you up." Mama hauled her to the sink and scrubbed water all over her face. A dish towel was applied next, and Mama set Tamika down, damp and pink cheeked. She looked better crust-free.

"You good, Dodge?" Cheryl asked me.

I nodded.

"Okay. Let's get your bags."

Amid the whirlwind of readying Tamika and Shamisha for school, I walked out to Cheryl's car to collect my duffel bag and backpack - all my belongings in the world. I said goodbye to Cheryl like I'd done 51 other times, and I didn't even watch her drive away. I hauled in my bags and set them on the top of the television. It was the only spot in the house I trusted.

"Mama," Jorge begged as she pushed him out the door. "Mama, make Bianca wash clothes. The washer works. She just told you it was broken because she's lazy, Mama."

"Okay okay okay," Mama shoved a backpack into his chest. "Go to school. I have to call her right now." She guided the three children out the door and closed it behind them, then pulled the receiver off a green phone on the wall and started shouting Spanish words into it. Besides "Bianca!" I didn't understand a thing. I realized I'd have to learn Spanish.

26

Laundry

Bianca arrived ten minutes later, a skinny Hispanic woman in sweats. She skulked in, glazed over. Had she gotten high first thing that morning or had she partied all night? Mama gave Bianca a scowl and stared her up and down. Then she started on a tirade in Spanish, and Bianca listlessly settled into a kitchen chair and took the scolding without answering a word. Finally Mama turned to me.

"I have to go to work. Can you make Jason a bottle?"

I nodded.

"And Bianca has to wash his diapers, okay?" Mama turned to the woman slumped at the kitchen table. "Wash his diapers, Bianca!" Then she marched out and slammed the door.

As soon as Mama disappeared, Bianca made her way to the couch in the living room and lowered herself onto it. I think she fell asleep before her head hit the cushions.

I trudged through the small house and opened every cupboard and door. The kitchen and living room filled the front of the house, with the front door smack in the middle between them. Straight across from the front door, a hallway ran toward the back of the house and dead-ended with Mama's big bedroom. Two bedrooms sat on the right side of the hall and a big bathroom/ laundry room sat on the left. Just past the bathroom, I found a hall closet and a door that opened outside. That was it. That was the whole house.

I walked out that hallway door onto a small concrete patio. Steel clothesline posts stood upright at the back of the lot, but the cord had broken and lay limp in the dirt between them. The rest of the narrow yard gazed back at me all bleak and barren, mottled by broken toys and weeds.

I peeked through a hole in the fence into the neighbor's beautiful back yard. He had a patio surrounded by giant pots filled with flowers. Lemon trees shaded the grass. Palm trees graced the sky above me as I turned around and around. I liked the neighborhood itself, but my new weedy, ugly back yard needed love.

"What a dismal place." This was it, though. This is what I'd asked for. Mama was a single mother, and Bianca obviously wasn't helping.

I returned to my new bedroom, where little Jason wiggled and sat up. I reached out my arms to him, and he pulled his little shoulder up and frowned away from me. "Get lost," his pouty face said.

"Hi Jason," I smiled at him. "Do you want those old diapers off?"

He considered me a second, then he nodded.

I lay him on his back, pulled off his plastic pants, and unpinned his diapers. They were soaked. I ran them to the washing machine in the bathroom and dropped them in.

Time to get potty trained, kid. He had a rash, so I washed him off in the bathtub and let him run around naked.

I jogged into the kitchen and rummaged through the cupboards. Canned food and a bag of spilled flour and rice… there was nothing good in there. At the top of the refrigerator, I found a box of Nilla Wafers. Haha!

"Jason!" I handed the little boy one cookie. He smiled and shoved it into his mouth. "Jason. If you go poop on the toilet, I'll give you another cookie. Okay?" I set him on the toilet and let him suck on his cookie chunk.

Next, I peeled the sheets and blankets off all the kids' beds and dragged them into the bathroom. I filled the washing machine with sheets, dumped in powdered soap, and turned the knob. Water began to fill the machine. Phew.

Jason sat on the toilet and watched all this with interest. I jogged into the kitchen and hunted under the sink for bleach or Pine-Sol, anything I could use as a disinfectant. Lysol spray. Good. I grabbed the bottle and sprayed down all four of the mattresses. Jason slid off the toilet and threw himself repeatedly onto the pile of blankets on the bathroom floor. I looked into the toilet. It was empty.

Maybe I should feed him. I just didn't want to find a little poopie pie party on the kitchen floor in an hour.

I pulled a towel off the wall rack to dry off the mattresses. Plastic covering on the girls' mattresses made this easy, but the ones on the bunk bed had to air dry. I opened the windows to let in a breeze. Rains earlier that week had washed any hints of hazy smog from the sky, and rich blue spread out above me.

Spare sheets. I hunted through the bedroom closets and bathroom shelves and hall closet and found nothing. Under the beds? No spare sheets for the kids' beds. No mattress covers either.

I scrubbed Jason's little hands in the bathroom sink and set him at the table while I scrambled us up a few eggs. Jason stood on a chair and used his newly clean fingers to stuff eggs into his mouth. That worked for me. He drank some water, and we sat on the carpet in our bedroom and sorted through the piles of stuff.

Dirty clothes, one pile. Baby toys, one pile. Coloring books, blocks, screwdrivers and nails and other things that didn't belong with baby toys, Candy Land game pieces and Sorry cards. The clothes and every single stuffed animal ended up on the bathroom floor in front of the washer. The same thing happened in the girls' room. Barbie dolls with matted hair and beads and coloring books and crayons and hair things and Cooties body parts and ponies and trucks and cars and trash and erasers and Play-Doh. Augh! They had mashed Play-Doh into the carpet!

Jason helped by taking items back out of the piles. He generously scattered the Candy Land pieces when I wasn't looking.

I asked the naked boy, "Jason, do you have to go poop?"

He shook his head.

"Tell me if you have to go poop. If you go in the toilet, I'll give you a cookie, right? You're a big boy now. Are you a baby who has to wear diapers?"

He shook his head, "No."

"That's right! You're a big boy! And you want a cookie. So, go poop in the toilet."

He ran into the bathroom and climbed up on the commode. I hoped he'd actually go.

I got a mixing bowl of warm water and poured in a little Lysol, then I dropped all the plastic toys I could find into it. I was tempted to throw away the Barbies with their matted hair, but I didn't. Somebody would wail and cry for those Barbie dolls, I just knew it, so I washed them with all the other toys. I washed out the toy buckets and bins, and I set the disinfected, scrubbed toys on towels to dry.

Jason returned and dumped over the Lysol bowl for me.

"Jason..." I groaned. Well. The carpets needed to be cleaned too.

By that time, the first load of sheets had finished, so I dragged in a chair and climbed up to pull out the clean sheets. I had to bend half my body into the washer to pull the sheets from the bottom, but I did it. Then, I hopped down and shoved the sheets into the dryer. I quickly filled the washer with a load of blankets and started it.

Then I hit a roadblock. The dryer didn't work. Nope. It made a horrible crunching noise when I turned it on, so I opened the door to shut it off. I'd have to use the clothesline.

I trotted out to the backyard and surveyed the cord in the dirt.

Yeah. Yeah, I could fix it.

While Jason played with toys in the weeds, I spent time untying the cord from one of the posts. I climbed on a chair and used a fork to loosen those knots, and it took forever. Plenty of line dangled at the end, though, past the knots. Once I'd finally wrestled the cord loose from the post, I gathered the two cord ends in the middle of the yard and tied those two sliced ends together. Then, I wrapped the end back around the steel post, heaving on it as hard as I could with my 7 ½ years of strength to make the cord as taut as possible. I tied it up and surveyed my work. I had one cord, just one line 15 feet long. It drooped a little in the middle, but it provided enough room to hang those sheets.

By the time I'd tossed the sheets over the line and straightened them, the washing machine had spun to a stop. I stuck Jason on the potty again, added more blankets to the washer and started the third load.

The sun shone down that February day in North Hollywood, warming the back yard to about 65 degrees by mid-morning. The sheets dried fast enough, and the dust didn't even kick up. Hoorah.

"Poop." Jason spoke his first word to me in the hall.

He'd slid off the toilet and left a smear, but that was better than a poopie party. He'd done it. He'd succeeded in his mission.

"Good job, Jason!" I cleaned off the toilet, then set him back up on it and got him all wiped up. "Good job! You have to tell me when you're done next time. Tell me, 'I'm all done!'"

We washed our hands, and I gave him his Nilla Wafer. "You're a big boy now!"

Serious, he nodded with the cookie in his mouth.

I spent the next four hours cleaning those rooms and washing clothes, and Jason helped me by pulling all the pots and pans out of a lower cupboard and banging on them in the kitchen. There were no clothes pins, so I just draped little shirts and pants over the line. After a bit, I flipped the clothes over, like floppy pancakes, so that the damp underside of the shirts and pants could dry faster. I ended up laying out the tiny socks on the patio, because they kept falling into the weeds.

I did hit a few problems. First, I ran out of laundry powder. I stared in dejection at the cardboard in the bottom of the box and thought I should go meet the neighbors. Jason and I visited eight houses with a Tupperware bowl and laundry cup, and we begged a cup of detergent at each house. Two elderly neighbors donated despite broken English; I *so* needed to learn Spanish. Jason and I had success, though! We soon collected enough detergent for four more loads, which was about all I needed at that point.

My second problem was ... no mattress covers for the beds. I couldn't bear to make the beds with those thin sheets on bare plastic. It was a fact of the universe that fitted sheets wore out faster than flat sheets, and people always had more flat sheets than they needed. I'd take advantage of that.

I visited neighbors in the other direction this time, travelling door-to-door with my most hopeful attitude. "Good morning, do you have any top sheets you don't need anymore? I'm doing a project." I did learn *sábana*, the Spanish word for "bed sheet."

This time, I found two Jewish women who asked if I was making costumes for Purim. Why not? I'd never celebrated Purim in my life, but huzzah!

After six houses, I found one wrinkled old woman who said, "Just a minute." She brought me back a multicolored pile of cotton flat sheets and dumped them into my arms. "Take them away. You just freed up a shelf in my hall closet." I hauled home this great treasure, and I made all the beds.

As the afternoon warmed, I woke Bianca to deal with the bucket of dirty diapers in the bathroom.

"I'm not touching those things, Bianca. That's too gross. And you need to scrub the bathroom too. Mama's going to be so mad that I cleaned the house while you slept on the couch the whole time."

The vacuum disappointed me. I tried to vacuum the carpets in the bedrooms, but that vacuum didn't suck. It sucked, because it didn't suck. So. Carpets would have to wait another day.

In the kitchen, I returned the pots and pans to the cupboard, but I didn't do the dishes. Those all had to wait. By the time I'd put away the toys and books and crayons and games and folded the clean clothes and made neat piles on Momma's bed…by the time I'd washed and dried all the blankets and made up the beds with clean sheets, complete with folded sheets underneath acting as mattress covers… by the time I'd bathed Jason, tucked him into fresh shorts and put him in bed with a bottle, I wanted to collapse. I took a shower, pulled on clean clothes, and snuggled with Jason in our nice fresh bed.

"We need to rent a carpet cleaner," I told Jason as I dropped off to sleep. "Wash the carpets."

I discovered several things about Mama that day. First, she wasn't a stupid person. She didn't believe Bianca for a moment when Bianca claimed credit for all the cleaning. I awoke in the early evening when I heard yammering in the kitchen.

"Dodge!" Mama called me. "DODGE!" I slipped out of bed and stumbled back down the hall.

"Yes, Mama?"

"Did you help Bianca do the laundry?"

I shook my head. "No, Mama. I did the laundry while Bianca slept all morning."

Bianca's eyes opened wide, and she began explaining, pointing at me and pointing at the bathroom. Spanish or not, I could tell she was lying her guts out.

"Is it true?" Mama asked me. "Did the landlord come by and fix the washer and dryer? Finally! I have been asking him for two weeks!"

"The dryer works now, doesn't it, Bianca?"

She nodded up and down, then spoke with a heavy accent, "Yes, the washer and dryer works. I cannot do laundry because they do not works, and the landlord comes by and fix them, and that's why I do laundry."

I shook my head. "No, Mama. The landlord didn't come by, and the dryer isn't fixed. I dried everything on the clothesline out back."

I led them down the hallway to the back door, and Mama saw the last of the kids' clothes hanging in the dimming evening light.

We walked back inside and Bianca shoved me ahead of her.

"Bianca cleaned the bathroom, though," I told Mama. "At least she was supposed to. If the diapers are washed, she's the one that washed them. I wasn't going to touch the diapers."

Mama glared at Bianca, then went off on her in Spanish. That seemed to make up the bulk of their relationship – Mama bellowing at Bianca in words I couldn't understand.

"Did Bianca make the beds, Dodge?"

"No, Mama. You know she didn't. And I tried to vacuum, but the vacuum is broken. If you're paying Bianca, I think you should stop. We could use that money to buy a vacuum and rent a carpet cleaner at the grocery store."

Bianca understood that all right. She marched my way with a hand up ready to smack me, so I dodged and dashed out the front door. I found the three other children home from school and playing in the yard. Bianca chugged my way, all red-faced and furious. She chased me out to the street, and I laughed at her.

"Go home, Bianca!" I dodged her again and ran back inside to Mama, where I shut and locked the door. Bianca banged on the other side, screaming profanities in Spanish. It's easy to tell when someone's cursing at you, no matter what the language is.

I took a deep breath. "I'll get the kitchen and floors all scrubbed up tomorrow. And we really need a carpet cleaner. The carpets in the kids' rooms are gross."

Mama grinned down at me. "Good Lord. Cheryl told me over and over, 'Oh, he's like another adult. Mia, you want him, because he'll be a big help to you!' She kept saying that, and I didn't believe her. She practically begged me to take you, but I thought, 'No little boy will be a big help to me!' Jorge is a good boy, but he would never say, 'Oh, tomorrow I'm going to scrub the kitchen. Tomorrow let's wash the carpets.'" Mama laughed out loud, a big cheerful laugh.

I smiled. "You're my mama now. This is my home. I want our home to be nice."

Bianca's screams muffled through the door.

"Will you tell Bianca to go home now?" I asked Mama. "Did she even clean the bathroom?"

Mama and I both walked down the hall and peeked through the door. Crud still covered the sink and the mirror. The tub had been filled with water, and diapers soaked in it.

"I'll clean the bathroom too. Sometime this week."

"Thank you." Mama sighed. Then she bit her lip. "Please wash my sheets and blankets too?"

I nodded. "Yes, Mama. But only if you tell Bianca not to come back. And I need more laundry detergent."

27 כז

Community

Within three days, I had cleaned all the carpets, washed all the tiled floors, wiped all the dirty smudges off the walls and thoroughly cleaned and organized the kitchen. Jason and I pulled every jar of pickles and every bit of Tupperware out of the refrigerator. Armed with a cloth and bucket of Lysol water, I scoured the fridge front to back and washed all the drawers. I attacked the couch upholstery with the beautiful carpet cleaner, and it made such a difference! I stopped feeling afraid to touch the furniture. I even washed all the dusty crud and fingerprints off the windows.

Jason made some mistakes, but by the end of the week we were out of Nilla Wafers, and he faithfully climbed on the potty himself every day. Mama put him in diapers for bedtime, now that she had clean diapers to pin on him. By the end of the month, his diapers were dry every morning, so she stopped bothering.

Mama took us all shopping for Valentine's Day, and she got Jason big boy underwear. I'd outgrown my first set, so I begged for Captain America underclothes. I know it sounds silly, but they soothed my soul somehow. And since I got Captain America, of course Jorge had to get Spider-Man. He ran around the house that night, shooting webs and jumping off the couch.

After a week, I called Cheryl and urged her to stop by. "Mama makes the kids put their stuff away before they go to bed. She's gotten super intense about it. They take baths every night."

"And Mia? Is she good to you?"

"Yeah, she's a warm, sweet person. She just has to work all day."

I didn't tell Cheryl that we'd fired Bianca. I didn't tell her I stayed home alone with Jason.

Mama came home tired in the evenings, so meals became my next project. She bought a lot of chicken and rice and beans, so Monday night when Mama opened the door after work, Jorge and I grinned all big and showed her the chicken and rice we'd made. The girls played with their ugly Barbie dolls in the other room, and we played as chefs.

I liked Jorge a lot. Maybe he lacked genius superpowers, but he had a good thinker in his head. We spoke directly to each other and said exactly what we thought, and I liked that. I recognized in Jorge the maturity that forms in children forced into roles of responsibility. He complained every day about school, but he had a practical mind.

When I suggested we start making dinner, Jorge jumped on it. I had no clue we'd discovered his special passion; Jorge loved to prepare food. At first, he watched me and did what I asked, but before long he figured out how to make things on his own.

"Just read the cookbook," he said, like it was no big deal. Either I had great teaching skills or Jorge innately understood cuisine, but he did a remarkably good job with or without me. He didn't get bored with it, either, and over the months and years he became a thoughtful chef. Early on, we produced tacos one night and vegetable soup the next, chicken enchiladas and chili. Jorge was the salad king right off; I never met a kid who loved fresh vegetables more than he did.

He got irritated when I hovered. I watched nervously as he climbed on a chair with a big knife to slice up bell peppers on the cutting board.

"I won't chop off my fingers, *pendejo*," Jorge snarled. "I know how to cut things."

I let him alone and watched as he cautiously pushed that butcher knife through carrots and cucumbers. He'd moved in with Mama first, and he was four months older than I was. I had no authority over him. Jorge never did chop open an artery and bleed to death, but one week after my arrival, he slipped while slicing an onion and gashed his left thumb. Blood dripped everywhere.

He hollered, "Oh wow. Oh wow! A little help here!"

Tamika saw the blood from her perch at the table. She burst into shrieking laughter and scurried into the other room. No clue. Maybe she thought Jorge was playing a joke.

I slammed open the dish towel drawer and clasped the towel around Jorge's thumb.

"Hold this tight!"

The blood stopped splashing across the floor while I ran to the bathroom for medical supplies. I found a mostly empty box of Band-Aids, one that still held butterfly bandages.

"Good good." I adored butterfly bandages. I performed emergency first aid in the end, filling the wound with crazy glue and bandaging it closed. We wiped the blood off the counter and floor, then I threw away the red-splattered onion and started again. The spaghetti turned out great, and the girls didn't tell Mama on us.

I couldn't stop Jorge from cutting up vegetables or cheese, but he listened to my pointers. "Cut the onion in half first, so there's a nice fat bottom on it. That way it won't roll."

He grinned, "Like Mama?"

We both giggled, but it was lighthearted. We both loved Mama.

Mama worried at first. We didn't tell her about the few dishes we broke or the food we burned or other mistakes we made. We didn't mention the wounds we gave ourselves. As weeks passed, she relaxed and grew accustomed to order in her domain.

In a perfect world, no authorities should have given Mama charge of five children all under eight-years-old. We clearly shouldn't have stayed alone in the afternoon, cooking on the stove by ourselves. Mama had no capacity to care for us and raise us by herself while working all day, and she couldn't afford to pay for reliable adult help. But, she trusted a scarred up little foster child, and we made it work.

Jorge wanted order and peace too, and we plotted to give ourselves the home we both needed. We took the little kids outside and played hide-and-seek and tag and CIA, spying on the other houses in the neighborhood. We turned off the television after cartoons were over and read books together. I saw in Jorge's eyes a calm that hadn't existed before. That peace on his face satisfied something deep inside me.

Not that the little girls didn't fight and scream and try to claw each other's eyes out. Not that they didn't change their clothes five times an afternoon and leave them scattered everywhere. Not that Jason didn't sit and wail over stupid things.

Jorge kept failing math until I wrestled with him and insisted we go over his math homework every afternoon together. I conquered him and sat on his chest.

He shouted, "Fine! But you have to let me teach you Spanish!"

"Okay!" I shouted back. "I wanted to learn Spanish anyway!"

"Good! Get off me!"

"Okay!"

On Sundays, Mama marched us down to the Catholic church for Mass. She wanted Jorge and me to take catechism classes, but we both refused. She threatened us and pleaded, but it was the one area we plain defied her. We had our separate reasons for resisting, and neither of us gave in. Neither of us wanted to give up our Saturdays.

I said, "We go to Mass! We believe Jesus paid for our sins; we're not going to Hell."

She didn't look so sure.

"We'll read the Bible every night before bed!" Jorge told her.

Mama still didn't look sure.

I had reserved Saturdays for my visits to Dr. Wilkins! And Jorge couldn't bear taking classes on the weekends that were his sanctuary from school. So, Mama gave us both a break. She took the little kids for bus rides on Saturdays, Jorge stayed home and watched television, and I took off toward Burbank.

But that's how I got my family.

Then, Jorge and I found something unexpected. We found our community.

I told Jorge we had to celebrate Purim so I wasn't a complete liar about the bed sheets. I didn't know what to do, so little Jason and I took a morning to interrogate our Jewish neighbors. The ladies gave me a list of ideas about dressing up and making food.

But then it rained Purim weekend. So much rain.

Jorge decided to bake cupcakes, and the twins helped us decorate them with mangled frosting and heaps of sprinkles. We dressed up in our bed sheets to look like two Esthers and a Mordecai, a baby Persian king and a no-good rotten Haman. During a break in the downpour, we toted those cupcakes around to our neighbors, Jews and Gentiles alike. Delighted, the Jewish ladies gabbed and gabbed and fussed over us. They pulled us into their homes and fed us these triangle-shaped date pastries and played music for us. Soon the little kids ran around and chased each other until they tripped over their bed sheets and their costumes came off.

That night, Mama tried to read the book of Esther for us while we colored at the coffee table. She only made it through two chapters, though, because the girls got energetic in their booing of Haman in chapter three. That's what the old ladies had told us to do: we had to boo the bad guy. Over and over, Mama told the girls to quiet down, because she couldn't read through all their booing. After they went to bed, Mama finished the story for Jorge and me. And it was so great! Intrigue! Good guys! Bad guys! Irony! How had I never heard the story of Esther before?

Something so small as dressing up on Purim opened our door to the neighborhood. I felt more connection to the folks around me than I'd had since I'd lived on my own street 30-odd years in the future. With that little act, my family grew and spread. The folks next-door urged us to pick their oranges and lemons. The Jewish ladies waved at us whenever we walked by.

The celebration affected Jorge a lot. One little old Hispanic man stood and talked in Spanish with Jorge for 20 minutes the day we brought those cupcakes between the rain showers. The man wanted somebody to talk to, even a seven-year-old kid. It moved Jorge.

"My *abuelo* died last year," Jorge confessed to me that night. "I didn't even get to see him for two years, because..." He looked away from me.

"Because your mom?"

He nodded. "Because my mom ran away. He was in a home, and then he died, and I didn't even get to see him. I think I'll go visit Mr. Sanchez again tomorrow."

Jorge didn't have to say more than that. It was easy to fill in all the blanks for him. I had Dr. Wilkins, didn't I?

Something sparked inside Jorge because of it - because of Purim and the old Jewish ladies and Mr. Sanchez - and it didn't take much for his spark to poof into flames inside me too.

"You know what?" Jorge said. "We need to make our place great. You and me, we both been in bad places, and this is a good place. We need to make our neighborhood the best place to live anywhere. I want everybody in the whole world to wish they lived here."

We sat at the kitchen table, eating tacos we'd made, and my heart broke open. In that moment, I felt the sweet pain of true connection. Good one, Jorge. I wanted to have the best neighborhood ever too.

Jorge and I brainstormed and penciled out ways to improve the little world where we lived. We could walk dogs. We could check in on the old people now and then.

Jorge finished a bite of his taco. "You know what we should do? We should put a garden in our front yard, something that's easy to water. Garden boxes. We can grow vegetables for food, and if we make our front yard pretty, it makes the whole neighborhood better."

Jorge liked his idea a lot. It involved wood and construction and screws and dirt – all things that appealed to him.

"Let's go out tomorrow and collect boards," I said. "We can find all kinds of broken boards at construction sites."

But this was another occasion in which my 20-20 hindsight failed me. There was no exploring construction sites the next day.

28

Storm

I awoke on the morning of March 1st to thunderclaps that shook the house.

Shamisha ran into my room and pulled me out of bed. "Look!" She bounced up and down on her toes, pointing out the window where rain pelted the neighbor's house. Fat drops of water bounced and sprayed on the roof tiles. Winds gusted past us, whistling, shaking the telephone poles. Lightning flashed, and Shamisha tugged and tugged me up and out of the room. Clouds darkened the house, and I flipped on the light just as the electricity flickered and shut off.

Mama marched down the hall. "I don't like this. This isn't good."

"The power is out!" Jorge declared in triumph. "You think school is cancelled?"

"I don't know," Mama murmured.

"Can we stay home anyway! I'll make breakfast! And we'll all get into Mama's bed and tell ghost stories!" Jorge ran to the stove to put on hot water, but of course the stove didn't work without electricity.

All six of us huddled in the living room and watched the storm out the windows. Mama collected candles and placed them in the kitchen and the bathroom to add light to those darker rooms. A booming rumbled far away. We didn't know it, but a tornado bounced around in downtown Los Angeles 12 miles south of us, tearing up homes and businesses and leaving a big hole in the roof of the L.A. Convention Center. Another tornado hit out in Pasadena, and mud slides dropped houses down hillsides and overwhelmed portions of the Pacific Coast Highway. In various towns around L.A. County, roofs collapsed under the water, and floods washed homes away. Thousands of people had to be evacuated.

We gathered up on the couch under blankets and admired the roaring storm. When it started to hail, we jumped up and pressed our noses against the cold windows. Hailstones smashed and bounced across the road outside, leaving chunks as big as golf balls. Thrilled, the girls bounced up and down, up and down. Tireless pistons.

I later learned that Queen Elizabeth II had come to visit, and the Navy provided her with a bus to traverse the flooded streets in Long Beach on her way to meet with President Reagan.

We didn't get washed away, and our little North Hollywood home wasn't sucked up in a tornado. A minor earthquake rumbled through in the middle of the day as an added bonus. Shamisha hugged Jason through the scariest rain-pounding, rumbling moments, but even he seemed to cautiously enjoy the excitement.

Mama made turkey sandwiches, and we shared some of Mama's precious orange pop. We all snuggled together in a pile on Mama's bed, and she told us the scariest ghost stories I'd ever heard.

The storm may have destroyed some people's lives, but it provided Jorge and me with all kinds of treasures. After dinner that week, Jorge and I explored the streets for garden box materials. We found bits of metal roofing and a half roll of heavy plastic sheeting on the side of the road. Huge industrial dumpsters offered us gifts of lumber, and day after day we dragged home ugly boards and sheets of shingles.

I begged Mama for a few dollars, and we returned from a yard sale victorious with a hammer and roofing nails, a hand saw and screws and screw bits. Jorge's Mr. Sanchez lent us a screw gun and a shovel, and soon we had everything we needed. We used a string to make straight lines, and we dug holes and planted our posts. Our boards weren't cedar or pressure treated, and I feared they'd rot away. We lined the inside of the boxes with plastic sheets or corrugated roofing. We nailed the asphalt shingles on the outside of the boxes so the wood wouldn't weather to dirt in just a few years.

Jorge and I built three garden boxes, all equal sizes, all the same distance apart, and we added cardboard and crumpled old newspapers and branches to the bottom. Then, we hauled soil from vacant lots to dump into them. That took a lot of work, so we finally decided to move dirt from our own back yard. We dug a pit on one side of the lot and hauled a wagon full at a time until our 4x8-foot garden boxes were half full.

The girls helped us move the dirt from the back yard. "Please let us pull the wagon!" Tamika begged. "Pleeeeeeease!"

"I don't know." Jorge frowned, absolutely pulling a Tom Sawyer on her. "I don't know if you're strong enough. The wagon might tip over."

"We're strong!" Shamisha stood proud, hands on her hips. "We're so strong! We're so strong we can do it."

Jorge shook his head. "No, you'll give up. You'll get tired and go inside to watch cartoons."

"No we won't! You jerk, we're not lazy!" The girls didn't give up. They pulled that wagon from the back to the front 20 times. Endless energy. I couldn't believe their stubborn stamina.

While other children played on their Ataris, Jorge and I trekked around to our neighbors and collected grass clippings. We dumped them in our boxes, along with any food scraps or eggshells or coffee grounds that anybody would give us. There were no farms around us. I didn't know a single person with chickens or goats for manure, but the closest pet shop donated several bags of stinky shredded paper and a variety of dead feeder fish and frogs. All of it went in our garden boxes. We covered the top of our organic matter with more dirt from the back yard, turned it all over with the shovel, then poured water on it with the hose. Soil. We were determined to build soil.

I begged Mama for another few dollars and ordered packages of red wigglers, just to make sure our gardens had worms. When they came, Shamisha made a practical observation.

"We gotta cover them up or the birds will eat them."

She and Tamika used their hands to dig trenches down the middle of our boxes and hid every worm under the soil. They got sticks to guard their worms from birds. Jorge and I tried to stay serious about it, but the girl soldiers taunted and threatened the birds, and we had to go inside to hide our laughter.

"I'll knock you in the head, you stupid robin."

"I'll turn you inside out and pull that worm right through you."

"You best stay in that tree, grub gobbler."

"That's right, grub gobbler! Earwig eater."

"Snake sniffer!"

Mama bought us seedlings for tomatoes and bell peppers, squash, cucumbers and beans. We planted onion seeds and cilantro and basil and oregano. We dug a few holes in the backyard and filled them with our souped up soil and planted cantaloupe and watermelon where they'd have room to grow and spread.

The whole project took us about four weeks, but we worked with a steady obsession, and Mama didn't stop us. At the end, we returned the drill and shovel to Mr. Sanchez, along with a pile of cookies as a thank you.

Of course, we now had a big pit in the back yard, about six feet wide and two feet deep. Lumpy. Ugly. Jorge and I stood over it one day, and we both had the same idea. We lined our pit with some of our plastic sheeting and filled it a foot deep with water for the kids to splash in on hot days. We had ourselves a pool.

In the summer, we picked tomatoes and peppers and cantaloupes. Sunflowers towered over our walkway. In the winter, we had turnips and winter squash, lettuce and spinach and cabbages. Our neighbor next-door gave us free reign to pick his oranges, and we gave him free reign to pick our carrots.

Foster kids often go back to their biological parents, or something goes wrong and they're moved to another house. Not us. Mama kept us all. Jason's parents had died. The girls' auntie never came for them, and Jorge's mother appeared to have run away forever.

And so it went for two years. Jason grew into a four-year-old ready to attend preschool. Tamika and Shamisha told hilarious stories. Jorge got better at math, and I learned to speak broken Spanish.

Studio City

I'm getting ahead of myself. I skipped a few important facts about those two years, so I'd better back up a bit before I tell what happened with Tiberius.

First, I started college at age eight. I took classes starting in the fall of 1983, but I don't want to bother you too much about it. I wish I could tell you I had adventures at school, but I didn't. No nuclear scientists created giant mutant lizards in the basement, much to my disappointment. I dropped Jason off with a neighbor during the mornings, and I took British Lit and Physics and Art one semester or Calculus and Spanish and European History another. Not too many classes, and lots of review. I sat in the lecture halls, and my feet barely reached the floor.

I felt embarrassed around the other students at first, but they made me a bit of a celebrity. One group of 20-somethings invited me to eat lunch with them every day, and they shared their cafeteria food with me. The girls told me I was cute and asked how I got the cool war paint scars on my cheekbone. They called me a "heartbreaker," which made me laugh. Sometimes I forgot I really did look like a boy.

I studied the two pink, mostly-parallel knife scars on my face and realized they sorta resembled one stripe of war paint. Maybe. No, not really.

Omygoodness. The worst thing, the thing I'd forgotten, was that I couldn't buy a laptop in 1983 and had no access to the Internet. I had to do all my research at the library, using *books*. I had to write out rough drafts by hand, then type up papers on an electric typewriter.

Yeesh. It took so much time! The library did have desktop computers with writing programs, but they were always being used by someone bigger.

No professor ever smiled when I appeared in their classrooms, by the way. They never seemed happy to see me that first day. I didn't want them asking for my mom in front of everybody, so I always tried to go up and speak to them right away.

"Hi. I'm Dodge Journey Spicer. You see me there on your list? That's me. No, sir, I'm not here with a parent; I'm a student. Um, yes, they call me a prodigy, but… what? Yes, I know my presidents. The one on the ten-dollar bill? That's … that's Alexander Hamilton, but he wasn't a president. Oh. That's Benjamin Franklin. You carry around $100 bills in your wallet? Nope, he wasn't a president either. No, sir, neither of them. Yes, hahaha, I do eat a lot of vegetables. Yes, my mom is proud of me."

They all asked me questions, those professors. It didn't matter what they looked like: tall, short, fat thin, black, white, male, female, ugly, charming, doofy, clean-cut. They all wanted to test me at the beginning, just to see if I was real.

"Hi. I'm Dodge Journey Spicer. I'm there on your list for this class. I'm eight-years-old. Yes, I like British authors very much. Favorites? C.S. Lewis and Roald Dahl. No, no not Ronald. Roald. Roald Dahl. He wrote *Charlie and the Chocolate Factory*? He's so much fun. In fact, I just realized that he's still alive. What? Oh, I've read Jane Austen and Shakespeare, and I like Dickens too. Yes ma'am, *Oliver Twist* and *David Copperfield* and *Nicholas Nickleby*… Maybe because he writes about orphans a lot? Yes, I can go sit down now."

Good old Roald Dahl. I discovered a gloriously chaotic treasure in the form of Dutton's Books a few blocks from our house - a quiet place of my own. I walked through the store's front door on Laurel Canyon Boulevard into a maze of shelves and stacks of printed joy. I often took Jason with me, and we read children's books together. When I needed alone time, I tucked myself away with *The BFG* or *James and the Giant Peach.* I needed Roald Dahl's cheery humor after research papers and derivatives.

Dave Dutton and his wife Judy ran the store, and Dave's blue eyes fascinated me. He had bright blue eyes, almost icy blue, eyes that adored books even more than I did.

"Here's a new one, Dodge." Dave handed me Roald Dahl's book *The Witches* one day. That tickled me. It was about a little boy who got metamorphosed into a mouse at a witch convention. With his new mouse body he could jump and sneak and swing by his tail, but he still had the brain of a boy. He decided to feed the witches their own mouse potion, and he eliminated the witch problem in England.

I grinned and thanked Dave. I didn't tell him that I'd gone through a metamorphosis of my own. I just curled up in a corner to enjoy my new book.

I told you, though, I don't want to bother you about all that. Far more interesting things happened during the two years I lived with Mama.

Like the day I met Denzel.

Seriously. Serious as *The Equalizer*.

One pleasant March evening, shortly after Jorge turned eight, we children ate our vegetable beef soup and munched our bread, and then two of us – we won't say who – started fighting over whether it was time to pull the new pudding out of the fridge.

Mama declared, "All of you, go for a walk! I cannot handle you all arguing over stupid things!" Then she chased us out the door.

We oldest four stumbled down the sidewalk, leaving Jason behind in the house.

"I told you it had to stay in there longer," Shamisha sniffed.

"I knowww," Tamika answered. "I just wanted to taste it. I just wanted to check."

"I wish we could go play basketball. Do we have a basketball?" I asked nobody in particular.

Jorge said, "There's a park. On the other side of the highway."

We tramped down back streets onto Magnolia Boulevard and out to the park, block after block after block due east. When we reached the grass, the kids dashed after each other, screaming and doing the things they were supposed to do at a park on a pleasant evening in March.

I liked this green oasis. Giant sycamores offered a pleasant shade over the picnic benches, and Jorge chased the girls around and around the peeling white tree trunks. After a bit, they all ran for the swings and slides, and I followed them past the baseball backstop.

I paused at the tall chain link caging around the basketball courts, where a guy inside shot baskets by himself. Chain link metal pressed hard and cool into my forehead, and I watched him in his shorts and tube socks, doing his thing.

Bored. Poor. I wished I had a basketball of my own.

Then he did a thing. The guy. He jumped up and made a shot, and his face flashed at me.

No. Way.

"Denzel?"

He didn't hear me, so I walked around to the other side of the backboard to get a better view of his face through the fence. I had to make sure.

He made another shot, and wow. He looked young. So young. Just a young black guy at a park shooting baskets. No big deal. Was he even famous yet? Did anybody know who he was?

I looked over my shoulder at the others; Tamika had managed to climb onto a swing without killing herself.

The man saw me, then went back to shooting baskets. How old was he? Was he even 30 yet? I thought of *The Book of Eli*, when he fought a dozen men in a post-apocalyptic bar. He was a 55-year-old dude in that. A deliciously scary warrior on a mission.

I watched him, my face denting into the chain link fencing, and I realized something. Something immense. I knew this man's future! I could quote movies he hadn't made! I knew the name of his firstborn son! I clung to the fence, frozen, unable to think of a word to say to him. I couldn't shout out, "Hey! Buddy! You're going to win your first Oscar in a few years!" I couldn't say that. It wasn't fair to tell him that.

I walked away. I had to. I had to leave before I said something disastrous.

Still, I couldn't help my excitement. I jogged over to the kids. "Hey guys. Guys."

Jorge pulled Shamisha backward out of the swing, but he let go of her too soon, and she fell on her rump in a poof of dust.

"Owww!"

Always a force, Tamika shouted at Jorge. "Why you drop her!"

"He didn't do it on purpose," I said.

"Yes he did!"

Shamisha got up, pouty. Jorge whopped the dust off the seat of her pants, and she turned to punch him in the chest.

"You didn't even help her up!"

"You guys! Listen. Tamika. Listen. There's a movie star over there."

That caught their attention.

"What?"

"That guy right there. Shooting baskets. He's a movie star."

"What movie star?"

"Probably the greatest movie star ever."

Without waiting for more information, Tamika ran right over and shoved her face against the fencing. I expected her to have a little more sense of awe, but she didn't know who he was.

"What's happenin!" Tamika shouted into the basketball court. "Hey. Hey! What's happenin!"

Jorge and Shamisha followed her over, and I followed them. They weren't intimidated like I was.

"You in movies?" Tamika bawled. "Dodge say you in movies!"

"Tamika! Shhh. Leave him alone."

She spun to me. "Why?"

Denzel held the basketball against his side with one arm.

Tamika ignored me. "You the greatest movie star in the whole world? Dodge say so."

Denzel actually laughed. Right out loud. One of his big, all teeth laughs. "Greatest movie star in the world? Who is Dodge?"

All three kids pointed at me.

I shrugged, embarrassed. "Hi." That's not exactly what I'd said. But, she wasn't wrong.

He couldn't be famous yet. There was nobody around, crowding, shoving papers at him to autograph. It was only 1983.

He raised his eyebrows at me. "You saw *Carbon Copy*? You liked that?"

I didn't know what he was talking about, but a flood of his movies rippled through my head. I wanted to tell him! I wanted to break my vow of silence about all things future! So, I grabbed my face to shut my mouth. I had to keep my mouth shut, so I kept my face firmly clasped in my hands.

"Drugs are bad for you." Denzel's voice entered my bubble. "Don't you listen to Nancy Reagan?"

That made me snort, so I finally relaxed and confessed, "You're a good actor. I like watching you." Then, I sucked air into my lungs until I couldn't hold any more. I didn't dare say anything else.

Jorge watched me, silent, puzzled.

"Are you on TV?" Shamisha asked.

The man raised his eyebrows. "Yes, I am. I'm on a hospital show called *St. Elsewhere*. Does your friend here like doctor shows?"

"Is that why you like him, Dodge? Cuz he's on a doctor show?" Shamisha turned back to the man through the fence. "Dodge is gonna be a doctor."

"Yeah!" Tamika said. "Dodge don't even go to school because he has to go to college when school starts again. Do you watch doctor shows, Dodge?"

Denzel didn't believe them. "He's going to college? Is that what he told you?" He frowned right at me. "You telling these girls stories?"

I gaped like a moron, wide-eyed, wanting to drop into a hole. My favorite actor stood right in front of me, and I couldn't think of a thing to say.

Jorge looked from Denzel to me and back again. He didn't want to hide in a hole. He wasn't intimidated and shy. He was insta-angry that Denzel had called me a liar.

"Dodge is our brother! And he's a genius. He already passed high school. And he's going to college in the fall, because he's a genius. I bet he knows more doctor things than you do!"

Gosh. Thank you, Jorge.

I didn't want Jorge to fight Denzel there in the park, though, right through the fencing. I had to stop wilting like a sunstruck flower.

"It's okay, Jorge. It's okay. You guys, this is Mr. Washington. He's gonna be one of the greatest actors ever. Mr. Washington, this is my brother Jorge and my sisters Shamisha and Tamika. You guys, you'll see. He'll be in so many movies." I dared look him in the face. "You're going to be in so many movies. I just know it."

"You just know it, huh?" He raised his eyebrows at me, a very Denzel look.

"Yes, sir. You're a good actor."

I nodded at him. And he nodded back, and then he shook his head and smiled away from me.

That's when I dared to ask. "Could we... could we play basketball with you?"

So, we attacked my favorite actor, who worked two miles down the road at CBS/Fox Studios where they filmed the nighttime medical drama *St. Elsewhere*. Every once in awhile, we found him down at the park shooting baskets. Jorge and the twins jumped on him sometimes and wrestled him into the grass, and he played monster and chased them and swung them through the air. Sometimes he let me go one-on-one against him in basketball. But mostly he didn't.

I never told him the future, but I wanted to every time.

On May 16, 1983, Mama and the kids and I watched Michael Jackson do the moonwalk for the first time while he sang "Billie

Jean" on NBC. The rest of the week, the girls and Jorge tried sliding backward across the kitchen floor. So funny. I couldn't wait until the Thriller music video came out so we could all do the dance.

That accidental meeting with Denzel gave me an idea, though. I knew which actors became famous in advance, before the rest of the world knew them, and that could be fun! I started looking up folks in the phone book, people who might need a little encouragement. People I'd always wanted to meet.

Some future-stars were impossible. Five million Samuel Jacksons were listed in the Los Angeles white pages. Or 12. But DiCaprio? That was a unique name! I found little Leo's mom in the phone book that summer and hunted him down at his house in West Hollywood. I didn't gush on my fellow eight-year-old. No, I called him names and tried to pick a fight with him. He called me names back, and I laughed so hard. So hard. I didn't tell him about his future. We had fun taunting each other, then I got on the bus and went home.

It wasn't easy to track people down, because a lot of actors were plain too young. Scarlett Johansson, Ryan Gosling, Chris Hemsworth, were they even born yet? I couldn't find Keanu Reeves or Whitney Houston. Eminem lived in Detroit. Christ Pratt and I grew up a few miles from each other in Washington, but the summer of 1983? He hadn't even started preschool.

After I met Denzel, I convinced Mama to let me stay up to watch *St. Elsewhere*. It didn't come on until 10:00 p.m., but she finally gave in and went to bed while I watched it alone on Tuesday nights. I had never seen one episode of *St. Elsewhere*, and I recognized young actors. Oh look! It's David Morse from *The Green Mile*. And Howie Mandel with hair!

Mama bought me a used bicycle for my eighth birthday, and I rode it to school in the fall. Its red paint had faded, and cracks in the handle grips had to be wrapped up with electric tape, but it proved a durable and zippy form of transportation. After my classes, I liked to pedal down to the CBS/Fox Studios complex just to hang around outside the wall. Studio City was a busy place with mile after mile of shops lining Ventura Boulevard, but if the River had water in it, I'd sit on a quiet bank and do my homework. The L.A. River was just a huge concrete trough that funneled floodwaters out of the city, but I liked it. Sometimes ducks and herons enjoyed the shallow water, which soothed me immensely. I'd left my home in the mountains for a highly populated smog bowl, and I no longer saw deer in my front yard. I liked it there under the trees along the edge of the concrete river.

Bruce Paltrow's daughter Gwyneth walked right past me once, but I didn't say anything to stop her. She was a few years older, and I felt shy. Another day, a ridiculously young Mark Harmon walked past, and I shouted at him.

"Hey Mark!"

He stopped on the walking path.

I waved. "Hi." Then I shut up.

The man surprised me by returning to where I sat. I had settled under a eucalyptus tree to read my physics textbook in the shade. He squinted down at it.

"Shouldn't you be reading comic books?"

I nodded.

"Are you purposely, willingly reading about Newton?" He looked closer at my book.

I nodded again.

"Isn't..." He closed his eyes, his faced scrunched a little. "Isn't the whole point of skipping school to *skip* school?"

I laughed. I forgot that normal kids my age were sitting in third grade classrooms reciting their times tables. I hated telling people I took college classes. I needed some sort of schtick, some joke to make people laugh, but I couldn't think of anything fast enough.

"Hey!" I changed the subject. "Hey, are you working over at the studios now? Are you shooting a television show?"

"Yeah, but I have some hours free. Sooo... just stretching my legs."

"Are you doing *St. Elsewhere* or... or *Falcon Crest*... or *Newhart?*"

"*St. Elsewhere.*"

"Oh cool! My friend Denzel's on that show. By the way, I really liked you in that thing, that movie you did."

He chuckled. "Thanks. Well. Enjoy your Newton."

Then, he walked off.

"Mark Mark Mark," I whispered as he strolled away. "In a few years, you're going to be the scariest Ted Bundy ever." It had taken me years to get over him as Ted Bundy. Years. But, then he became Jethro Gibbs of *NCIS* and made it all better.

Early in 1984, Mark saw me walking down the sidewalk, and he let me enter with him through the gate and gave me a tour of the CBS/Fox studio world, with its huge, barn-like sound stages and streets with names like "Gunsmoke Avenue." I learned that they still had the lagoon for *Gilligan's Island* hidden back behind that red brick wall. I sat at the edge of the beach and ate my lunch and, let me tell you, it was weird to munch on my tuna fish sandwich at Gilligan's lagoon, then look up at big, tan stage buildings on the other side.

I thanked Mark for the tour. I considered telling him things about the future, about the Summer Olympics or Michael Jordan. I wanted to tell him all about Michael Jordan. I might have told him about Michael Jordan. Or. Maybe I didn't.

Look. In the big scheme of things, it didn't matter whether I played basketball with Denzel or bantered with Mark Harmon, but I enjoyed these small perks of living in North Hollywood.

Bets

I needed money. I had ideas, big ideas about the things I could develop and build and do. As I lay awake at night with little Jason snuggled up beside me, I imagined all the ways I could save lives if I just had some money. I wanted to start homes for battered women. I wanted to build big, comfortable houses surrounded by gardens as homes for women and children rescued from human trafficking, places where they could rest and heal. Places where they could paint or care for animals and plant flowers and learn to be people again. I wanted to give homeless people jobs.

All I had to do was earn a few hundred dollars, bet on Mike Tyson, invest in the stock market, and in 25 years I'd be rich enough to build facilities for rescued people. It sounded like an awesome 25-year plan.

It wasn't so easy to make money, though. When Jorge and I built garden boxes around the neighborhood, we did it for free. We did it for our people, for our community. We didn't charge the old folks to walk their dogs, because we chose to help them on purpose, just to be good friends. Some older gentlemen handed us a dollar here or there, tucking them into our pockets.

"*Gracias. Gracias, abuelo.*"

I needed to figure out how to get an income, and I could only make colorful fires for the neighbors two or three times.

Jorge and I set up a lemonade stand, but not a single person stopped by. Not one. The twins took over, and they must have had sales magnetism. In two days, those girls sold 36 cups of lemonade - and tips! They got tips! They paid us back for the cups we'd bought, and then they split the $16 they had left. That night, they strutted around the house with their cash, boasting to the house until Mama confiscated their money and tucked it away in jars on the shelf in her closet.

I started asking my professors if I could clean their houses. "For five dollars, I will mop and vacuum your house once a week. I'll do your dusting. I'm the best deal in town. I can organize your garage, change your oil. Any unpleasant job that you need done, I can do it."

"No, Dodge." My history teacher shook his head when I asked him. "I like your attitude, kiddo, but no."

I finally convinced two professors and a lab assistant to let me clean their bathrooms or pick up their backyard dog poop. I did a good job so they kept me on, but it turned out the best funds came from typing up papers for my fellow students. I charged $5 to proofread a paper for grammar and punctuation, wording, whatever, and another $5 to type it up. Their trust was almost superstitious. It shocked me how many young adults were perfectly happy to pay an eight-year-old to produce neatly typed, well-edited reports for them to hand in. On Tuesday and Thursday mornings, I proofread papers on the couch while Jason played with his toys and watched Sesame Street. It almost made me feel like an adult again.

I felt a little like an adult with Mama too. I loved my big, soft Mama. I snuggled up next to her on the couch in the evenings and listened about her day. She got my jokes, and I got hers, and so many nights we talked and giggled like two schoolgirls.

I wanted to tell her I was a girl. So many times I almost told her. I should have. I should have just told her.

The war with Tiberius wasn't my fault, though. It was her fault. And it was Tiberius who caused all the trouble. Still, I think it would have helped if Mama had known I was a girl.

I'm sorry, I'm getting ahead of myself again.

For the summer of 1984, we improved our little pool in the back yard, daring to fill it up higher so the girls and Jason could learn to swim. The younger kids splashed so much that we had hardly any water left in the pool at the end of each day, but it helped water the melon vines that spread all over the backyard.

For my ninth birthday, Jorge and I sneaked down the road to go night-swimming. One of Jorge's teachers had left town for the week, and Jorge boldly pulled back the pool cover to expose beautiful, warm water. We kept quiet, because I really did *not* want to get caught that time. Mama would have killed us if the cops brought us home, so we took care to swim at a low volume.

The moon wasn't completely full that night, but it was still big and bright. We dried off after midnight and sat on the pool chairs with our towels wrapped around us. From his backpack, Jorge pulled out small berry pies he'd made and even a candle for me to blow out. The pies had smashed a little, but they tasted great.

"Happy birthday, Dodge." Jorge smiled in the moonlight, so proud.

Thank you, Jorge. Thank you for the best ninth birthday.

Okay, Mama wouldn't have killed us. That gentle soul never once hit any of us, but we still didn't like to make her mad. She'd scold us or send us to our rooms in great shame. If we really upset her, she might start weeping in the living room, and none of us wanted that, not even Tamika.

I learned that Mama was raised near the coast of Colombia and had moved to the United States just after she'd turned 18. She rarely talked about her childhood, and Jorge told me not to bring it up. "Her family all died, and she wanted to start her life brand new." She did bring a bit of Colombia to us, though. She cooked Colombian meals on the weekends, which usually involved chicken and corn meal and beans and rice. And Mama loved her coffee, she really did.

The 1984 Olympics came to Los Angeles that summer, and that offered Jorge and me one of our bigger opportunities for adventure. The world was arriving in our great city, and Jorge and I had a chance to watch the games live, right in front of our faces. That's what we wanted. We wanted to breath the aromas of sweat and muscle rub and gaze on as the world's greatest athletes pummeled each other raw.

It also offered me opportunities for making bets! I lay awake trying to remember the 1984 Summer Olypics. Who won which events?

Huge disappointment, though. Our neighbor with the orange and lemon trees received his tickets in June, and I learned in horror that they'd gone on sale a full year earlier in the summer of 1983. What's more, they were issued to specific individuals and weren't transferable. The committee didn't want people buying up tons of tickets and scalping them, so I couldn't find tickets through the newspaper.

The neighbor lent me his game schedule, and Jorge and I found refuge under the knarled oak tree behind a house for sale. That oak tree was our quiet spot, our hiding place, the place where we escaped the girls' ever-listening ears and shared our secrets. We settled down between its roots and studied over the schedule for Olympic events. We found out the games weren't held at one single building; they were spread out all over southern California.

"We'll have to sneak in," Jorge whispered.

"Sneak in? Are you kidding?"

"You're a genius. Why else are you a genius if you can't sneak us into the Olympics?"

Oh. Oh, Jorge. Challenge me, will you? "Okay. Where do you want to go?"

"How about wrestling?" Jorge chewed his upper lip.

"No. No, we can't get all the way to the Anaheim Convention Center. And we're not going to Long Beach. Or Coto de Caza or any other place that takes half a day to get to."

"Oh! Soccer! Let's watch soccer."

"That's at the Rose Bowl out in Pasadena." Could we sneak into the Rose Bowl? How could we do that? "The first match is July 29th, but it doesn't start until 7:30 p.m."

"How do we do it?" Jorge chewed his lip. "How do we sneak in?"

"My mother always said that if you're somewhere you're not supposed to be, just act like you belong and people won't bother you."

Jorge grimaced in disbelief. "Your mother taught you that?"

"She sure did."

So, Jorge and I took the bus out to Pasadena on Sunday, July 29th, after Mass, after lunch. Mama rented movies for the kids to watch on VHS, and we escaped. And boy, it was a long bus ride. Jorge and I had read through most of *The BFG* by 2:30 when we arrived at the empty Rose Bowl parking lots. Bright daylight. And hot.

We casually walked around, from ticketing gate to ticketing gate, looking for weaknesses in the iron fencing. Tall, spiky-topped gates blocked every entrance. The spaces between the bars were too narrow for us to slide through, and we had *not* metamorphosed into mice, but I finally saw our opportunity at a vehicle gate.

"Look. We can squeeze under."

The road drooped away under the middle of the gate, and it gave us at least eight inches of clearance. We were skinny nine-year-old kids, and if our heads could get under that gate, our whole bodies would follow. Jorge went first, because he was bigger. He squeezed under and reached his hand out for our backpack. I shoved it to him as heat broiled up from the pavement, then I slipped my head under and kicked at Jorge as he dragged me across the searing pebbly asphalt.

Jorge didn't care about my scraped knees. "We're in."

Not quite. We had to race across an open space to dive under some bushes, because there were more doors, more gates.

"Where do the soccer teams come in?" That's what I wanted to know. At least we were shaded under those bushes in our little leafy cave.

We had awhile to wait, so we shared the backpack as a pillow and took a nap. When we started to hear noises outside, just a few people talking, rumbling, we poked our heads out and surveyed the situation. Somebody had propped doors open, and that's what we needed.

Time for my great plan. We pulled flattened candy boxes from our backpack and gave them their 3D forms. M&Ms. Skittles. Snickers. Three boxes each. We taped the corners, sneaked out of the bushes, and boldly walked through the main doors, our arms full of "candy." We were with the concessions people. We belonged.

Three men in blue and white tracksuits strolled past us. Soccer suits. Jorge waved with genuine excitement. "Hi!"

One fellow pointed, all serious. "*Ehi ragazzi, datecene un po' di quelli.*"

No idea what he said. The other two men laughed, though, so we smiled and walked on. I had sneaked into dozens of pools, so I thought I'd be fairly cool and calm, but I had legitimate fear. Like I said, it made a difference when we didn't want to get caught.

As we approached one of the concession places, a burly fellow shook his head at us, and we froze, eyes wide, arms full.

"You're in the wrong place, boys. You with Pete? You gotta keep walking." Then, he gave us directions. Which was awesome. We now had a name to use. We're with Pete. Have you seen Pete? We need to find Pete.

We never reached Pete, but we found a tunnel out to the field wide open, and we used it. It took us 30 seconds in the tunnel to break down our candy boxes and stash them in our backpack, and then we were free. The vast green appeared below us, fresh and bright, waiting for the gladiators to appear in their soccer shorts. We ran way up to the top of the stadium and sat in seats and finished our book.

And that's when Jorge learned I was a girl.

Of course he did. He was going to figure it out at some point.

I said, "Shoot. I gotta go to the bathroom."

Jorge's eyes went wide. "We can't. We can't go back down. If they ask for our tickets..."

He was right.

"Just pee over there against the wall. Nobody will know."

"That's gross. I'm not gonna do that."

Jorge smiled big. "If I drink 32 ounces of pop, I can write my whole name. Jorge Tomás Louis Augustín Diaz." He said it giggling.

"Whatever. No you can't."

"You drank that huge thing of 7-Up on the bus. Write your name."

"I don't want to."

Jorge kept laughing to himself.

I rolled my eyes. "You can't do all five of your names anyway."

"You're so weird. I've never seen you pee outside, not even once. Are you messed up? Did it get chopped off or something?"

"No."

"Do your name then. It's like signing you were here."

"No! I'm not desecrating this honored place!"

He was going to find out eventually. Everybody would find out in a couple of years.

"There are enough people here now. Let's go get better seats." Without waiting for him, I jumped two steps at a time down the stadium stairs.

"You're so weird!" Jorge bellowed behind me.

I found a half empty row closer to the field and scooted down it. Jorge plopped beside me. Boy, I had to go so badly. I'd have to find some woman going to the bathroom with a child and casually glom onto her.

I confessed then. "I *can't* pee my name. I don't have the right parts."

Jorge's eyebrows wrinkled. He didn't know if he'd heard me right.

"You don't have... you don't have boy parts?"

I shook my head, and Jorge kept frowning.

"Are you messing with me?"

I shook my head again. "I'm. I'm... I never had them."

Then Jorge surprised me, because he laughed.

"Ohhh..." he slumped forward. "Gosh, I'm so glad! Thank God."

"You're glad?"

"Yeah, I can't tell you how much. For real, you're a girl?"

I nodded.

"What a relief! What a relief! I thought I was crazy! It's not that you're not tough, because you *are*. For a long time I thought you were a boy, especially with those cool scars on your face. But there's something... there's something I don't even know how to explain. Like. I look at you sometimes, and I get this idea that you're a girl. The other day one of the guys from school asked who you were, and I almost told him you were my sister. I didn't say it, but it almost came out."

I held out my hand to him, and he shook it.

"Good job."

"Haahah!!!" He laughed again. "I knew it! Why, though? You should tell Mama! You should tell the kids too."

"I know. I know! Let me finish up at school and get all my classes out of the way. Then I'll come clean. They think I'm a boy too."

Jorge laughed again. "I don't care. I think it's too hilarious. I was so worried, though. I felt bad that I kept thinking you were a girl. So, I'm glad you are one after all."

"Don't blow my cover, okay? You can't go saying I'm your sister."

"I can't tell them you're my brother, though."

That was true. "Okay. Tell them I'm your best friend."

"Sure. I mean. You are."

That night we watched Italy beat Egypt 1-0 along with 37,430 other people. People who'd paid for their tickets.

That was the only time we successfully sneaked in. We got turned away at the big pool at USC. Super disappointing ride home.

However! It turned out that Dr. Wilkins had tickets! All kinds of tickets! Apparently, being a Hollywood composer had its benefits. He took me to a horse jumping contest at the racetrack in Arcadia, and he took Jorge to watch judo matches. He got both of us into the men's gymnastics floor exercises at UCLA, and Jorge gaped, mesmerized as men bounced and flipped across the mat with flexibility and power.

"We gotta learn to do that," he breathed, and I agreed.

Back in our neighborhood, I bet our neighbor with the orange and lemon trees that Mary Lou Retton would win the woman's gymnastics all-around. I didn't say I knew she'd get a perfect 10 on her final vault. I still felt that sort of thing was too risky. But! I made a few other bets on the 1984 Summer Olympics, and my money jar kept filling up.

31 ƖƐ

Tiberius

Two sets of scars. I didn't need any more.

In September of 1984, Jeopardy broke my heart again. It finally came on television, and I immediately tried to get on the show. but there were no plans for a Kid's Week. They told me I had to be 18 to try out.

In deep mourning, I bought a whole half-gallon of Rocky Road ice cream. Jorge and I plopped on the sidewalk outside Dutton's Books and ate the whole thing. Then, we sneaked into *A Soldier's Story* so we could watch our man Denzel in a movie.

By mid-December of 1984, I'd saved up $662 from 16 months of cleaning bathrooms and editing papers. I decided I could spare $50 on presents for the family. I couldn't afford any big gifts, but I bought everybody fun toys - like yo-yos and wooden flutes and super bounce balls. I got a basketball and a soccer ball for the whole family and stuff to decorate cookies for Christmas. In excitement, I found Dr. Wilkins at his apartment.

"Mama has been making so much food, and we get presents Christmas Eve, but she doesn't fill up stockings. So, this year we'll have full stockings, and Mama will be so surprised! And look!" I showed him the mugs I'd found for 25 cents each at the thrift store. "Look at Mama's mug with the Mama Bear on it. It's so huge! This thing has to hold 24 ounces of coffee. She'll love it."

Dr. Wilkins watched me display my bags of gifts, and he did a strange thing. He took the bags out of my hands and set them down on the ground. Then, he pulled me over to him and gave me a rare hug. "You did a good job."

He held me out by my shoulders and got all serious. "I don't think it's safe for you to go carrying all this stuff home on your bike. Let me give you a ride home."

"You don't have a car."

"We'll take the bus together. You shouldn't carry all of it alone."

On Christmas Eve, I sneaked out and stuffed our stockings with the extra toys I'd bought. I added candy canes to our little Christmas tree and set out the basketball and soccer ball. I hung more candy canes in random places all over the living room, then snuggled back in my bunk.

We had great fun Christmas morning. None of us expected robots or computers or trips to Acapulco. The kids delighted in the silly toys and new board games we'd received from the Colombian "baby Jesus" the night before. Mama immediately filled her giant mug with coffee and sat there drinking it proudly. She made us waffles and we sprayed mountains of whipped cream on them. Then we filled our new mugs with hot cocoa and stirred our drinks with the peppermint sticks.

About 10:00 a.m., somebody knocked on the front door. The girls both raced to answer it and stuck their heads through the doorway.

"There's nobody here," Tamika said.

Then Shamisha screamed. "Ohmygosh! Ohmygoshohmygosh!!! Look! Look!"

Jorge and Jason and I all ran out, and there – lined up next to the house – leaned four brand new bicycles with big bows on them, along with a Big Wheel for Jason. A giant sheet of butcher paper had been taped to the house, and in bright green and gold paint it bellowed, "Ho! Ho! Ho! Merry Christmas!"

The girls bounced up and down like little bugs, dashing back and forth from bike to bike in admiration.

"Shuhchuhhwiiinn," Tamika read. "Mine says Schwinn on it."

"They have our names!" Shamisha shouted. "Look! You get the baby blue, and I get the purple. And, hey! Hey Jorge! Yours is green, and Dodge, yours is red! Ahhhhhh!! This is so rad!!!"

I ran my hands across the bright red, shiny paint on my new bike. I fingered the brakes on the handlebars - handlebars free of electric tape. I pressed the foamy seat with my thumb and tried to figure out the gear-change system. Jorge's bike was completely different than mine, all pimped out with pegs and shocks. He'd gotten a freestyle BMX bike, one he could use to do jumps and stunts. Mine was built for speed. And I laughed, because it was a girl's bike.

Jorge surprised me, all hunched over. His chest heaved up and down. Tears dripped down his cheeks, and he knelt on the ground and hugged the frame of that green bike. He'd probably never received so glorious a Christmas present in all his life.

I thanked our secret Santa that next Saturday. And I dropped off my new Rubik's Cube at his house for safe keeping. Mike sent me a Rubik's Cube for Christmas, and *that* was the gift that made me teary-eyed. Silly Mike. I wondered when I'd get to see him again.

December 16, 1984

Dear Dodge,

I got your letter and your gardens sound a m a z i n g. I wish we could grow year-round gardens here, but... you know... it snows. Aunt Mindy's been wanting to build a greenhouse since 1972, so maybe this next spring I'll stop being a bum and I'll help her by building one. I did go see her at Thanksgiving, so I don't need lectures from you about how I travel too much annd never visit and I'm a terrible nephew. She sends her love.

Here, I finally bought one of these for you. You probably already have three of them and you can solve them in 12 seconds like the kids in the competitions, but I wanted you to have one that I —me, myself—bought you. It's your Rubik's Cube from Mike, and you can't let kids get jelly fingers all over it, right? Put it behind a glass case and save it, because it's likely the only Christmas gift I'll ever give you. Merry Christmas.

I might be moving to Baltimore next June. Not sure if I'm excited by it, but I'll be near the ocean. I'll keep you posted.

Enjoy that 60F winter weather of yours. ☺

Love, Mike

See. All these little details are important, because our lives were good. We weren't rich. We had a lot of kids in a small house, but we were happy. Then, a few days after that Christmas in 1984, Mama did the worst thing ever. She got herself a stupid boyfriend.

Mama had gentlemen callers sometimes. She was only about 30, so of course she'd gone out looking for Mr. Right. Carlos hung around during the fall of 1983. Montel took Mama out a few times in the summer of 1984, but she'd never had a serious boyfriend. We kept her busy, and she didn't have time for dealing with gooey men.

Then, in late December, Tiberius white-knighted into our lives, and Mama's heart clearly thud thud thudded in her chest. She'd met him at a work Christmas party, and I understood her attraction to him. The guy had biceps, and he wore snug T-shirts to show them off. He stood about 6'2" and fit neatly into the tall, dark, handsome category. He drove a jazzy Pontiac. Mama got herself dressed up for him on Friday nights, and they stayed out until 2:00 in the morning. Jorge and I lay awake, unable to sleep until Tiberius brought Mama home safely.

Tiberius seemed nice enough, and he spent a lot of time with us the week between Christmas and New Year's. He'd drop onto his stomach in the living room and crash trucks together with four-year-old Jason. He'd swoop the girls onto his shoulders and run around the house with them, neighing like a horse. He complimented Jorge about the gardens, and they went out together to pick lettuce leaves or pull up carrots for dinner. Jorge's whole face beamed, so proud, the first time he and Tiberius came into the kitchen from the garden. Poor Jorge had missed having a dad, and a big black man who played trucks with Jason and horsey with the twins and appreciated good steamed spinach? That man blessed Jorge's heart.

Tiberius had a good job too. He worked as an electrician and made enough money to take Mama out to nice restaurants. He bought her new skirts and bright, colorful blouses. He kissed her and told her she looked beautiful. He showed no signs of drug use, I never saw him drunk, and he seemed like a good choice. I *wanted* him to be a good choice. I wanted him to be everything we needed him to be.

One single problem upset the whole mom-and-dad family thing that Tiberius had developing with Mama. Me.

I didn't do anything different than normal. Jorge and I still made dinner. We still worked to make sure everybody did their chores and finished their homework and got to bed on time. I provided free babysitting anytime Tiberius wanted to take Mama out on the town. When he spent the night in early January, I didn't say a thing to him. I didn't ask him to help with rent. I didn't ask him to buy groceries. I didn't interrogate him about his intentions.

I did quietly ask Mama, "What are you doing having a man spend the night? You've only known him a few weeks!"

She didn't get mad at me for asking. She just blushed and shrugged, embarrassed. "I know, I know, *mijo*. I know I shouldn't, but I couldn't help myself. He's so beautiful."

It didn't stop. Before long, Tiberius and Mama had a sleepover most nights.

Look, I wanted Mama to have a good man. I wanted her to find somebody who loved her, but I couldn't relax around her boyfriend. He didn't like me for some reason, and it became clearer the more time he spent at our house. I plain offended him. He liked Jorge. He liked Tamika. He liked Shamisha. He doted on Jason. But, when I walked into the room, he stiffened.

Mama left for work at 8:00 every morning and returned home by 6:00 every evening, but Tiberius started arriving while Jorge and I still worked on dinner. If Jorge beat me home, I'd find him with Tiberius, laughing and carrying on in the kitchen as they prepared food. If I ran into the house before Jorge, Tiberius always sent me out.

I tried to stay out of his way. I watched Jason at home all day on Tuesdays and Thursdays that semester, but other days I made excuses to Jorge that I had a lot of schoolwork to do and needed to make late use of the library. It didn't seem to bother Jorge at all, because I hadn't abandoned him. He had Tiberius now.

Of course, Mama told me off in Spanish when I came home too late, because I'd worried her. And if I worried her, then Tiberius took me out back and told me off in English.

I couldn't win.

At first, I thought we faced a male dominance problem. I'm sure that was a big part of it, besides the trouble that Tiberius saw me as his competition for Mama's affection and resented my whole genius-child status. I know Mama bragged on me a lot, and I sensed that irritated him. But, the frosting on the cake turned out to be something more basic; he didn't like my pale skin.

I couldn't believe it! My whole life, I'd agreed we should judge the content of a person's character and not the color of his skin, and it shocked me that Tiberius cared about some white kid living in his girlfriend's house. I know that was naïve of me. I know. But, we had neighbors of every skin shade, and nobody cared - not that I ever saw. We treated each other like human beings. You know, just people, and we had a good community going on. I guessed Tiberius had grown up in a different kind of neighborhood.

I wanted him to like me. It *grieved* me that he didn't like me. I wanted a dad too, and Tiberius had all kinds of good things going on. But nothing I did pleased him.

One particular Wednesday, I biked home early with plans to gulp down a snack and hide in my room with schoolwork until dinnertime. The Pontiac was parked out front, and Tiberius sat on the couch watching TV when I walked through the door.

"Hi," I greeted him. He only grunted in response.

I'd worked through lunch that day, so I pulled out turkey and bread to make myself a sandwich.

Tiberius immediately barked from the living room. "Get out of the kitchen. You can wait for supper."

I hadn't eaten a thing all day, and my stomach ached. "I didn't get to have lunch. Don't worry, I won't spoil my dinner."

He didn't settle down and watch his show like a normal person. Instead, Tiberius bolted off the couch, and it took three seconds for him to cross from the living room into the kitchen. I backed toward the sink because he came at me like a bus.

He stood there above me, so tall, so much bigger than I was. "Oh, I see, pretty boy. You like arguing, like you're a full-grown man."

My mouth opened and closed like a fish. I glanced around for a way to escape; he filled the whole kitchen. "No disrespect, Tiberius."

"But, you just argued with me," he pushed. "How can you say you respect me if you're arguing with me?"

I said nothing. I couldn't win this conversation.

"No, don't hunch there like a rabbit. I want you to tell me how you could possibly respect me if you're willing to open your mouth at me. You get any closer to that sink, you're going down the drain. Are you late for a very important date there, white rabbit?"

I watched his boots, waiting. Waiting for him to leave me alone.

"What? You had a mouth on you about a minute ago. Don't have you have a mouth now?"

I'm not kidding. Tiberius intimidated me, and I looked up and down and everywhere but into his face. If I'd stood a foot taller, if I were a full-grown man, I'd have decked him. But, I wasn't either of those things, so I cowered and concentrated on the dark leather of his footwear.

"I apologize for talking back to you."

"Oh, you apologize now? Now you want to apologize."

He dug two fingers under my chin and forced me to meet his eyes.

"How'd you get those scars on your face, pretty boy?"

I hated his eyes on me. He stared at my right cheek, and I focused on the evening stubble on his jaw.

"Did your daddy do that to you? He didn't want a pretty boy, so he carved your face? Carved it like a rabbit."

I thought of my father, my quiet, creative dad always living off in his imagination, and anger flashed up, a bubble of hot water that popped and splashed. Tiberius misunderstood my surge of emotion, and a grin spread across his face.

"He did, didn't he?" Tiberius cursed and sneered a half-smile sneer. He opened his hand and wrapped it around my chin. "Listen up, you broken saltine. This is my home now, and I'm the man in charge here. Does that process in your brain? Does that process? Good. If you want to test me on that, then you go right on ahead and test me."

He gripped my jaw tighter.

"I mean, we could give you matching scars on the other side of your face." He stared me down. "How's that sound? Get you all evened out?"

He forced his dark eyes on mine, holding me captive before he dropped his hand and took a small step to the side. "Get out of my face."

I ran and hid in my bed, under the covers and everything. They offered no real protection, but covers always made me feel better.

Later that evening, I climbed up and knelt on the bathroom sink to study myself in the mirror. I tried to see the pretty boy Tiberius saw, and I didn't. I had nice blue eyes under my cropped hair, but freckles sanded my nose. By late spring, I'd have a whole freckle beach across my square face. No matter how much Jorge liked them, my scars weren't pretty. If I didn't know better, I'd have believed I was a boy myself.

"A white genius girl might not be so bad," I thought. "He might not hate me if he knows I'm a girl." Then again, maybe he was looking for excuses to hate me. Maybe he'd treat me worse if he knew.

I honestly wanted to come clean to Mama, but I had to do it without Tiberius around.

That big man still loved on Jason. He gushed over the girls and buddied up with Jorge. Mama glowed and sparkled when he walked into the room, and I knew he made her happy. After that day, though, Tiberius sought a reason to pop me. I made sure to pack my lunch every day. I tried my best to avoid him, but he didn't make it easy.

He bellowed from Mama's room one evening. "Dodge! Get in here!"

Mama had stepped out to the store for coffee and milk, leaving him to sit with us. I walked in and Tiberius demanded, "Did you fold these clothes?" He shoved a fistful of shirts in my face. His shirts. His shirts that I'd washed and dried and folded and placed on Mama's bed the way she'd asked me to.

I turned and shut the door to keep his words inside the room. "Yes. I folded those."

"Why are you lying to me?"

"What?"

"You said you folded these, but they're not folded." He dropped them on the floor. "If you had folded them, they wouldn't be in a pile on the floor right now."

I stared at the shirts, maroon and black and bright yellow. This was so much worse than a schoolyard bully.

"What are you staring at? Pick them up!"

I reached down and scooped them into my arms. Whatever I could do to appease him, that's what I wanted to do. "How would you like your shirts folded, Tiberius?"

He cursed at me. "It's not about what I want. It's about folding them right!"

"Would you…" I tried to think of the politest way to ask. "Are you willing to show me how to fold them?"

He glared at me, hating me. He plain hated me.

I looked deep into the anger of those eyes and projected it onto the months ahead, and my heart slumped. He wouldn't like me any better in a month. Not in a month or a year. The tension promised only to worsen, and I recognized that nothing I tried was going to make him accept me.

"How are we going to fix this?" I dropped all my defenses and asked the question honestly. "I want peace. I want to fold your shirts right. You make Mama happy. I want that."

"You want to make peace around here?"

I nodded.

227

He frowned like I was stupid. "Then, leave. You're in the system. Get another home." He said it abruptly and harshly. Final answer.

Until that moment, I'd hoped to smooth things over with him. I'd given him space. I'd let him have the alpha male position and had been willing to help him win the affection of my brothers and sisters. *That* was what he wanted? To get rid of me?

No. No. NO.

All my intimidation evaporated in that moment. I was done with home-hopping! He was *not* going to swoop in from nowhere and take my family from me!

"I lived in 51 homes before I came here." I met his eyes. "I have a family now." Mama and Jorge and the girls and Jason were my family. We had built our life, just like the garden boxes outside. We'd built our family and watered it and made it healthy, and that's why it was good. "*We* did all the hard work, and you think you're gonna come into our home and kick me out?" With unexpected calm, I told him, "Take off, Tiberius."

Only I didn't say "take."

I expected a negative reaction. I expected rage. Instead, a weird satisfaction entered his face, a glint of victory. The next moment passed in slow motion, but I couldn't move fast enough to avoid it. He reached his hand back, and I watched it. His great, big hand rose up, and I watched it swing back down until it crashed like a train into the side of my head. The floor left my feet, and I flew right through the air, sailing across the room until I hit the carpet. I slid to a stop and lay there, stunned, waiting for the pain in my head to dim. I'd heard the term, "That rung my bell," before, and it made sense. I understood all those cartoons where the characters see birds or stars circling around their heads. Man, Tiberius hit hard.

When I finally focused above me, he looked the happiest I'd ever seen him. Genuinely. He watched me wipe my face with my T-shirt, clearly entertained as I struggled to stand up.

"Hey, Dodge," he grinned. "We can do this every night."

Of course, I wanted to tell Mama what had happened, to warn that her boyfriend planned to get rid of me. I wanted to tell her that he'd knocked me across the room, but when she came home all happy and singing with groceries, I had no chance to talk to her. Tiberius didn't let me. He dominated her time all evening.

By the next day, he'd already given his twisted rendition of what had happened, and it was no good. She pulled me aside before breakfast and scolded me for telling Tiberius to "take off," and when I tried to explain, she wouldn't listen.

"I don't want your excuses. Tiberius is very good to us. I know he's a new man in the house and you're not used to it, but you need to treat him with respect. You can't say rude things and not expect consequences, Dodge."

"But Mama. He almost knocked my head off. Are you going to let him do that?"

She softened. "I don't want him to hit you. I will tell him he can't hit you. But, you shouldn't give him a reason!"

Gah!

She knew me. Mama knew me, and Tiberius wasn't going to be able to get rid of me as easily as he hoped. But he started trying.

February. What was it with February? It was like I'd moved right back in with Ashlynn and Ted, but back then I'd only stuck around to protect Donnielle. This was entirely different, because I wasn't going anywhere.

Tiberius couldn't make me abandon Jason, my little man, or the crazy twins! Or Jorge, my brother and best friend. I loved my big soft Mama, with her sweet and honest heart. She and I no longer joked together on the couch at night, and I missed snuggling up beside her after the kids went to bed. I'd always felt safe with her there, secure and warm and safe. Tiberius had already stolen my quiet time with Mama, and now he wanted to kick me out of her life?

That wasn't the worst of it. He slandered me. He didn't make a frontal assault on me in Mama's presence, because he knew Mama loved and admired me, but he made mean jokes about me to the younger kids. I heard him rumbling to Mama in her room at bedtime, and from the tones I knew he made wise-sounding arguments that smeared my character with grays and tans. He didn't try to paint me as pure evil, because Mama knew better. Instead, he sprayed drops of dirty paint at me. It was the frog in the hot water trick.

Mama loved me. She did. But, she had tumbled into the worst kind of passion for her big, handsome electrician. She had longed for a good guy. She had wanted to bring a dad into our family, and every kid in the home liked him but me.

What to do? What to do? How to beat Tiberius?

I couldn't shy away anymore. It did no good to hide. I had to fight back, but I had to do it wisely and shine as the best version of myself.

229

So, I focused on being the happy Dodge, the fun and responsible Dodge. I picked wildflowers in the vacant lot on our street and vased them up to grace the table. I gave the girls more attention than ever. I kissed Mama's neck when I walked into the house and greeted my nemesis cheerfully.

"Hi Tiberius! How was your day?"

When he tried to complain about me, Mama blew him off. I loved her so much!

"Tiberius!" I heard her in the kitchen. "You're too suspicious! That child is the kindest, most generous boy in the world. The very first week he came here, he cleaned the whole entire house himself. You need to trust me, *querido*. You have nothing to worry about with him. He's a jewel."

Haha!

Still. I couldn't let him catch me alone. He freely manhandled and demeaned me, with no pretense that I'd committed a crime. We both understood we played a game of skill, and if I was foolish enough to let him corner me, then – boom – I lost that round. It was his job to trick Mama into sending me away. It was my job to spend time with the whole family while avoiding accidental alone time with my enemy.

Thank God for my dear Dr. Wilkins, my friend, my solid place. I biked out toward Burbank every Saturday and enjoyed Dr. Wilkins' clever humor and got in my piano lesson for the week. And therapy. I got some therapy too.

Doc was insistent. "You have to be honest with your mother. You need to sit down with her and explain what's going on, because she's responsible for you. She has to send him away."

"Tell her that."

"She knows. She just doesn't know. You know?"

"You're no help at all!"

"She loves you." Doc brushed his beard smooth with one hand. He always did that when he was thinking serious thinks. "She's an intelligent woman. Give her some credit, and tell her everything he's been doing."

"I don't get time alone with her anymore."

"You should tell your case worker then."

"She might move me!"

"Well, you can always stay with me," Dr. Wilkins shrugged. "You don't *have* to go back there. It's okay to hide out for awhile."

"No! That's the whole point. He's trying to get me to go away, and I can't let him. Maybe I'll push his buttons some night, and he'll beat the daylights out of me, and then I can call the cops."

Doc's eyes opened wide. "Don't you dare."

"But, that will work. It worked with Ted. See? It'll be over then."

"What if he permanently damages you? What if he kills you?"

"Good grief. He's not gonna kill me. He's not a murderer."

Doc insisted I act rationally. "Talk to your mother. Tell her the truth. The *whole* truth, young lady."

I looked at him, and he looked at me.

His way was more reasonable. I hoped it would work.

32

Fence

I couldn't get Mama alone. I pushed through the next couple of weeks, winning a battle here and losing another there. I kept hoping Tiberius would give in and just accept me, that he'd recognize me as a force for good, but animosity smoldered in his eyes whenever he looked my way. It amazed me that Mama didn't notice.

Tiberius took Mama out in late February, like he often did. I looked forward to their date nights, because I could relax with my little family for a few precious hours. They surprised me by returning early on this specific night. I hauled the garbage to the can at 9:00 p.m. and found the Pontiac already parked at our curb, empty. I looked up the sidewalk. Tiberius escorted Mama to the front door and held it open for her. He whispered in her ear and closed the door behind her.

I sprinted down the street in my bare feet, and in thirty seconds I had zig-zagged through yards and over Mr. Sanchez's back wall. Cool grass greeted me on the other side, where I paused to breathe and think. I had to get to my window. It wouldn't work to disappear into the night for hours, because Mama would worry. I'd only delay the confrontation anyway; my enemy would stand sentry until I returned. If I ran away and never came back? That's exactly what he wanted! That meant I had to get to my window and slip inside, and I had to do it fast.

I skirted through back yards and climbed our fence, then dropped lightly onto the dirt and tiptoed around the boards that covered our empty pool pit. Somebody had locked the back door, so I carefully opened the side gate slowly…slowly… to avoid any squeaks.

The gate came to life and disobeyed me. I lost hold of the plank as the whole door banged my shoulder and knocked me down, and Tiberius caught my shirt before I hit the ground. He yanked me up, grasped me victoriously by the arm, and walked me past my window and out into the street where defeat pulled all the strength from my body. What was his problem!

The man's big fingers bit into my arm, as though he were trying to pinch it off altogether, as though all his frustrations focused on that small area of my body. I tugged away from him, and he grabbed even harder, causing real agony along my bicep.

"Pretty boy, what should I do with you?" Tiberius forced me along, and I trotted to keep up with him. The smooth pavement cooled my feet, and I tried to concentrate on that. After a few yards, he drew me off the road into the vacant lot, and I had to deal with gravel and last year's pokey dead grass.

"Start a new life somewhere, all bright and shiny," Tiberius urged me. "Find some nice white family that wants you. Go get you some people in Beverly Hills or Sherman Oaks, rich folks excited to raise a boy wonder genius. Buy you a Cadillac for your 16th birthday. Send you to USC so you can become a doctor. That's what you want, right? To be the world's youngest doctor?"

Doogie Howser dashed through my mind again. How old was Doogie when he graduated med school? No. Doogie Howser wasn't on television yet, and he wasn't a real person.

The pain in my right bicep yelled out as we reached the fence at the back of the lot. Tiberius jerked me around and dug his fingers into my other arm. I wanted to pull away from that mean grip, to get him to release me. He squatted down until his eyes lowered to my level, and his breath warmed my cheeks and forehead. It smelled sweet, the sweet smell of…maybe rum? A streetlight dimly lit the lot, but Tiberius faced me away from the light, and darkness smothered his expression. I strained to make out his eyes as he backed me up and banged me against wooden planks.

"You're a smart boy, right?" His voice was low and husky. "Mia's always going on and on about how smart you are." He mocked me, "Ooh, it's a nine-year-old going to college, making everybody so proud. So, listen to me really good here. Are you listening?"

"Yes." You've got me shoved against a fence while you breathe in my face, you big lug. I hear you.

"Nah, I don't think you're listening, because you can't seem to get facts straight. Maybe you're stupid after all. Mia doesn't want to send you back, but if you don't leave on your own, pretty boy, I guess I'll have to make you disappear."

I wanted to see his face. I squinted into the darkness, waiting for my eyes to dilate, waiting to see the outline of his cheeks. Only his eyes appeared, his faint white eyes, almost pixelated in the night.

"You could accept me." I didn't think before I said it, but it's what I wanted. It's what I really meant. "You could be my dad too." Just quit it, Tiberius. Stop being like this.

A strange gurgle started in his throat and got stuck there, but I couldn't see any expression on his face. His dim eyes narrowed and disappeared altogether.

It was a blink. A flicker as time slowed. Pictures began to sweep before my mental eyes, a montage of memories, as though my brain thought I was about to die and wanted me to recall the totality of my life in the time it took Tiberius to close his eyes and open them again.

Will Smith's opening song to *The Fresh Prince of Bel-Air* bounced into my head, so friendly, so fun. "Now this is a story all about how my life got flipped-turned upside down." Why couldn't Mama have dated somebody like Uncle Phil from *The Fresh Prince*? The happy Neverland of TV sitcoms had nothing to do with this moment at the back of a vacant lot. They didn't fit, and I felt lied-to, as though fun and jokes didn't exist in the real world. In the real world, my arms wailed at me and begged for release. In the real world, I had to lose my family over and over again.

Or Jassy Mercer's dad! Why couldn't Mama date somebody like Mr. Mercer? He'd worked for Boeing when we were growing up in Everett, and Jassy and her brother Tyler always bought brand name clothes from the mall. Man, Jassy was beautiful. She swept in like an African princess while I always dressed like the freckled farm girl. Their mom gave my mom bags of hand-me-downs every year, and those clothes from Jassy's parents were like a birthday and Christmas wrapped into one. Tyler owned so many pairs of Nikes, he never wore them out. Every year I grew into his almost-new Nikes.

Jassy kept a horse at the stables down the road. She could do back handsprings and hands-free roundoffs, and it wasn't until I grew up that I appreciated how much money her parents invested in equestrian and gymnastics lessons.

Those things weren't what mattered to me, though. I liked Jassy's dad because he was nice to me. That's all. Once, I walked in to find him watching *Gone With the Wind* of all things. While I waited for Jassy to get ready, I sat and enjoyed his movie with him. He looked down at me sitting on his couch and said, "I love this movie. This is one of my favorite movies." That fun, warm moment stuck with me forever.

Why not somebody like Mr. Mercer? Why Tiberius!

My mom? She didn't even learn to read until the sixth grade. It took seven years in the L.A. school system for a teacher to realize this girl couldn't read. Finally, that one teacher explained, "B says buh. G says guh," and Mom said, "Well, why didn't anybody ever tell me that!" She started learning to read that day, but she never did well in school. All my life, she worked low-paying jobs because she'd dropped out of high school. I grew up taking care of my little brothers and sisters, sometimes all of us crammed into one bedroom, because that's what Mom could afford.

I wanted to tell Tiberius. I wanted him to understand me.

Mom hated her poor education, so she taught me to read when I was small. She worked through lists of spelling words with me and told funny stories to help me learn my states and capitals. I worked hard in high school, earned A's and won a few scholarships. I travelled all over after I graduated from college. Then, I got a solid job, bought a house and things were fine.

That was the American dream, right? Work hard and make a life for yourself?

Tiberius had the American dream going on. He had a solid job. He had strength and good looks and money. I didn't understand!

A bruising pain in my shoulder blades called me back. The 24 frames-per-second of my thoughts flipped to the end of the reel, and I returned to the man before me. His long blink ended, and rough boards ground into my shoulders.

Recent rains had cleaned the air, and a cool night breeze brushed across my lips. "Why do you hate me so much?" I whispered.

Tiberius spoke into the darkness without hesitation. "You make the house look bad. I don't like the way you make the house look."

"What? Nobody cares that Mama's got a multi-colored family. The whole neighborhood knows us."

"You don't get it, do you?" His eyes narrowed in the darkness. "I'm not a teenage girl, worried about what people *think*. What matters is what I think, and what I think about my house. And what I want in my house. My house. That's what matters. So, you either leave or you'll disappear. Those are your choices."

He thumped me against the fence again, and I longed for him to unclasp his fingers and let me go.

"You'll make me disappear?" He'd said that earlier, hadn't he?

"They'll say you ran away. Foster kids do that, don't they. They run away." He was telling me.

"I don't believe you. You're not gonna murder a child."

He drew so near that his nose nearly touched mine. The warmth from his face brushed over my cheeks, and with an intensity I didn't expect, he growled. "It's all I think about." And he laughed. Like... like he meant it.

I thought back to Jeremy. He'd dreamed about slicing me up. He'd practiced all day so he could get good at it. Were there really so many people out there like Jeremy, like Ted? People who daydreamed about horrible things?

It was like I'd lost all my self-control, and my real thoughts kept falling out. "You'll get caught. If you kill me, they'll find my body. They always do, and then they'll -"

I didn't finish, because Tiberius grabbed my throat and started to squeeze. I could tell he wasn't using all his strength. I knew he meant only to scare me, to show his power over me, to remind me that he could do what he said. In my head, I understood that, but it still worked, and the terror overwhelmed me. I felt the anger in his hands, his thumbs on my trachea, pushing. I couldn't breathe, and pressure filled my skull. I kicked and fought at him, grabbing his hands with my own, scratching and gouging him with my nails. It was like scratching a rock.

When he let go, I rolled down into the pokey grass and sucked in breaths. Tears sprung out my eyes, and I struggled to pull air into my lungs. I coughed, and each breath hurt my throat. He hadn't broken my windpipe. He hadn't knocked me out, but he could have done it, and we both knew it.

"You have nine more years, Dodge. Nine years to build another family. Monday you'll call your social worker and ask her to move you. And if you don't listen, if you make me get rid of you, appreciate something. Mia will think you ran away, and they won't ever find the body. Ever."

Ten minutes later, I lay in bed snuggled beside Jason. Maybe I'd made a mistake standing against Tiberius. It would be better for the whole family if I did leave. They could all enjoy their mom and dad and non-white children, and their lives could merrily roll along.

I wrapped my arms around Jason and pulled his limp body closer - my living teddy bear. What could I do? What move should I make? Maybe I'd have to call Cheryl and have her come get me. I couldn't beat Tiberius. He'd find a way to win.

Jorge whispered above me. "I can hear you."

That startled me. I didn't even know he'd gone to bed.

"What do you hear?" I whispered back.

"You're crying like a little girl."

He said it so simply, I let myself go. "I *am* a little girl." My voice cracked, and I rolled my face into my pillow to deaden the sound. My throat hurt, and the pressure of not crying built up and made my throat hurt more. I held my pillow over my face and let the misery seep out.

Jorge took deep breaths. "I know Tiberius bullies you, Dodge. He keeps saying nasty things about you when you're not around, and I know he hurts you when it's just you and him."

"Oh." I let the tears drain into my pillow. Tears of stress and tears of release. I should have known better. I'd forgotten that Jorge had lived his own painful life before coming to Mama's house, and he paid attention to everything.

"Why didn't you ever ask for my help! Why are you trying so hard to hide it?" Genuine confusion piqued Jorge's voice. "Why would you do that?"

"Because Tiberius is good to you," I croaked. "I didn't want to spoil it for you."

"*Geez* are you an idiot sometimes." I could almost hear his head shake above me. "If he's mean to you, he's not being good to me."

I laughed then, a light laugh that I also hid in my pillow.

"Let me help you get rid of him!" Jorge whispered. "I think it's time we got rid of him."

I nodded and pulled Jason close again. "Yeah. Let's do that."

"Okay," said Jorge. "I gotta think."

33 ƐƐ

Sabotage

Jorge said nothing to me about Tiberius the next morning. He dropped out of bed and wandered down to the kitchen to cut up strawberries and oranges for breakfast. The girls had already sneaked out of bed to watch Saturday morning cartoons, and they sat in front of the television like lumps, like sprouting potatoes - all eyes.

"You guys want French toast?"

They focused on Bugs Bunny and didn't answer me.

Mama liked French toast and sausage, so I pulled down a square dish and set a pan on the stove.

Jorge finished cutting up fruit and set a plate on the table. He didn't interrupt the girls' show because they'd wail, and if they wailed, that would wake up Mama and Tiberius. Jorge wisely waited until a commercial before he walked in and turned it off.

"C'mon and eat up real quick," he told them softly. "Then you can turn the TV back on."

"We wanna eat in the living room," they whispered.

"No. Mama said so cuz you guys leave your dishes everywhere."

"Fiiiiiiine." Tamika slumped to her seat at the table and stuffed an orange slice into her mouth. She turned to Shamisha and gave her a big orange-peel smile.

I dropped three pieces of sodden toast into sizzling butter, then grabbed a fork to eat with the girls.

Tamika pointed at me. "Hey Dodge. What's up with your arm?"

"What?"

"Your arm's all bruised."

Sure enough, four long, purple-brownish spots hopped down my bicep. I remembered the night before and Tiberius' cruel grip as he bounced me against the fence.

I pulled away from her, but Shamisha slid off her chair and grabbed my other arm. "What are those?" She poked at the spots.

Jorge raised his eyebrows at me. "Big hands. Big fingers?"

"Oh yeah!" Tamika tried to put her little fingers in the bruises. "Look, look! It was a big dude. His hands were so huge."

I pulled away. "Leave me alone."

Shamisha clung to me and tried to put her fingers into the spots on my other arm. I wrestled away from them and ran to the living room. The girls chased me, giggling. They jumped on me and knocked me onto the couch, and in a moment they were on top of me, laughing and grabbing at my arms with their small hands.

"Who squeezed your arm like that?" Shamisha said. "That's so weird."

"Shhh!" Jorge shook his head at them. "Look. Somebody's been picking on Dodge, and we're gonna get rid of him."

"Who's been picking on Dodge?" Shamisha asked.

"Keep your voice down," Jorge urged. "*Somebody's* been mean for a long time, and Dodge is too brave to tell anybody. But, we won't let *somebody* do that anymore."

Tamika wrapped her arms around my chest. "I'm sorry, Dodge. If I saw Somebody, I'd punch him right in the head for you."

I hugged her back, holding her close, feeling her cornrows against my cheek. "Thanks, Tammy. That would rock awesome sauce."

"Pow!" Shamisha grinned.

I grinned back. "Oh! The French toast!" I shoved them off and ran to the kitchen to flip it over.

Back at the table, the girls munched on their fruit. I made a pile of food, and soon Mama and Tiberius emerged, rubbing their heads and faces. I ran into my room, pulled Jason out of bed, and brought him out to the table to eat his strawberries.

"Where's the coffee, Dodge?" Tiberius slid French toast onto his plate.

I kissed Mama and hustled to get the coffee going.

Ideas boiled away in Jorge's brain, I could tell, and he started by getting us out of the house. As I flipped on the coffee maker, Jorge said, "We already ate, Mama, so we're gonna go play at the park. Right, Dodge? The park?" He physically grabbed the girls and dragged them out the door. "Bye Mama!"

Tiberius stopped me with a hand on my chest. "Take Jason. And send the kids home at 11:30. It's family day."

We jumped on our bikes and zoomed through back roads. When we reached the park, Jason hopped off the pegs of Jorge's bike, and Jorge threw his bike down in the middle of the grass.

As the girls dropped their bikes, Jorge said, "Okay you guys. You want to know who's been picking on Dodge and hurting him and calling him names?"

No. I didn't want him to do this.

"Who?" The girls wanted to know.

"It's somebody who was pretending to be our friend. But, he's not our friend. He's a fake."

"Jason, you want me to push you on the swings?"

Talking about Tiberius gave me anxiety. I scooped Jason onto my back and swung him around me and set him back down. He ran off to the swings, and I followed him. Jorge could explain why we had to get rid of Tiberius, but I needed to figure out how to do it. I had to tell Mama that he'd threatened to murder me. I had to tell Mama that. I had to call Cheryl and tell her to talk to Mama. I'd been afraid to tell Cheryl, but maybe she could help Mama see that Tiberius wasn't who she thought he was.

"Higher, Dodge!" Jason swooped up and back, up and back. He was happy for me to push him forever, and it gave me time to think.

I looked over a few times while Jorge and the twins engaged in deep discussions in the grass. Sometimes the girls jumped up and talked with their arms, and sometimes they dropped back down and listened to Jorge. I pushed Jason for a long time, and they talked for a long time, and I finally started to wonder what they were saying.

I finally caught Jason around the middle and pulled him off the swing. "You wanna go chase Jorge?"

Happy with that, he ran back ahead of me.

"We have a plan, Dodge!" Tamika grinned when we returned. "It's going to be so great!"

Of course, they were children. I should have guessed their ideas to banish Tiberius would be the kind produced in children's minds. As I think about it, though, their plan worked. Not in the way they intended or expected, but … oh well.

On Saturdays, Jorge had traditionally crashed on the couch to watch television and vegetate in peace. I had traditionally gone off to visit Dr. Wilkins, and Mama had traditionally taken the younger three on a bus ride to eat at McDonald's or go to the zoo or hike around Griffith Park or whatever it was they did. We continued this pattern, and when the other kids biked west to go home, I pedaled east. The air breezed all lovely past my ears as I zoomed along, and I felt alive and free flying down the road.

I had no clue the kids went straight back to implement their great plan. All that time they'd hunched together on the grass, they'd dreamed up a series of pranks on Tiberius. I thought ... I don't know what I thought. I heard about the pranks later, and their energetic creativity impressed me. Maybe not their *wisdom*, but they definitely earned an A for effort.

At lunch, Tiberius opened his tuna sandwich to sprinkle salt, and the whole shaker of salt dumped out in a pile on his tuna. He had to throw away that sandwich and get another one. Not too big a deal.

A short time later, Tiberius grabbed a clean shirt out of his dresser drawer, and cayenne pepper puffed everywhere when he unfolded it.

"He coughed and sneezed for minutes," Jorge later confessed to me with unsuppressed glee. "His eyes watered! It was great."

The kids wanted to make Tiberius go away. That was the idea - to make him feel unwelcome, to communicate that the whole house was hostile toward him, to punish him for hurting me. I don't think they expected him to get angry, they just wanted to chase him off.

Mama and Tiberius prepared to take the younger kids on their bus ride, but when Tiberius stuck his feet in his shoes, he found the toes filled with toothpaste.

Jorge told me, "He didn't yell at us or anything. He just said swear words under his breath and cleaned out his shoes."

Mama and Tiberius took the children out for ice cream, but the girls kept jumping to sit on Tiberius' feet, wrapping their arms around his calves so that he had to walk with giggling ankle weights. When he told them to stop and get off, they just shrieked with delight, as though the whole thing were a colossal joke. They disobeyed him all morning, and only when Mama jumped in did the girls calm down and behave.

Twins even mocked him. Running ahead of the two adults, the girls claimed to have sung, "Tiberius is a pain, he has a little brain. Tiberius is a jerk. He can't get to work. Tiberius is so dumb. He thinks his toe's his thumb." Insulting rhymes over and over again. I don't know where they got the moxie.

As soon as they reached home, Mama begged Jorge to take the kids away. "Take Jason. Take the girls. Take yourselves out of this house. I don't want to see you home until dinnertime."

But, it didn't get better, because Jorge had spent the afternoon planting bombs at the house. When Tiberius opened the freezer, he found all his beer cans slushy with mostly frozen beer. (It was the first thing Jorge had done that morning. I think that small, vengeful act of sticking all the beer in the freezer spawned Jorge's ultimate plan of sabotage.)

Tiberius took a shower to find that his shampoo had been dumped down the drain. And the towels were all wet in the washing machine. And his shaving cream and razors and aftershave had gone missing, along with every pair of his boxers. By this time, Tiberius wanted to kill somebody.

Of course, Jorge had overlooked his game's potential for negative results. He assumed Tiberius would *know* that he and the girls were behind the sabotage. As a climax, Jorge intended to announce in front of Mama that they were kicking Tiberius out! That was Jorge's plan, and I felt humble gratitude when I heard about it. Jorge and the girls did all of that because we were family, because they loved me. They chose me. They chose me over Tiberius, and I wanted to hug them forever.

Of course, it didn't work out the way Jorge planned. Things like that never do.

34 ⅊Ɛ

Vete

I shoved through the front door at 6:00 p.m. with no knowledge of the great sabotage plot. I had no idea that Tiberius assumed I'd been the evil archvillain behind it all, or that my presumed disrespect had pumped rage through him all day. I parked my bike and walked into the house, expecting Mama making dinner. Instead, Mama sat at the table with Tiberius, trying to soothe him. Like a clueless match, I entered this powder keg.

"Hi." I walked across the kitchen to pour a glass of Kool-Aid.

Tiberius started yelling before I reached the fridge. I would tell you what he said, but I don't remember it. His voice banged into my ears, but the words didn't register as pictures in my head. I couldn't understand him. He made too much noise, and he didn't form his sentences well. Profanities poured from his mouth, enraged, bitter words, and none of them made sense to me.

I stood in the middle of the kitchen and looked back and forth between him and Mama.

Tiberius finally paused to breathe, and I asked, "Mama, what's wrong? What happened?"

"Baby, baby please calm down. Tiberius baby, it's okay." Mama looked at me. "All those pranks you did, Dodge. They were bad. I know you were trying to be funny, but they were bad things to do."

I didn't know what she meant. "Mama. I didn't pull any pranks."

Tiberius reached out one arm, grabbed me by the front of my shirt, and yanked me right up to him. The front of my shirt. That was his go-to. He growled, "Boy, in two seconds, I'm gonna put you through that wall."

I leaned away from him, stiff through my whole body. "I've been gone all afternoon, Mama." I whispered, as though I could avoid death by speaking softly. "I went to visit Dr. Wilkins."

Tiberius raised his hand above me, and I thought he really would knock me through the wall. I cringed away from one of his ringing blows, but he stopped himself. Instead, he grasped the cloth at my chest with both hands and shook me.

Mama's eyes widened in alarm. His fury surprised her, and she tried to calm him. "They were practical jokes, my love. He's just a boy playing jokes."

"Disrespectful!" Tiberius raised his voice. The shirt dug into my armpits. "Boy, you have giant gonads to fill my shoes with toothpaste. Pouring pepper in all my shirts. What was it you said to me? This was *your* family?"

"Dodge!" Shock stretched Mama's face. "*Mijo*, don't you know that I love Tiberius? Why would you say terrible things to him?"

I leaned away from the man's hot breath.

"Poured salt on my sandwich!"

"He's trying to get rid of me. He choked me last night, Mama. He threatened to kill me."

"All my boxers gone. All of them."

"Look, Mama. Look at my arms."

"Stop lying!" Tiberius roared.

Grief wrung Mama's face. "Dodge, if you did those things, please be honest and tell him you're sorry."

"Mama. Mama listen."

"And what's this! What is this? Where did you get all this money?"

It was like he reached in and grabbed a handful of my intestines. I watched, paralyzed, as Tiberius stretched across the table and snagged a jar. My jar. My jar of savings from 18 months of tediously typing papers and cleaning dog poop. His eyes reflected a glint of victory as he set down the secret weapon he'd been holding.

"Dodge," Mama's brown eyes opened wide with concern. "Where did you get that money?"

I stared in real fear at my jar of hard work. "How did you get that?" I'd hidden it in my closet, high up behind a stack of text books. Snooping. He'd been snooping through my things!

"There's $700 here, Dodge." Tiberius thunked the jar down in front of him. "Didn't I tell you, Mia? I told you I kept missing money."

"I worked for that money. I've been working - ever since I started school! That's my money!"

Tiberius pulled a wallet from his back pocket and flipped it open.

"Remember the $50 I had last night, Mia? It's gone. I told you!" Then he reached into my jar and pulled out handfuls of my cash. Tens, 20s, 100s. In my face.

I almost grabbed his arm. "Don't Tiberius! Please don't! Mama, stop him!"

He piled up the bills and stuffed them into his wallet, like he really thought they were his! Like I owed him in some rage-filled, vengeful place in his brain.

"Mama! He's been trying to get rid of me! Last night he knocked me against a fence and said he'd kill me! He's been trying to trick you! He's trying to force me to leave, and now he's stealing my money!"

"Stop LYING!" Tiberius turned and smacked me then, right in front of Mama. His hand cracked me across the side of the head, and my cheek bounced off the table. I hit the tiled floor on my side, but I knew better than to stay down. I made myself scramble up, grabbed Mama's shirt and pulled myself to her.

"That boy has been a liar since I first met him, Mia! If we're going to make this work, he needs-"

Mama surprised me then. She surprised us both. She jumped up and grabbed my pile of Roald Dahl paperbacks from the edge of the table and shouted, "Out!" Then Mama, who never got more savage than bellowing in Spanish, raised a copy of *James and the Giant Peach* and hucked it at her man's head.

"What?" Tiberius ducked as the book flew past his ear.

"You hit this little boy like that? Get out right now!" *Danny The Champion of the World* slapped him in the chest a moment later, and he tossed up his arms to protect himself from *The BFG*.

"He's lying to you, though!"

"If he took a crap in your shoes, Tiberius, you don't slap a child to the ground like that! You don't lose your temper over children's jokes! Get out!" Then, the Spanish started. I stood behind her, and she lambasted the violent man in her kitchen. She grabbed his shirt with both hands and jerked him toward the door. Mama weighed less than Tiberius, but she leveraged her mass in that moment of rage.

"¡Vete!" She shoved him. "¡Fuera de aquí!"

Tiberius resisted. He tried to apologize, to speak softly to her, to take it back. She wasn't having any of it. The Spanish got louder, and she propelled him out the front door.

"It'll be okay," he told her from the front steps. "We'll work it out."

"Don't come back!" Mama slammed the door shut.

She firmly twisted the deadbolt, then turned and uprighted her chair. She plopped down, muttering angry Spanish words.

"*Ven aquí ahora*," she ordered.

I obeyed and stood before her. She clasped my ears with her soft hands and tilted my face toward her. My head still rang from the blow and all the noise.

"He should not hit you like that." Mama frowned at my cheek.

"See my arms?" I mumbled. "He grabbed me last night. He said he'd murder me and make my body disappear."

"Shh shhh..." She urged me to be quiet, then placed her own warm fingers on the brown spots along my bicep. "Your jokes were rude and mean, but they were just jokes."

"He took my money, Mama! That was my money!"

"Did you sneak it from him?"

"Never! Have I ever sneaked it from you?"

I hadn't, and she knew it.

"Mama, I worked so hard, and he just robbed me! And he knew he was stealing it!"

"His money kept missing."

"*No.*" How could I make her see? To get that everything he did was a lie? My head ached so much. "And ask Jorge about the jokes."

Mama wasn't ready to believe me about anything. "Why? Why would Jorge play tricks on Tiberius?"

"Because Jorge is my brother." I mumbled it into her silky, flowery shirt. I just wanted her to hold me and protect me.

"What?" She didn't understand.

I didn't want to talk. I had no energy. "Jorge and the girls didn't want him to hurt me anymore."

Mama's voice choked. "But why do you disrespect him all the time, Dodge? Why do you say terrible things to him? You should not have said those things." Mama took several deep breaths, trying not to cry. The events of that day had slapped her as violently as Tiberius had slapped me, and she'd thrown out a man she adored.

I wanted to hug Mama and comfort her. In fact, I *didn't* want her to be alone. I'd put up with Tiberius because I wanted her to be happy, but Tiberius would have broken her heart with or without me. He'd tried to tear us apart and obviously didn't care about Mama one bit.

I wanted to yell at Tiberius and beat him up and punish him for

246

doing Mama that way – building up her hopes and then stomping them to bits like eggshells. I wanted to throat punch him per Doc's orders.

"Mama." I grabbed her hand and held it tight. "I want you to find a good man to love you. But Tiberius decided he was gonna hate me from the beginning, and I couldn't make him stop."

And so, I held her, and she held me, and we both cried together for a little while.

The four kids returned home an hour later. Mama asked if they'd pulled those pranks, and the girls surprised her by bouncing up and down on their toes.

"Did it work! Did we make him go away?"

"Why!" Mama wailed in obvious remorse. She'd thrown out her boyfriend in a moment of rage, but I could tell she didn't really want him gone. She'd started to remember how sweet he'd been and forget that he'd knocked my face against a table.

"He's a showman, Mama," Jorge told her. "It's like covering a pile of dog poop with a silk handkerchief. He kept hitting Dodge! He wanted to get rid of one of your kids."

I sat next to her at the table, and I brushed her hair back with my hand. I kissed below her ear and gave her a hug. "I don't want you to be alone, Mama."

Mama nodded. She understood. She suffered from a broken heart, that's all.

"He's gonna come back," Jorge whispered as soon as we were alone. "They always come back."

"Yeah, I know."

"What are we gonna do? How do we keep him away?"

"You tell Mama that he's the liar, and I'm not. You keep telling her that he's the bad guy. She has to be the one to refuse him."

So, Jorge and I waited for Tiberius to show up at the door. We waited for him to appear on the front steps to woo her back. He'd pulled $420 out of my jar, and I resigned to losing it forever if that meant never seeing him again. Jorge and I both knew he wouldn't give up easily, though, and at least three times a day, Jorge told Mama she'd made the right decision. He told her she was a good mama. He was proud of her.

Two days later, Tiberius called during dinner. We all sat around the table, watching Mama as she listened and talked. I couldn't hear what he said, but I understood that he was asking her to lunch. She frowned and struggled, but in the end she said, "No. I don't want to see you." And she hung up.

I jumped up and hugged her hard. "Mama, that was so brave!"

Shamisha gave her a hug too. "You're beautiful, Mama. And your heart is made of strawberries."

"All the men want to get with you, Mama," Tamika said. "I see them looking at you. Mmm mmm. You gotta find the right one."

That night Jorge and I talked for a long time after Jason fell asleep.

I told Jorge. "You know, Tiberius could have gone to Cheryl and complained that Mama doesn't have enough room for all of us. I'm not supposed to be sleeping with Jason. I'm not supposed to be watching Jason alone all day. If he was smarter, he would've convinced Cheryl to come get me."

Jorge sighed. "I'm glad he didn't."

"I feel so relaxed now. It's like I've been under a brick wall for two months, and now it's gone."

"I know," Jorge said. "I felt it too. I just ignored it for a long time."

Two sets of scars.

35 ‮35‬

Bruce

I found my dear Dr. Wilkins in a foul mood that next Saturday. He said, "Let's go for a walk and have lunch! I'm 68-years-old, and if I want a Reuben sandwich, nobody can tell me I can't have one."

"I won't stop you."

"I've been eating bran-this and salad-that because my doctor says so, but I don't see the point in extending my life if I'm forced to eat miserable food all the time."

I'd contemplated leaking my superpowers to Doc. I'd longed to share my time-flexible inside jokes with him, but I also didn't want to disrupt his safe and ordered reality. I'd already dragged him into enough of my craziness.

We left my bike inside his apartment building and strolled down the sidewalk to a café, where he ordered a Reuben with an iced tea, and I ordered a fat cheeseburger with a 7-Up, and we talked and laughed like we always did.

"So, young lady! I honestly don't know how you can fool anybody anymore, *Yentl*."

I smiled. "People are starting to see it for themselves."

"Why hasn't your mother figured it out?" Dr. Wilkins shook his head. "She's intelligent. She lives with you."

"Well, the differences in cultures and backgrounds and all that... and, you know, the state thinks I'm a boy. My documents say I'm a boy."

The doctor took an enormous bite of his sandwich and closed his eyes in pleasure. When he spoke, it was from the side of his mouth. "It's just wonderful to take huge bites. My mother would disapprove, but I no longer care if it's polite, It's glorious to fill one's mouth with food."

"Jorge knows I'm a girl. Did I tell you that? He figured it out a long time ago, and I've *almost* told Mama so many times, but I'm afraid she'll get all protective of me. Also, I don't want to sleep in the girls' room. Also, she might think I'm really a liar after all, because Tiberius tried to convince her I was the devil in disguise."

The old gentleman swallowed and took a drink of his tea. "You are a liar. Liar liar pants on fire, hanging on a telephone wire."

"I've thought about it a lot. Maybe Tiberius wouldn't have hated me so much if he knew I was a girl."

"You know better than that." Doc wiped his beard clean.

I took a bite of burger. We both ate thoughtfully, watching the street outside our window. I *did* like my mouth full of food. I chewed away and reached out to take a drink of 7-Up as a familiar face walked by the window.

I lived in film studio land, and sometimes I recognized people, like the guy who did deodorant commercials or the character actor who played an annoying accountant. Those folks went to bookstores and supermarkets like everybody else, and I noticed them. At least, I thought I knew them. In 1983, I'd known Denzel shooting baskets because he'd burned a spot in my brain for 30 years. Sometimes I saw actors, but I wasn't as sure. Was that really the deodorant commercial guy, or was my brain overworking?

The face that passed our window was another brain-branded face. He looked exactly like a young Bruce Willis. So much like him, I had to make sure. I wasn't going to let Mr. *Die Hard* himself stroll by without a double-check.

"I'll be right back." I waved at Doc without explanation, jumped up and dashed out the door and down the sidewalk.

I trotted up beside him. "Bruce?" If I was wrong, if he didn't stop... He turned! He turned and frowned down at me! Yes! Haha!

"Hi Bruce!" I couldn't help myself. This was ridiculous behavior, because actors were just people. Just normal people who took showers and ate sandwiches. But, it was Bruce Willis! "How old are you? You're turning, what... 30-years-old? Wow, you have so much hair!"

Good grief, I had no brains in my head.

Bruce looked up the sidewalk behind me and rotated slowly in a circle to see who else might be accosting him. An old woman walked her spaniel up the road, and that was it. "Excuse me?"

I stared up at his face, my heart pumping like bricks in my chest. "Are you... are you famous yet?"

I'm not proud of any of this. I turned into an utter loser, and I'm embarrassed that I have to relate it to you. I had never bothered the deodorant actor or the annoying accountant actor. Or even Gwyneth Paltrow.

He frowned at me. "Am I famous yet?" He looked around again. "Are you messing with me? Scott! Did Scott send you?"

I shook my head so quickly his face blurred above me. I had to think quickly. What had Bruce Willis done in 1985? "No! No, I just... I think *Moonlighting* is a fantastic show, and you're amazing."

"Oh," he nodded, as though I'd answered his question. "Oh, you watched the pilot already."

My head kept shaking, because I'd screwed up again. "It isn't on television yet? I'm sorry. I'm a moron."

"Yeah, the pilot's on TV tomorrow. Is tomorrow Sunday?" He scratched the underside of his chin. "Yeah, tomorrow. If you were able to see it already, that's great. So you liked it? I think it's a lot of fun myself, you know? Not the same basic detective show."

I'd watched *Moonlighting* faithfully from age 10 onward, when all the world was falling in love with detective David Addison. I agreed with Bruce. "Your character is hilarious. David runs his mouth, and it makes me laugh. Is... is this your first show? Have you been in any movies?"

"Nah, this is it," Bruce chuckled. "It's a kick in the pants, though. I hope people enjoy it."

I nodded energetically. "It'll be a big hit, and in a year, you'll be so famous that *everybody* will know you on the street."

"You think so, huh?" Bruce looked down at me. "I appreciate that, kid. No, I really do."

I wanted so badly to give him a hug. So badly, but I forced myself to stand back and let him be. "Well, I better let you go. Thanks for stopping."

He grinned back at me. "Thanks for stopping me."

I thought I'd die.

Sighhh. I headed back toward the café, where Dr. Wilkins had to be wondering why I'd dashed off. I watched the sidewalk pass under my sneakers, square by square. Don't step on a crack or you'll break your mother's back.

Seeing actors before they were famous. Such a crazy thing. They weren't hidden away in their mansions before they were famous. They walked down the sidewalk like regular people.

I had no reason to watch for danger. I had thirty more feet to the door of the café where Dr. Wilkins chewed on his sandwich. I hadn't been gone more than two minutes, and the streets were quiet that Saturday morning. No gang members shot at each other. No dogs growled or dark clouds glowered overhead. The sun shone pleasantly that morning of March 2nd, and I glowed over meeting a favorite actor. The warmth of it still danced in my heart, and what happened next seemed so incredibly rude, so messed up, so out of place in that cheerful, friendly morning.

With no warning, a massive hand clapped around my face, warm and meaty. A bear's arm wrapped around my middle, and I was hefted against a chest like a wall. The surprise was so sharp, I couldn't accept it as reality. I thought, "This is the wrong dream," as though a nightmare had invaded my perfectly good sleep.

But, it wasn't a dream. And I couldn't breathe.

A narrow alley loomed between the café and the building next to it, hardly wide enough for the few garbage cans stashed there. A giant gripped me and hauled me out of the sunlight into that tunnel, and it took me about three seconds to understand that I faced danger, that I had to fight. I started wriggling. I kicked the heels of both my feet into my captor's thighs, stretching down, trying to catch him in the knee. He held me too high for that, but I could tell my heel punches smarted, because he barked out and cursed at me. And that's when I knew. It was Tiberius.

My eyes went wide. Had he stalked me? Had he followed me around? Terror. He had plans for me. Bad plans. Bad bad plans. I had to get away from him right now!

I couldn't reach his knee, so I pulled up and focused higher. Wham. Wham. On the third kick, I caught him square in the groin, and he grunted and bent over. He didn't let go, but he wrapped both his arms around me, freeing my mouth.

"Help!" I screamed with all my might. "Help! Ahhhhhhhhh! Help!" I kept screaming while I thrashed and kicked and tried to make him let me go.

Still half doubled-over, Tiberius set me on the pavement, then he turned me around and punched me flat in the side of the head. This wasn't an open-handed slap, but a real, full-on man punch. My left cheek exploded, and I crashed into the metal can behind me. I knew that he hadn't hit me full power. If he weren't doubled over, if he'd put his whole weight into it, that punch could have killed me. I tried to get back up, but Tiberius grabbed my arm. His fist smashed into the side of my head again, harder this time, and the world flashed black as my skin split and my cheekbone shattered.

Tiberius clung to my T-shirt and refused to let go. I couldn't use my eyes right, and two versions of his angry face filled my vision. A heavy pain pumped through my skull, and I wanted to sit down. No, I had to keep fighting. I didn't want to die like that, punched into brain death by Tiberius in a stupid alley in Burbank! He paused to lean sideways against the wall, and I took advantage of that moment. I fell backwards away from his hand and, as my T-shirt jolted against his fist, I kicked straight up and caught him in the groin again. I'm convinced he spoke and words came out, but I only heard the orange pressure of pain and blood and confusion.

"Help!" I cried through the dizzying misery in my face. "Help!!"

I couldn't focus on anything. Up became down and the blur of a wall dangled above me. I wanted to spill to the ground, but Tiberius wrapped his big hands around my neck and squeezed. This time, he didn't hold back. Stars sparkled in the air around me, and my ears filled with a high-pitched hum. My left cheek felt ready to pop off, and I thought he'd break right through my neck and snap my head clean off.

The next moment, a giant "WHACK!" broke the grip on my throat, and I was yanked down against the pavement. My attacker cowered in a shadowy haze above me. A second "WHACK" echoed in our alley, and Tiberius' hands released altogether. He twisted around to face his new enemy, and I dropped away onto my back.

A shadow man stood above us, armed with a random chunk of lumber. "C'mon, honey," he beckoned to me. "Go. Quick."

I had to get out of the alley. I had to move. Roll over. Crawl. Crawl to the wall of the building. I knew I needed to get away, to get out of there, but I couldn't see through the agony in my head. Focus on my hands, on moving them across the pavement. Hard pavement. Little rocks. I reached the wall and cautiously walked my hands up cool white concrete, using its guidance to raise myself to my knees. I leaned against that wall - so dizzy. Colors blurred in the world around me, and I struggled to keep vertical. I had to get to the sidewalk, out into the open.

A crunching sound told me that Tiberius had gotten cracked with that board again.

Scuffling. Feet scraping rocks across the pavement. Strong arms wrapped around me, arms that scooped me up and out of the alley, around the corner into full sunlight. I reached out and grasped his shirt as he set me on my feet. The pounding pressure in my head and face overwhelmed me, and I fought a longing to sink to my knees. Hands gently pressed my temples and turned my head. My left eye had swollen shut and I couldn't see him.

"Sweetheart, we have to get you to a hospital."

I recognized his voice, and my blurred mind told me it made sense. I knew that voice for a reason.

A cry burst from Dr. Wilkins a few feet away. "Dear God!" His form grayed the light to my right eye. "What happened!"

My rescuer took care of the talking. "Some guy had her down in the alley there. We need to get this little girl to a doctor."

Dr. Wilkins disappeared from my sight. "I don't have a car."

"Then we need an ambulance. C'mon, kiddo. Let's get you to where you can sit down."

He carried me into the café and settled me in the nearest booth. Above me, a waitress yelped, "What happened!"

"Call an ambulance," Dr. Wilkins urged her, his voice rough as he gathered my hands in his. "It's okay, Dodge. You'll be okay."

"Doc," I mumbled. "Tiberius. Followed me."

"Oh, Dodge. Dodge, I'm sorry. I'm so sorry. I thought it was over. I thought he was gone!"

"Tiberius? Who's Tiberius?"

I breathed through my lips. "Doc. Bruce. From New Jersey, like you."

I started to drift off, but Bruce snapped his fingers in front of my face. "No no no. Don't do that. Stay awake. You have a concussion, honey. You need to stay awake."

I did. I remained conscious all the way to the hospital. But even with my good eye open, I still saw my enemy's face and felt his hands around my throat.

36 ∂Ɛ

Gauze

Mama patted my hand beside the hospital bed. I heard her voice and felt her presence in my dreams. When I opened my eyes and saw her, I wanted to throw my arms around her neck. Tears had streaked makeup down her cheeks, and her eyes puffed up swollen and red.

"Hi Mama," I whispered. Thickness weighed down my brain, and a mass of something covered one side of my head.

A wonderful smile spread over Mama's face. She dabbed her eyes with a soggy wad of tissue. "My poor baby. My poor baby, you're awake!"

I breathed out, "You need more Kleenex, Mama."

She collected a large handful of tissues but continued to cry. And then she got angry. "What were you doing! What were you doing out in Burbank! This nice man calls me and tells me you were attacked in an alley." She broke down and berated me in Spanish. "*¡No puedo creer que seas tan loco e irresponsable, y te fueras tan lejos de casa! Mírate, todo herido. Estás castigado. ¡Te encerraré en tu habitación todo el verano!*"

I reached out for her hand. She gave it, and I held it to my chest. I wanted to snuggle next to her, to kiss her face and wrap myself up in her softness, but my head still felt too heavy to move. My throat ached, and it hurt to talk aloud. "It's okay," I whispered. "You don't have to lock me away in my room all summer, Mama. I wasn't being crazy or irresponsible."

"It's not okay! All these bad things! It's because I didn't make you go to catechism classes! I should have made you go!"

I wanted to laugh, but my face ached and my head ached. I reached up and touched the soft gauze bandages that covered my left

255

cheek and wondered what I looked like. At least I could see out of my left eye again.

"Mama. Is there a mirror?"

Mama wasn't finished. "Why do you smile like that? You will go nowhere by yourself anymore, you bad very bad boy. You will be locked in your room!"

Even propped on pillows, my head weighed down my face. My eyebrows tried to press my eyes shut. "Please don't scold me, Mama."

Tears trickled down her dear brown cheeks. She held my hand to her lips. "I only scold you because you worry me so much."

An urgency hit me. "Mama, listen. Tiberius did it."

"What?" She looked confused. "What did Tiberius do?"

"In the alley. Tiberius dragged me into the alley."

"No! Tiberius would not do that!"

I took a deep breath. "Yes, he would, Mama. I know it makes you sad, but he said he'd kill me."

Mama cried, "I don't understand! How could a wonderful man be so evil! What did you do to him?"

I lay back and muttered my thoughts out loud, letting my head and eyes rest. "He followed me... waited to find me alone. Blames me 'cause you kicked him out. Doesn't blame himself."

Mama started to sob, and I reached out to pat her arm.

"He said that you hated *him* and wanted to get rid of *him*. Maybe you are lying. You are so smart! You could be a very smart liar!"

I opened my eyes at that. I lay in a hospital bed with a broken face. "Do you even hear yourself?"

Doc walked in then, pale and disheveled. His wrinkles seemed deeper than normal.

"Mama. Dr. Wilkins." I didn't have to move to croak out my few words. "He's the friend I go see on Saturdays."

Mama dried her eyes again. She made an effort to compose herself for company. "You are the piano teacher? You are the one who called me?"

"I'm so sorry," Dr. Wilkins apologized to Mama. "Dodge was only outside for a minute. It happened in a minute."

"Wait. What's today?" I didn't know how long I'd slept.

Mama tried to hush me. "Don't talk. You need to rest."

"Saturday?"

"It's Sunday." Mama motioned for me to be quiet.

"Mama, a show starts tonight. Watch it with me? The lead actor stopped Tiberius."

Dr. Wilkins shook his head in disbelief. "Lead actor? You and your movie stars. I don't understand you, you genius you. I've watched people fawn all over the nastiest people just because they were famous. I'm a respected composer! My music warms television scenes. You hear my jingles in commercials, but you don't trip all over yourself when I come around."

I laughed, and it hurt. I had to laugh with my face relaxed so that a "huh huh huh" came out, and that made me laugh more, and it hurt more.

Then I realized something.

"Doc, Bruce saw my attacker. Mama won't believe it was Tiberius."

Mama started to protest, but I kept going.

"Bruce will identify him. We have pictures of Tiberius at our house. Have you called the police?"

Dr. Wilkins waved his hands for me to calm down. "Shh. Shh. Relax, little one. We'll take care of everything. Calm your spinning mind. Right now, you need to rest, and I need to go home and get some sleep, and your mother needs to check on her children."

"Okay." My head relaxed into the pillow. "I'll rest if you take care of it."

Alone in the hospital that night, Sunday, March 3rd, 1985, I watched the very first episode of *Moonlighting* as The ABC Sunday Night Movie. I hadn't told Bruce, but I'd never actually watched that episode before.

37 ٣٧

Anna

The hospital released me two days later, just in time to watch Bruce's second episode from home. Tuesday nights now meant *St. Elsewhere* and *Moonlighting*.

Surgeons had used titanium plates to repair my cheekbone, which tickled Jorge. "You're a cyborg!" Jorge gushed when I got home. "You have metal inside your face!"

"They have to remove the plates in six weeks, though," I warned him. "Because my cheeks are still growing."

"Ohhh…" That disappointed Jorge so much. "At least you'll have a cool scar on the side of your face. You'll look so tough, nobody will want to mess with you."

I already had scars on my face. I didn't need any more scars on my face. One day I hoped to reach the year 2020 and replace the "me" that had disappeared into the past. It did no good to pile up a host of unexplainable marks to mar my previously unmarred face. Five years. I'd survived a measly five years back in time, and I'd already collected an unreasonable number of mars.

Mama turned to the children. "All you bouncing monsters, listen! Nobody is allowed to jump on Dodge! Nobody is allowed to wrestle with him. His face can be injured very easily." She urged me to sit up on the couch while she stuffed cushions behind me. Then she brought me some iced tea and dragged the coffee table over so I could reach it. "Oh, *mijo*. How are you going to ride your bike to school?"

"My legs aren't broken, Mama. But I should call all my professors about my absence so I don't lose points. And, Mama? Please make sure all the doors and windows are locked. Close the curtains. I don't want anybody to see inside our house."

I'd felt safe in the hospital, but now I genuinely feared Tiberius would show up to finish the job. I could not perish here in the 1980s! I had a family in the future who needed me, and I couldn't vanish one day with no explanation. I needed to survive the next 35 years!

Tiberius attacked me over and over in heated dreams on the couch that night. Finally, I lay awake in the darkness, breathing deep breaths to calm my heart. I worked over my situation and realized a few things. First, he wouldn't try to kill me with other people nearby. That's why he'd hunted me down in Burbank and waited for me to be alone. But! But he'd find a way to disappear me if I let him. I couldn't identify him if I were dead, stuffed into plastic garbage bags in some dumpster, headed for a landfill. Alive, though? My existence threatened him.

That meant I couldn't stay home alone. I had two months left of classes, two months of riding back and forth to school to finish up the semester. Tiberius knew that too.

I lay awake, thinking. Thinking thinking. I called up Dr. Wilkins as soon as the sun glimmered in the morning.

"Have you heard anything? Did they catch him? Did they go to his work and find him and arrest him?

Dr. Wilkins sighed on the other end of the phone. "They haven't told me anything, Dodge."

I hated it. My home no longer felt safe! I needed to hide.

I called Pastor Jack and explained the whole situation to him. He offered to let me stay with him and Anna until law enforcement caught Tiberius. He prayed with me over the phone, which made me feel a little better, but I still checked every lock in the house after I hung up with him. Then, I hid away in Mama's room with the door locked.

I even scooted under Mama's bed to pull out the little black case that held her handgun. I loaded the magazine with 9mm rounds and set it on the nightstand beside me. Finally, finally, I managed to doze off until Jorge and the girls got home from school. I unlocked the front door for them, ushered them in, then locked the door behind them. I hid the gun away for their sakes, but I still buried myself in Mama's room for the rest of the evening.

Mama found me huddled in her bed when she got home. She sat beside me and wrapped a gentle arm around my back. "Don't be sad, Dodge. You're okay, *mijo*. Your face will heal."

"It's not that, Mama. I'm just so scared. I'm scared Tiberius will show up and try to kill me again." I'd bravely moved from home to home for years. I'd faced dangers every week, but it was like I'd used up all my reserves of courage. Tiberius had pounded the last of it out of me and left me a gushy, mushy, fearful mess.

"He won't, baby. He won't." I know she was trying to comfort me, but she wasn't really listening.

"Yes!" I shouted. "Yes he will! He's going to try to kill me. Why don't you believe me? How long have you known me? How long! You know him two months, and you believe him instead of me? I tell you a man wants to kill me, and you think it's nothing!"

That startled her. "Okay. Okay okay, Dodge. I believe you."

Emotion rose in my chest and created more pressure in my head, which hurt my aching face. "He ruined our home. I don't feel safe here anymore. I have to go stay with somebody else until he's caught." He had won! He'd gotten me to leave!

Mama took my hand, concerned. "No, you don't have to go away, Dodge. You'll be safe here."

"I won't be safe if he knows where I am. I won't be safe here alone all day. I won't be safe riding my bike to school. Pastor Jack offered to let me come stay with him for a little bit, and maybe I should."

Mama slumped. Her big, warm shoulders drooped, and she took a deep breath. She reached over and gently wiped a tear off my good cheek. "Okay. And when you know you're safe, you come home?"

"Okay."

She looked miserable. "I am sorry. I'm sorry I brought home a man that would do this to you."

"Oh Mama. How could you have known? Just don't let him come back."

That evening, Denzel stopped by with flowers from the whole crew of *St. Elsewhere*. I sat there reading through all the names and pushing wet out of my eyes. He spent time telling me jokes and silly stories, and I appreciated every moment of it.

After he left, I yelled at Jorge for telling on me. "He didn't have to know I got beat up! You didn't have to tell him!"

Jorge just grinned. "You have metal in your face."

The next morning, Pastor Jack picked me up and drove me away to his home up north where Anna tucked me into a spare room, and I finally slept and slept. I still had to tell myself that Tiberius wouldn't magically appear, wouldn't break in to strangle me, but I relaxed enough to sleep through the night.

I only dared feel safe as days passed. One day and another and another without incident. I enjoyed my quiet afternoons with Anna, and I didn't cook a single meal. I offered to help with the dishes, but she just smiled and chatted with me while she washed up all the dishes herself.

The doctor removed my stitches the next week, and I felt good enough to return to school. Jack dropped me off every day when he drove to work, and Anna picked me up early afternoons. My face healed and I felt protected and barricaded away from danger, although I missed the bandages that hid the black eye and gash in my face. A Halloween zombie gazed back at me from the mirror, and I begged Anna to buy me an eye patch so I could look like a pirate and not a raggedy, busted up boy.

After that first week, I called the Burbank Police Department, but they had no useful information for me. Mama gave Jack the number for Tiberius' job, but when Jack called them, they said nobody by that name worked there. It seemed so hopeless.

The fear dissipated but never evaporated altogether. Wednesday of my second week back at school, I heard a knock at Jack and Anna's door, and I didn't know whether to peek out the window or run to my bed in the guest room. I sat frozen over my math book at the dining room table. Anna walked through, and I shouted spontaneously, "Be careful! Don't open the door!"

Anna listened, but she didn't share my terror. She removed her glasses and peeked through the eyehole to spy out our visitor, then she looked back across the living room at me. "I think it's safe." She replaced the glasses on her face and opened the door, and … ohhh… who walked in but the awesome guy himself.

"Bruce!" I stood up from my chair.

He walked in, embarrassed and out of place. "I'm sorry to show up like this," he apologized to Anna. "I would have called, but I didn't know your… Do you mind if I talk to this young lady a little?"

"Not at all." Anna looked at me. "Do you want to talk to him?"

She knew I did! I'd already told her all about him, and I'd made her watch *Moonlighting* with me.

"You're a tough person to track down," Bruce approached me. "I know that's the point, but you did a good job."

I nodded again.

"Wow, your face is looking better. You're healing up pretty good."

I felt in my pocket for my eye patch but decided to leave it off; he'd already seen my ugly. "Um. Happy Birthday." It was March 20th, and that meant he'd turned 30-years-old the day before.

"See! That's it right there. That's the reason I want to talk to you. You know what? The Monday after we met, I went to the studio and asked around about you. I figured somebody could tell me how you were doing after that attack in the alley. But, you know what?"

I knew what. "And nobody knew anything about me."

Bruce gave large, slow nods. "That's right. Not a soul had heard of a little girl named Dodge. Nobody. So, that didn't make any sense. You know what else didn't make sense?"

I could think of a few things.

"New Jersey. You knew I came from New Jersey."

I shrugged and slid back into my seat. "Your accent."

"Okay. But my birthday. How do you know my birthday?" He shook his head. "I'm sorry. I know you're still recovering, and I didn't mean to come in here to interrogate you. But. But, there are things that don't add up, and it's been driving me nuts."

I'd been so careful with Denzel and Mark Harmon. I'd been so careful. Why hadn't I been careful with Bruce? What was wrong with me? I needed to change the subject.

"I'm glad you came by. You know what Tiberius looks like. You can identify him. You can testify against him."

"Yeah yeah yeah. I'll do all that." Bruce looked hard at me. "And I'm glad you're doing okay. But answer the question. How did you know about the show already? Your foster mother tells me you're a genius, and I believe that, but I want to know if you're a sneaky sneaky genius child criminal."

I glanced over at Anna, who gave me a look that said, "Well?" She knew a few things about me from Jack. I scratched my chin and perused my math homework.

"Nah nah nah," Bruce said. "Eyes up here, genius child who gets away with murder. By the way, I found out today your foster mother thinks you're a boy!"

"She thinks you're a boy?" Anna said.

I nodded. "Well, the school does too. I was dressed in boy clothes when I entered the foster system, and I've just... kept it up." I winced at Bruce. "Did you tell-?"

He shook his head. "No, I didn't give up your rotten secret. Dr. Wilkins warned me about it before I went over to your house. I don't know how she doesn't already know, though. She lives with you! I thought you were doing some pixie rock star thing with the short hair."

"Expectations. She expects a boy, so that's what she sees. You had no expectations. You just saw."

He stood above me. "Look, I don't care. I'll testify for you and help put away that creep who tried to strangle you." He turned to Anna. "He's really a bad guy."

Anna nodded.

He explained to Anna, "I went over all the ways she could know me. I thought maybe her grandma knew my mom or something like that. But Mia says she's an orphan and grew up here. Is that right?"

Anna nodded again. "She has an odd situation. I knew her mom years ago when she was little. But, yes, she's lost her parents."

I turned to that gracious woman. "Anna, do you mind too much if Mr. Willis stays for a few minutes? Can we get you something, Mr. Willis? Maybe a glass of water or cookies and milk or something? You want to sit down?"

Anna headed into the kitchen. "I'll get you both lemonade."

Bruce pulled out the chair across from me and settled into it. He grimaced. "C'mon. Don't do the 'Mr. Willis' thing, you con artist."

I studied the familiar face across the table. So young. So much hair! He wore a plain black T-shirt, and he sat with his elbows on the table, eyebrows raised, waiting. Waiting for me to say something. Good grief, what could I tell him? The whole thing made me grumpy, and he could see it; he saw my distaste for this lousy job he'd given me, and he didn't care.

"So? How did you know me on the street?"

It was the obvious question. I'd screwed up. I'd complimented him on a show that hadn't come into the public eye. I'd recognized a guy nobody should have recognized, and the moment overwhelmed me.

"I can't believe I'm sitting here with you, talking to you about this," I muttered out loud. "I'm sitting with Bruce Willis. That's crazy. That's so crazy. I've been so careful, and I threw it all away. Because I like you."

"Kid."

"I've known Dr. Wilkins since I was six-years-old, and I still haven't given him the answer to what you're asking me. But you know what? I don't know what happens to him in the future. But you, I do. I know all kinds of things that happen to you in the future."

"You know what happens to me in the future?" He squinted.

I rested my face in my arms and moaned.

"You just run your mouth and horse manure falls out. Is that what this is?"

I pulled my head up. "It's true! I know about you, because you become super famous in the future, and I know the future."

Bruce sighed. "See, that's not how this works. I'm not leaving until you tell me the truth. You can't feed me a bunch of junk and expect me to say, 'Oh, okay. She knows the future, that explains everything,' and then I just go away."

I didn't back down. "It's why I recognized you on the street when you walked by. And why I would know something like your birthday. And that you used to stutter."

He jolted at that last bit. "Yeah! Things like that!" Bruce leaned up on his elbows to get closer to me. His green eyes opened wide so that his forehead wrinkled up, and he spoke in a low voice. "How did you know I stuttered? How would you know that!"

I met his gaze. He wouldn't believe the true answer to his question.

"How would you know about me!"

Anna placed large glasses of lemonade before us, and I waited for her to sit down. But, she didn't. She wandered back into the kitchen and abandoned me! Leaving me with Bruce Willis, who wanted to know the maddening, insane reality of my life. I met his eyes, and he raised his eyebrows. Waiting.

I hated this.

"I want to tell you my secret now," I whispered, a solemn, troubled child. I paused a beat while he waited for me to go on. "I see dead people." I snorted and blew out my lips! I couldn't do it! I tried to keep going, but laughter interrupted me "Hahah… They're walking around. They don't know they're dead!" I hid my face in my arms while my shoulders shook.

Of course he didn't get it. *The Sixth Sense* wouldn't come out for some 15 years. He couldn't get it. He folded his arms across his chest and frowned, waiting for me to stop acting my age.

"I'm sorry," I squeaked. "I'm sorry. 'Come out to the coast, we'll get together, have a few laughs.' Heeeee. 'Yippee Ki-Yay.' Say that." I tried to breathe. "Would you? Would you say, 'Yippee Ki-Yay' for me?" I tried to take in air. I tried to take in big breaths and calm myself while Bruce Willis glowered at me, irritated.

"I'm serious, kid."

"Oh, c'mon, Bruce. I have to tell you my huge secrets, and you won't even say 'Yippee Ki-Yay' for me?"

"What? Yippee Ki-Yay? What is that?"

I let myself get out all the giggles. I took a drink of my lemonade and used my arm to wipe my eyes dry. "I've been on edge since the day you saved me in the alley, and here you come in and now I can laugh. Thanks."

He groaned. "C'mon, Dodge. I just want to know. Do you have a pal at the studio? What's the deal? Do you sneak in and watch while we do scenes? Peek through files?"

"No." He wanted me to tell him that I was Harriet the Spy. I was a creeper. "No. I don't even know where the studios are."

"Okay."

"The truth? You want the truth? I've watched movies you haven't made yet, Bruce. I was quoting movies that haven't been written. I've seen interviews that you haven't given."

He sat back up, and his eyes narrowed.

"Wait. You're saying you're *from* the future? You know the future because you're from the future? That's your story?"

We sat and stared back at each other for a long moment. I finally nodded.

He repeated, "You're from the future?"

I nodded again.

Bruce studied me, shaking his head the whole time. "Yeah, I don't buy it."

"What don't you buy?"

"Saul said you were his foster kid when you were six. You'd just turned six. And he said he was your...14th foster home or something. You've been in foster care your whole life."

"Saul? You mean Dr. Wilkins?" I'd never thought about his first name before.

"Yeah. You're a foster kid. You're not from the future."

I closed my math book and shoved it in front of him. "What does this say?"

"It says *Calculus*."

"What rotten little 9-year-old foster child studies calculus?"

"A genius."

"Nobody is that huge a genius, Bruce. And I'm not really a genius anyway. The truth, the full truth? The truth is that I already grew up once. That's the truth. I was a chemist, and I ran a geochemistry assay lab. I got married and had three kids, and my oldest son's birthday is March 19th. Which is why I remember your birthday. And one day - for no clear reason - I woke up four-years-old again back in 1980. Anna and Pastor Jack know, but they're the only ones. Not even Dr. Wilkins knows. And that's why I'm in foster care; I'm a duplicate of the original me without a duplicate set of my parents. I remember the future because it's my past."

Bruce scowled at me. He sat and scowled for a minute. Then, he reached across and grabbed my math book, flipped it open, and skimmed down the page. He slid my spiral notebook across the table and started thumbing through the pages, scanning over the work I had penciled out.

I kept on. "Listen. On the Fourth of July weekend this year, a movie comes out called *Back to the Future*. I've watched that movie probably 30 times. Michael J. Fox gets into a shiny DeLorean that's been made into a time machine, and he gets stuck back in 1955. He has to find a way to get back to 1985. But me? There was no time machine. There was no DeLorean, and I don't get to go back to the future. I just woke up one day in 1980 as a four-year-old living my life all over again."

"That… doesn't happen," Bruce shook his head. "That's not real."

"It does happen. It happened to me. It's real."

"Is this like an *Invasion of the Body Snatchers* thing? Did you take some kid's body? Are you an alien?"

I grinned. "What? No. No, I'm not an alien. I've watched you on David Letterman. I've watched you on *The Tonight Show*, and you talk about yourself. Like, when you were in school a Spanish teacher started calling you Bruno. You had to say *me llamo Bruno* – because Bruno is the Spanish version of Bruce."

"Shut up." He shoved his chair back and stood up. "Seriously."

I knew he married Demi Moore. I knew they had daughters. I knew his brother died. But, I couldn't tell him those things, because that was wrong. "It's 1985. Right?" I changed gears. "It's 1985 and this guy Mike Tyson is going to win all his fights this year. Every single one. He just goes out and bashes the snot out of his opponents."

"The snot?"

"Bam bam bam!! Mike Tyson. He's got heavy eyebrows and a lisp and he's short. But, it doesn't matter, he wins anyway. And Whitney Houston! Ever heard of Whitney Houston?"

Bruce shook his head.

"Ha! You will! And… New Coke! They bring out New Coke this summer, and it's sweet like Pepsi and everybody hates it. The public is going to have a loud hatred for New Coke. So, then Coke will go back to the old formula and call it 'Coca Cola Classic,' and people will buy it like crazy. I personally think the whole thing is brilliant marketing."

Bruce shook his head. He shook his head as he settled back into his chair across from me.

"I have all my lifetime of memories as an adult, Bruce, but I *feel* like a kid. It's weird, because I feel like I'm a child, a ridiculously smart child, and I have only a vague sense of what it was like to be an adult. Except that I know things. I like to play with Legos and watch cartoons and read silly kids books, but I know things. And I'm super irritated that I have to go through puberty all over again in a couple of years."

Bruce laughed spontaneously at that. Then, he stared into the air, into nothing for the longest time. Finally he said, "This boxer. Mike?"

"Tyson."

"Tyson. So, if I start watching his fights, you say he always wins."

"Yep. He'll be the heavyweight champion of the world next year."

"And Whitney Houston? Does he beat Mike Tyson?"

"Whitney Houston is a *she*, and she's a singer, and my friend Jassy Mercer got a Whitney Houston album for her 11th birthday. I mean, she'll get it this coming fall. In a few months, she and I, the original me, will be dancing all over her living room singing like we're in love with our teddy bears."

Bruce clasped his hands on top of his head. His head that still had hair on it. He got up and walked across the living room, back and forth. Back and forth.

"Say you're telling the truth. Which is nuts, and I don't believe it." He returned and sat back down. "Then…then…you have a cool gift!"

"I guess."

"It is a cool gift. An important gift! If you're from the future, you remember things. You could stop serial killers."

"It's not so easy. I don't remember enough."

"You remember New Coke!"

"Yeah, but what do you remember about the 1960s, Bruce? No, listen. Do you remember the date of the moon landing? When Neil Armstrong and Buzz Aldrin stepped out on the moon?"

Bruce stopped and thought about it. "It was July. In 1969."

"Okay, that's pretty good. But what if you had to remember the exact date?"

"It was a Sunday," Bruce added. "Ed Sullivan didn't come on. July… 20th? July 20th, 1969."

"All right, you totally ruined my point. But before Reagan got shot, I couldn't remember the date! I knew it was sometime in 1981 or 1982, but I couldn't remember anything else about it. Then one day it happened, and I had no way to warn anybody. I have to remember *details* to stop bad things from happening."

"But you knew Reagan would get shot! That's something."

"Or it's nothing! Several years from now, there'll be a bombing in Oklahoma City that kills a whole bunch of children, but I don't remember the date! I think it's 1995. I can't remember! They pinned it on a guy named Timothy McVeigh, so maybe I could tell the FBI to watch him. But, they can't surveil him for a whole year for no reason!"

"Still, you're smart. If you were a chemist, that means you were smart your first time around. You could figure it out."

My predicament was new to Bruce, but I'd been dealing with it for five years. "I think about it all the time, of course I do. But my memory isn't good enough."

He took a long drink from his glass and set it down again on the table. "This is really weird, kid."

I took a deep breath and reached for my glass too.

He thought a moment. "I become a big-time actor?"

"Huge. Way to go. Good for you."

Bruce held his empty lemonade glass and stared at the tabletop. I watched him working over the things I'd told him, and I felt peculiar because he seemed so familiar. As far as my unconscious brain was concerned, he'd been hanging out in my living room all my life. I'd been spending time with him through a box for 35 years. I'd never met him; he didn't know me from Eve, and I didn't know what he was like in real life, but my unconscious mind didn't know that. It recognized him and assumed we were friends. I felt warm and comfortable sitting across the table from him.

"I think you're being pessimistic about what you remember," he said finally. "What you know could be valuable, whether you realize it or not."

Was it valuable? Could I make a difference?

"Here's the thing, Bruce. I've wanted to stop terrorist attacks, but I've been wondering. What if I was *always* here all along, and so anything that I do contributes to how the future played out in the first place?"

"Hmmm. That's not what Kyle Reese told Sarah Connor."

"Forget Kyle Reese! *The Terminator* is just a movie, and the movies are always wrong! The machines don't take over and try to destroy us. There's no nuclear war. The world isn't flooded or iced over or taken over by apes. There's no global meltdown. Maybe everything I do only leads to what already happened!"

"But what if you could change one thing? One horrible thing? What if you knew the identity of the Zodiac Killer in the future, and you were able to tell the FBI and they could catch the guy?"

I thought of September 11th and the Twin Towers and Pentagon and smashed Flight 93 in Pennsylvania. I'd thought about them over and over again for five years. Could I stop the attacks? Did I have that power?

"I don't know if I can change a single thing. What if I can't?"

"Don't you have an obligation to try? At least try?" He stared at me with wide eyes until I finally nodded my head.

"Yes. Yes, of course. But I have to live long enough to get to the point it matters I know something."

"Okay I get it. But I'm here to help." Bruce's eyes shifted to the left side of my face, where my new crescent-moon scar still shone red.

I didn't know how to react to that. "You're here?"

He shrugged. "I'll wait for this Mike Tyson. Mike Tyson? And Whitney Houston to do their things. But I … I might believe you. And if you are who you say you are, you could be a real-life superhero. That's something you shouldn't waste."

"Well, thanks." I smiled wearily at him. I appreciated it. I knew his life was about to become exceptionally busy, and I already forgave him if he couldn't follow through with helping me, but I was grateful.

"Yippee-Ki-Yay," I said.

"Yippee-Ki-Yay," he repeated.

Aw yeah. That made my night.

38 8Ɛ

Run

I lived with Pastor Jack and Anna for two months. Two months. I missed Jorge and the girls and Jason. I missed Mama. I called and talked to them a lot, but I had to skip Jorge's 10th birthday, and that frustrated me. I bought G.I. Joes and mailed them to him, but I hated not being there.

I resented Tiberius for making my home unsafe. Mike Tyson had his first professional fight on March 6th, and I'd totally missed it in the middle of all this mess!

Otherwise, it was good to rest in a peaceful home. I enjoyed the quiet and calm. I got all my schoolwork done without Jason climbing up and over me, and it was easy to earn my straight A's. After six weeks, I had surgery to remove the metal plate, and I healed from that. A solid pink mark rounded the outside of my left eye and cheek, but it came to be part of my face, and I stopped staring at it every time I looked in the mirror.

I hadn't phoned Mama for a couple of weeks, until one day she called and asked me to come home.

"Did they catch Tiberius?" I asked, hopeful.

No, she said. They hadn't. "But, I think you are safe now."

"Is he dead?"

She laughed. "No. But, I want you to come home. I don't want you to worry anymore."

Jack and Anna had never once suggested I leave. In fact, they'd told me repeatedly I could stay as long as I needed, but I didn't like taking advantage of them. Tiberius had to have given up by now, right? Maybe he'd moved out of state. Maybe he'd fled to Costa Rica like a decent person.

The school semester ended. I pulled together my duffel bag of clothes and my Dodgers backpack, and Jack drove me to Mama's the next Sunday.

When we pulled up to my house, Jack got serious. "You sure you want to do this? If they haven't found Tiberius, that means he's still out there."

"I'm not injured anymore. I can keep my eyes open."

Jack didn't look happy. I hardly noticed his great lanky height or his huge forehead or his nose anymore. His good, honest face had concern all over it. "I mean it, Sadie. You don't have to go back yet. You can wait."

"I miss my brothers and sisters. I need them. And they need me. At least, I think they need me."

Jack nodded. "They need you whole and undamaged, dear."

"I know."

He got out and helped me unload my bike. "Sadie, hold on. Let me pray for you."

I genuinely loved it when Jack prayed. Some people pray, and you know they're just saying words, but Jack talked to God like he knew Him. Sometimes he and Anna bickered. Sometimes he forgot things. He was a normal human being, but something about him gave me a sense of security, as though big angels walked wherever he walked, and God Himself conducted his life. Or wrote the musical score. Something like that. I'd met too few people like Pastor Jack in my life, and it made me wish that I could be like him. I wanted big angels to follow me everywhere, and I wanted God Himself to be the conductor that directed the musical score of my life.

"Pray that God directs all my steps," I said. "And pray that they catch Tiberius. And pray that he doesn't hurt me again."

Jack did just that, then he gave me a final hug around my head. "Call me if you need anything."

While he watched, I slung my bags over my shoulder and walked my bike through the gate to park it with the other bikes in the back yard. I gave Jack a last wave through the gate and ran to the back door of the house.

"Hello Mama!" I jogged into an empty kitchen.

The silence shouted back at me. It was like I'd entered a house for sale. The kitchen sparkled. The floors had been swept and mopped. I peeked into the bedrooms, pleased to see the kids had vacuumed their carpets. Clothes hung in neat, orderly rows in the closets, and when I washed my hands in the bathroom, no toothpaste or grime coated the sink.

"Wow. They did so great."

That didn't seem right. I expected some clutter, some normal life messes. Maybe they'd cleaned up to surprise me.

I opened the back door and double-checked outside. Yep, the kids' bikes sat parked by the wall, like I'd thought. Maybe they'd gone on a Sunday afternoon outing. So strange, because they expected me home.

I returned inside and looked into Mama's room. Her sheets and blankets stretched flat and smooth across her freshly made bed. Her bed? Mama never made her bed. She washed the sheets every week or so, but daily bed-making did not happen. She didn't care.

Strange.

I decided to munch on cereal and watch TV while I waited for them to come home. I poured my sugary mini wheats into a bowl and reached into the fridge for the milk. As soon as I did, I couldn't breathe.

The world was filled with just the worst. The worst.

Cold air from the fridge wafted onto me for thirty seconds. It held me there, frozen. I finally ran down the hallway and slid open the drawers in Mama's dresser. Ten seconds later, I pulled on my backpack and ran out the back door to my bike.

"Mama!" I jumped on and pumped out to the road. "Never choose your hormones over your brains!"

I rode my bike east out to Toluca Lake then decided to catch a bus. I stuck my bike on the front and rode north. When I got off, I rode around until I found a little diner. There I sat in a corner and ate a bowl of soup and piles of saltines for hours. As dusk darkened the world outside, I used the counter phone to call Dr. Wilkins.

"Can I come over?"

"Dodge!" Doc yelped through the phone. "Your mother has been calling me all afternoon. Where are you?"

"Don't call her back, Doc."

"Okay, I won't."

"Can I come over?"

"Yes, of course!"

"I can be there in 20 minutes. We're synchronizing our watches.

Okay? In exactly 20 minutes at 8:35, I will show up at your back door, and you will be ready to let me in. Don't show yourself before that. Got it?"

"Yes, paranoid child."

"You told Mama you hadn't seen me?"

"Repeatedly."

"She let him into the house, Doc! She told me it was safe to come home, but that place is freaky clean and he's got his beer in the fridge and his clothes in the dresser, and I want to talk to Jorge and find out what's really going on, but I can't. Okay. I'll see you in 20 minutes."

"Ah, I see. Okay, 20 minutes. Go."

I rode through the neighborhoods, up and down, wasting time. I biked to Doc's building from the east, stashed my bike between the dumpster and wall, and 15 seconds overdue, I dashed up to the door. The good composer opened it and led me up to his apartment.

"Lock it," I said. "Quick. Quick."

Dr. Wilkins clicked the door and the deadbolts into place, and I dropped my bags by the piano.

Paranoid, yes. But rightfully!

"He's not out there waiting for me. He's probably at the house with Mama and the children. I know. I know. I know I'm being a lunatic, but I panicked."

Doc put a hand on my shoulder. "It's okay. I'm glad you came here."

I grabbed the Rubik's Cube that Mike had sent me, and I twisted it around and around until I made a flower on all sides. I kept it at Doc's, safe from jelly fingers, and it served the same purpose as a fidget spinner or squeeze ball in different decades. I twisted it around until I had a four-leaf clover in a blue background. Then I twisted it back so that all sides were solid. Then I twisted it into a four-leaf clover again.

"Do you want to talk about it?"

I shook my head. "Is it too late to play the piano? Will it make the neighbors mad?"

Doc smiled. "Yes, it will make the neighbors mad."

"Okay then." I twisted the Rubik's Cube back so that all the sides were solid. I made the checkerboard pattern, then I twisted them back.

"Are you hungry? Do you want to eat?"

"No, please."

"Would some tea help?"

I drew in a massive breath and let it out. "Okay."

We sipped our warm drinks at the table in the tiny kitchen, and Dr. Wilkins tried to joke with me. When that didn't work, he got practical. "You know, I really need to call your mother and let her know you're safe."

"No!" I insisted. "No! She let him in! Do not call her. I feel safe here only because he doesn't know where I am."

"Shh shhh. It's okay, I understand. I won't call."

"I need to talk to Jorge first. I'm so tired, though, Doc. I'm so tired. If you protect me, I'll feel safe enough to go to sleep."

I kissed that good, warm, wrinkled face, then I stumbled into my old bedroom and fell asleep in minutes.

I slept until 9:00 a.m. We sat at the table again the next morning over eggs and toast, and this time we talked it out.

"Okay! Let's help me get all of our facts straight," the wise man said. "You are supposed to be at your mother's house. Correct?"

"Correct."

"But, based on clues you spied when you walked in, you believe she has allowed the return of El Diablo."

"Roger that."

"Who tried to choke you to death in yonder alley in March." He waved his hand loosely in the direction of the café down the road.

"That's right."

"And this terrifies you."

"Obviously."

"Now! Your mother has urged you to return, despite these facts, because she believes the promises of El Diablo that it was all just a big misunderstanding, and he will not hurt you."

"You're so smart, Doc! I know that's what it is. He convinced her. She should know better! But, he still managed to convince her."

"Anything else?"

"I have superpowers."

"Well, we all knew that." He rolled his eyes.

I peered at him, wondering what he *did* know. He had brains in that aged head. "So, what do I do now, Doc?"

"I think you need to let your beloved mother know you're safe."

"Yes. But not yet."

"And Pastor Jack. Because she probably called him half a dozen times too."

"Of course! That's why I didn't call him yesterday."

"And ... the police. So, they can go find Tiberius. I believe he has

274

an outstanding warrant for his arrest."

"Oh! Good idea!"

"I always have good ideas."

"And Jorge," I said. "I want to find out if the kids are okay. As soon as possible. I want to talk to Jorge."

Dr. Wilkins agreed. "I think that's important, and we can manage it in a most surreptitious manner. First, call Pastor Jack and let him know you're safe. Then, give me the phone."

After I hung up with Jack, Dr. Wilkins began calling Mama. The answering machine beeped in his ear the first three times he tried throughout the day. At 3:30 p.m., one of the girls picked up, and Dr. Wilkins asked for Jorge.

"He's in his room," Tamika said cheerily. "But, Mama's here."

Dr. Wilkins talked to Mama and learned that they hadn't heard a word from me. "Maybe Dodge is in danger. Call the police." Clever Dr. Wilkins!

No. Mama believed that I was just being naughty and hiding out somewhere.

"Okay. Please call if Dodge returns." He hung up.

"Wow, she's home early. They're all home early," I said.

Dr. Wilkins phoned every two hours. At 9:30 p.m., he made his final call of the day, and Jorge answered.

"Hi Jorge," Dr. Wilkins nodded quickly at me. "Sorry it's late."

I slipped across the kitchen floor and stuck my head next to Doc's ear to listen in.

"No problemo." Jorge sounded tired. Listless.

"Jorge, I want to ask you about Dodge."

"I don't know where he is!" Jorge insisted, almost wailed, as though he'd been asked that question over and over and over. As though Dr. Wilkins had poked his sore spot.

"No, son, I know. I know. It's okay. It's not your fault."

"I don't know where he is," Jorge repeated, and I wanted to reach through the phone and hug him.

"Jorge, are you alone in the house right now?"

"No."

"Are the adults there?"

"Yeah, I'll get-"

"Wait. Wait, Jorge. It's you I want to talk to."

Jorge whimpered, "I haven't seen Dodge in two months."

"Shh. Shh. I believe you. Are you alone in the room?"

"Yes."

"Now, Jorge. Dodge always told me you were smart. Just listen. I want you to write down a number. Do you have a pencil?"

"Um. Yeah."

Doc spoke out the phone number twice, slowly. He then told Jorge, "Okay, stick that number in your pocket. The person on the other end will be able to help Dodge, but this is top secret stuff and you can't tell anybody. Not your Mama. Not your sisters. Nobody. Don't call from your house. As soon as you can sneak out to a pay phone, call the number. It doesn't matter how late you call. Call in the middle of the night if you have to wait to get out in secret. If you agree to do this, I want you to say, 'Yes, sir. We'll call if we hear from him.'"

"Yes, sir. We'll call if we hear from him."

"Good lad. Now hang up."

I'd been holding my breath throughout the conversation, and I let it all out.

"Whose number is that?" I panted. "Who will he call from the phone booth?"

"Me. It's my business line."

Oh.

Doc nodded. "And now we wait."

We tried to read, but neither of us could focus. In the end, Doc pulled out a deck of cards. We played cribbage for 90 long minutes while I felt guilt over Jorge. The grief in his voice made me wonder what took place the two days I'd been missing.

Dr. Wilkins was close to winning his third game against me when the phone rang.

Doc grasped the phone at his desk. "Hello?"

I rushed to his side to listen.

"Hi?" The boy's voice on the other end shivered with nerves. Or cold.

"Are you safe, Jorge?" Doc asked. "Are you safe? Are you alone? If you're not, press any button."

No buttons beeped in our ear. "I'm okay. I'm alone. Do you know where Dodge is?"

"She's just fine, Jorge. But, Dodge wants to know if you're okay. She's worried about you."

"Is she there? Can I talk to her?" Jorge asked honestly, a sob in his voice. "Can you put her on?"

Dr. Wilkins handed me the phone.

"Jorge, it's me. Are you all right?"

"I'm so glad it's you! I was so scared!"

"Has Tiberius hurt you?" I demanded.

"…He just wants to know where you are."

"He has! He's been hurting you!"

"You were supposed to come home yesterday, and we got home and you weren't there. But I was glad, Dodge! I was glad you left. I can't make Mama understand. She believes him and doesn't believe me. And you shouldn't be here!"

"Are the kids all safe?"

"Mama keeps telling me it will be okay, but she doesn't know he acts different when she's not around. He's always nice when she's there, but I never know how he's gonna be when she's gone. He loses his temper. He slapped Shamisha yesterday, and I wanted to kill him."

"He's got a warrant for his arrest, Jorge, and we're gonna call the cops to go get him. Does he stay at home all day? Is your schedule the same?"

"He's not there all day. He leaves in the morning, but he's there when I get home."

"Okay. Can you and the girls go to the park after school? Ride your bikes down to the park when school lets out, and when you get there, use a pay phone to call this number again."

"I can do that. But Dodge? Would you come see us at the park? Would you meet us there?"

I weighed the danger. "Sure, I'll meet you there. That's better than a phone call anyway. As soon as you get out of school, ride over there, and I'll meet you."

"Okay." Relief lightened Jorge's voice. "It's like there's a big hole at home since you left. Everybody misses you."

Tears rimmed up in my eyes. "Yeah, I miss you too." I had one more thing to say. "You know, when I came in yesterday, you guys had the house really clean. I mean. Really clean. I was impressed."

Jorge didn't say anything for a few seconds. "Yeah. It's cold out, and I gotta get some sleep. I'll see you tomorrow."

39 ୧ଽ

Volcano

Of course, things didn't work the way I intended. Not even a little bit. Dr. Wilkins and I reached the park at 3:30, and we waited and waited, expecting the kids to show up on their bikes around 4:00.

No. No Jorge and Tamika and Shamisha. By 4:30, it was clear something had gone wrong.

Maybe it was the security of Dr. Wilkins' presence, but I felt ten times safer than I had hiding in a booth with my soup and crackers the night before. I'd avoided Tiberius for so long, but here in the park with Doc, my fear melted away. Maybe the angels had showed up, I didn't know, but I'd gotten a small refill on my courage reserves.

"We need to go to my house," I told Doc.

"No."

"We have to," I insisted. "I'll go in the house and face him. He won't hurt me with Mama there, especially after he promised her I'd be safe. He's been trying to win her back. You make the phone call for the police to come get Tiberius, and I'll be there to make sure the kids are safe. Tiberius is so unpredictable, I just want to make sure they're out of the house when the cops come."

"Dodge Journey Spicer, I am not letting you go there alone."

"Call the house and ask if you can come and visit. Call after I get there. You can be excited I'm home safe And of course you'll want to see me."

"What if your mother doesn't want a visitor?"

"I'll sneak the kids out my bedroom window. Don't worry."

"They're not the ones I'm worried about."

"They are the ones that *I'm* worried about."

278

Doc's wrinkles deepened, if that were possible. He frowned down at me beside him on that park bench.

I threatened to go with or without him, and the old composer finally agreed with my plan. We took a bus to the convenience store three blocks from my house.

I urged him, "Please wait half an hour. Call the cops, then call Mama."

"Half an hour!"

"I can't just walk in there and pull the kids out. I have to play it cool. Give me a half hour."

"This is too much stress for an old man, Dodge. I play music for a reason. Pleasant, engaging music. I don't go on high-speed chases and punch bad guys."

On Sunday, I'd felt exposed and vulnerable. Mama had wanted me to come home right into whatever trap Tiberius had planned for me. Today, he didn't expect me, and that gave me an advantage.

I left Doc at the convenience store and trotted down our road, past the vacant lot where Tiberius had banged me against the fence. I ran up to the front door and tried the doorknob. Locked. Darn. I reached up and knocked.

Kids shouted inside. Mama opened the door, and tears erupted into her eyes. Tamika slid into the doorway next. She screamed and leaped at me, wrapping her arms around my neck. Shamisha jumped on me a moment later, and I had to grab the doorframe to stay on the steps. I laughed and held both girls as Mama's Spanish thundered down on me.

"Where's Jason!" I hauled the girls into the house "Jason! You here?"

"Dodge!" The little boy ran in, flung his arms around my waist, and we all flopped onto the kitchen floor, a pile of arms and legs and warmth and joy. For that little moment, that drop in time, Tiberius had no power. I had my family back, and I grabbed each one and kissed their faces over and over.

Mama watched us and began to laugh. Jorge joined her and grinned down at me on the floor. But, I saw it. I saw the strain around his eyes, the worry. He glanced down the hall and back at me, and I knew my enemy readied to emerge from his cave. I pulled Jason onto my lap and wrapped my arms around his warm little chest.

"You've got so many freckles!" Tamika laughed at me.

"So do you!"

"No, I don't," she grimaced. "You're weird."

Mama put her hands on her hips. "Come on, *mijo*. I want a hug too. And then I want to pinch off your head for scaring me for two days! Two days! I should lock you in your room for a month!"

I melted into Mama's softness and let her hold me, all the while knowing I'd have to face the dragon she'd let back into the house.

"I love you, Mama. I didn't mean to scare you. I was scared."

"I know, *mijo*. I know. But you don't have to be scared. I want you to trust me, baby."

As Mama pulled me into her, I faced her door at the end of the hall. I only watched a few more seconds before Tiberius emerged. He stepped out, slow, calm. He didn't breathe fire and smoke right then, but my face ached. My heart didn't care that loving family members surrounded me, it pumped blood harder just the same.

"Well!" Tiberius used his cheeriest voice, his face wide in a smile. "The prodigal has returned! Where's the fatted calf?"

I couldn't say a thing. Mama released me, and I stood and watched that big man walk toward me. I flashed back to the alley, and my cheek pounded. Songs on the radio could splash my memory with the smells of sunscreen and saltwater, but the sight of Tiberius washed woozy agony over me.

"So, you ran off and hid for two days." Tiberius nodded down at me, as friendly as can be. "You worried Mama, son. It was shameful to treat her that way."

Honestly bothered by that part of it, I turned to Mama. "I'm sorry. I really am sorry."

"Well, supper is ready!" Tiberius declared. "I think it's time we all sat down and enjoyed it. Dodge, help Jorge bring the food to the table."

Somebody had fried potatoes and onions and sausages and cut up a salad. Jorge and I set the table and carried dishes across the kitchen while Mama had the little ones wash their hands. I wanted to whisper my plan to Jorge, but Tiberius watched us too closely.

"Gentlemen, we're all going to be good?" The big man met my eyes first before he turned to Jorge. The hostility behind those eyes hadn't dissipated a smidge, and Jorge and I both saw it. Blinded by swirling, washing hormones and eternal hope, Mama couldn't see, and we knew that too. We complied by nodding our heads.

Which was a lie. I had every intention of causing problems after the wise doctor made his phone call. For the moment I sat at the table with Tamika on one side and Shamisha on the other. Jason climbed onto my lap, and we ate our food. Jason didn't adore the salad, but he obediently chewed on a few bites of lettuce. I nuzzled my face into his fuzzy hair, relishing those precious moments as the girls giggled and slipped food onto my plate. My heart swelled because I loved them so much.

"So, where did you go?" Tiberius finally asked as we munched our food. "Where does a boy go hang out for two days?"

Mama put her hand on his arm. "He's back. He's safe. I don't even care. I just wanted him home."

"I know Mia. I'm just curious. He – foof – disappears? Without leaving a note? Without calling?"

"I really am sorry I scared you, Mama."

Tiberius wiped his mouth with a paper napkin. "Let me think. What would my father have done if I'd been thoughtless like that?"

"Tiberius, please," Mama said again. "Please let it go. Dodge, we have cherry pie and ice cream."

"Would you like me to get it?"

Mama nodded. "Jorge, help him."

Jorge and I jumped up and moved pans and trays to the counter. The girls took the dirty plates to the sink, and I placed clean bowls around the table. Jorge brought out the dessert.

"Everybody hand your bowl to Tiberius. He can serve the pie and ice cream."

Did the twins and Jason notice the tension? Mama had to feel it. I knew she did, but she wanted her imagination to manifest as reality, no matter what her practical side said.

Jorge and I understood the full danger we faced, that a dragon, no, a *volcano* puffed at the end of the table, dishing cherry pie and ice cream into white Corelle bowls. Dragons might puff and breathe fire, but volcanoes blasted open sooner or later and - kaboom - annihilated everything around them.

My plate emptied, but I didn't see or taste my dessert. I watched the explosion of Mount St. Helens in my mind. Forests of trees flashed down like toothpicks before a scorching cloud of debris and ash. When my vision returned to the table, I found Tiberius' eyes focused on me. What had he planned?

"You want me and Dodge to do the dishes tonight, Mama?" Jorge asked. Good job, Jorge. We needed some side-by-side time.

Tiberius answered instead. "No, wash the dishes with Tamika.

Shamisha can clear the table. Mama and I need to talk to Dodge."

I saw Jorge's heart deflate. He didn't dare disobey, no matter how much we needed to talk. I clearly had to get us all sent to our rooms as soon as possible.

After dessert, Shamisha hopped up to clear dishes from the table. Tiberius gently took Mama's hand and led her to the living room, and the two of them settled onto the couch. Tiberius called me over, and I stood before them. Dr. Wilkins should be calling any minute now, but I had to resist the temptation to glance at the phone.

Sitting, that big man met me eye-to-eye, and he commanded the room. Mama held his hand, held the hand of my enemy. I smiled at her anyway. I loved her, and I wanted her to know it.

"Dodge, pay attention."

I turned my eyes back to the volcano.

"Things are going to be different from now on, you need to know that. You're out of school, so you'll be home every day to watch Jason. Mama and I don't want you going anywhere. You'll stay here, because this running off around the valley is crazy. You're nine-years-old."

Mama nodded earnestly. "It really is, baby. You go to Burbank! You go to Van Nuys! This is too dangerous."

"You need to stay close to home. If I go out on the steps and call for you, you have to be near enough to hear me. Like every other kid in this neighborhood."

I didn't bother to argue with him. I didn't respond at all.

Mama added, "I know you want your piano lessons, but it's too far! I don't want you riding your bike out there anymore."

I took a deep breath. What was Tiberius' goal in all of this? Was he trying to pick a fight? Smother me, hold me back, drive me crazy? Keep me close for easy harassment? It was Tiberius who got home early, not Mama.

"You can keep working on the garden," Tiberius said. "You can visit neighbors if you tell us where you're going first. But, I mean it, Dodge. You need to be able to hear us when we call."

You know what was messed up? I wanted to believe him. Tiberius sounded so reasonable, so parental, I almost doubted my memories. It took a quick flash back to our minute in the alley to keep the truth fresh, but Dr. Jekyll hid Mr. Hyde so well!

Did he seriously hope to fool me? Obviously, this was a ruse for Mama's sake, but he acted like he fully expected me to believe it too. I searched his face for a hint of honesty, a momentary break in the mask that hid his guilt. Nope, he faced me like an earnest father concerned about my safety.

It couldn't all be for show. This had to be a step in his runaway-Dodge plan. Stifle me with a million rules. Then dispose of me. Then tell Mama I ran away. I saw it, but I still felt moved by his concerned voice. He deserved an Oscar.

"Answer Tiberius, baby. I know you understand what he just said to you."

The phone rang.

"I'll get it!" Without waiting for permission, I ran to the phone and grabbed it off the hook.

"Hello? ... Oh, hi Dr. Wilkins!" I said it with natural enthusiasm. "Yes, sir. I'm home."

Doc's voice sounded anxious even through the receiver. "Dodge, I'm so sorry, I don't know Tiberius' full name. I called, and they want details about him that I don't know. I've never tipped off the police before!"

"Me either." That was a cruel blow. I glanced at the adults in the living room and remembered to keep my cover. "Yes, I know. I know Mama was worried about me."

"You don't have to stay there. Let me speak to your mother. I'll talk her into letting you spend a few days with me."

"Yes, Dr. Wilkins. She's here. Just a moment." I held the phone out to Mama. "He wants to talk to you."

Mama started to get up, but Tiberius placed his hand on her knee. "Just tell him Mama will call him back."

Geez, this guy. I *wanted* to throat punch him.

"Dr. Wilkins, Mama needs to call you back. Is there a number where she can reach you?" I grabbed a pencil and paper. "Okay. I'll write it down."

Dr. Wilkins read off the phone booth number and then hissed, "Am I actually supposed to sit by this payphone?"

"Yes, sir. She'll call you back."

"Dodge, you're driving me crazy. Are you safe? Are you getting the kids out?"

"I'm fine. I'll talk to you soon, Doc. Good night." I hung up and returned to the living room.

Tiberius continued his lecture while I stood before him. The police tip-off hadn't worked. They weren't coming. What should I do now?

"...I think you should be grounded to the house for the next week. Mia, what do you think?"

"You did scare us, Dodge. That was wrong of you."

Our simple little plan had failed. Should I pacify Tiberius? Should I make a fuss and get myself sent to my room? Should I encourage the volcanic eruption so that Mama wanted him gone too?

I wasn't really good at chess. I could play strategically for awhile, but then I always got impatient. I'd take out an enemy bishop even if it was protected by a rook so that mass slaughter followed. Then, after we'd wiped out half of each other's armies, I'd proceed with strategy again. I saw the net that Tiberius was stretching for me, and I made a decision. Dr. Wilkins would have forbidden it, but I was tired of the chess game.

"Tiberius, how many of the kids have you hit?"

He jerked up straight, but before he responded, I called out, "Shamisha! Come in here real quick!"

Like a peach, Shamisha trotted in.

"Did Tiberius slap you the other day?"

Shamisha stopped still, like a statue. She side-glanced at Tiberius, and then at Mama, and then at me, and she didn't say anything.

"It's okay, Shamisha. You can say it out loud. We already know the answer."

She only shook her head at me.

"He smacked you, didn't he? You can say it. It's true."

"Dodge." There was a warning in Tiberius' voice.

"See this scar on my face, Shamisha? Tiberius punched me. He broke my face, and I had to have surgery."

I saw the pressure building in the volcano on the couch. "Dodge, it's time for Shamisha to go to bed."

I nodded at her. "It's okay. Go on and go to your room."

She did. She ran.

"That wasn't Tiberius," Mama said from the couch. "Dodge, that wasn't Tiberius who did that to you."

I shouted across the kitchen. "Jorge! What did Tiberius do Sunday night when I didn't come home, and he couldn't find me. Did he whip you? What did he do?"

Jorge had his hands deep in suds. He twisted to look back at me, shock on his face.

I turned back to the couch, "They're terrified of him, Mama. He slapped Shamisha. I'm pretty sure he's been beating Jorge. He's sitting there, gaslighting like ExxonMobil, and one day he'll turn on you too."

"Exxon?" Magma heated my enemy's face, and veins bulged on his neck and forehead. Still, he held it in. He didn't explode. "Dodge, you're grounded for the next week. I think it's time you go to your room."

Leave the living room? "Okay."

Instead of heading down the hall, I jogged to Jorge and Tamika at the sink.

"Go to your room, Dodge!" Tiberius hollered behind me.

"Get Shamisha and Jason. All of you go out the window," I hissed to them. "Go to Mr. Sanchez's house and stay there."

"Now, Dodge!" Tiberius shoved off the couch and started my way. I dashed toward the hall, toward my room, but he grabbed my arm.

"When I tell you to do something…" Tiberius cut himself off as he hauled me back into the living room. He stood before Mama with my arm grasped in his fist. We stood there, he my accuser, and she the final judge.

Mama's brown eyes opened wide, so full of sadness that I wanted to hold her. "Dodge, why do you say terrible things about Tiberius? He loves these children. Your words are not true, Dodge."

"It's not about me, Mia," Tiberius shook his head. "I don't want him manipulating you."

"Mama, I'll go to my room. I just wanted to say good night to Tamika."

Grief tightened Mama's face and tears rose into her eyes again. "Tiberius. Please send him to his room. It's been a long day, and he's normally a very good boy."

Jorge and Tamika finished the dishes, and water sucked down the drain, a slurping sound that interrupted the tense silence.

"Let me help them wipe down the counters, Mama. And I'll go to my bedroom."

Tiberius refused to release my arm until Mama nodded at me. I ran in and grabbed a rag. "I've got a plan," I breathed to Jorge as I cleaned the counter beside him. "I can't do it until you guys leave. I'll meet you at Mr. Sanchez's house in 30 minutes."

"He's gonna kill you," Jorge whispered.

"I have a plan. I *need* you to get them out."

Jorge rinsed out the sink. I wiped down the rest of the counter and started on the stove top. As Jorge walked past me, he muttered, "Thirty minutes."

I didn't plan to take that long, but I needed Jorge to wait and not come back looking for me.

The children disappeared. The kitchen was clean, and I returned to the living room to burst the lid off that bubbling magma.

I faced Mama.

"Go to your room now, Dodge," she nodded at me.

I didn't go. "I love you, Mama. I think you're wonderful. You need to tell Tiberius to leave. You apologized for putting me in danger, and now you've let him back in."

He'd won her heart. She'd chosen to fully trust him instead of me. "Oh baby. Tiberius is a good man. You have been so bad, Dodge. Why are you so bad to him?"

Tiberius' breaths puffed faster, but I refused to look at him. I kept my eyes on Mama.

"Because he's evil. I don't understand why you believe him. He punched me, Mama. He broke my face. He choked me."

"I told you, Mia," Tiberius couldn't keep the rage out of his voice. "You've let him run around doing whatever he wants, and it's not about me. He has no respect for you."

"You are so rude. You are so rude, *mijo*."

I turned to the man himself. "Tiberius, you know you smashed my face, and now you're beating on these children. You know it, and I'm not going to let you do it anymore!"

That did it. Tiberius lunged for my arm, and I danced out of the way. He caught the back of my shirt and marched me toward the front door. "I need to have a talk with him, Mia."

I shoved away from him. "No! If he takes me outside, you'll never see me again. Mama!"

Tiberius jerked my shirt hard. "Better shut up, boy."

"He'll say I ran away, but he'll bury my body somewhere!"

I didn't know if he planned to end me right then, and I didn't care. I threw my arms up and thrashed and wriggled until I wriggled right out of my shirt.

Tiberius cursed and kicked at me, but I dodged and bolted to Mama's room and slammed the door. I turned the little knob lock and dove under the bed, pulling out the black case.

Tiberius stood on the other side of the door, and the knob rattled over and over again. "Boy, you better come out of there, or I'll break your legs. Open up!" He called me increasingly worse names, his voice growing louder and louder.

I set the small case on the bed and thumbed numbers into place on the combination lock. I'd shamed Mama the previous year when I'd found it, because she hadn't turned the numbers out of position. "Any of the kids could have opened it!" My hands shook badly now, and I had a hard time clicking open the clasps, but I managed and pulled out Mama's 9mm. It was big and heavy for me, but it would do the job.

From the kitchen, Mama begged Tiberius to calm down. Tiberius ignored her and thumped even louder, hammering the door, using colorful terms to threaten me with all of it - all the bad things.

I checked the magazine; it still held those few rounds I'd loaded in March. I didn't think I had time to load more, so I slammed it into the gun and pulled hard with my whole hand to jack a cartridge into the chamber. Then, I retreated to the back wall and waited for the inevitable. I had 12 feet, 12 feet between me and the violent force behind the door.

It came. Tiberius gave a heavy kick and the door broke open and bounced against the wall. I held that gun with both hands stretched out in front of me, and as soon as the door opened, I shot the ceiling above his head.

BAM!

The shot blasted through the room, through my eardrums, through my head, like a thunderclap in the brain. Darn! No ear protection!

Tiberius ducked and stared at the ceiling. Then, he yelled at me. "Dodge, you put that thing down!" That was the most real, the most authentic I'd ever seen Tiberius.

My ears sang as hairs in my inner ear died. I'd just destroyed my ability to hear at certain frequencies. Ear protection!

"Mama, call 911!" I called down the hall. "Call 911 now!" I kept my arms extended and pointed at the man's chest. In my memory, I heard the ancient principle: "Never point a gun at anything you don't intend to shoot."

"Get on the ground," I told Tiberius. "Get on the ground!"

He didn't move.

"Dodge. Put the gun down!"

I shot again.

Survival

Part of me honestly wanted to shoot him in the chest, center of mass, and just kill him. Bam bam bam - I wouldn't have to fight with him or deal with his crazy anymore. I'd legitimately claim self-defense, and I plain felt that Tiberius deserved a little killing.

There were a few things that stopped me. First, I worried that the bullet might zip straight through Tiberius and hit Mama down the hall behind him. Second, Mama still loved him, and I didn't want to shoot her lover right in front of her. Third, we'd have to move if I killed him, because Mama wouldn't sleep in a house where somebody had bled to death all over her bedroom floor.

I couldn't wing him and make him desperate. Tiberius needed to think he might survive. If he came at me, I had space. Two seconds. Two seconds to take him out. These thoughts flashed through my head as the high hum from the first gun blast rang in my ears.

So, I shot the floor at his feet.

He jumped back and cursed loudly. He wanted me. He wanted to grab me so badly.

"Your heart's next, *cabron*!"

Tiberius slowly lowered himself, his eyes on me the whole time.

"Stretch out your arms and legs and don't move. If you move, I will shoot you. I hope you move so I CAN SHOOT YOU!"

He believed me. We both knew he had good reason.

Mama's emotions leaked in from the kitchen, where she sobbed to the 911 operator. The big hand on her wall clock pointed to 6:15. How long would it take the police to get there?

Tiberius kept trying to talk to me, and I wanted to kick him in the head. But, I didn't. I stood against the wall and held the gun on him. I didn't want that big man to leap at me and make me shoot. Or worse, lunge and get ahold of me and bludgeon me to death.

"Are they coming, Mama?" I shouted.

She appeared cautiously at the end of the hall. "Oh Dodge!" She pleaded, "You will be in so much trouble when the police get here. Put down the gun!"

"Stay there, Mama. If he moves, I have to kill him so he can't hurt me!"

Anything. Anything to keep that big man still.

"Sing something, Tiberius. Sing a song."

He didn't like that idea. "A song?"

"To pass the time. Because if you move, I will shoot you. Or tell a joke. Do you know a good joke? Tell me a joke so that I don't have to shoot you."

"You don't want to do that, Dodge. Put down the gun."

"*No me tientes!*"

"You want a joke? I'll tell you a joke. You, Dodge. You're a joke."

"Now we're getting somewhere. Tell another one."

He cursed several times, but then he astonished me by telling an actual joke. A kid's joke.

"All right. What is Yoda's last name?"

"I don't know. What's Yoda's last name?"

"Lay-hee-hoo."

I gave a nervous chuckle. "That's pretty good. Any others?"

He cursed at me again. "I'm the joke king! I have more jokes than you have days in your life. Why do bees have sticky hair? They use honeycombs. Why are peppers good at archery? Cuz they habanero!"

That night, the police response time for a nine-year-old holding a gun on a grown man was a little over seven minutes. Seven long long minutes. I started singing Christmas carols, because we both knew the words, and that made the time pass more quickly. I wanted to keep Tiberius' mind occupied so he couldn't plot against me.

We finished "The First Noel," and Tiberius started on me.

"Boy, you sure screwed up. The police will shoot you when they get here."

I said nothing. Another song. I needed another song.

"They'll see you holding that gun. I'm on the ground. They'll see you holding that gun, and they'll shoot you dead."

"They're not gonna shoot a kid."

"You think they'll believe you? Nobody will believe you. Look at you, scars all over your face like a street fighter. Like a little gangster."

As the police pulled up outside, I realized they really might see me as the perpetrator and not the victim. I kept my eyes on Tiberius.

"Mama! Tell them I won't shoot Tiberius if he leaves me alone!"

She opened the door and slipped out to talk. Tiberius kept smiling up at me, a nasty, mocking smile. "They're gonna lock you up, boy. Little gangster foster brat, shooting up a house."

Lyrics bounced into my head, and I giggled out loud in tension. "'I'm the kind of G the little homies wanna be like.'" I laughed. "'On my knees in the night saying prayers in the street light.'"

"Man, you're crazy." Tiberius said that one like he meant it.

Another car pulled up outside. The police rumbled with Mama at the front of the house, and I realized I had to end it. "Go ahead and leave," I told Tiberius. "Back out on your hands and knees."

Instead, Tiberius shouted. "Help! He's lost his mind!"

"Tiberius. Get out of here."

"You're a criminal, Dodge. They all know it now."

I took a step forward. "Then maybe I'll just kill you."

BAM! I missed his left shoulder - not by much.

Tiberius cursed and backed up.

"Keep going!"

"You're psycho!" He muttered insults all the way down the hall. As soon as the door opened and Tiberius was in view of the outside world, I ran to the window and wriggled it open.

"I'm throwing the gun out the window! Hey! Hey everybody! I'm throwing the gun out! Do you hear me!!"

I released the magazine and jacked the round out of the chamber. I threw the gun as hard as I could at the fence beside the house. Then I threw the magazine. "Do you hear me! The gun is outside! I threw it outside!"

The jacked bullet on the carpet. A bullet that didn't kill Tiberius. I lifted Mama's bed cover and stuffed the cartridge under her mattress to keep it safe. If I was on my way to juvenile detention, I didn't want that bullet taken from me.

What should I do now? I looked like a bad kid gone nuts, but I was only nine-years-old. Nobody wanted to shoot me. Right? I ran to the front of the house and banged on the door. "I threw the gun out the window!" I bellowed. "I threw the gun away. I want to come outside now!"

I waited a few moments.

"You want to come outside?" A male voice shouted.

"Yes, please! I threw the gun out Mama's window."

"Okay, son. Open the door slowly."

"Okay."

Nine-year-olds were still little kids. I slowly opened the door and stuck both my hands out to show they were empty. The door opened all the way, and I stood there, a small person wearing nothing but blue shorts and tennis shoes.

An ambulance pulled up across from our house. Three police cars already filled both sides of the street. Mama sobbed into Tiberius' chest on the far side of the garden boxes, and my ears still rang from the gun blasts.

I wanted them to handcuff Tiberius right away, but they didn't. Mama's wailing on the phone had prepared them to stop a homicidal child, not a grown man. Her weeping explanation in the front yard placed all the blame on me.

One older black officer took charge. "All right. Family members back inside."

I retreated into the kitchen. A younger officer led Tiberius to the living room, and I expected my enemy to argue, to fight, to run away. I expected him to act like a man who hated cops, who faced arrest for attempted murder. He didn't. Tiberius behaved perfectly calm and reasonable.

"He has a warrant for his arrest!" I told one of the policemen.

The older black officer pointed me down the hall. "Let's go talk." He said it in obvious anger, and the badge on his chest labelled him a lieutenant. Wow. I'd earned a lieutenant? We returned to Mama's room, and he tried to close the door behind us. The frame was broken, so it didn't click shut.

"Take a seat." He pointed to Mama's bed. I perched on the corner of the bed while he surveyed Mama's room. He grimaced at the hole in the ceiling. A small, clean hole. I wanted to warn him about Tiberius, but I'd heard the fury in his voice.

"Young man. Guns are not toys. This is not a game. Last week those men out there, right out there, responded to a call where an 11-year-old accidentally shot and killed his brother. That boy will have to live the rest of his life knowing he killed his own brother! Do you have a clue how serious this is!"

I feared what Tiberius was telling the other cop, but I listened to the officer's lecture. He was going to give it, and I got it. The officer made perfectly valid points.

"Never ever use a gun to handle a disagreement, young man. Do you understand me?"

"Please, Lieutenant-"

"Do you understand me!"

"Yes, sir. I understand."

"Do you?"

I nodded. "Yes, sir. I only did it to protect myself."

"You shot holes in the house to protect yourself?"

"The man your officer has in the next room?" I pointed. "I'm little and I can't fight him! I had to make him believe I'd shoot him, or he was gonna beat me to death."

The officer asked direct questions. "Did you leave for two days without telling your foster mother where you went?"

"Oh. Yes, sir. I did."

"Was your foster father about to take you outside to talk to you about it? Out front? And beat you *to death* in front of the neighbors?"

He clearly didn't believe that.

"He's not my foster father. He's just her boyfriend."

That enraged him even more. "And you were willing to shoot him. Shoot a man! Because you were in trouble for running away?"

I'd been through foster homes where a lot of people had yelled at me, and I'd learned to relax my wild emotions. The more tense the situation, the more vital it was to give people space. I deserved to cry, to shout, but that wasn't how the world worked. It was an injustice of the universe that when you needed help the most, when circumstances were the worst, you had to stay calm for folks to listen.

I looked at him for some silent seconds.

"Because you were in trouble," he repeated.

"Lieutenant, please listen. Please." I pointed at my cheek. "Last time he beat me up, he broke my face and tried to choke me to death. He did it outside in Burbank, at noon and everything. He really does have a warrant. Please don't leave here without arresting him. That's why I pulled the gun on him – so that you could come and arrest him."

The officer frowned in aggravation, but he used a finger to beckon me closer. I obeyed, and he examined the pink crescent moon on the side of my face.

"Did he make these marks on your cheek?" The lieutenant

thumbed my right cheekbone.

"No, sir. That was a foster brother awhile back." I stood in my shorts, shirtless, my back exposed. "And the ones on my back were a different foster father."

The lieutenant turned me slowly in place, and when I met his eyes again, they had softened. He pulled out a little notepad and started writing. "Go ahead and sit back down."

The lieutenant asked me questions until I had given him the full story of Tiberius' time in our lives: the harassment and threats and other attacks. I listed all the violence that Tiberius had promised 15 minutes earlier while he banged on the door.

"Why didn't you shoot him?"

I recognized he was probing my psychology, but it still sounded like a funny question. I admitted, "I don't want to kill anybody. I had to act tough because I needed him to stay still, but I'm glad he listened and didn't move."

"Even after what he did to you?"

"I don't want to hurt people. And Mama's in love with him."

After the officer wrote it all down, he took me to the ambulance so the paramedics could look me over.

The EMTs treated me kindly while they did a survey of my body. I had to answer questions about my three sets of scars again, because they wanted to know. The youngest guy wouldn't let it go. He kept probing, digging, asking questions I didn't want to answer.

I asked him, "Did you ever consider getting foster kids? The world needs more good foster parents." Whenever I met decent people, I'd say, "You should become a foster parent. We need people who will protect us. We need a family."

One of the police cars pulled away, but the lieutenant and two other officers continued to talk to Mama and Tiberius. "Why aren't they arresting him?" I asked the young paramedic. He didn't know either.

Tiberius had reason to be calm.

One of the younger cops walked back over. "We ran his ID, and your foster father doesn't have any warrants. Are you sure he was the one who attacked you in Burbank? Because your foster mother says he wasn't."

Oh my goodness. This was ridiculous.

"Except that he *was*," I told the young cop. "Mama doesn't believe me, because she loves him." Where was Dr. Wilkins?

"If you feel like you're in danger, we'll take you into custody," the young man said. "We're talking to your social worker right now."

No no no. No, I couldn't leave the kids alone with Tiberius. "There are other children, officer. Other children are in danger."

He looked up and around. "Others?"

Wait. They were all foster kids. They were foster kids too! Had I made a terminal error? With all my brilliance and foreknowledge, all my years of living, my superpowers, had I completely screwed up? Had I let Tiberius win?

I looked down the road toward Mr. Sanchez's house, and there they came, slowly walking home. The twins dashed behind the orange tree and peeked out. Jorge had hold of Jason's hand and strained his neck to see inside the house before he got there.

I'd made a mistake. We were about to be broken up and parceled out to different homes. I'd just let Tiberius destroy our family!

When they saw it was safe, the girls dashed around and around the cars, delighted by all the excitement. Jorge ran inside and found Mama sobbing to my lieutenant with her confused explanations. I only heard the varying pitches of her voice, but I doubted she sat there defending me.

"C'mon," the young cop took hold of my arm. "Don't worry. You're not arrested. But the lieutenant wants you in his car for now."

"Wait. Wait a minute. I can't go anywhere yet."

"You're not going 'anywhere yet.' He only wants me to keep you outside the house and safe."

He led me to the lieutenant's car and put me inside. Then he closed the door, clunk, which locked me in. I stayed on my knees, keeping watch out the window for Dr. Wilkins. Was he still waiting by the pay phone?

The lieutenant had served the City of Los Angeles a long time, and he knew how people worked. He could see through the deceivers of the world, and he wasn't somebody to play with. Still, he might have believed my big, well-spoken enemy if it hadn't been for Jorge.

Jorge later told me what happened inside the house. He stood in the kitchen and listened to Mama for a minute. Then, he jumped in. "No, Mama! Tiberius is the best liar I ever met. I didn't want Dodge to come home because Tiberius hurts Dodge all the time!"

Jorge said that right out loud, as though Tiberius didn't stand a few feet away, and that moved the officers to lead Jorge and the girls into a bedroom to question them separately. Jorge told me, "I said that you took care of everybody. I told them I hated Tiberius for hurting you and hoped they put him in jail forever."

I hugged him tighter than he liked when he told me that. "You're a good big brother, Jorge."

It turned out his legal name wasn't Tiberius at all, and that's why his record showed up all pretty and clean. When the children kept calling him "Tiberius" the lieutenant had the sense to look him up by his alias. Boom. There was the warrant. They finally arrested him and placed him in the back of the other cruiser across the street.

Even then, Tiberius winked at me through the glass. He winked and mouthed at me, "I'll get out."

That's when Dr. Wilkins knocked on my car window, obviously eager to find me alive. He had to go find an officer to release me, but as soon as I was out of the cruiser, I grabbed the front of his fuzzy vest. "I'm so sorry to do that to you. It's okay. Nobody was hurt."

The sun had set that May evening, and the sky glowed orange over the date palms and reflected in the windshields of the police cars. Poor Doc had been waiting at that phone booth, and I apologized to him. "I feel bad I couldn't call you back. I didn't have a chance."

He dismissed all that. "Where is your shirt!" He held me out at arm's length. "That's it! That's it. Where's your mother?"

"It's okay, Doc. Doc! It's okay!"

He didn't answer me. I followed him into the house, where Mama still sobbed, traumatized.

Mama looked up at Dr. Wilkins as he walked through the door. "I don't know what to do with him anymore." She wiped her eyes with her fingers. "Shooting a gun in the house like that!"

Doc turned to me in the doorway, astonished. "You discharged a gun in your house?"

I nodded.

"I can't believe you, Dodge! I should never let you fly solo!"

"You scared me!" Mama yelled at me, "You are a crazy boy! They've arrested Tiberius, are you happy now?" She continued to weep, and I wanted to find her something to weep into. My white shirt lay on the floor near the door, so I handed it to her.

"Who are you?" the lieutenant asked Dr. Wilkins, one more body in the small kitchen.

"I'm Dodge's piano teacher." He turned to Mama. "Do they know Tiberius attacked Dodge in the alley? I was there that day."

"We know about it," the lieutenant said.

"Dodge, look. You need to tell your mother the full truth. Now."

I met Doc's serious eyes and looked over at Shamisha and Tamika on the couch. "Here, Mama. Please don't cry." I wanted to stroke her back and comfort her, but Doc had put me on the spot. I would either traumatize her more in the future or get it all out right here. Right now, as the orange glow faded in the sky through the kitchen window. I looked at Doc, then the officers, and then at Jorge.

"Mama, I didn't want to scare you. I just wanted to stop Tiberius. I'm not bad, and I'm not crazy." I looked up at the lieutenant. "And I'm not...I'm not even a boy."

Jorge's eyes widened.

"I've been wanting to tell you for a long time, Mama, but I never knew how to do it."

At first I didn't think Mama even heard. She continued to wipe her face with my T-shirt. She finally spoke. "What do you mean? You're not a boy? You are a terrible boy. You are a crazy, dangerous boy."

"I'm not. I'm not terrible, and I'm not crazy or dangerous. And. I'm not a boy. I'm a girl."

I apologized to the lieutenant with my eyes, but he only looked confused, like he was trying to see it. With my short haircut and no shirt, my freckles and scars, I camouflaged well.

Mama peered at me, her swollen eyes half closed, as though she didn't know who I was, as though she didn't recognize me as a person she knew, let alone a person she loved.

"Cheryl needs to come get you," she choked into my shirt. "They called Cheryl. She needs to come take you away. I can't have you anymore."

I stared. "No, Mama! You don't need to send me away! Tiberius is gone now. He's the one who was trying to get rid of me!"

She shook her head. She shook her head over and over. "I should have. He was right. I should have sent you back." Then Mama turned away from me and hid her face.

I gaped at her back as an indescribable awfulness overwhelmed my insides. I didn't have enough room in my small chest for the waves of feelings that rolled through me. I had let her in! Deep past the scabs over my heart, past all my protections! The rejection, the frustration and injustice swelled up and suffocated me, and I couldn't breathe. I wrapped my arms around myself and looked at the floor tiles. If I looked anywhere else, the next drop of emotion would have burst me to pieces.

Jorge exploded on my behalf. "No, Mama! You're the one that let Tiberius back in! You're the one that believed him when you should have believed Dodge! He beat her up, and you *let* him! He bullied her and choked her and punched her, and you refused to believe her, so why should she tell you the truth about anything!"

Big choking sobs rolled up inside me and forced their way out. I couldn't stop them.

Mama squinted. "You knew? You knew Dodge is a girl?"

"You were supposed to protect her!" Jorge shouted. "And if you're sending her away, then I'm going too!"

I couldn't be there anymore. I shoved past Dr. Wilkins and ran. No shirt. I didn't care.

Jorge found me 20 minutes later, my cheeks stained and red and my nose plugged. His face appeared around our twisted old oak. The house still hadn't sold. I said nothing as Jorge walked around the tree and sat beside me for a silent minute. Then, he scooted right up and wrapped his arms around me.

"I thought you were brave." He patted my back. It was a gentle, steady pat, and it was the most comforting gift anybody could have given me in that moment.

"Mama doesn't want me anymore." I leaned into him and blubbed into his chest.

Jorge kept patting me. "It's okay. It's okay, Dodge."

"I did it all wrong. I let him win."

"There there. He didn't win."

"He did! I let him!"

"No, he didn't. Shhh. I'm here, Dodge. I want you."

Pressure filled my head again. "I want you too, Jorge."

Jorge let me relax with his 10-year-old arms around me, and we sat there quietly. He rubbed my back until I breathed steadily again.

"C'mon," Jorge finally whispered. "We have to go. He's waiting."

"Who?"

"That cop. Don't worry. He doesn't want to put you in jail." He rubbed the hair on the top of my head. "Yeah. Dr. Wilkins told them it was okay. He told Cheryl he'd take us both." Jorge paused. "You know, Dr. Wilkins is smart. He said nice things about you, but he was kind to Mama at the same time."

I rubbed my eyes with the back of my hand.

Jorge laughed. "I wish I could have been there to see it when you shot a hole in the ceiling! I wish I could have seen the look on his face!"

"I made him tell jokes and sing Christmas carols." I giggled through my stuffed nose.

"Jokes? You made him tell jokes? That's the best thing I've ever heard." He helped me get up and walked me around to meet with the lieutenant.

Dr. Wilkins replaced my bed at the Burbank apartment with a bunk bed, and Jorge and I enjoyed merry times with the composer. Dr. Wilkins plied his magic on Jorge, who decided that learning to play the piano was fun, though it didn't make up for no television.

During the next few weeks, Jorge and I rode the city bus home to Mama's every morning, whether she wanted us there or not. Jorge and the twins finished up the year at their school. I dropped Jason off at Mrs. Davis' house for Mama and spent some hours with him. I wasn't about to lose the girls and Jason, no matter what Mama did.

But she broke my heart. She wouldn't talk to me for weeks, and it grieved me. It grieved me every day. I finally stopped her in the living room before she left for work one morning.

"Will you wait a minute?" I stood in front of her. "Just stop! I'm sorry. I never told you I was a girl, and I'm sorry. But, I'm still here."

She gazed sadly at me.

"I don't want to move back, Mama. It's good with Dr. Wilkins, but I want you to know I'm sorry. And I love you. I love you a lot."

"I'm sorry too." She nodded, and tears rose up in her eyes. "And I love you too. You ... you have to give me time. I need time!"

"That's fine. You can have time." And I gave her a hug.

In June, the elementary school let out for the summer, freeing Jorge from his educational misery. More importantly, Dr. Wilkins, Jorge, and I all attended Tiberius' preliminary hearing. The district attorney produced a pile of hospital records and police reports. The court agreed the D.A. had sufficient evidence to take his case to trial, and they set the court date for August.

And that's when I made a decision.

One evening in late June, Dr. Wilkins and Jorge and I sat around the little table in the kitchen, eating our dinner.

"We need a vacation," I announced.

"A vacation?" Jorge said.

"Yes. I have a proposal."

Jorge and I had experimented with ravioli, and it turned out surprisingly okay. Dr. Wilkins forked a piece of the homemade pasta and placed it in his mouth. He chewed thoroughly and swallowed, then he took a sip of his chardonnay. "I'm waiting, Dodge. I'm waiting to hear what you propose."

"I propose that we purchase bus tickets to New Jersey. I've saved up $335, and I propose that we place large bets on a 19-year-old boxer named Mike Tyson. He's going to conquer John Alderson on July 11th in Atlantic City."

"That's your proposal?" Dr. Wilkins calmly stabbed another piece of ravioli.

"Yep. It's precisely why I saved up that $335. And then he will conquer Larry Sims in Poughkeepsie, New York on July 19th."

"I see," said the old composer.

"You're so weird, Dodge," Jorge said. "I never knew a girl who liked boxing."

I smiled. "It's the eye of the tiger. It's the thrill of the fight. And if my calculations are correct, Mike Tyson K.O.s his opponents a whole bunch of fights in a row. Bam bam!!"

Jorge scraped his plate. "What? You can't calculate things like that."

"Ah ah ah," Dr. Wilkins reproved Jorge. "Doubt her not. She has superpowers."

I nodded. "I do. I have superpowers."

Jorge rolled his eyes.

"Also, I called to find out where Mike Tyson's fights would be. That's how I know where his fights are."

"Will I get charged for that long-distance call?"

I winced. "Uhhh… more like six long-distance calls."

"What about the girls and Jason?" Jorge didn't want to leave them. He was always the good brother.

"We won't stay away long. I hoped we could find a bookie and then, um, set it up long distance? Dr. Wilkins, can you do that? Get yourself a few bookies who can place bets for you no matter where the fight is?"

"I have no clue, dear. I'm sure there are people who do those things."

"But, listen. On our way from Atlantic City to Poughkeepsie, we'll stop in New York City to visit Donald Trump."

Dr. Wilkins chuckled at that. "Stop and see Donald Trump? That's right. It's like going to Coney Island and getting on a ride. We'll just buy tickets!"

I grinned. "I've written him letters since I was eight, telling him about my great genius and asking him to pay my tuition to USC."

"She has superpowers," Jorge reminded our guardian.

"Donald Trump knows I'm a foster child attending college, and that's good enough for him. Then! After we've bet enough times on Mike Tyson, we should have a sizeable amount of cash to drop on the stock market."

"Oh, of course." Doc sipped his wine. "Which stocks will we be choosing in the stock market?"

"Microsoft. As soon as they go public. So, we'll have to get in touch with somebody who can help us do that."

Jorge asked, "Microsoft? What's that?"

"Computer software. According to my super careful calculations, Microsoft will be highly successful."

"Microsoft," muttered Dr. Wilkins. He confessed, "You know, I've never touched a computer."

"That's okay. You don't have to own one to buy stock in it."

"Maybe we can visit Donald Trump for my birthday."

"Dodge, dear. You really will need an appointment."

"He said he'd tell his secretary to expect your call, Doc."

"I thought we were going to watch *Back to the Future* for your birthday," Jorge reminded me.

"Both. We'll do both."

"I guess I'll call my niece in Cape May and warn her I'm coming to visit."

"My friend Mike moved to Baltimore. He might want to drive out to Atlantic City too."

"And... are we treating you like a boy or a girl?" Jorge asked.

"A girl. I'll have to get used to wearing shirts all the time. Dr. Wilkins tattled on me to Cheryl like a big tattletale, and I think they're having my birth certificate updated."

Dr. Wilkins swallowed the last of his wine. "Microsoft."

I'd survived into June of 1985. Only 35 years to go.

Epilogue

I reached into my front pocket and pulled out a 9mm cartridge. It lay in my hand, all coppery and harmless.

"February 2, 2020." Jorge wrote the date in his spiral notebook. The bus rumbled, and his printing bumped a bit on the page. Jorge's writing was never tidy anyway. "That's 02 02 20 20. That's a mirror." Jorge squinted at the paper. "The numbers mirror each other. Did you notice that?"

"Yeah. It's kinda fun, huh?" I rolled the round between my fingers. I liked having it with me. It gave me a kind of comfort.

Across the aisle, Dr. Wilkins had covered his eyes with his hat, and a soft snore emanated from him.

Jorge elbowed me. "So, you're saying this 44-year-old lady should have woken up on 02 02 20 20 and she woke up on 02 02 1980. But... that ruins the mirror!"

"No, it's arithmetic. What is 20 plus 20?"

"Forty."

"Yeah. And what's 2 plus 2?"

"Four."

"Right. She went back in time 40 years to when she was 4."

"But she went back to 1980. That's *no bueno*."

"And what's 40 times two?"

"Eighty."

"Yeah, and it's her second time around doing it. So, it's the start of her 40 times two."

Jorge looked puzzled. "But, it would have to be her 4th birthday. Was she born on February 2nd?"

"No. She was born July 15th."

"That's... that's not exactly four then. It's four and... six months and... some days."

"Oh. I never thought about it. I guess you're right."

"And there's no two or four in July 15th."

"No... but..." I thought about it. "But, 7 plus 15 makes 22."

"Yeah it does."

I looked at Jorge. "Oh! And she was born in 1975! Check this out! If you add up one, nine, seven, and five, it also equals 22. And 22 plus 22 is 44."

"Hahahah! You're good! That's awesome."

He was right about the "four and six months and some days" thing though. It didn't make sense. "How many days are there from July 15th to February 2nd? Jorge, can I have the pencil?" I shoved the 9 mm round back into my front pocket.

From July 15th to July 31st was 16 days. There were 31 days in August, 30 in September, 31 in October, 30 in November, 31 days in December, and 31 days in January. Plus the two days to Groundhog Day. I wrote out:

$$
\begin{array}{r}
16 \\
31 \\
30 \\
31 \\
30 \\
31 \\
31 \\
\underline{2} \\
\end{array}
$$

"Hey Jorge. If she was born on July 15th, she would have been 44 and 202 days old when she went back in time."

"You mean, she'd be 44 and 0202 days old," Jorge corrected. "And she would have gone back in time to when she was 4 and 0202 days old."

"Or... Except that 202 is already a mirror. It's a mirror of itself."

"So, there's 202 twice. When she was 44 and when she was 4."

"She was a perfect storm of doubles, wasn't she?" I scanned across our list of twos and fours.

"And she gets to live her life all over again. She's the doubles queen."

"She's the doubles queen."

"Hey Dodge."

"Yeah Jorge?"

"Isn't your birthday July 15th?"

"Yep."

"Hey! Wouldn't that be the greatest thing ever if it happened to you? Maybe one day when you're 44, you'll wake up on Groundhog Day as a four-year-old."

I thought of the bullet in my pocket. "I don't know, Jorge. I don't think it would be the greatest thing ever."

"Yeah, it would! I hope it happens to you. If it does, will you look me up?"

"Of course, Jorge. I'll hang out with you all the time."

To Be Continued...

About the Author

Amy Joy Hess is a chemist and paleontologist, editor and teacher who lives in the mountains of North Idaho. She bears a nitric acid burn on her wrist, and there's scar in her palm from an ice accident on Diamond Lake when she was 11. She loves all her children, both biological and collected, and a variety of students at the high school call her, "Mom."

"I can't wait until the kids are all grown and we have the house to ourselves," her husband Blade said one day.

"Honey, I'm sorry," she said with compassion. "You married me when we had six kids living here. When the children grow up, I've long planned to take in foster kids. What made you ever think we'd have the house to ourselves? How did that even enter your head?"

Blade said nothing.

It's something they'll have to talk about.

Amy Joy lives in a house she bought in their small mountain town. Should she disappear one day in early February, don't worry too much. She might be crossing the Caspian Sea or hiking down mountains in Nepal. She'll get home as soon as she can.